continued . . .

War of the Roses: Bloodline

THE CONQUEROR SERIES

"Iggulden writes with sweep and immediacy."

—*The Christian Science Monitor*

"Authentically detailed historical drama."

—*Booklist*

"Borrowing from history and legend, Iggulden reimagines the iconic conqueror on a more human scale—larger-than-life surely, but accessible and even sympathetic. Iggulden's Genghis is shaping up as a triumph of historical fiction."

—*Publishers Weekly* (starred review)

"Readers who enjoy well-researched tales of historical adventure with an emphasis on political intrigue, exotic settings, and military conflict will enjoy the ride."

—*Library Journal*

"A rip-roarin' read, and inspiration to go and sack a few cities on your own."

—*Kirkus Reviews*

THE EMPEROR SERIES

"A swashbuckling adventure story . . . dramatic historical fiction to keep adults turning pages like enthralled kids . . . Iggulden is a grand storyteller."

—*USA Today*

"Fast-moving, action-oriented . . . weaving an intricate and compelling tapestry of Roman underling and slave life."

—*Publishers Weekly*

"*Emperor* is stunning. . . . Words like 'brilliant,' 'sumptuous,' and 'enchanting' jostle to be used, but scarcely convey the way Iggulden brings . . . the tale to life."

—*Los Angeles Times*

"A brilliant, tough-as-nails story. I wish I'd written it. It left me wanting more. A novel of vivid characters, stunning action and unrelenting pace."

—Bernard Cornwell, *New York Times*–bestselling author of *The Pagan Land*

TITLES BY CONN IGGULDEN

THE WARS OF THE ROSES SERIES
Stormbird
Margaret of Anjou
Bloodline

THE EMPEROR SERIES
The Gates of Rome   *The Gods of War*
The Death of Kings   *The Blood of Gods*
The Field of Swords

THE CONQUEROR SERIES
Wolf of the Plains   *Empire of Silver*
Lords of the Bow   *Conqueror*
Bones of the Hills

QUICK READS
Blackwater
Quantum of Tweed

BY CONN IGGULDEN AND HAL IGGULDEN
The Dangerous Book for Boys
The Pocket Dangerous Book for Boys: Things to Do
The Pocket Dangerous Book for Boys: Things to Know
The Dangerous Book for Boys Yearbook

BY CONN IGGULDEN AND DAVID IGGULDEN
The Dangerous Book of Heroes

BY CONN IGGULDEN AND ILLUSTRATED BY LIZZY DUNCAN
Tollins: Explosive Tales for Children
Tollins 2: Dynamite Tales

Wars of the Roses
STORMBIRD

Conn Iggulden

G. P. Putnam's Sons
New York

PUTNAM

G. P. Putnam's Sons
Publishers Since 1838
An imprint of Penguin Random House LLC
375 Hudson Street
New York, New York 10014

The Library of Congress has catalogued the G. P. Putnam's Sons hardcover edition as follows:

Iggulden, Conn.
Wars of the Roses : stormbird / Conn Iggulden.
p.   cm.
ISBN 9780399165368
1. Great Britain—History—Henry VII, 1485–1509—Fiction.   I. Title.
II. Title: Stormbird.
PR6109.G47W37   2014   2013042790
823'.92—dc23

First G. P. Putnam's Sons hardcover edition / July 2014
First Berkley trade paperback edition / May 2015
First G. P. Putnam's Sons trade paperback edition / May 2017
G. P. Putnam's Sons trade paperback edition ISBN / 9780425275443

Printed in the United States of America
7   9   10   8

Cover illustration by Vince McIndo
Author and title type by Carol Kemp
Series title type by Charles Stewart
Interior illustrated map *London/Windsor* and illustrated *Royal Lines of England Family Tree*
copyright © 2013 by Andrew Farmer

To Mark Griffith,
a descendant of John of Gaunt

ACKNOWLEDGMENTS

Thanks are due to Victoria Hobbs, Alex Clarke, Nita Taublib, and Tim Waller, skillful guides for each stage of the book's development. Any errors that remain are my own. Thanks are also due to Clive Room, who accompanied me to castles and cathedrals, demonstrating a vast knowledge of the period. I just couldn't stop him.

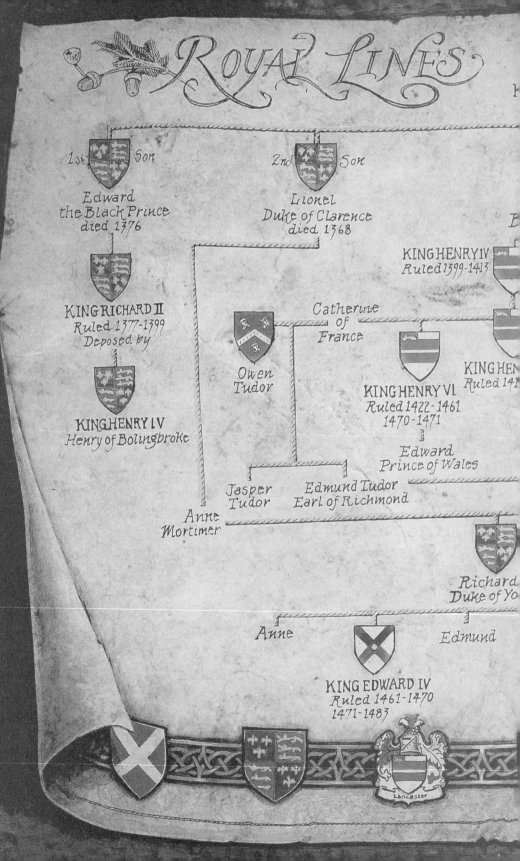

ROYAL LINES

1st Son

Edward
the Black Prince
died 1376

2nd Son

Lionel
Duke of Clarence
died 1368

KING HENRY IV
Ruled 1399-1413

KING RICHARD II
Ruled 1377-1399
Deposed by

Catherine
of
France

Owen
Tudor

KING HENRY VI
Ruled 1422-1461
1470-1471

KING HEN
Ruled 141

KING HENRY IV
Henry of Bolingbroke

Edward
Prince of Wales

Jasper
Tudor

Edmund Tudor
Earl of Richmond

Anne
Mortimer

Richard
Duke of Yo

Anne

Edmund

KING EDWARD IV
Ruled 1461-1470
1471-1483

Lancaster

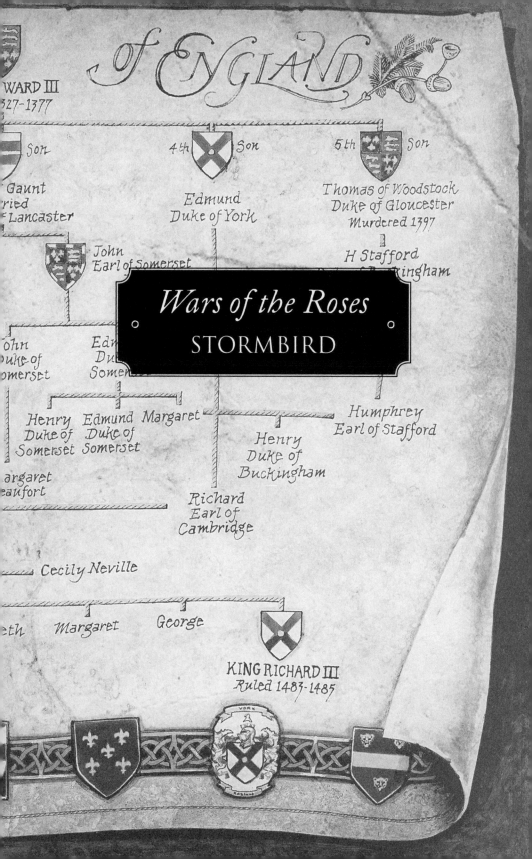

MAPS AND FAMILY TREES

MAPS

FAMILY TREES

England at the time of the Wars of the Roses

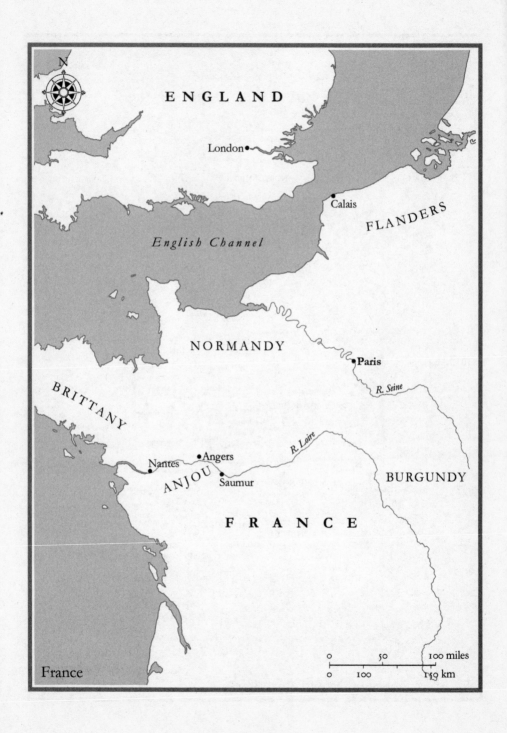

N

ENGLAND

London

English Channel

Calais

FLANDERS

NORMANDY

Paris

R. Seine

BRITTANY

Nantes

Angers

R. Loire

BURGUNDY

ANJOU

Saumur

FRANCE

0   50   100 miles

0   100   150 km

France

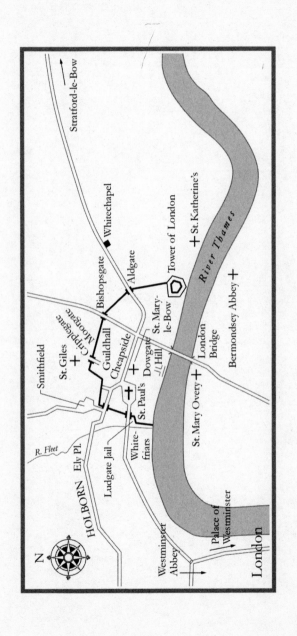

Royal Lines of England

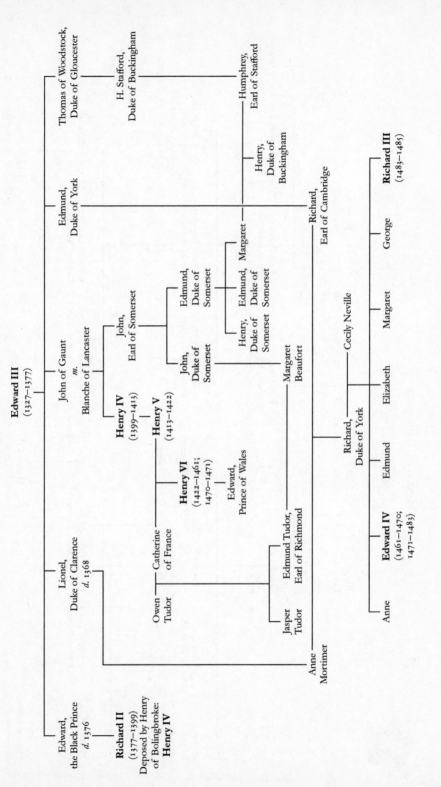

House of Lancaster

King Edward III

John of Gaunt, Duke of Lancaster

1. Blanche of Lancaster = **John of Gaunt, Duke of Lancaster** = 2. Constance, daughter of Peter the Cruel, King of Castile and Leon = 3. Katherine Swynford

From 2. Constance:
- Katherine, *m.* Henry III, King of Castile and Leon

From 3. Katherine Swynford:
- John Beaufort, Earl of Somerset and Marquis of Dorset
- Henry Beaufort, Bishop of Winchester, and Cardinal
- Thomas Beaufort, Duke of Exeter

Children of John Beaufort, Earl of Somerset and Marquis of Dorset:
- John Beaufort, Duke of Somerset
- Edmund Beaufort, Duke of Somerset
- Joan Beaufort, *m.* James I, King of Scots

Children of John Beaufort, Duke of Somerset:
- Margaret Beaufort

Children of Edmund Beaufort, Duke of Somerset:
- Henry Beaufort, Duke of Somerset
- Edmund Beaufort, Duke of Somerset
- Margaret Beaufort, *m.* Henry Stafford, Duke of Buckingham

From 1. Blanche of Lancaster:

Henry IV

Children of Henry IV:
- Humphrey, Duke of Gloucester
- John, Duke of Bedford
- **Henry V**, *m.* Catherine of France
- Thomas, Duke of Clarence

Catherine of France = Owen Tudor
- Edmund Tudor, Earl of Richmond
- Jasper Tudor, Earl of Pembroke

Henry VI, *m.* Margaret of Anjou
- Edward, Prince of Wales

Margaret Beaufort = Edmund Tudor, Earl of Richmond →
Henry VII, *m.* Elizabeth of York
- **Henry VIII**

House of York

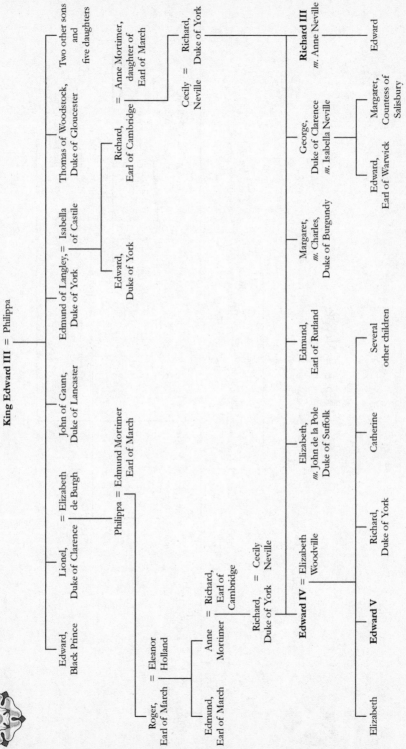

King Edward III = Philippa

Edward, Black Prince

Lionel, Duke of Clarence = Elizabeth de Burgh

John of Gaunt, Duke of Lancaster

Edmund of Langley, Duke of York = Isabella of Castile

Thomas of Woodstock, Duke of Gloucester

Two other sons and five daughters

Philippa = Edmund Mortimer Earl of March

Edward, Duke of York

Richard, Earl of Cambridge = Anne Mortimer, daughter of Earl of March

Roger, Earl of March = Eleanor Holland

Edmund, Earl of March

Anne Mortimer = Richard, Earl of Cambridge

Richard, Duke of York = Cecily Neville

Cecily Neville = Richard, Duke of York

Edward IV = Elizabeth Woodville

Edmund, Earl of Rutland

Elizabeth, m. John de la Pole Duke of Suffolk

Margaret, m. Charles, Duke of Burgundy

George, Duke of Clarence m. Isabella Neville

Richard III m. Anne Neville

Edward, Earl of Warwick

Margaret, Countess of Salisbury

Edward

Elizabeth

Edward V

Richard, Duke of York

Catherine

Several other children

House of Neville

Ralph Neville = Joan Beaufort, daughter of John of Gaunt

Richard, Duke of York = Cecily Neville

Richard, Earl of Salisbury = Alice, daughter of Thomas Montacute, Earl of Salisbury

Edmund, Earl of Rutland

Edward IV

George, Duke of Clarence

Richard III

Richard, Earl of Warwick and Salisbury, "The Kingmaker" = Alice, sister and heiress of Henry Beauchamp, Earl and Duke of Warwick

John, Marquess of Montacute

George, Archbishop of York

George, Duke of Clarence = Isabella

Anne = Edward, Prince of Wales

= **Richard III**

George, Duke of Bedford

House of Beaufort

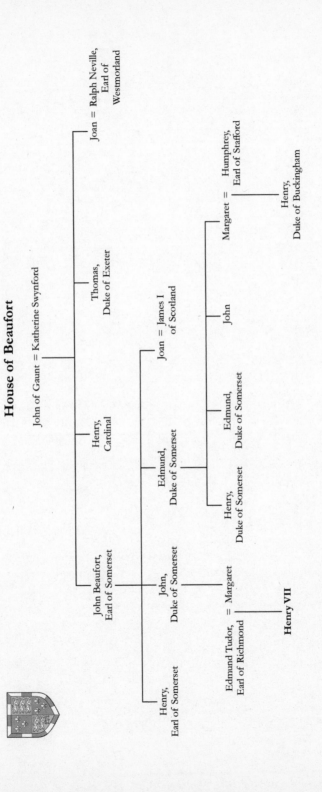

John of Gaunt = Katherine Swynford

- Joan = Ralph Neville, Earl of Westmorland
- Thomas, Duke of Exeter
- Henry, Cardinal
- John Beaufort, Earl of Somerset

Henry, Earl of Somerset

John, Duke of Somerset

Edmund Tudor, = Margaret
Earl of Richmond

Henry VII

Edmund, Duke of Somerset

- Joan = James I of Scotland
- Henry, Duke of Somerset
- Edmund, Duke of Somerset
- John
- Margaret = Humphrey, Earl of Stafford

Henry, Duke of Buckingham

PROLOGUE

Bowls of dark royal blood lay beneath the bed, forgotten by the physician. Alice Perrers rested on a chair, panting from the effort of wrestling the King of England into his armor. The air in the room was sour with sweat and death, and Edward lay like his own effigy, pale and white-bearded.

There were tears in Alice's eyes as she looked on him. The blow that had struck Edward down had come from a clear spring sky, unseen and terrible on a warm wind. Gently, she leaned forward and wiped spittle from the side of his drooping mouth. He had been so strong once, a man among men who could fight from dawn till dusk. His armor gleamed, yet it was marked and scarred like the flesh it covered. Underneath it, muscle and bone had wasted away.

She waited for him to open his eyes, unsure how much he still understood. His awareness came and went, moments of fading life that grew fewer and shorter as the days progressed. At dawn, he'd woken and whispered for his armor to be put on. The doctor had jumped up from his chair, fetching another of his filthy drafts for the king to drink. Weak as a child, Edward had waved away the stinking mixture, beginning to choke when the man continued to press the bowl against his mouth. Alice had felt her resolve firm when she saw that. Over the doctor's furious protests, she'd shooed him out of the king's rooms, snapping her apron at him and ignoring his threats until she was able to close the door on his back.

Edward had watched her lift his chain mail from the armor tree. He'd smiled for a moment, then his blue eyes had closed and he'd sagged back into the pillows. For the next hour, she'd grown pink at the labor, wiping her forehead with the back of her hand as she struggled with leather ties and metal, heaving the old man back and forth without his aid. Yet her brother was a knight, and it was not the first time she'd dressed a man for war.

By the time she pulled the metal gauntlets over his hands and sat back, he was barely aware, groaning softly as he drifted. His fingers twitched on the crumpled blankets until she gasped and stood, realizing what he wanted. Alice reached out to the great sword standing against the wall of the room, having to use both arms to place it where his hand could take the hilt. There had been a time when Edward had wielded that blade as if it had no weight at all. She wiped hot tears as his hand closed on it in a spasm, the gauntlet creaking in the silence.

He looked like a king once more. It was done. She nodded to herself, pleased that when the time came, he would be seen as he had lived. Reaching for a comb from her pocket, she began to smooth out the white beard and hair where they had become matted and tangled. It would not be long. His face drooped on one side, as if warm wax had melted, and his breath came in crackling gasps.

At twenty-eight, she was almost forty years younger than the king, but until his illness, Edward had been vigorous and strong, as if he might live forever. He had ruled all her life, and no one she knew could remember his father, nor the great Hammer of the Scots who had ruled before him. The Plantagenet family had left a mark on England and torn France apart in battles no one thought they could win.

Her comb snagged in his beard. Blue eyes opened at her touch and, from that ravaged body, her king looked up at her. Alice shuddered under the fierce gaze that had brought its own form of weakness in her for so long.

"I am here, Edward," she said, almost in a whisper. "I am here. You are not alone."

Part of his face pulled into a grimace, and he raised his good left arm to grip her hand and lower it, with its comb held tight. Each breath was drawn roughly in, and his skin flushed with the effort of trying to speak. Alice leaned close to hear the mush of words.

"Where are my sons?" he said, raising his head so that it left the pillow, then falling back. His right hand trembled on the sword hilt, taking comfort from it.

"They are coming, Edward. I've sent runners for John, to bring him back from the hunt. Edmund and Thomas are in the far wing. They are all coming."

As she spoke, she could hear a clatter of footsteps and the rumble of men's voices. She knew his sons well, and she prepared herself, knowing her moments of intimacy were at an end.

"They will send me away, my love, but I will not go far."

She reached down and kissed him on the lips, feeling the unnatural heat on his bitter breath.

As she sat back, she could make out the braying voice of Edmund, telling the other two of some wager he had made. She only wished the oldest brother could have been among them, but the Black Prince had died just a year before, never to inherit his father's kingdom. She thought the loss of the heir to the throne had been the first blow that led to all the rest. A father should not lose sons before him, she thought. It was a cruel thing to bear, for man or king.

The door came open with a crash that made Alice start. The three men who entered all resembled their father in different ways. With the blood of old Longshanks running in them, they were some of the tallest men she had ever seen, filling the room and crowding her even before they spoke.

Edmund of York was slim and black-haired, glowering as he saw the woman sitting with his father. He had never approved of his father's mistresses and, as Alice rose and stood meekly, his brows came down in a sour expression. At his side, John of Gaunt wore the same beard as his father, though it was still rich and black and cut to a sharp point that hid his throat from sight. The brothers loomed over their father, looking down on him as his eyes drifted closed once more.

Alice trembled. The king had been her protector while she amassed a fortune. She had grown wealthy from her association, but she was well aware that any one of the men in the room could order her taken on a whim, her possessions and lands forfeited on nothing more than their word. The title of duke was still so new that no one had tested their authority. They stood over earls and barons almost as kings in their own right, finding their peers and equals only in that room, on that day.

Two heads of the five great houses were absent. Lionel, Duke of Clarence, had died eight years before, leaving only a baby daughter. The son of the Black Prince was a ten-year-old boy. Richard had inherited his father's Duchy of Cornwall, just as he would inherit the kingdom itself. Alice had met both children, and she only hoped Richard would survive his powerful uncles long enough to become king. In her private thoughts, she wouldn't have wagered a penny on his chances.

The youngest of the three was Thomas, Duke of Gloucester. Perhaps because he was closest to her in age, he had always treated Alice kindly. He was the only one to acknowledge her as she stood and trembled.

"I know you have been a comfort to my father, Lady Perrers," Thomas said. "But this is a time for his family."

Alice blinked through tears, grateful for the kindness. Edmund of York spoke before she could respond.

"He means you should get out, girl," he said. He didn't look at her, his gaze held by the figure of his father lying in his armor on the pale sheets. "Off with you."

Alice left quickly at that, dabbing at her eyes. The door stood open and she looked back at the three sons standing over the dying king. She closed the door gently and sobbed as she walked away into the Palace of Sheen.

Alone, the brothers were silent for a long time. Their father had been the anchor on their lives, the one constant in a turbulent world. He had ruled for fifty years and the country had grown strong and rich under his hand. None of them could imagine a future without him.

"Should there not be a priest?" Edmund demanded suddenly. "It's an ill thing to have our father attended by a whore in his last moments." He didn't see his brother John scowl at the loudness of his voice. Edmund barked at the world with every word, unable to speak quietly, or at least unwilling.

"He can be called yet for the last rites," John replied, deliberately gentling his tone. "We passed him in prayer in the little room outside. He'll wait a while longer, for us."

The silence fell again, but Edmund shifted and sighed. He looked down at the still figure, seeing the chest rise and fall, the breaths audible with a deep crackle in the lungs.

"I don't see—" he began.

"Peace, brother," John said softly, interrupting. "Just . . . *peace*. He called for his armor and his sword. It won't be long now."

John closed his eyes in irritation for a moment as his younger brother looked round and found a chair to suit him, dragging it close to the bed with a screeching sound.

"There's no need to stand, is there?" Edmund said smugly. "I can at least be comfortable." He rested his hands on his knees, looking across at his father before turning his head. When he spoke again, his voice had lost its usual stridency. "I can hardly believe it. He was always so strong."

John of Gaunt rested his hand on Edmund's shoulder.

"I know, brother. I love him, too."

Thomas frowned at both of them.

"Will you have him die with your empty chatter ringing in his ears?" he said sternly. "Give him silence or prayer, either one."

John gripped Edmund's shoulder more strongly, as he sensed his brother would reply. To his relief, Edmund subsided with ill grace. John let his hand fall and Edmund looked up, irritated by the touch even as it ended. He glared at his older brother.

"Have you thought, John, that there is just a boy now between you and the crown? If it weren't for dear little Richard, you would be king tomorrow."

The other two spoke at once in anger, telling Edmund to shut his mouth. He shrugged at them.

"God knows the houses of York and Gloucester won't see the throne come to them, but you, John? You are just a hair's breadth from being royal and touched by God. If it were me, I'd be thinking of that."

"It should have been Edward," Thomas snapped. "Or Lionel, if he'd lived. Edward's son Richard is the only male line and that's all there is, Edmund. God, I don't know how you have the gall to say such a thing while our father lies on his deathbed. And I don't know how you can call the true royal line a 'hair's breadth,' either. Hold your wind, brother. I'm sick of hearing you. There is only one line. There is only one king."

The old man on the bed opened his eyes and turned his head. They all saw the movement, and Edmund's tart reply died on his lips. As one, they leaned in close to hear as their father smiled weakly, the expression twisting the good half of his face into a rictus that revealed dark yellow teeth.

"Come to watch me die?" King Edward asked.

They smiled at the gleam of life and John felt his eyes fill with unwanted tears, so that his vision swam.

"I was dreaming, lads. I was dreaming of a green field and riding across it." The king's voice was thin and reedy, so high and weak that they could barely hear. Yet in his eyes they saw the man they had known before. He was still there, watching them.

"Where is Edward?" the king said. "Why isn't he here?"

John rubbed fiercely at his tears.

"He's gone, Father. Last year. His son Richard will be king."

"Ah. I miss him. I saw him fight in France, did you know?"

"I know, Father," John replied. "I know."

"The French knights overran where he stood, yelling and smashing through. Edward stood alone, with just a few of his men. My barons asked me if I wanted to send knights to help him, to help my firstborn son. He was sixteen years old then. Do you know what I said to them?"

"You said no, Father," John whispered.

The old man laughed in short breaths, his face darkening.

"I said no. I said he had to win his spurs." His eyes turned up to the ceiling, lost in the memory. "And he did! He fought his way clear and returned to my side. I knew he would be king then. I knew it. Is he coming?"

"He's not coming, Father. He's gone and his son will be king."

"Yes, I'm sorry. I knew. I loved him, that boy, that brave boy. I loved him."

The king breathed out and out and out, until all breath was gone. The brothers waited in terrible silence, and John sobbed, putting his arm over his eyes. King Edward the Third was dead, and the stillness was like a weight on them all.

"Fetch the priest for the last rites," John said. He reached down to close his father's eyes, already lacking the spark of will.

One by one, the three brothers bowed to kiss their father's forehead, to touch his flesh for the last time. They left him there as the priest bustled in, and they walked out into the June sunshine and the rest of their lives.

PART ONE

ANNO DOMINI 1443

*Sixty-six years after the death
of Edward III*

o o o

Woe to thee, O land,

when thy king is a child.

ECCLESIASTES 10:16

CHAPTER 1

England was cold that month. The frost made the paths shine whitely in the darkness, clinging to the trees in drooping webs of ice. Guardsmen hunched and shivered as they kept watch over the battlements. In the highest rooms, the wind sobbed and whistled as it creased around the stones. The fire in the chamber might as well have been a painting for all the warmth it brought.

"I remember Prince Hal, William! I remember the lion! Just ten more years and he'd have had the rest of France at his feet. Henry of Monmouth was my king, no other. God knows I would follow his son, but this boy is not his father. You know it. Instead of a lion of England, we have a dear white lamb to lead us in prayer. Christ, it makes me want to weep."

"Derry, please! Your voice carries. And I won't listen to blasphemy. I don't allow it in my men, and I expect better from you."

The younger man stopped his pacing and looked up, a hard light in his eyes. He took two quick steps and stood very close, his arms slightly bent as they hung at his sides. He was half a head shorter than Lord

Suffolk, but he was powerfully built and fit. Anger and strength simmered in him, always close to the surface.

"I *swear* I've never been closer to knocking you out, William," he said. "The listeners are *my* men. Do you think I'm trying to trap you? Is that it? Let them hear. They know what I'll do if they repeat a single word." With one heavy fist, he thumped Suffolk lightly on the shoulder, turning away the man's frown with a laugh.

"Blasphemy? You've been a soldier all your life, William, but you talk like a soft-faced priest. I could still put you on your backside, William. That's the difference between you and me. You'll fight well enough when you're told, but *I* fight because I like it. That's why this falls to me, William. That's why I'll be the one who finds the right spot for the knife and sticks it in. We don't need pious *gentlemen*, William, not for this. We need a man like me, a man who can see weakness and isn't afraid to thumb its eyes out."

Lord Suffolk glowered, taking a deep breath. When the king's spymaster was in full flow, he could mix insults and compliments in a great flood of bitter vitriol. If a man took offense, Suffolk told himself, he'd never get anything done. He suspected Derihew Brewer knew the limits of his temper very well.

"We may not need a gentleman, Derry, but we do need a lord to deal with the French. You wrote to *me*, remember? I crossed the sea and left my responsibilities in Orléans to listen to you. So I would appreciate it if you'd share your plans, or I'll go back to the coast."

"That's it, isn't it? I come up with the answers and I'm to give them to my fine noble friend so he can reap all the glory? So they can say, 'That William Pole, that Earl Suffolk, he's a *right* sharp one,' while Derry Brewer is forgotten."

"William *de la* Pole, Derry, as you know very well."

Derry replied through clenched teeth, his voice close to a snarl.

"Oh, yes? You think this is the time to have a nice French-sounding name, do you? I thought you had more wits, I really did. Thing is, William, I'll do it anyway, because I care what happens to that little lamb who rules us. And I don't want to see my country ripped apart by fools and cocky bastards. I do have an idea, though you won't like it. I just need to know you understand the stakes."

"I understand them," Suffolk said, his gray eyes hard and cold.

Derry grinned at him without a trace of humor, revealing the whitest teeth Suffolk could remember seeing on a grown man.

"No, you don't," he said with a sneer. "The whole country is waiting for young Henry to be half the man his dad was, to finish the glorious work that took half of France and made their precious Dauphin prince run like a little girl. They're *waiting*, William. The king is twenty-two and his father was a *proper* fighter at that age. Remember? Old Henry would have torn their lungs out and worn 'em as gloves, just to keep his hands warm. Not the lamb, though. Not his boy. The lamb can't lead and the lamb can't fight. He can't even grow a beard, William! When they realize he ain't *never* coming, we're all done, understand? When the French stop trembling in terror about King Harry, the lion of bloody England, coming back, it's all finished. Maybe in a year or two, there'll be a French army clustering like wasps to come for a day out in London. A nice bit of rape and slaughter and we'll be taking off our caps and bowing whenever we hear a French voice. You want that for your daughters, William? For your sons? Those are your stakes, William *English* Pole."

"Then *tell* me how we can bring them to truce," Suffolk said slowly and with force.

At forty-six, he was a large man, with a mass of iron-gray hair that spread out from his wide head and fell almost to his shoulders. He'd put on bulk in the previous few years, and next to Derry he felt old. His right shoulder ached on most days and one of his legs had been badly gashed years before so that the muscle never healed properly. He limped in winter and he could feel it sending fingers of pain up his leg as he stood in the cold room. His temper was growing short.

"That's what the boy said to me," Derry replied. "'Bring me a truce, Derry,' he says. 'Bring me peace.' *Peace* when we could take it all with one good season of fighting. It turned my stomach—and his poor old dad must be turning in his grave. I've spent more time in the archives than any man with red blood should ever be asked to do. But I found it, William Pole. I found something the French won't turn down. You'll take it to them and they'll fret and worry, but they won't be able to resist. He'll get his truce."

"And will you share this revelation?" Suffolk asked, holding his temper with difficulty. The man was infuriating, but Derry would not be rushed and there was still the suspicion that the spymaster enjoyed having an earl wait on his word. Suffolk resolved not to give Derry the satisfaction of showing impatience. He crossed the room to pour himself a cup of water from a jug, draining it in quick swallows.

"Our Henry wants a wife," Derry replied. "They'd see hell freeze before they give him a royal princess like they did with his father. No, the French king will keep his daughters close by for Frenchmen, so I won't even give him the pleasure of turning us down. But there is one other house, William—Anjou. The duke there has paper claims to Naples, Sicily, and Jerusalem. Old René calls himself a king and he's ruined his family trying to claim his rights for ten years now. He's paid ransoms greater than you or I will ever see, William. And he has two daughters, one of them unpromised and thirteen."

Suffolk shook his head, refilling the cup. He had sworn off wine and beer, but this was one time when he truly missed the stuff.

"I *know* Duke René of Anjou," he said. "He hates the English. His mother was a great friend of that girl, Joan of Arc—and you'll recall, Derry, that we burned her."

"No more than right," Derry snapped. "You were there, you saw her. That little bitch was in league with someone, even if it wasn't the Devil himself. No, you're not seeing it, William. René has the ear of his king. That French peacock owes René of Anjou his crown, *everything*. Didn't René's mother give him sanctuary when he tucked up his skirts and ran? Didn't she send little Joan of Arc to Orléans to shame them into attacking? That family kept France in French hands, or at least the arse end of it. Anjou is the key to the whole lock, William. The French king married René's sister, for Christ's sake! That's the family that can put pressure on their little royal—and they're the ones with an unmarried daughter. They are the way in, I'm *telling* you. I've looked at them all, William, every French 'lord' with three pigs and two servants. Margaret of Anjou *is* a princess; her father beggared himself to prove it."

Suffolk sighed. It was late and he was weary.

"Derry, it's no good, even if you're right. I've met the duke more than once. I remember him complaining to me that English soldiers laughed at his order of chivalry. He was most offended, I recall."

"He should not have called it the Order of the Croissant, then, should he?"

"It's no stranger than the Order of the Garter, is it? Either way, Derry, he won't give us a daughter, certainly not in exchange for a truce. He might take a fortune for her, if things are as bad as you say, but a truce? They aren't all fools, Derry. We haven't had a campaign for a decade and every year it gets just a little harder to hold the land we have. They have an ambassador here and I'm sure he tells them everything he sees."

"He tells them what I let him see; don't you worry about *that*. I have that perfumed boy sewn up tight. But I haven't told you what we'll offer to make old René sweat and pull on his king's sleeve, just begging his monarch to accept our terms. He's poor as a blind archer without the rents from his ancestral lands. And why is that? Because *we* own them. He has a couple of derelict old castles that look out on the best farmland in France, with good Englishmen and soldiers enjoying it for him. Maine and Anjou entire, William. That will bring him to the table fast enough. That will win us our truce. Ten years? We'll demand twenty and a bloody princess. And René of Anjou has the king's ear. The snail-eaters will fall over themselves to say yes."

Suffolk rubbed his eyes in frustration. He could feel the taste of wine in his mouth, though he had not touched a drop for more than a year.

"This is madness. You'd have me give away a quarter of our land in France?"

"You think I like it, William?" Derry demanded angrily. "You think I haven't sweated for months looking for a better path? The king said, 'Bring me a truce, Derry'—well, this is it. This is the only thing that will do it, and, believe me, if there was another way, I'd have found it by now. If he could use his father's sword—Christ, if he could even lift it—I wouldn't be having this conversation with you. You and I would be out once more, with the horns blowing and the French on the run. If he can't do that—and he *can't*, William, you've seen him—then this is the only way to peace. We'll find him a wife as well, to conceal the rest."

"Have you told the king?" Suffolk asked, already knowing the answer.

"If I had, he'd agree, wouldn't he?" Derry replied bitterly. "'You know best, Derry,' 'If you think so, Derry.' You know how he talks. I could get him to say yes to anything. Trouble is, so can anyone else. He's weak like that, William. All we can do is get him a wife, bide our time, and wait for a strong son." He saw Suffolk's dubious expression and he snorted. "It worked for Edward, didn't it? The hammer of the bloody Scots had a weak son, but his grandson? I wish I'd known a king like that. No, I *did* know a king like that. I knew Harry. I knew the lion of bloody Agincourt, and maybe that's all a man can hope for in one lifetime. But while we wait for a proper monarch, we have to have a truce. The beardless boy isn't up to anything else."

"Have you even seen a picture of this princess?" Suffolk asked, staring off into the distance.

Derry laughed scornfully.

"Margaret? You like them young, do you? And you a married man, William Pole! What does it matter what she looks like? She's almost fourteen and a virgin; that's all that matters. She could be covered in warts and moles and our Henry would say, 'If you think I should, Derry,' and that's the truth of it."

Derry came to stand at Suffolk's shoulder, noting to himself how the older man seemed more bowed down than he had when he'd entered.

"They know you in France, William. They knew your father and your brother—and they know your family has paid its dues. They'll listen to you, if you take this to them. We'll still have the north and all the coast. We'll still have Calais and Normandy, Picardy, Brittany— all the way to Paris. If we could hold all that and Maine and Anjou as well, I'd be raising the flags and marching with you. But we can't."

"I'll need to hear this from the king before I go back," Suffolk said, his eyes bleak.

Derry looked away uncomfortably.

"All right, William. I understand. But you know . . . No, all right. You'll find him in the chapel. Maybe you can interrupt his prayers, I don't know. He'll agree with me, William. He always bloody agrees."

ACROSS A SWATH of frozen, crunching grass, the two men walked in darkness to the Windsor chapel, dedicated to the Blessed Virgin, Edward the Confessor, and St. George. In starlight, with his breath misting before him, Derry nodded to the guards at the outer door as they passed through into a candlelit interior that was almost as cold as the night outside.

The chapel seemed empty at first, though Suffolk sensed and then caught glimpses of men standing among the statues. In dark robes, they were almost invisible until they moved. Footsteps on stone echoed in the silence as the watchers walked toward the two men, faces hard with their responsibility. Twice, Derry had to wait until he was recognized before he could make his way along the nave toward the lone figure at prayer.

The monarch's seat was almost enclosed in carved and gilded wood, lit by dim lamps hanging far above. Henry knelt there with his hands out in front of him, tight-clenched and rigid. His eyes were closed, and Derry sighed softly to himself. For a time, he and Suffolk just stood and waited, gazing on the upraised face of a boy, lit gold in the darkness. The king looked angelic, but it broke both their hearts to see how young he seemed, how frail. It was said his birth had been a trial for his French mother. She had been lucky to survive, and the boy had been born blue and choking. Nine months later and his father, Henry V, was dead, torn from life by simple sickness after surviving a lifetime of war. There were some who said it was a blessing that the battle king had not lived to see his son become a man.

In the gloom, Derry and Suffolk looked at each other in silence, sharing the same sense of loss. Derry leaned close.

"It could be hours yet," he whispered into Suffolk's ear. "You'll have to interrupt or we'll be here till morning."

In response, Suffolk cleared his throat, the sound louder than he had intended in the echoing silence. The king's eyes fluttered open, as if he was returning from very far away. Slowly, Henry turned his head, taking in the two men standing there. He blinked, then smiled at them both, crossing himself and muttering a final prayer before rising on legs made stiff from hours of stillness.

Suffolk watched his king fumble with the latch of the monarch's seat before stepping down and approaching him. Henry left the pool of light behind so that they could not see his face as he came close.

Both men knelt, Suffolk's knees protesting. Henry chuckled over their bowed heads.

"My heart is full to see you, Lord Suffolk. Come, now, stand up. The floor is too cold for old men. I'm sure that's right. I hear my chambermaid complaining, though she doesn't know I'm there. She's younger than you, I think. Up, both of you, before you catch a chill."

As Derry stood, he opened the lamp he carried, spreading light across the chapel. The king was dressed in the simplest of clothes, just plain dark wool and blunt leather shoes like any townsman. He wore no gold and, with the look of a boy, he might have been an apprentice in some trade that did not require too much strength.

Suffolk searched the young man's face for some trace of the father, but the eyes were guileless and the frame was slender, showing no sign of the massive strength of his bloodline. Suffolk almost missed the bandages on Henry's hands. His gaze snagged on them and Henry held them up into the light, his face flushing.

"Sword practice, Lord Suffolk. Old Marsden says they'll harden, but they just bleed and bleed. I thought for a while . . ." He caught himself, raising one bound finger to tap lightly at his mouth. "No, you have not come from France to see my hands. Have you?"

"No, Your Grace," Suffolk answered gently. "Can you grant me a moment? I have been talking to Master Brewer about the future."

"No beer from Derry!" Henry said. "The only Master Brewer with no beer!"

It was an old jest, but both the older men chuckled dutifully. Henry beamed at them.

"In truth, I cannot go from this place. I am allowed to take a break each hour, for water or to fill a pot, but then I must return to my prayers. Cardinal Beaufort told me the secret and the burden is not too great."

"The secret, Your Grace?"

"That the French can't come while a king prays, Lord Suffolk! With my hands, even bandaged as they are, I hold them back. Isn't that a wonderful thing?"

Suffolk breathed slowly in and out, silently cursing the young man's great-uncle for his foolishness. There was no purpose in having Henry waste his nights in such a way, though Suffolk imagined it made it easier for those around him. Somewhere nearby, Cardinal Beaufort would be sleeping. Suffolk resolved to wake him up and have him join the boy in prayers. A king's prayers could only be gilded by those of a cardinal, after all.

Derry had been listening closely, waiting to speak.

"I'll clear the men away, my lord Suffolk. Your Grace, with your permission? This is a private matter, best not overheard."

Henry gestured for him to carry on while Suffolk smiled at the formal tone. For all Derry's bitterness and scorn, he was cautious in the presence of the king. There would be no blasphemy in that chapel, not from him.

The king seemed not to notice the half-dozen men Derry ushered out of the chapel into the frozen night. Suffolk was cynical enough to suspect one or two remained in the darkest alcoves, but Derry knew his own men and Henry's patience was already wearing thin, his gaze drifting back to his place of prayer.

Suffolk felt a surge of affection for the young king. He had watched Henry grow with the hopes of an entire country on his shoulders. Suffolk had seen those hopes falter and then crumble into disappointment. He could only guess how hard it had been for the boy himself. Henry was not stupid, for all his strangeness. He would have heard every barbed comment made about him over the years.

"Your Grace, Master Brewer has vouchsafed a plan to bargain for a wife and a truce together, in exchange for two great provinces of France. He believes the French will deliver a truce in exchange for Maine and Anjou."

"A wife?" Henry said, blinking.

"Yes, Your Grace, as the family in question has a suitable daughter. I wanted . . ." Suffolk hesitated. He could not ask whether the king understood what he was saying. "Your Grace, there are English subjects living in both Maine and Anjou. They would be evicted if we give them up. I wanted to ask if it isn't too high a price to pay for a truce."

"We must have a truce, Lord Suffolk. We must. My uncle the cardinal says so. Master Brewer agrees with him—though he has no beer! Tell me of the wife. Is there a picture?"

Suffolk closed his eyes for an instant before opening them.

"I will have one made, Your Grace. The truce, though. Maine and Anjou are the southern quarter of our lands in France. Together, they are as great as *Wales*, Your Grace. If we give such a tract of land away . . ."

"What is her name, this girl? I cannot call her 'girl' or even 'wife,' now, can I, Lord Suffolk?"

"No, Your Grace. Her name is Margaret. Margaret of Anjou."

"You will go to France, Lord Suffolk, and you will see her for me. When you return, I shall want to hear every detail."

Suffolk hid his frustration.

"Your Grace, do I have it right that you are willing to lose lands in France for peace?"

To his surprise, the king leaned in close to reply, his pale blue eyes gleaming.

"As you say, Lord Suffolk. We must have a truce. I depend on you to carry out my wishes. Bring me a picture of her."

Derry had returned while the conversation went on, his face carefully blank.

"I'm sure His Royal Highness would like to return to his prayers now, Lord Suffolk."

"I would, yes," Henry replied, holding up one bandaged hand in farewell. Suffolk could see a dark red stain at the center of the palm.

They bowed deeply to the young King of England as he walked back to his place and knelt, his eyes closing slowly, his fingers lacing together like a lock.

CHAPTER 2

Margaret let out a gasp as a hurrying figure thumped into her and they both went sprawling. She had a blurred sense of tight-drawn brown hair and a smell of healthy sweat and then she went down with a yelp. A copper pot crashed to the courtyard stones with a noise so great it hurt her ears. As Margaret fell, the maid flailed to catch the pot but only sent it spinning.

The maid looked up angrily, her mouth opening on a curse. As she saw Margaret's fine red dress and billowing white sleeves, the blood drained from her face, stealing away the flush from the kitchens. For an instant, her eyes flickered to the path, considering whether she could run. With so many strange faces in the castle, there was at least a chance the girl wouldn't recognize her again.

With a sigh, the maid wiped her hands on an apron. The kitchen mistress had warned her about the brothers and the father, but she'd said the youngest girl was a sweet little thing. She reached down to help Margaret to her feet.

"I'm sorry about that, dear. I shouldn't have been running, but it's all a rush today. Are you hurt?"

"No, I don't think so," Margaret replied dubiously. Her side ached and she thought she had scraped an elbow, but the woman was already shifting from foot to foot, wanting to be off. Back on her feet, Margaret smiled at her, seeing the gleam of sweat on the young woman's face.

"My name is Margaret," she said, remembering her lessons. "May I know your name?"

"Simone, my lady. But I must get back to the kitchens. There's a thousand things to do still, with the king coming."

Margaret saw the handle of the pot sticking out of the trimmed hedge by her foot and picked it up. To her pleasure, the woman curtsied as she took it back. They shared a smile before the maid vanished at only a fraction less than her original speed. Margaret was left alone to stare after her. Saumur Castle had not been this busy for years, and she could hear her father's deep voice raised somewhere nearby. If he saw her, he would put her to work, she was certain, so she headed in the opposite direction.

Her father's sudden return to Saumur had brought Margaret to bitter, furious tears more than once. She resented him as she would have resented any stranger who arrived with such airs, assuming all his rights as lord and master of her home. Over the decade of his absence, her mother had spoken often of his great bravery and honor, but Margaret had seen the blank spaces on yellowing plaster as paintings and statues were quietly taken and sold. The collection of jewelry had been the last to go, and she'd observed her mother's pain as men from Paris arrived to appraise the best pieces, staring through their little tubes and counting out coins. Every year had brought fewer luxuries and comforts, until Saumur was stripped of anything beautiful, revealed in cold stones. Margaret had grown to hate her father by then, without knowing him at all. Even the servants had been dismissed one by one, with whole sections of the castle closed and left to grow blue with mildew.

She looked up at the thought, wondering if she could get up to the east wing without being spotted and put to a task. There were mice running freely in one of the tower rooms, making their little nests in old couches and chairs. She had a pocket full of crumbs to entice them out, and she could spend the afternoon there. It had become her refuge, a hiding place that no one knew about, not even her sister Yolande.

When Margaret had seen the men from Paris counting the books in her father's beautiful library, she'd crept in at night and taken as many as she could carry, stealing them away to the tower room before they could vanish. She felt no guilt about it, even when her father returned and his booming orders echoed around her home. Margaret didn't really understand what a ransom was, or why they'd had to pay one to get him back, but she cherished the books she'd saved, even the one the mice had found and nibbled.

Saumur was a maze of back stairs and passages, the legacy of four centuries of building and expansion that meant some corridors came to a stop for no clear reason, while certain rooms could only be reached by passing through half a dozen others. Yet it had been her world for as long as she could remember. Margaret knew every route and, after rubbing her elbow, she went quickly, crossing a corridor and clattering through a wide, empty room paneled in oak. If her mother saw her running, there would be harsh words. Margaret caught herself dreading the footsteps of her governess as well, before she remembered that terror of her youth had been dismissed with all the others.

Two flights of wooden stairs brought her up to a landing that led straight across to the east tower. The ancient floorboards were bowed and twisted there, rising away from the joists below. Margaret had lost entire afternoons stepping on them in complicated patterns, making them speak in their creaking voices. She called it the Crow Room for the sound they made.

Panting lightly, she paused under the eaves to look out across the upper hall, as she always did. There was something special in being able to lean over the vast space, up at the level of the chandeliers, with their fat yellow candles. She wondered who would light them for the king's visit now that the tallowmen no longer called, but she supposed her father would have thought of it. He'd found the gold somewhere to hire all the new servants. The castle teemed with them like the mice in the tower, rushing hither and yon on unknown errands and all strangers to her.

Onward through the library, which made her shiver now that it was bare and cold. Yolande said some great houses had libraries on the ground floor, but even when they had been rich, her father had cared little for books. The shelves were thick with dust as she passed, idly drawing a face with a finger before hurrying on. At the library window, she looked down on a courtyard and scowled at the sight of her brothers practicing sword drills. John was battering little Louis to his knees and laughing at the same time. Nicholas was standing to one side, his sword tip trailing in the dust as he yelled encouragement to them both. With a glance around to make sure no one was watching, Margaret pointed her finger at her oldest brother and cursed him, calling on God to give John a rash in his private region. It didn't seem to affect his cheerful blows, but he deserved it for the pinch he'd given her that morning.

To her horror, John suddenly looked up, his gaze fastening on hers. He gave a great shout that she could hear even through the diamonds of glass. Margaret froze. Her brothers liked to chase her, imitating hunting horns with their mouths and hands while they ran her down through the rooms and corridors of the castle. Surely they would be too busy with the king coming? Her heart sank as she saw John break off and point, then all three went charging from sight below. Margaret gave up on the idea of going to her secret room. They had not discovered it yet, but if they came to the library, they would hunt all around that part of the castle. It would be better to lead them far away.

She ran, holding her skirt high and cursing them all with rashes and spots. The last time, they'd forced her into one of the great kitchen cauldrons and threatened to light the fire.

"Maman!" Margaret yelled. "Mamaaan!"

At full speed, she barely seemed to touch the steps, using her arms to guide her as she hurtled down a floor and cut across a corridor to her mother's suite of rooms. A startled maid jumped back with a mop and bucket as Margaret shot past. She could hear her brothers hallooing somewhere on the floor below, but she didn't pause, jumping down three steps that appeared in the floor in front of her, then up another three, some ancient facet of the castle's construction that had no clear purpose. Gasping for breath, she darted into her mother's dressing rooms, looking wildly around for sanctuary. She saw a huge and heavy wardrobe and, quick as winking, opened the door and shoved herself into the back, comforted by the odor of her mother's perfume and the thick furs.

Silence came, though she could still hear John calling her name in the distance. Margaret fought not to cough in the dust she had raised. She heard footsteps enter the room and held herself as still as any statue. It was not beyond John to send Nicholas or little Louis out in another direction, while John crashed around and gulled her into a feeling of safety. Margaret held her breath and closed her eyes. The wardrobe was at least warm and they surely wouldn't dare search for her in their mother's rooms.

The footsteps came closer and, with no warning, the door of the wardrobe creaked open. Margaret blinked at her father in the light.

"What are you *doing* in here, girl?" he demanded. "Do you not know the king is coming? If you have time for games, by God, you have too *much* time."

"Yes, sir, I'm sorry. John was chasing me and—"

"Your hands are filthy! Just look at the marks you have made! *Look* at them, Margaret! Running around like a street urchin with the king on his way!"

Margaret dipped her head, clambering out of the wardrobe and closing the door carefully behind her. It was true that her palms were black with grime, picked up in her wild scramble through the upper rooms. Resentment grew in her. Lord René may have been her father, but she had no memories of him, none at all. He was just a great white slug of a man who had come into her home and ordered her mother about like a servant. His face was unnaturally pale, perhaps from his years languishing in prison. His eyes were gray and cold, half hidden by heavy, unwrinkled lower lids, so that he always seemed to be peering over them. He had clearly not starved in the prison, she thought. That much was obvious. He'd complained to his wife about the tailor's fees for letting out his clothing, leaving her in tears.

"If I had a moment to spare, I'd have you whipped, Margaret! Those dresses will all have to be cleaned."

He shouted and gestured angrily for some time, while Margaret stood with her head bowed, trying to look suitably ashamed. There had been maids and house servants once, to scrub every stone and polish all the fine French oak. If dust lay thick now, whose fault was that, if not the man who had ruined Saumur for his vanity? Margaret had listened to him complaining to her mother about the state of the castle, but without an army of servants, Saumur was just too big to keep clean.

Margaret remembered to nod as her father raged. He called himself the King of Jerusalem, Naples, and Sicily, places she had never seen. She supposed it made her a princess, but she couldn't be certain. After all, he'd failed to win any of them, and a paper claim was worthless when he could only froth and strut and write furious letters. She hated him. As she stood there, she flushed at the memory of a conversation with her mother. Margaret had demanded to know why he couldn't just leave again. In response, her mother's mouth had pinched tight like a drawstring purse and she had spoken more harshly than Margaret could remember before.

Margaret sensed the slug was coming to the end of his tirade.

"Yes, sir," she said humbly.

"What?" he demanded, his voice rising. "What do you *mean*, 'Yes, sir'? Have you even been listening?" Spots of color bloomed on his white cheeks as his temper flared. "Just get out!" he snapped. "I don't want to see your face unless I call for you, do you understand? I have better things to do today than teach you the manners you obviously lack. Running wild! When the king is gone, I will consider some punishment you won't forget so easily. Go! Get out!"

Margaret fled, red-faced and trembling. She passed her brother Louis in the corridor outside, and for once he looked sympathetic.

"John's looking for you in the banqueting hall," he murmured. "If you want to avoid him, I'd go round by the kitchen."

Margaret shrugged. Louis thought he was clever, but she knew him too well. John would be in the kitchen, or close by, that much was obvious. They would not be able to put her in a cauldron, not with so many staff preparing a king's feast, but no doubt her brother would have thought of something equally unpleasant. With dignity, Margaret walked rather than ran, struggling with tears she could hardly understand. It didn't matter to her that the slug was angry; why would it? She resolved to find her mother, somewhere at the center of the bustle and noise that had been quiet just a few days before. Where *had* all the servants come from? There was no money for them and nothing left to sell.

By sunset, her brothers had given up their hunt in order to dress for the feast. The population of Saumur Castle had increased even more as King Charles sent his own staff ahead. As well as the cooks hired from noble houses and the local village, there were now master chefs check-ing every stage of the preparation and half a dozen men in black cloth examining every room for spies or assassins. For once, her father said nothing as his guards were questioned and organized by the king's men. The local villages all knew by then that there would be a royal visit. As darkness fell, with swallows wheeling and darting through the sky, the farmers had come in from their crofts and fields with their families. They stood on the verges of the road to Saumur, craning their necks to catch the first glimpse of royalty. The men removed their hats as the king passed, waving them in the air and cheering.

King Charles's arrival had not been as impressive as Margaret thought it would be. She'd watched from the tower window as a small group of horsemen came riding along the road from the south. There had been no more than twenty of them, clustered around a slender, dark-haired figure wearing a pale blue cloak. The king did not stop to acknowledge the peasants, as far as she could see. Margaret wondered if he thought the world was filled with cheering people, as if they were part of the landscape, like trees or rivers.

As the royal group rode through the main gate, Margaret had leaned out of the open window to watch. The king had seemed rather ordinary to her as he dismounted in the courtyard and handed his reins to a servant. His men were hard-faced and serious, more than one looking around with an expression of distaste. Margaret resented them immediately. She had watched her father come out and bow to the king before they went inside. René's voice carried up to the windows, loud and coarse. He tried too hard, Margaret thought. A man like the king would surely be weary of flattery.

The feast was a misery, with Margaret and Yolande banished to the far end of a long table, wearing stiff dresses that smelled of camphor and cedarwood and were far too precious to stain. Her brothers sat farther up the table, turning their heads to the king like travelers facing a good inn fire. As the oldest, John even attempted conversation, though his efforts were so stilted and formal that they made Margaret want to giggle. The atmosphere was unbearably stuffy, and of course her sister Yolande pinched her under the table to make her cry out and shame herself. Margaret poked her with a fork from a set of dining silver she had never seen before.

She knew she was not allowed to speak; her mother, Isabelle, had been quite clear about that. So she sat in silence as the wine flowed and the king favored her father or John with an occasional smile between courses.

Margaret thought King Charles was too thin and long-nosed to be handsome. His eyes were small black beads, and his eyebrows were thin lines, almost as if they had been plucked. She'd hoped he would be a man of panache and charisma, or at least wearing a crown of some kind. Instead, the king fiddled nervously with food that obviously didn't please him and merely raised the corners of his lips when he attempted to smile.

Her father filled the silences with stories and reminiscences of court, keeping up a stream of inane chatter that made Margaret embarrassed for him. The only excitement had come when her father's waving hands had knocked over a cup of wine, but the servants moved in swiftly and made it all vanish. Margaret could read the king's boredom, even if Lord René couldn't. She picked at each course, wondering at the cost of it all. The hall was lit with expensive fresh tapers and even white candles, which were usually only brought out at Christmas. She supposed the costs would mean months of hardship to come, when the king had gone. She tried to enjoy it all, but the sight of her father's long head bobbing in laughter just made her angry. Margaret sipped her cider, hoping they would become aware of her disapproval and perhaps even abashed. It was a fine thought, that they would look up and see the stern girl, then glance at plates heaped with food they would scarcely touch before the next course came. She knew that King Charles had met Joan of Arc, and she longed to ask the man about her.

At the king's side, her aunt Marie listened to René with a disapproving expression much like Margaret's own. Again and again, Margaret saw her aunt's gaze drift to her mother's throat, where no jewels lay. That was one thing René had not been able to borrow for the dinner. Her mother's jewels had all gone to finance his failed campaigns. As the king's wife, Aunt Marie wore a splendid set of rubies that dripped right down between her bosoms. Margaret tried not to stare, but they were meant to attract attention, weren't they? She would have thought a married woman would not want men to stare at her bosoms in such a way, but apparently she did. Marie and René had grown up in Saumur, and Margaret saw her aunt's assessing eye flicker from the bare ears and throat of her mother to the enormous tapestries hanging along the walls. Margaret wondered if she would recognize any of them. Like the servants, they were borrowed or leased for a few days only. She could almost hear her aunt's thoughts clicking away like a little abacus. Her mother always said Marie had a hard heart, but she had won a king with it and all the luxury of his life.

Not for the first time, Margaret wondered what could have brought King Charles to Saumur Castle. She knew there would be no serious talk during the dinner, perhaps not even until the king had rested or hunted the following day. Margaret resolved to visit the balcony above the upper hall when she was allowed to go to bed. Her father took honored guests in there to enjoy the great fire and a selection of his better wines. At the thought, she leaned closer to Yolande, just as the girl was trying to tweak her bare arm in pure mischief.

"I'll twist your ear and make you shriek if you do, Yolande," she muttered.

Her sister pulled her hand back sharply from where it had been creeping over the table. At fifteen, Yolande was perhaps her closest companion, though of late she had taken on the airs and graces of a young woman, telling Margaret pompously that she couldn't play childish games anymore. Yolande had even given her a beautiful painted doll, spoiling the gift with a dismissive comment on baby things she no longer needed.

"Will you come up the back stairs with me after the feast, to listen at the balcony? By the Crow Room."

Yolande considered, tilting her head slightly as she weighed her exciting new sense of adulthood against her desire to see the king speak to their father in private.

"For a little while, perhaps. I know you get frightened in the dark."

"That's you, Yolande, and you know it. I'm not afraid of spiders, either, even the big ones. You'll come, then?"

Margaret could sense her mother's disapproving stare turned on her, and she applied herself to some cut fruit on a bed of ice. The slender pieces were half frozen and delicious, and she could hardly remember when a meal had finished with such fine things.

"I'll come," Yolande whispered.

Margaret reached out and rested her hand on her sister's, knowing better than to risk her mother's wrath with another word. Her father was telling some tedious story about one of his tenant farmers, and the king chuckled, sending a ripple of laughter down the table. The meal had surely been a success, but Margaret knew he hadn't come to Saumur for wine and food. With her head low, she looked up the table at the King of France. He looked so very ordinary, but John, Louis, and Nicholas were apparently fascinated by him, ignoring their food at the slightest comment from his royal lips. Margaret smiled to herself, knowing she would mock them for it in the morning. It would pay them back for hunting her like a little fox.

CHAPTER 3

The Crow Room was silent as Margaret moved across it in bare feet. She'd spent part of the previous summer sketching the floor in charcoal on the back of an old map, marking each groaning joint or board with tiny crosses. The light from the fire in the upper hall spilled up over the balcony, and she crossed it like a dancer, taking exaggerated steps in a pattern that matched the one she saw in her memory. The crows remained silent, and she reached the balcony in triumph, turning back to gesture to Yolande.

Lit by flickering gold and shadow, her sister fluttered her hands in frustration, but she had caught the same illicit excitement and crept out across the polished boards, wincing with Margaret as they groaned under her. The two girls froze at every sound, but their father and the king were oblivious. The fire huffed and crackled, and an old house always moved and shifted in the night. René of Anjou didn't look up as Yolande settled herself beside her sister and peered down through the upright wooden balusters on to the scene below.

The upper hall had survived the stripping of Saumur almost intact. Perhaps because it remained the heart and center of the family seat, its tapestries and oak furniture had been safe from the men of Paris. The fireplace was big enough for a grown man to walk into without dipping his head. A log the size of a small couch burned merrily there, heating black iron pokers laid across it until the tips glowed gold. King Charles sat in a huge padded chair drawn close to the flames, while her father stood and fussed with cups and bottles. Margaret watched in fascination as René plunged one of the pokers into a goblet of wine for his king, sending up a hiss of steam and sweetening the air. She could smell cloves and cinnamon, and her mouth quirked as she imagined the taste of it. The heat did not reach as far as her hiding place, unfortunately. The stones of the castle sucked warmth away, especially at night. Margaret shivered as she sat there with her legs curled up to one side, ready to dart away from the light if her father looked up.

Both men had changed their clothes, she saw. Her father wore a quilted sleeping robe over loose trousers and felt shoes. In the flickering light she thought it made him look like a sorcerer, gesturing with steam and fire over the cups. The king wore a heavy garment of some shimmering material, belted at his waist. The fanciful idea pleased her, that she was witness to some arcane rite between magic workers. Her father's unctuous tones shattered the illusion.

"You have brought them to this position, Your Majesty, no other. If you had not secured Orléans and strengthened the army into the force it has become, they would not be pleading for a truce now. This is a sign of our strength and their weakness. They have come to us, Your Majesty, as supplicants. It is all to your glory and the glory of France."

"Perhaps, René. Perhaps you are right. Yet they are cunning and clever—like Jews, almost. If I were dying of thirst and an Englishman offered me a cup of water, I would hesitate and look for the advantage it brought him. My father was more trusting, and they repaid his goodwill with deceit."

"Your Majesty, I agree with you. I hope I am never so trusting as to shake the hand of an English lord without checking my pockets afterward! Yet we have the report of your ambassador. He said their king hardly spoke to him at all and he was rushed in and out of the royal presence as if the room was on fire. This Henry is not the man his father was, or he would have renewed their wanton destruction years ago. I believe this is an offer made from weakness—and in that weakness, we can regain lands lost to us. For Anjou, Your Majesty, but also for France. Can we afford to ignore such an opportunity?"

"That is *exactly* why I suspect a trap," King Charles said sourly, sipping his hot wine and breathing in the steam. "Oh, I can well believe they want a French princess to improve their polluted line further, to bless it with better blood. I have seen two sisters given over to English hands, René. My father was . . . inconstant in his final years. I am certain he did not fully understand the danger of giving Isabelle to their King Richard, or my beloved Catherine to the English butcher. Is it so surprising that they now claim my own throne, my own inheritance? The impudence, René! The boy Henry is a man of two halves: one angel, one devil. To think I have an English king as my nephew! The saints must laugh, or weep—I don't know."

The king drained his cup, his long nose dipping into the vessel. He made a face as he reached the dregs and wiped a purple line from his lips with his sleeve. He gestured idly, lost in thought, as Margaret's father refilled the cup and brought another poker out of the rack in the fire.

"I do not want to strengthen their claim with one more drop of French blood, Lord Anjou. Will you have me disinherit my own children for a foreign king? And for what? Little Anjou? Maine? A truce? I would rather gather my army and kick them black and blue until they fall into the sea. That is the answer I want to give, not a truce. Where is the honor in that? Where is the dignity while they sell wheat and salt peas in Calais and polish their boots on French tables? It is not to be borne, René."

Above, Margaret watched her father's expression change, unseen by the gloomy king. René was thinking hard, choosing his words with great care. She knew her mother had been feeding him oil and senna pods for his constipation, one legacy of his imprisonment he seemed to have brought home with him. The heavy white face was flushed with wine or the heat from the fire, and he did look congested, she thought, a man stuffed full of something unpleasant. Her dislike only deepened, and, against reason, she hoped he would be disappointed, whatever it was he wanted.

"Your Majesty, I am at your command in all things. If you say it is to be war, I will have the army march against the English in spring. Perhaps we will have the luck of Orléans once again."

"Or perhaps the luck of Agincourt," King Charles replied, his voice sour. For a moment, his arm jerked, as if he was considering throwing his cup into the fire. He controlled himself with a visible effort. "If I could be certain of victory, I would raise the flags tomorrow, I swear it." He brooded for a time, staring into the flames as they shifted and flickered. "Yet I have seen them fight, the English. I remember those red-faced, shouting animals roaring in triumph. They have no culture, but their men are savage. *You* know, René. You have seen them, those ham hocks with their swords and bows, those great fat blunderers who know nothing but slaughter." He waved a hand in irritation at dark memories, but Margaret's father dared to interrupt before the king could ruin all his hopes and plans.

"What a triumph it would be to take back a quarter of their land in France without even a battle, Your Majesty! For a mere promise of truce and a marriage, we will win more than anyone has in a decade or longer against them. They have no lion of England any longer, and we would have denied them the heart of France."

King Charles snorted.

"You are too obvious, René. I see very well that you want your family lands returned to you. The benefit is clear to your line. Less so to mine!"

"Your Majesty, I cannot disagree. You see clearer and further than I could ever do. Yet I can serve you better with the wealth of Anjou and Maine in my hands. I can repay my debts to the Crown with those rents, Your Majesty. Our gain is their loss, and even an acre of France is worth a little risk, I am certain." He warmed to his theme, seeing the king's grudging approval. "An acre of France returned is worth a great deal, Your Majesty, still more when it is returned from the old enemy. That is a victory, whether it is brought about by French negotiation or French blood. Your lords will see only that you have won land back from the English."

The king sighed to himself, setting his cup down on the stone floor to rub his eyes.

"Your daughter will be an English queen, of course, if I agree to this. I take it she is of sound character?"

"Your Majesty, she is the very soul of demure nobility. It can only strengthen your position to have a loyal member of my family in the English court."

"Yes . . . there is that," Charles said. "But it is close to incestuous, René, is it not? King Henry is already my nephew. Your daughters are my nieces. I would have to apply to the Pope for special dispensation—and that has its costs, at least if we want it granted within the decade."

René smiled at the signs of progress. He knew the English would send to Rome for the dispensation if he demanded it. He was also aware that his king was bargaining for a tithe in exchange for his agreement. The fact that Saumur's treasure rooms were filled with empty sacks and spiders bothered him not at all. He could borrow more, from the Jews.

"My lord, it would be an honor to meet those costs, of course. I sense we are very close to a solution."

Slowly, Charles dipped his head, his mouth working as if he had found a morsel in his back teeth.

"Very well, I will be guided by you in this, René. You will be lord of Anjou and Maine once more. I trust you will be suitably grateful."

René knelt, reaching for the king's hand and pressing it to his lips.

"I am your man, Your Majesty. You may depend on me for any task, even to my life's blood."

Far above their heads, Margaret's eyes were round and wide as she turned away. Yolande was staring, her mouth hanging open. Reaching out, Margaret closed it gently with a finger.

"I am already promised," Yolande whispered. "Father would not break my engagement."

In silent accord, they crept back from the light, with Margaret wincing as the boards complained under them. Away from the balcony, the two sisters stood up in the gloom. Yolande was trembling in excitement, and she gripped her sister's hands, almost hopping in place, as if she wanted to dance.

"You'll marry a king, Margaret. It *has* to be you."

"An English king," Margaret replied doubtfully. She had always known her husband would be chosen for her, but she had assumed her mother would make the choice, or at least be involved in it. She looked irritably at her sister, bouncing like a robin in the shadows.

"I have been bargained for like a prize heifer, Yolande. You heard them. It is . . . overwhelming."

Yolande drew her still farther away, into another room that was even darker without the spilled gleam from the balcony. In pale moonlight, she embraced her sister.

"You will be a *queen*, Margaret. That is what matters. Their Henry is young, at least. You could have been given to some fat old lord. Are you not thrilled? When we are grown, I will have to bow to you when we meet. Our brothers will have to bow to you!"

A slow smile spread across Margaret's face at the thought of her brother John being forced to acknowledge her superior rank. It was a pleasant image.

"I could have some English guardsman stuff him in a cauldron, perhaps," she said, giggling.

"You could, and no one would stop you because you would be a queen."

Some of Yolande's uncomplicated pleasure reached her, and the two girls held hands in the darkness.

THE CITY OF ANGERS was beautiful in the evening. Though it was the capital of Anjou and so under English authority, the inhabitants rarely encountered the foreign oppressors, outside of the courts and tax-gatherers. Reuben Moselle had invited many of the English merchants to his house on the river, as he did every year. In trade alone, the party always paid for itself, and he considered it a fair investment.

In comparison to the French and English, he dressed very simply, in dark colors. It had long been a habit of his not to show his wealth in his attire. It did not matter that he could have bought and sold many of the men in the room, or that a third of them owed him a fortune in gold, land, or liens on their businesses. Away from his bank or in it, he was the soul of modesty.

He noted that his wife was talking to Lord York, making him welcome in their home. Sara was a treasure, finding it far easier than Reuben did to speak to the bluff English rulers. On the whole, Reuben preferred the French, whose subtle minds were more suited to the nuances of business. Yet York commanded the English soldiers in Normandy and had been invited as a matter of course. The man controlled contracts for vast sums, just to feed his men-at-arms. Reuben sighed as he rehearsed his English and approached them through the crowd.

"Milord York," he said, smiling. "I see you have met my wife. It is a great honor to have you in my home."

The nobleman turned to see who had addressed him, and Reuben forced himself to smile under a stare that was full of disdain. The moment seemed to last a long time; then York inclined his head in acknowledgment, the spell broken.

"Ah, the host," York said without noticeable warmth. "Monsieur Moselle, may I introduce my wife, Duchess Cecily?"

"Mon plaisir, madame," Reuben said, bowing.

She did not extend her hand, and he was caught in the act of reaching for it, covering his confusion by fiddling with his wineglass. Diamonds sparkled at her throat, and she seemed well suited to her English husband, with cold eyes and thin lips that did not smile. Everything about her looked stern and humorless, Reuben thought. Her eyebrows had been plucked almost to nothing, and across her white forehead she wore a band of lace sewn with gems.

"You have a fine house, monsieur," the duchess said. "My husband tells me you are in trade." She spoke the word as if she could hardly bear to dirty her lips with it.

"Thank you, madame. I have a small bank and supply house, a local affair, for the most part. Your husband's valiant soldiers must be kept fed and warm in the winter. It falls to me to provide some of their comforts."

"For a fortune in gold," York added. "I have been considering other suppliers, Monsieur Moselle, but this is not the place to discuss such things."

Reuben blinked at the tone, though he had heard it before in men of all stations.

"I hope I can dissuade you, milord. It has been a profitable association for us both."

The wife's mouth twisted at the mention of profit, but Reuben continued to smile, trying hard to be a good host.

"Dinner will be served very soon, madame. I hope you enjoy what small pleasures we can provide. If you have a moment, the orangerie is lovely at night."

Reuben was at the point of excusing himself when he heard coarse voices raised in the garden. He pursed his lips tight, hiding his irritation behind the wineglass as he sipped from it. One of the local farmers had been trying for some time to bring him in front of a magistrate. It was a trivial matter, and Reuben knew the city officials too well to be worried about some poor peasant with a grievance. It was not impossible that the fool had come to the annual party to cause a disturbance. He tilted his head, exchanging a glance with his wife that showed she understood.

"I should go and see to my other guests. Lady York, milord. I'm very sorry."

The noise was increasing, and he could see dozens of heads turning. Reuben moved smoothly through the crowd, smiling and making his excuses as he went. His wife would entertain the English lord and his cold wife, making them both welcome, he thought. Sara was God's gift to a devout man.

The house had once belonged to a French baron, a family fallen on hard times and forced to sell their properties after disasters in battle. Reuben had bought it outright, much to the disgust of local noble families who objected to a Jew owning a Christian home. Yet the English were more relaxed about such things, or at least easy to bribe.

Reuben reached the great windows in clear glass that opened out onto the lawn. They were folded back that night, to let in the warm air. He frowned as he saw soldiers standing with their boots on the neatly trimmed grass. His guests were all listening, of course, so he kept his voice calm and low.

"Gentlemen, as you can see, I am in the middle of a private dinner for friends. Can this not wait until tomorrow morning?"

"Are you Reuben Moselle?" one of the soldiers asked. The voice contained a sneer, but Reuben dealt with that every day, and his pleasant expression didn't falter.

"I am. You are standing in my home, sir."

"You do well for yourself," the soldier replied, looking into the hall.

Reuben cleared his throat, feeling the first tingle of nervousness. The man was confident, where usually he might have expected a certain wariness around wealth and power.

"May I have the honor of knowing your name in return?" Reuben said, his voice shading into coldness. The soldier did not deserve his courtesy, but there were still too many interested heads turned in his direction.

"Captain Recine of Saumur, Monsieur Moselle. I have orders for your arrest."

"Pardon? On what charge? This is a mistake, Captain, I assure you. The magistrate is inside, in fact. Allow me to take you to him and he will explain—"

"I have my orders, monsieur. An accusation has been made, at *département* level. You'll come with me now. You can explain yourself to the judge."

Reuben stared at the soldier. The man had dirty hands and his uniform stank, but there was still that unsettling confidence about him. Three more men showed yellow teeth at his back, enjoying the discomfort they were causing. The thought of being forced to go with such men made Reuben begin to sweat.

"I wonder if I can be of help, Monsieur Moselle?" a voice said at his shoulder.

He turned to see the figure of Lord York standing there with a glass of wine in his hand. Reuben breathed in relief. The English noble looked like a soldier, with his jutting chin and wide shoulders. The French soldiers were instantly more respectful.

"This . . . captain is saying I am to be arrested, Lord York," Reuben said quickly, deliberately using the title. "He has not yet mentioned the charge, but I am certain there has been some sort of mistake."

"I see. What *is* the charge?" York said.

Reuben could see the soldier consider an insolent reply, but then the man shrugged. It was not wise to irritate a man of York's reputation and influence, at least not for a lowly captain.

"Blasphemy and witchcraft, milord. He'll have to answer at the court in Nantes."

Reuben felt his mouth fall open in surprise.

"Blasphemy and . . . This is madness, monsieur! Who is my accuser?"

"Not my place to say," the soldier replied. He was watching Lord York, fully aware that the man could choose to interfere. Reuben, too, turned to the Englishman.

"My lord, if you will have them return tomorrow morning, I am certain I can find witnesses and assurances that will reveal this for the falsehood it is."

York looked down on him and his eyes glittered in the lamplight.

"It does not strike me as a matter for English law, Monsieur Moselle. This is no business of mine."

The captain smiled wider at hearing that. He stepped forward and took Reuben by the arm in a firm grip.

"Begging your indulgence, monsieur. Come with me now. I don't want to have to drag you." The grip grew stronger, giving the lie to his words. Reuben stumbled with it, unable to believe what was happening.

"The magistrate is in my house, Captain! Will you at least let me bring him out to you? He will explain it all."

"It's not a local matter, monsieur. Why don't you say something else and give me the pleasure of knocking your teeth into the back of your throat?"

Reuben shook his head, mute with fear. He was fifty years old and already breathing hard. The violent threat astonished him.

Richard, Duke of York, watched his host being taken away with something like amusement. He saw his wife come through the crowd to stand at his shoulder, her expression delighted as the elderly man stumbled out through the gardens with his captors.

"I thought this evening would be terribly dull," she said. "That is the only way to deal with Jews. They grow too bold unless they are reminded of their station. I hope they beat him for his insolence."

"I'm sure they will, my dear," he said, amused.

In the main hall, they both heard a shriek as the news reached Reuben's wife. Cecily smiled.

"I think I would like to see the orangerie," she said, extending her arm for her husband to guide her inside.

"The charges are rather serious, my dear," York said thoughtfully. "I could buy the house for you, if you wish. Angers is splendid in summer and I have no property here."

Her thin lips curled as she shook her head.

"Better to have it burned and rebuilt, after the previous owner," she replied, making him laugh as they went in.

CHAPTER 4

Reuben tasted blood in his mouth as he staggered sideways across the road. He could smell the unwashed crowd that bayed and spat at him, calling him "Christ killer" and "blasphemer," their faces red with righteous indignation. Some of them threw stones and cold, wet filth that struck him on the chest and slithered inside his open shirt.

Reuben ignored the outraged citizens. They could hardly hurt him worse than he had been already. Every part of him was bruised or battered and one of his eyes was just a sticky blind mass that seeped a trail of fluid down his cheek. He limped as he was shoved along the streets of Nantes, crying out as his feet bled through the wrappings and left red prints on the stones behind him.

He had lost something in the months of torture and imprisonment. Not his faith. He had never doubted for a moment that his enemies would receive the same punishments. God would seek them out and bow their heads with hot iron. Yet his belief in any sense of decency in men had been crushed along with his feet. No one had come to speak for him or to claim him from the courts. He knew at least a dozen men with the authority and wealth to secure his release, but they had all stayed silent as news of his terrible crimes became known. Reuben shook his head wearily, washed through with a sense of fatalism. There was no sense to any of it. As if a man of his standing would spend his evenings drinking the blood of Christian children! Not when there was good red wine in his cellar.

The charges had been so monstrous that at first he had been certain they would be revealed as lies. No sensible man could believe any of it. Yet the city judges had screwed up their fat mouths as they stared down at the broken, battered figure dragged up from the cells. They looked on him with disgust on their faces, as if he had somehow chosen to become the shambling, stinking thing the court inquisitors had made of him. Wearing black caps, the judges had pronounced a sentence of death by flaying, with every sign of satisfaction at a job well done.

Reuben had learned a sort of courage in his cell, with the boot they made him wear that could be wound tighter and tighter until his bones creaked and broke. In all his life, he had never had the strength or the wind to fight. With what God had given him, he had made himself wealthy: with his intellect, secretly scorning those who paraded their ability to lift lengths of iron into the air and swing them. Yet when the pain was unbearable, when he had stripped his throat raw with screaming, he had still not confessed. It was a stubbornness he had not known was in him, perhaps the only way left to show his contempt. He had wanted to meet his execution with that shred of pride still intact, like a last thread of gold in a worn cloak.

The senior judge from Nantes had come to the cell after many days. Jean Marisse looked like a cadaver, holding a pomander of dry petals to his nose against the stink. Masked in dried blood and his own filth, Reuben had glared up at him through his one good eye, hoping to shame Marisse with something like dignity. He could not speak by then. His teeth had all been broken, and he could barely take in the slop of porridge they brought each day to keep him alive.

"I see the Devil's pride is still in him," Jean Marisse had said to the guards.

Reuben had stared in dull hatred. He knew Jean Marisse, as he knew all the officials of the region. It had once seemed a profitable enterprise to learn their habits, though it had not saved him. The man had a reputation among the whores of the town as one who preferred to whip rather than kiss. There was even talk of a girl who had died after an evening with him. Marisse's wife would have been scandalized at the news, Reuben was certain. His mind had swirled with his own accusations, but there was no one to listen and his tongue had been pulled to its full extent and mangled with pincers designed for the purpose.

"Your questioners tell me you will not confess to your sins," Jean Marisse had said. "Can you hear me, Monsieur Moselle? They say you will not sign anything, though they have left your right hand untouched for that purpose. Do you not understand this could all end? Your fate has already been written, as sure as sunset. There is nothing left for you. Confess and seek absolution. Our Lord is a merciful God, though I do not expect one of you Abrahams to understand. It is written that you must burn for your heresies, but who can say, truly? If you repent, if you confess, He may yet spare you the fires of hell."

Reuben remembered staring back. He'd felt as if he could channel all his pain into his gaze, until it would strip away the man's lies and flesh and open him down to the bone. Marisse already looked like a corpse, with his thin face and skin like wrinkled yellow parchment. Yet God did not strike him down. Jean Marisse had thrust out his chin, as if the silence itself was a challenge to his authority.

"Your property is forfeit, you understand? No man may profit from an association with the Devil. Your wife and children will have to make their own way in the world. You have made it hard enough for them with your rites and secret magic. We have a witness, Monsieur Moselle, a Christian of good standing and unimpeachable honor. Do you understand? There is no hope for you in this world. Who will take in your family now, when you are gone? Shall they continue to suffer for what you have done? Heaven cries out, Reuben Moselle. It cries out against the pain of innocents. Confess, man—and this will end!"

In the street, Reuben staggered against a shouting peasant, his broken foot betraying him. The burly apprentice struck out immediately, cracking Reuben's head back and sending a fresh flow of blood spattering from his nose. He saw bright drops of it gleam on the straw and filth that made up the road to the town square. One of the guards snarled at the apprentice, shoving him back into the crowd with a pike pole held across his chest. Reuben heard the man cackle even so, delighted to be able to tell his friends he had landed a stroke on the Jew's head.

He staggered on, his mind fluttering in and out of clarity. The road seemed to go on forever, and every step was lined with townspeople come to see him die. Some snot-nosed urchin stuck out a foot and Reuben fell with a grunt, his knees striking the stones so that a lance of pain went up his legs. The crowd laughed, delighted that some part of the scene would play out in front of them. The ones pressed six-deep along the route at that stage could not afford to bribe their way into the main square.

Reuben felt a strong arm lift him up, accompanied by a smell of garlic and onions that he knew well from the prison. He tried to thank the guard for his help, but his words were unintelligible.

"On your feet," the man growled at him. "It's not far now."

Reuben remembered Jean Marisse leaning over him in his cell, like a crow examining a body for some part still worth eating.

"There are some who wonder how a Jew could carry out such filthy spells and rituals without his wife and children knowing. Do you understand me, Monsieur Moselle? There are some who whisper that the wife is surely as guilty as the husband, that the children must be as tainted as the father. They are saying it would be a crime to let them go free. If you do not confess, it will be my duty to bring them here to these cells, to put them to the question. Can you imagine what it would be like for a woman, Monsieur Moselle? Or a child? Can you conceive of their terror? Yet evil cannot be allowed to take root. Weeds must be torn out and cast on the fire before they spread their seed on the wind. Do you understand, monsieur? Sign the confession and this will end. All this will end."

Just a year before, Reuben would have laughed at such a threat. He'd had friends and wealth then, even influence. The world had been an ordered place where innocent men did not find themselves held down and screaming as strangers worked on them, with no one coming to help or one word of comfort to be had. He'd learned what evil really was in the cells beneath the prison yard at Nantes. Hope had died in him as his flesh was burned and broken.

He'd signed. The memory was clear in his mind, looking down on his own shaking hand as he put his name to lies without bothering to read them. Jean Marisse had smiled, his lips peeling back from rotting teeth as he'd leaned close. Reuben still remembered his warm breath and the fact that the judge's voice had been almost kind.

"You have done well, monsieur," Marisse had said. "There is no shame in telling the truth at last. Take comfort in that."

The town square was packed with onlookers, leaving only a narrow path between ranks of guards. Reuben shuddered as he saw cauldrons of bubbling water on either side of a raised platform. The manner of his death had been described to him with relish by his torturers. It had amused them to make sure he understood what awaited. Boiling water would be poured over his skin, searing it from the bones and making it easier to strip long pieces of steaming flesh from his arms and chest. It would be hours of impossible torment for the pleasure of the crowd. Reuben knew with a shudder that he could *not* bear it. He saw himself becoming a screaming animal before them all, with all his dignity ripped away. He dared not think of his wife or his daughters. They would not be abandoned, he told himself, shaking. His brother would surely take them in.

Even the thoughts of his enemies had to be squashed down to a small corner of his mind. He was half certain he knew the architect of his fall, for all the good it did him. Duke René of Anjou had borrowed fortunes in the months before his arrest, against the security of Saumur Castle. The first tranche of repayment had been due around the time the soldiers came to arrest him. Reuben's wife had advised against making the loan, saying it was well known that the Anjou family had no money, but then a lord like René of Anjou could ruin a man just as easily for a refusal.

As Reuben was bound to poles facing the crowd, he tried to resist the gibbering terror that screamed inside him. It would be hard, as hard as they could make it. He could only wish for his heart to give way, the frightened, leaping thing that pounded in his chest.

The men on the platform were all locals, paid a few silver deniers for the day's work. Reuben did not know any of the faces, for which he was thankful. It was hard enough to have strangers howling and raging at him. He did not think he could stand to see the faces of men he knew. As his limbs were fastened in place with harsh tugging, the crowd pressed in to see his wounds, pointing them out in fascination.

His gaze swept across the empty, roaring faces, then stopped suddenly, the mist clearing from his good eye. A balcony hung over the square and a small group of men and women rested there, watching the proceedings and talking among themselves. Reuben knew Lord York even before the man saw him looking and met his stare with interest. Reuben saw the man catch his wife's attention, and she, too, looked over the railing, pressing her hand to her mouth in delighted awe as his bony chest was revealed.

Reuben looked down, his humiliation complete. The men on the platform had stripped his shirt away, revealing a mass of colorful bruises in all shades of yellow and purple, down almost to black where his ribs had been kicked and cracked.

"*Baruch dayan emet,*" Reuben muttered, pronouncing the words with difficulty. The crowd did not hear him bless the only true judge that mattered. He tried to press them away from him, closing his eyes as the first clay jugs were dipped into bubbling water and the long knives were shown to the crowd. He knew he could not bear it, but neither could he die, until they let him.

PORTSMOUTH was loud with street criers and the bustle of one of the kingdom's great ports. Despite the anonymity of the busy street, Derry Brewer had insisted on emptying the inn of all customers and staff before he spoke a word of private business. He had three burly guards outside, facing disgruntled patrons unable even to finish their beers.

Derry crossed to the bar and sniffed at a jug before pouring dark ale into a big wooden mug. He raised it up in a mock toast as he sat back down and drank a deep draft. Lord Suffolk poured from the jug of water on the table, emptying his cup and smacking his lips as he refilled it. Eyeing him, Derry pulled a satchel around from his back and rootled around in its depths. He held up a roll of parchment, sealed with wax and wrapped in a gold ribbon.

"It seems the Pope is willing enough, William. I am amazed at such a spiritual man finding some purpose for the chest of silver we sent him, but perhaps it will go to the poor, no?"

Suffolk chose not to dignify the mocking question with an answer. He took another long drink to wash the taste of sea salt from his mouth. He'd spent the last six months traveling back and forth from France so often that the Portsmouth dockers greeted him by name as they doffed their hats. He was weary beyond belief, sick of discussions and arguments in two languages. He eyed the bound roll in Derry's hands, aware that it signaled a fast-approaching reality.

"No congratulations?" Derry said cheerfully. "No 'Well done, Derry'? I am disappointed in you, William Pole. There's not many men could have pulled this off in such a time, but I have, haven't I? The French looked for foxes and found only innocent chickens, just like we wanted. The marriage will go ahead, and all we need to do now is mention casually to the English living in Maine and Anjou that their service is no longer appreciated by the Crown. In short, that they can fuck off."

Suffolk winced, both at the word and the truth of it. The English in Anjou and Maine ran businesses and huge estates. From noble lords with power and influence to the lowest apprentices, they would all be enraged when a French army came to evict them.

"There is one thing, though, William. One delicate little matter that I hesitate to bring up to a noble lord of your exalted station in life."

"What *is* it, Derry?" Suffolk said, tired of the games. His cup of water was empty again, but the jug was dry. Derry swirled his ale around in the mug, staring at the liquid as it moved.

"They've asked for the marriage to take place in the cathedral at Tours, that's what. Land that will have the French army camped outside, ready to take possession of the price of the truce, that's what! I'm not letting Henry walk in there, William, not while there's life in me."

"You're not *letting* him?" Suffolk replied, raising an eyebrow.

"You know what I mean. It would be like dangling a bit of beefsteak in front of a cat. They'll never let him out of their clutches, I'm telling you now."

"So change the venue. Insist on Calais, perhaps. If he's not safe there, he wouldn't be safe getting married in England."

"Those letters you have carried for months were not just makeweight, William Pole. They wouldn't accept Calais, where their royals would be surrounded by an English army. I wonder why that is? Here's a thought. Could it be for the same reason we wouldn't agree to Tours? Give me credit for having some wits, William. I tried to insist, but they wouldn't budge a bloody inch. Either way, no matter where we hold it, we have another problem, don't we? Our Henry can't be allowed to speak to the French king. Just a short chat with the lamb and they'll be blowing their own bloody trumpets and looking across the Channel."

"Ah. Yes, that is a problem. In Tours or Calais. I can't see . . . Is there not some neutral position, halfway between the two?"

Derry looked up scornfully at the older man.

"What a shame I never had your fine mind to help me when I was poring over the maps looking for just such a place. The answer is no, William. There is English territory and French territory. There *is* no in-between. Either we give way or they do, or the whole thing comes to a stop and there'll be no marriage and no truce. Oh, and we haven't solved the problem of the lamb having to remain silent for the entire service, either. Do you think he'll accept that, William? Or is it more likely that he'll tell them he holds their ships back with his bloody hands each night? What do you think?"

William saw Derry was smiling even as he announced the certain failure of months of work.

"You have a solution," he said. "Is that it?"

Derry raised his beer again, swallowing deeply and putting it down empty.

"Nice drop, that. Yes, I have an answer to your prayers, William Pole. Or an answer to his royal ones, maybe. He'll get married at Tours, all right. He just won't be there."

"What? Is this some sort of riddle, Derry?" He saw the other man's eyes grow cold, and he swallowed.

"I don't like being doubted, William Pole. I told you I had an answer and there aren't three other men in England who could have thought their way through the wisps of fog the French have wrapped around this. You know what they're like, so cocksure of their own superiority that they can hardly believe we keep thrashing them. It takes a certain kind of arrogance to ignore getting your backside tanned for you so many times, but they do manage it. Don't ask me how." He looked at the confusion in Lord Suffolk's expression and shook his head.

"You're too kind for all this, William. It's what I like about you, mainly, but you need to be an adder-tongued bastard to get one by those sods. We'll agree to the church in Tours, but our little lamb will be ill at the last moment, when it's too late to call it off. That's the sort of news that will set their own tongues wagging with excitement." He attempted an atrocious French accent as he went on. "'Lak 'is fadder! 'Ee is tekken with the sickness! *Peut-être* 'ee will not live.' But you'll be there to exchange rings and vows in his place, William. You'll marry little Margaret *for* him."

"I *will not*," Suffolk said firmly. "I'm already married! How can something like that even be legal? I'm forty-seven, Derry, and married!"

"Yes, you said. I wish I had considered it before. Honestly, William, I don't think you have the brains of a fish. It's just for show, isn't it? A service in Tours, with you standing in for Henry, then a real marriage when she is safely home in England. All legal. They'll go along because it will have taken them months just to sort out the places at the wedding dinner. We'll present it so they have no choices left but one."

"Dear Lord," William said faintly. "Someone will have to let her know, the girl."

"No, that is one thing we *won't* do. If she's told before the wedding day, the French king will have time to call it all off. Now, look, William. We've brought this gilded peacock to the table. I am not letting him get away now. No, this is the only way. They find out on the day and the service goes ahead with you. Isn't that a reason to have a beer for once, William? This is Kentish malted ale, you know, a farthing a pint if I was paying. They do nice chops and kidneys here as well, once I let them back in. Let's toast your second wedding day, William Pole. Doesn't your heart sing like a bleedin' lark at the thought? Mine *certainly* does."

CHAPTER 5

The summer sun rose over a clear horizon at Windsor, lighting the great walls in red-gold as the town around it grew busy. Richard of York was dusty and tired after a long ride from the coast, but simmering anger lent him the energy to banish weariness. The three soldiers with him were all veterans of fighting in France, hard men in well-worn leather and mail, chosen for their size and the ability to intimidate. It was not difficult to guess why the duke had summoned three of the most brutal soldiers under his command for the night crossing and hard ride. Someone, somewhere needed killing, or at least the threat of it. His men were enjoying the sense of authority that came from being in a duke's wake. They exchanged glances of amusement as their patron bullied his way past two outer rings of castle guards. York didn't suffer fools, and he would not be balked in his desire to see the king that morning.

Somewhere close by, they could hear orders being roared and the tramp and jingle of marching soldiers. York's movement toward the king's private rooms was about to be met by armed men. The three with him loosened their swords in the scabbards, cracking knuckles and necks in anticipation. They had not spent years getting soft in England like the king's guards. They were enjoying the prospect of meeting men they felt were only barely on the same side.

The duke loped forward, his strides long and sure. He saw two solid-looking pikemen guarding a doorway ahead and drew to a halt as he came right up to them.

"Stand aside. I'm York, on urgent business for the king."

The guards stiffened, their eyes staring. One of them glanced at his companion and the man shifted his grip on the pike uncomfortably. He was due to come off watch as soon as the sun cleared the battlements, and he looked irritably at the gold thread showing on the horizon. Just a few minutes more and he would have been in the guardhouse, eating his breakfast and wondering what all the noise was about.

"My lord, I have no orders to admit you," the guard said. He swallowed nervously as York turned his full glare on him.

"That is the nature of urgent business. Get out of my way, or I'll have you flogged."

The guard swallowed and opened his mouth to reply, already shaking his head. As he began to repeat himself, York's temper surged and broke. He gestured sharply and one of his men grabbed the guard by the throat with a gauntleted hand, pushing him off his feet as he crashed back against the door. The sound was loud, echoing around the outer walls. Someone walking up there yelled an alarm.

The guard struggled wildly, and his companion jerked his pike down. Another of York's men stepped inside the range of the heavy iron head and thumped a blow to the man's chin that sent the pike and its owner clattering to the ground. The first guard was dispatched as quickly, with two fast punches that spread his nose across his face.

A troop of running guards appeared around a corner fifty yards away, led by a red-faced sergeant with his sword drawn. York glanced coldly in their direction as he opened the door and went through.

Inside, he stopped, looking back.

"Francis, hold the door. You two, come with me," he ordered.

The biggest of the three men pressed his weight against the door, dropping the locking bar and holding it in place with both hands. It shuddered immediately as someone crashed against it from outside. Without another word, the duke broke into a run through the rooms beyond. The king's private suite lay ahead, and he knew Windsor well enough not to hesitate. At speed, he went across a tall-ceilinged empty hall and up a flight of steps, then skidded to a halt, his men almost running into him. The three of them stood, breathing hard, as York stared at the sight of Derihew Brewer leaning back against a low stone window that looked out over the vast hunting park of Windsor.

"Morning, my lord. I'm afraid the king isn't feeling well enough for visitors, if that's who you're after."

"Stand up when you're talking to me, Brewer," the duke retorted, coming farther into the room and stopping. His gaze swept around suspiciously, looking for some explanation for the spymaster's confidence. With a sigh, Derry pushed himself away from the windowsill and yawned. On the floor below, they could all hear a rhythmic thumping as the guards outside began to batter the door down.

Derry glanced out of the window at files of soldiers running in all directions.

"Bit of a brawl out there this morning, my lord. Your work, is it?"

York eyed the door that he knew led directly to the king's apartments. It was solidly shut against him, with only Derry in the waiting room. Yet something about the man's insolent smile pricked at his nerves.

"I've come to see the king," the duke said. "Go in and announce me, or I'll do it myself."

"No, I don't think I'll be doing that, Richard, old son. And I don't think you will, either. The king calls for *you*, or you don't come. Has he called for you? No? Then you know what you can do with yourself, don't you?"

As Derry spoke, York's face grew dark with affronted rage. His men were as surprised as he was to hear a lord addressed by his common name. Both men stepped toward Derry, and he squared up to them, still smiling strangely.

"Lay a hand on me, lads, please. See what you get."

"Wait," York ordered. He could not shake the feeling that he was being trapped, that something was wrong. It was almost the sense of having eyes on him that he could not see. The two soldiers loomed over Derry, though he was as wide as either of them at the shoulder.

"Good to see you still have a few wits knocking about," Derry said. "Now, lads, that door downstairs won't last longer than a heartbeat. If I'm not here to stop them cutting you down, I don't think your master's title will hold them back, do you? Not next to the king's rooms, it won't."

York swore to himself, suddenly understanding that Derry was deliberately wasting time. He strode to the oak door, determined to see the king that morning, no matter what else happened.

As he moved, something flashed past him. A cracking sound like a beam breaking made him jerk to a stop, his hand still out to take the door's handle. York stared at the black iron bolt sticking out of the oak at head height.

"That's the only warning, Richard, old son," he heard Derry say. "The next one goes through your neck."

The duke spun round in time to see a ribbon of dark purple curtain flutter to the ground. In its fall, it revealed a long slit that ran around the ceiling on one side, almost for the full length of the room. Three men lay flat in the gap, so that he could see only their heads and shoulders, as well as the terrible weapons they were aiming at him. Two of the three watched him coldly as they stared down the sights of crossbows. The third shuffled back on his elbows to reload. York gaped up at the men, seeing the sunlight gleam on the polished bolt tips. He swallowed as Derry laughed.

"I told you, Richard. The king calls or you *don't* come."

Below their feet, a great crash told them the outer door had given way at last. The two soldiers with the duke exchanged a worried glance, their good mood evaporating.

"Lads, *lads*!" Derry said, taking a pace toward them. "I'm sure your *armed* presence near the *king* is just a misunderstanding! No, *don't* back away from me. I have a few things I'd like to say to you before we're done."

The clatter of running soldiers grew louder, and voices shouted a challenge as men poured into the room.

"I'd lie down if I was you," Derry told the two soldiers.

They dropped quickly, holding their hands out empty so as not to be run through by one of the red-faced bawling men as they came in. York remained standing and folded his arms, watching with cold eyes. He knew none of the men-at-arms would dare touch him. When his soldiers were trussed securely on the floor, they all seemed to look to Derry for new orders.

"That's better, Richard," Derry said. "Isn't that better? I think it is. Now, I don't want to be the one responsible for waking the king up this morning, if we haven't already. How about we take this outside? Quiet as mice now, lads."

The duke strode through the assembled guards with his face a shade of dark red. No one stopped him from heading down the stairs. To Derry's eyes at least, it was almost comical the way the guards picked up their prisoners as quietly as possible and trooped back down after him.

York did not pause at the body of his biggest soldier by the shattered outer door. His man Francis had his throat slashed open and lay in a spreading pool of blood. York stepped over him without a downward glance. The bound prisoners moaned in fear as they saw their companion, so that one of the guards reached down and cuffed the closest one hard across the face.

The sun was bright after the gloom of the inner rooms. Derry strolled out behind them all and was immediately approached by the sergeant-at-arms, a man who sported a huge white mustache and practically shook with anger. Derry accepted his salute.

"No harm done, Hobbs. Your men deserve a pint on me tonight."

"I wanted to thank you, sir, for the warning," the sergeant said, glowering at York as he stood watching. For all the gulf between their ranks, the security of Windsor was the sergeant's personal responsibility, and he was furious at the assault on it.

"It's no more than my job, Hobbs," Derry replied. "You've one body to clear away, but that's all. I think our point has been made."

"As you say, sir, though I don't like to think how far he reached. I will still make an official complaint if you don't mind, sir. This is not to be borne, and the king will hear of it." He spoke for the duke's benefit, though York listened without any visible reaction.

"Take our pair of trussed chickens to the guardhouse, would you, Hobbs? I'd like a word with them before I send them back to their ship. I'll deal with his lordship myself."

"Right you are, sir. Thank you, sir."

With a final glare hot enough to melt iron, the old soldier marched his men away, leaving Derry and York alone.

"I wonder, Brewer, if you can survive having me as an enemy," York said. He had lost his red flush, but his eyes glittered with malice.

"Oh, I daresay I can, but then I've known much more dangerous men than you, you pompous prick."

There was no one to hear, and Derry's mask of wry good nature dropped away as he faced the duke and stood threateningly close to him.

"You should have stayed in France and carried out your king's orders," Derry said, poking him in the chest with a stiff finger.

York clenched his fists in rage, but he knew Derry would beat him into the ground at the slightest provocation. The king's spymaster was known to frequent the fight rings in London. It was the sort of rumor he made sure all his enemies heard.

"*Are* they his orders?" York grated. "A wedding and a truce? My men to remain in Calais? I *command* the army, Brewer. Yet I get no word until now. Who will protect the king if his soldiers are three hundred miles to the north? Have you even thought of that?"

"The orders were genuine?" Derry asked innocently.

York sneered.

"The *seals* were correct, Brewer, as I'm sure you know. I wouldn't be surprised to hear it was your hand on them, melting the wax. I'm not the only one who thinks you have too much control over King Henry. You have no real rank, no title, yet you issue commands in his name. Who can say if they have truly come from the king? And if you poke your finger at me again, I will see you hanged."

"I could have a title," Derry replied. "He's offered me one before. I think, though, that I'm perfectly happy as I am, for the moment. Perhaps I'll retire as Duke of York, who knows?"

"You couldn't fill my shoes, Brewer. You couldn't even fill my codpiece, you lowborn—" The duke was interrupted as Derry barked a laugh at him.

"Your codpiece! That's a fine jest. Now, why don't you go back to your ship? You're due at the king's wedding next month. I don't want you to miss it."

"Will you be there?" York asked, his gaze sharpening.

Derry didn't miss the implication. It was one thing to scorn the man's authority in Windsor, while surrounded by the king's guards. It was quite another to consider how the Duke of York might act in France.

"I wouldn't be absent for such a joyous occasion," Derry replied. He watched as York smiled at the thought.

"I'll have my personal guard with me, Brewer. Those pretty orders don't prevent that. With so many bandits on the roads, I won't feel comfortable with less than a thousand men, maybe more. I'll speak to the king then. I wonder if he knows half the games you play."

"Alas, I am but the agent of the royal will," Derry said with a smirk that hid his dismay at the threat. "I believe the king desires a few years of peace and a wife, but who can know his mind, truly?"

"You don't fool me, Brewer. Nor that bootlicker Suffolk. Whatever you've offered the French, whatever you've concocted between you, you're both wrong! That's the worst of it. If we offer a truce, do you think the French will leave us in peace? It makes us look weak. If this goes ahead, we'll be at war before the summer is over, you poor dullard."

"I am tempted to risk the king's anger just to see you knocked out on this grass, my lord," Derry said, standing very close to the other man. "Give me a moment to consider the pros and cons, would you? I would enjoy breaking that sharp beak of yours, but then you are a duke and you have a certain level of protection, even after the prick you made of yourself this morning. Of course, I could always say you took a tumble when the guards chased you away."

"Say what you like, Brewer. Your threats and prods don't frighten me. I'll see you again, in France."

"Oh, are you off, then? Very well. I'll send your men on in a while. I'll look forward to continuing our chat at the wedding."

York marched away back to the main entrance of the castle. Derry watched him go, a thoughtful expression on his face. It had been a little closer than he'd hoped. He'd heard the duke was coming two nights before, but the guards at the outer gate should have been warned. York should never have reached the inner keep, never mind the door to the king's own rooms. As it happened, Henry was still praying in the chapel, but the duke didn't have that vital piece of information.

For a moment, Derry considered the conversation. He had no regrets. A man like York would have tried to get him killed just for the scene at the king's rooms. It didn't matter that Derry had made it worse with insults and threats. It couldn't *be* worse. He sighed to himself. Yet he couldn't let the outraged duke see the king, either. York would have had Henry agreeing to everything and the whole subtle arrangement and months of negotiations would have been wasted. Derry had known when he woke up that it would be a bad day. So far, it had met his expectations in every aspect. He wondered what odds he could get on surviving the wedding in Tours. With a rueful expression, he realized he should make preparations for not coming back.

He remembered old Bertle doing just the same on more than one occasion. The spymaster before him had survived three attempts at poison and one man waiting for him in his rooms with a dagger. That was just part of the job, Derry recalled him saying. A useful man made enemies—that was all there was to it. If you were useful to kings, your enemies would be quality. Derry smiled at the memory of the old man speaking the word with relish.

"Look at his clothes, lads. Look at this knife! *Quality*, lads," he'd said, grinning proudly at them as he stood over the body of the man found in his rooms. "What a compliment to me that they sent such a gentleman!"

Old Bertle may have been an evil sod, but Derry had liked him from the start. They'd shared a delight in making other men dance, men who never even knew the choices they made were not their own. Bertle had seen it as an art. For a young man like Derry, fresh from war in France, Bertle's teachings had been like water to a dry soul.

Derry took a deep breath, feeling calm return to him. When Bertle summoned his six best men and gave his authority to one of them, you knew things were serious, that he might not be coming back from wherever the work took him. Each time it was a different man, so that they were never sure which one of them was truly his chosen successor. Yet after a dozen close shaves, the old man had died in his bed, slipping peacefully into sleep. Derry had paid three physicians to check the corpse for poisons, just to be sure he didn't have to track someone down.

At peace once more, Derry cracked his knuckles as he strolled toward the guardhouse. It wouldn't make things any worse for him to give the two soldiers a proper beating. He was certainly in the right mood for it.

IT PROMISED to be a glorious summer's day as the sun rose, with the air already warm and the skies clear. In Saumur Castle, Margaret was up before the light. She was not sure if she had slept at all, after so long lying in the heat and darkness, her mind filled with visions of her husband and not a little fear. Her fourteenth birthday had passed a few months before, almost unremarked. Yet Margaret had noticed, not least because she had begun to bleed the following morning. The shock of that was still with her as she bathed and checked herself in the light of a night lamp. Her maid had told her it would come each month, a few miserable days of bundling rags into her undergarments. It seemed a symbol of change to her, of things going so fast that she could barely take in a new discovery without a dozen others clamoring for her attention. Were her breasts fuller? She thought they were, and used a looking glass to pinch and squeeze them into something like a cleavage.

The castle was not silent that day, even at so early an hour. Like mice in the walls, Margaret could already hear distant voices and footsteps and doors slamming. Her father had spent gold like a river over the previous months, employing a vast staff and even bringing dressmakers from Paris to do their best with his daughter's skinny frame. Seamstresses had been working every night in the castle rooms, sewing and cutting cloth for her sister and three cousins, who had traveled from the south to accompany her at the ceremony. Over the previous days, Margaret had found the girls slightly irritating as they preened and giggled around her, but somehow she had gone from knowing the wedding was far off to the actual morning, without any sense of how the time had vanished. It was still hard to believe today was the day she would marry a king of England. What would he be like? The thought was so terrifying she could not give voice to it. Everyone said his father had been a brute, a savage who spoke French like a dithering geck. Would the son be the same? She tried to imagine an Englishman holding her in his powerful arms and her imagination failed. It was just too strange.

"Good morning, my . . . husband," she said slowly.

Her English was good, so her old governess had said, but then the woman had been paid to teach her. Margaret blushed furiously at the thought of sounding like a fool in front of King Henry.

Standing in front of the glass, she frowned at her tangle of brown hair.

"I do take thee to be my husband," she murmured.

These were the last moments she would have alone, she knew. As soon as the maids heard her moving, they would descend in a flock to primp and color and dress her. She held her breath at the thought, listening with half an ear for the first footsteps outside.

When the knock came, Margaret jumped, gathering a sheet around her. She crossed quickly to the door.

"Yes?" she whispered. The sun was not yet up. Surely it could not be time already?

"It's Yolande," she heard. "I can't sleep."

Margaret cracked open the door and let her in, pushing it gently shut behind her.

"I *think* I slept," Margaret whispered. "I remember a strange dream, so I must have dozed for a while."

"Are you excited?"

Yolande was staring at her with fascination, and Margaret drew the sheet around her shoulders with some attempt at modesty.

"I am terrified. What if he does not like me? What if I say the wrong words and everyone laughs? The king will be there, Yolande."

"Two kings!" Yolande said. "And half the noblemen of France and England. It will be marvelous, Margaret. My Frederick will be there!" She sighed deliberately, swirling her nightshift hem over the oak floorboards. "He will look very handsome, I know. I would have married him this year if not for this, but . . . Oh, Margaret, I did not mean anything by that! I am content to wait. At least Father has restored some of the wealth we lost. It would have been a pauper's wedding last year. I just hope he has left enough to marry me to Frederick. I will be a countess, Margaret, but you will be a queen. Only of England, of course, but still a queen. Today!" Yolande gasped as it sank in. "You will be a queen today, Margaret! Can you conceive?"

"I believe I can bear one or two," Margaret said wryly.

Yolande looked blank at her pun, and Margaret laughed. Her expression changed on the instant to one of panic as she heard trotting footsteps in the corridor outside.

"They're coming, Yolande. Bloody hell, I'm not ready for them!"

"Blerdy 'ell?"

"It's an English saying. John told it to me. Bloody *hell*. It's like *sacré bleu!* he said, a curse."

Yolande beamed at her sister.

"Bloody hell, I like it!"

The door opened to admit an apparently endless stream of maids, bearing steaming buckets of water and armfuls of strange-looking implements to work on her hair and face. Margaret blushed again, resigned to hours of discomfort before she would be allowed into the public gaze.

"Bloody hell!" Yolande murmured again at her shoulder, awed as the room filled with bustling women.

CHAPTER 6

With the sun setting, Derry let his head sag as the cart trundled along the road, cursing occasionally as the wheels dipped into holes and sent him lurching from one side to the other. He had been on the road for eighteen days, hitching rides whenever he could, with his nerves jangling each time he heard hooves. He hadn't relaxed for a moment since his confrontation with the Duke of York and had certainly not taken the threat lightly. His own network of informers and spies around the fortress of Calais had brought him unpleasant news. The duke's men were making no secret of the fact that they wanted a word with Derry Brewer. From a professional point of view, it was interesting to be on the other side of an effort to track him down, instead of being the one pulling the strings. That was little comfort as Derry scratched a dozen flea bites in the back of the creaking wagon.

The drover currently staring into the middle distance was not one of his men. Like hundreds of other travelers coming south from Normandy for a gawk at kings, Derry had paid a few coins for a spot on the cart and given up on the thought of riding hard and fast into Anjou.

He'd slipped York's men easily enough in the port, but then Calais was always full of bustling crowds. The tracks and lanes leading south into Anjou were a better place to pick up a lone traveler, without fuss or witnesses. At least the wedding would be over before he saw another sunset. Derry hadn't dared use an inn for as long as he'd been on the road. It was too easy to imagine a quick sweep picking him up while he snored unaware. Instead, he'd slept in ditches and stables for two weeks—and smelled like it. He hadn't meant to cut it quite so close, but his means of travel were all slow, hardly faster than walking. He'd kept count of the mornings, and he knew the marriage was taking place the next day. It was almost an agony to know he was almost there. He could sense York's nets closing around him with every mile.

Derry rubbed a grimy hand over his face, reminding himself that he looked more like a peasant than most of the real ones. A battered straw hat drooped over his eyes, and his clothes had never been washed since the day they'd come off the loom. It was a disguise he'd used before, and he relied on the stink and filth to keep him safe.

As he trundled south, he'd seen riders coming past in the duke's livery half a dozen times. Derry had been careful to stick his head out and watch them, just as any farmer would do. The cold-eyed men had stared at everyone they passed, searching for a glimpse of the king's spymaster.

He'd decided he'd use his razor on them if he was spotted. It was a finger-width line of the finest steel, with a tortoiseshell handle. If they found him, he'd vowed to make them kill him by the road rather than suffer the duke's torturers or, worse, the man's smug pleasure in landing such a fish. Yet the duke's men hadn't stopped at the sight of one more grubby peasant staring from the back of an oxcart.

It could have been humiliating to be forced to go south in such a way, but in fact Derry enjoyed the game. He thought it was that part of him that had drawn old Bertle's attention, when Derry was just another informer and ex-soldier, with his knees showing through torn trousers. Derry had been running a little fight ring in the London rookeries, with his hand in the pockets of all the men involved. It had earned him a fair bit, as he'd combined setting the odds with rigging the matches, giving strict orders to whichever fighter would win or lose.

He'd only met Bertle once before the night the old man had come to one of his fights. Dressed in his dusty blacks, Bertle had paid for a penny seat and watched it all: from the finger signals Derry gave the fighters, to the chalkboard of odds and how they shifted. When the crowd went home, the old man remained, coming up to him with a gleam in his eye as Derry paid four or five bruised and battered men their share of the takings. Recognizing him, Derry had waved off the lads who might have shoved him out into the night and just let Bertle sit and observe. It had been after midnight when they'd cleared the warehouse of all sign that it had been used. Whoever the owner was, he didn't know he'd hosted fights that night. He'd never know unless he found blood under the fresh sawdust, but either way, they never used the same place twice.

Even then, Derry had sensed Bertle's amusement and delight at mixing with the rough fight crowd. He'd let all the others go until the old man was the only one remaining.

"What is it, then, you old sod?" Derry had said to him at last. He remembered Bertle's slow smile then, a hard little man who'd seen most kinds of evil and shrugged at them all.

"Proper little king-thief, ain't you, son?" Bertle had said.

"I do all right. I don't cross the gangs, or not often. I make a living."

"You do it for coin, then, do you? To make an honest crust?"

"Man has to eat," Derry shot back.

Bertle had just waited, raising his eyebrows. Derry still remembered the way the old man's face creased in delight when he'd given an honest answer. He still didn't know why he had.

"I do it because it's fun, you old devil, all right? Because no matter who wins, I *always* do. Satisfied?"

"Maybe. Come and see me tomorrow, Derry Brewer. I might have a job or two for you, something *worth* doing."

The old man had shuffled off into the night, leaving Derry staring after him. He'd been certain he wouldn't go, of course. Yet he had gone anyway, just to see.

Derry shook off the daze of memories, knowing he couldn't just drift while the ox ambled along. He'd thought through a lot of lines to say when he strolled up to the Duke of York at the wedding. As long as he could find a place to wash and change first, of course. The grubby sack he rested on was filled with carefully folded garments, good enough to transform him if he could just get there with his throat uncut. He wondered what the farmer thought of the strange passenger who looked like he couldn't afford a meal, but could still pay good silver to ride through the night. Derry grinned to himself at the thought, glancing up at the man's wide back. The road had cleared as the sun set, but they'd rolled on, as Derry needed to be there. He'd even dozed, rocked to sleep by the cart and only waking once when the ox let out a tumultuous fart like the crack of doom. It had Derry chuckling into his sack at the sheer silliness of his position.

The eastern sky lightened in shades of gray long before he could see the burning line of the sun. Derry had been to Anjou a few times in his travels, placing and taking messages from men in his employ. He knew there had been a trial and execution of some Jewish moneylender a month or so before, and he had a rough idea of the debts incurred by René of Anjou. The man had secured his position with a bit of ruthlessness Derry could appreciate, but he wondered idly if he should investigate the man's holdings a little further. Before the rents from Anjou and Maine came in, he'd be vulnerable. A couple of burned shops, perhaps a crop sowed with salt so that it rotted in the fields—

the possibilities were endless. With just a little push, René of Anjou might have to come begging to his daughter's new husband for a loan—and then they'd have a lever into the French court. That was assuming Derry could survive the wedding day, of course. The lords Suffolk and Somerset had their instructions if Derry didn't arrive, but knowing that was hardly a comfort.

As dawn came, the drover insisted he had to rest, feed, and water the great black ox that had ambled its way south for two days. Derry could see the double tower of the cathedral of Tours standing above the fields in the distance. It could not be more than a few miles away. With a sigh, he jumped down from the cart and stretched his legs and back. The road was mercifully empty in both directions. He assumed those who had traveled to see the wedding were all there by then. He was the only one still on the road, with the possible exception of the duke's riders still searching the countryside for him.

Even as he had the thought, he caught a glimpse of a dust cloud in the distance and ran for the verge, jumping into a bank of wild grasses almost as high as his head.

"Three silver deniers if you say nothing," he called out in French, digging himself in as deep as he could. It would have surprised Lord Suffolk to hear Derry's perfect fluency in that language.

"Eleven," the drover replied as he attached a feed bag to the slobbering mouth of his ox.

Derry half rose in indignation.

"Eleven! You could buy another ox with eleven, you bastard!"

"Eleven is the price," the man said, without looking round. "They're getting closer, my fine English lord."

"I'm not a lord," Derry grated from the long grass. "Eleven, then. My word on it."

The sun had risen, and he chafed at every lost moment. He could not take another step toward the cathedral with riders in sight. He wondered if he could creep away on his hands and knees, but if they saw the grasses move from the height of a saddle, it would be all over and done for Derry Brewer. He remained where he was, trying to ignore the flies and bright green grasshoppers that crept and buzzed around him.

He dropped his head right down when he heard the jingle and clatter of horsemen approaching the cart. They were so close he felt he could have reached out and touched them. He heard a braying English voice speaking execrable French as it shot questions at the drover. Derry breathed out in relief as the man said he had seen no one. The riders didn't waste much time on one more grubby peasant and his ox. They trotted on quickly, so that silence returned to the roadside and Derry could hear birdsong and bees once again. He stood up, looking after the troop as they disappeared in the direction he wanted to go.

"Eleven deniers," the drover said, holding out a great spade of a hand.

Derry reached into his sack and counted out the coins. He handed them over.

"Some would call this robbery," he said.

The man only shrugged, smiling slightly at the wage he had earned for himself. As he turned back to the cart, he didn't see Derry draw a polished wooden club from his sack. One blow to the base of the man's neck sent the drover staggering. Derry rapped him again on the dome of his skull, watching him fold with satisfaction.

"They would be wrong," Derry told the unconscious figure. "That was just force majeure negotiation. *This* is robbery."

He took his coins back and eyed the road to Tours and the risen sun. The ox chewed contentedly, looking at him through long lashes that would have suited a beautiful woman. The cart was too slow, Derry decided. He'd just have to run the last few miles.

Leaving the drover to wake in his own time, Derry set off, pounding down the road to Tours. After only a short way, he cursed aloud and came back. The drover was groaning, already beginning to wake.

"You must have a lot of bone in that big head," Derry told him. He counted out three silver coins and placed them in the man's hand, folding the fingers over.

"This is just because you remind me of my old dad, not because I'm going soft," he muttered. "All right?"

The drover opened one eye and looked blearily at him.

"All right, then," Derry said. He took a deep breath and began to run.

MARGARET HARDLY dared move in the dress. The new cloth itched and felt strange on her, as stiff as if she were dressed in boards. Yet she could not deny it looked magnificent in the long glass. Seed pearls were sewn onto every exposed part, so that they rattled whenever she moved. The veil was as thin as spiderweb, and she marveled at being able to see through it. She could no longer bend to look at the perfect satin slippers she wore underneath. Her feet seemed far away, as if they belonged to someone else, while she had been reduced to a head, perched on acres of white cloth. Only the servant fanning at her kept sweat from breaking out as the heat of the day rose.

Margaret was flushed by the time she was finally allowed to come out into the sunshine. Saumur Castle was the best part of forty miles from the cathedral at Tours, and a grand carriage waited for her in the courtyard. It gleamed with polish and new black paint, drawn by two matched geldings in glossy brown. A canopy had been erected over the open seats, to protect her from dust as they rode.

Her mother came out of the main house, approaching with both

pride and strain written clearly in her expression. Margaret stood awkwardly as her dress was tweaked and tugged into the perfect position
to take her seat.

"Keep your head high and don't slouch," her mother said. "The
dignity of the family rides with you today, Margaret. Do not shame us.
Yolande! Help your sister."

Yolande scurried forward, lifting armfuls of cloth to prevent them
from dragging on the stones as Margaret took careful steps. A footman
she did not know helped her up the step and, with a gasp, she ducked
through the gap and almost fell onto the bench inside. She was in, with
Yolande fussing around to arrange the train in such a way that it would
not wrinkle too badly. Another carriage was already waiting to enter
the courtyard, and it felt as if the entire staff were coming out to wave
her off. Margaret concentrated on breathing shallowly, feeling dizzy
from the constriction. She could not have slouched if she'd wanted to:
the panels of the dress held her upright. She raised a hand to the lines
of maids and footmen and they cheered her dutifully. Her gaze fell on
one she did know, from running into her during the king's visit. That
young woman was smiling and waving a handkerchief with tears in her
eyes. Margaret felt like a painted doll compared to the little girl she
had been then.

Bright-eyed and panting, Yolande clambered in to sit at her side.

"This is incredible," she said, looking all around. "It's all for you!
Are you excited?"

Margaret searched inside herself and found only nervousness. She
made a rueful face in reply. Perhaps she would be excited on the road,
but she was about to marry a young man she had never seen. Would
this English Henry be as nervous? She doubted it. Her future husband
was a king and used to grand occasions.

Two more footmen in black, polished boots and spotless livery took their positions on either side of the carriage. In theory, they would repel any thieves or bandits on the road, but there was no real danger. The carriage driver was a large florid man who bowed elaborately to the two girls before taking his seat and arranging a long whip with a dangling cord at the tip.

Somehow the carriages began moving before Margaret was ready. She saw the walls of Saumur passing and leaned as far over as she could to wave good-bye to her mother. Her father and brothers had gone ahead the previous day. This morning was for the women of the household, but it had come and gone so quickly she could not comprehend it. All the hours since waking seemed to have been compressed into moments, and she wanted to call out for the driver to stop, her mind flitting through a thousand things she was meant to remember.

She saw her mother signaling to the next carriage, her mind already on the gaggle of cousins and the vast labor going on to prepare Saumur for a wedding feast that evening. Margaret sat back, seeing two more of the carriages waiting patiently to take guests to Tours. As she and her sister trundled out onto the road, Margaret listened to the driver clicking his tongue and making the whip snap so that the horses lurched into a trot in perfect unison. She gasped with pleasure at the breath of wind on her face. It would be hours yet till she saw the cathedral. For the first time, she felt a pleasurable tingle of anticipation.

As the carriage left Saumur land through the northern gate, the road widened. Both girls were awed at the crowd lining the verges. No one had bothered to tell Margaret of the numbers who had traveled just to see her. English and French alike stood waving their caps and cheering, calling her name. Margaret blushed prettily, and they craned their necks and laughed in the sunshine.

"Bloody hell," Yolande muttered in delight. "This is wonderful."

Suffolk did his best to hide his worry as he stood in front of the cathedral. He stared up at the double tower as if he found it interesting, doing anything he could to seem relaxed and untroubled. His new trousers and tunic itched, though he fancied he looked slimmer than usual in the cut. He was forced to mop his face as the weight of his cloak seemed to grow heavier with every passing hour, the fur trim tickling his throat. The English style of layered cloth was out of place in a French summer, but he noticed the French were dressed just as warmly, so that they were almost as red-faced as the English nobles already drunk on fortified wine.

Suffolk envied York his trim frame as he caught sight of the man striding through the crowd and stopping to give orders to one of his men-at-arms. The duke had brought a huge personal guard with him, more than all the other English lords put together. Even so, it was dwarfed by the number of French soldiers camped around the town.

Suffolk watched as York's man saluted and rushed off on some errand. Suffolk clasped his hands behind his back and tried to look fascinated by the Gothic towers and ornate stonework. He wished his wife had come, but Alice had been scandalized at the very thought. It had been hard enough explaining that he would marry a fourteen-year-old French princess that day, if it all came off. Having his own wife there as well would be a mockery of the church, or so she'd said, at some length.

A greater mockery would be the slaughter that could very well erupt at the slightest provocation, Suffolk thought. For the moment, York's men were studiously ignoring the French soldiers around Tours, while their noble masters strolled and talked. Suffolk knew the French were there to take command of Anjou and Maine the moment the service was over. He would have loved to tell York, especially after suffering the man's meaningful glances to the distant soldiers. York felt his caution was utterly vindicated by the presence of such a French force. As they'd passed briefly in the churchyard, he'd hissed a question, demanding to know how Suffolk thought just a few guards could have protected King Henry. Suffolk had only been able to mumble helplessly that there would surely be no danger on a wedding day. York had glared at him, visibly suspicious, as he bustled away.

It was a fraught situation, and Suffolk's nerves wound tighter and tighter with every passing hour. York didn't know the king would not be coming, and now there were two armies facing each other in the fields. All it would take was for some idiot to call the wrong insult or play some vicious prank and no force on earth or in heaven would prevent a battle. Suffolk used a soft cloth to wipe his face once more.

As he murmured something inane to another guest, Suffolk saw York change direction to approach him across the churchyard.

"Come on, Derry," Suffolk said softly in English, making the closest French noble squint at him in confusion. "I need you here. Come on." He beamed at the duke as he halted.

"Richard! What a wonderful day we have for it. Have you news of the king?"

York looked sourly at the older man.

"I was coming to ask just that, William. I have no word from the ports that he is even on his way. Have you seen Derry Brewer?"

"Not yet. Perhaps he is with the king. I think they were coming over together."

York scowled to himself, staring over the crowd of French and English noble families, all enjoying the sunshine.

"I can't understand it. Unless he's grown wings, he should be well on the road by now. My men would hardly have missed a royal party passing through Calais, but I've heard nothing."

"They could be outrunning the messengers, Richard. Have you thought of that? I'm sure they'll be here in time."

"This has Brewer's hands all over it," York said angrily. "Secret routes and subterfuge, as if even the king's own lords cannot be trusted. Your friend Brewer will look a fool if the king's party is ambushed and taken while we stand here in our finery."

"I'm sure that won't happen. Derry merely seeks to keep the king from harm, as do we all."

"I won't be happy until he's safely married and on the road home. You've seen the soldiers they have camped all around us? Thank God I brought so many with me! This is a dangerous situation, William. I have too few men to hold them if they make a surprise attack."

"I'm sure they are only here to protect King Charles and his lords," Suffolk lied nervously. He dreaded the moment when the full details of the marriage agreement would be revealed. He had to hope the French king would not make too much of a show as he took command of his new territories. Knowing the French as he did, William de la Pole suspected that was a very vain hope indeed.

"The town is like an armed camp and the French king isn't even here yet," York said. "I'm missing something, William. On your honor, will you tell me I'm worrying over nothing?"

"I . . . I can't say, Richard." He saw the duke's eyes narrow.

"*Can't?* There *is* something, then, something I haven't been told. I need to know, William, if I'm to protect the King of England on French soil. Do you understand? I cannot be caught asleep if there are plans afoot of which I know absolutely nothing. *Damn* that Derry! Tell me, Lord Suffolk. What have I not been told?"

A great roar went up along the road west. Suffolk looked toward it in relief, taking out his handkerchief to mop his brow.

"Who is that?" he said. "Surely not the bride yet. Is it the French king?"

"Or King Henry," York replied, watching him closely.

"Yes, yes, of course," Suffolk said, sweating heavily. "It could be Henry arriving. I had better go and see, if you will excuse me."

York watched the older man walk stiffly away. He shook his head in disgust, summoning a guard to his side with a sharp gesture.

"Check the outskirts once more. I want Derry Brewer to be taken quietly. Bring word to me as soon as you have him."

"Yes, my lord."

The guard saluted smartly and trotted away. York's expression soured as he heard the crowd's shout and understood that the French king had arrived at Tours. The sun was at noon and there was still no sign of the bridegroom or the bride.

DERRY DID HIS BEST to stroll as he walked through the field of French soldiers, all resting and eating lunch in the sun. The last time he'd seen that many together in one place had been a battlefield, and the memories were unpleasant. He knew very well why they were there. The cheerful groups gossiping and chewing hard bread would become a military force again when orders came to take back the vast territories of Maine and Anjou.

Derry had expected to be challenged, but on instinct he'd lifted a heavy tureen of soup at the outskirts and staggered on with it. That simple prop had brought him right through the heart of the encampment. There were dozens of other servants fetching and carrying for the troops, and whenever he felt a suspicious gaze, he stopped and allowed men to fill their bowls, smiling and bowing to them like a simpleminded mute.

By noon, he was through the camp and able at last to give the now-empty cauldron to a group of elderly women and walk on. The French king's carriages had been sighted on the road, and no one was watching the bedraggled figure wandering away from the camp.

Derry walked as far as he dared down the road, until he saw clusters of soldiers by the cathedral itself. It was just a short sprint away, but he knew he wouldn't make it. Derry looked around to see if anyone had eyes on him, then dropped suddenly into a ditch by an ancient wooden gate, where the grasses grew thick.

Smug with satisfaction at having walked through a French army, Derry watched soldiers stop and search two carts that trundled past them. York's men seemed to be everywhere. Derry made a face as he felt ditch water seeping through his clothes, but he held his sack out of it and kept well down, using the gatepost as cover and waiting for his moment. The men-at-arms stayed clear of the actual cathedral, he noted. The church building had its own gardens, with a wall and gate. If he could just get through that outer boundary, he'd be in the clear. Cathedrals in France or England were all built along the same lines, he told himself. He'd be familiar enough with the layout if he could get inside.

Peering through fronds of dead grass, Derry could see the pretty birds of the wedding party, out in the sunshine of the churchyard. They were so close! He could almost see individual faces. For a moment, he was tempted simply to stand up and call to one of his allies, like Suffolk. York would surely not have him taken in public. Derry looked down at his sodden breeches and black fingers. He was as filthy as only days on the road could make him. If a peasant looking as rough as he did approached the wedding group, soldiers would grab him and bear him off before half the nobles even knew what was happening. Either way, it did not suit his sense of style to be manhandled by guards while he yelled for Suffolk. Derry was still determined to walk up to Richard of York in his best clothes and act as if it had all been easy.

Old Bertle had always enjoyed his sense of style. In memory of the spymaster, he'd do it with a flourish.

Derry raised his head a fraction, watching a pair of guards who had taken a position solidly in front of the cathedral gate in the wall. They were sharing a pie and standing close together as they broke it apart with their fingers and chewed.

Beyond that wall lay the bishop's own residence, with kitchens and pantries and drawing rooms fit for any lord. Derry widened his eyes, trying to keep watch for the other groups of soldiers on their rounds. Inch by inch, he reached into his sack for his heavy club. It couldn't be the razor, not against English soldiers—and not on church ground. The sort of murky world he usually inhabited would only get him hanged in the bright light of a French day. Yet the thought of trying to go through two armed soldiers with just a slab of wood was more than daunting. One, yes, he could always surprise one with a rap behind the ear, but he couldn't allow the alarm to go up or he was finished.

The sun moved into the afternoon as Derry lay there, growing frantic. Three times, half a dozen soldiers in English tabards of gold and red came marching round the cathedral boundary. They carried the sort of bows they'd made famous at Agincourt, and Derry knew they could spit a rabbit at a hundred paces, never mind a full-grown man. He was almost invisible in his tattered brown cloth, but he still held his breath as they passed just twenty yards from him, knowing the hunters among them would spot even a twitch in the long grass.

Time crept by with aching slowness. Something large crawled across Derry's face, and he ignored it as it bit him on the neck and stayed there to suck his blood. There was only one thing that could distract the guards around the cathedral, and he was waiting for it before he could move.

It came at two hours past noon, as far as he could judge from the sun. Men and women from the local villages began to swirl along the road and he could hear distant cheering. In a few moments, there was movement everywhere, with excited people running to get the best position to see the bridal carriages arrive. Derry stood up as a group of them went past him, using them to block the sight of England's spymaster rising red-faced from a stinking ditch. He strode toward the guards at the gate and silently blessed the bride as he saw both men were looking west themselves. They had never seen a princess before, and this one would be Queen of England.

Derry stepped around a running child and brought his wooden club across the ear of one of the guards. The man slumped as if his legs had been cut and the other one was just turning in dawning surprise when Derry brought his stick back and smacked it across the man's temple. The guard let out a grunt as he fell and Derry was certain he heard an English voice exclaim in shock nearby. He kicked open the gate and rushed inside, already pulling the grubby hat from his head and tossing it into a neatly trimmed bush.

The bishop's apartments were separate from the cathedral, and he ignored the path leading to them, heading instead to the vestry. Derry was willing to kick any door down by then, but it opened easily as he worked the latch and he was inside. He looked up slowly to see the enormous pink bulk of a French bishop, standing in what looked like white undergarments. Another cleric stood gaping, a long white cloth in his hands.

"My lord bishop, I apologize for disturbing you. I am late for the wedding, but Lord Suffolk will vouch for me."

As he spoke, Derry yanked fine clothing from his sack, and it was only the sight of fur trim that stopped the bishop from calling for help.

Derry felt a thump against the door at his back and turned swiftly to drop a locking bar across.

"May I trouble you further for a jug of water? The bride is here and I fear I am too travel-stained to be seen."

The two stunned clergymen looked at him, then the bishop gestured weakly to another room. Derry charged through to where a wide bowl waited on a marble dresser. He turned the water and a washcloth black as he rubbed himself down and stripped as fast as he could.

When he came out, the bishop was alone, his servant presumably gone out to check the bona fides of the stranger who had burst in on them. The bishop looked even bigger in his formal robes, a great tent of a man who watched with interest as Derry smoothed down his hair with a wet hand and shoved his crumpled sack in a corner.

"God bless you, Your Excellency," Derry said. "I thought I wasn't going to make it for a time."

He walked out into the church.

"There he is!" a voice shouted in English.

Without looking back for the source of the call, Derry broke into a full sprint down the long nave, toward the sunlit door at the far end.

CHAPTER 7

Margaret's carriage pulled up in front of the cathedral, turning a wide circle. The crowd cheered and Margaret blushed prettily as she and Yolande were helped down. The gossamer veil covered her face, but she could see them all clearly through it. They had come to that place for her. Her nervousness increased as she saw King Charles beaming to one side with her aunt Marie.

Her own smile grew strained under the veil as she caught sight of her father standing at the king's shoulder, wearing a blood-red coat over cream breeches and polished black boots. The cloth was layered in patterns of gold thread, and he bulged both over and under the stiff material. Yet René of Anjou looked smugly happy at the presence of so many fine nobles at his daughter's wedding. As she curtsied to both men, Margaret wondered if her father cared at all about the ceremony, or whether he thought only of the lands he had won back to his family estate.

As Margaret rose, another man came through the crowd and bowed deeply. He was tall and wide-shouldered, his hair the color of iron. His clothes were less gaudy than those of her father or the king, and somehow Margaret knew him as English even before he kissed her hand and spoke.

"Princess Margaret, it is a great honor," he said. "I am Suffolk, but it would be my honor if you would call me William." To her surprise, he bowed again and she realized the big English lord was almost as nervous as she was.

As he was about to speak once more, her sister Yolande extended her hand, palm downward, then giggled as Suffolk tried to kiss it and bow for a third time.

"You must be Princess Yolande, my dear. I am at your service, of course," he said. His eyes came back to Margaret, and he bit his lower lip.

"I wonder if you would be so good as to grant me a word in private, my lady? I have some news you must hear before the ceremony."

Margaret looked up to see her father and King Charles exchanging a confused glance.

"What is this, Lord Suffolk?" René said, bustling forward. "It is not seemly to delay the ceremony. Where is the bridegroom? Is he close by?"

Margaret's heart sank as her father spoke. The English king was not there? She had visions of returning unwed to Saumur Castle, the subject of mockery and sly whispers for the rest of her life. She suddenly wanted to cry and felt Yolande's hand take hers and squeeze it in silent support.

"Your Majesty, my lord Anjou, I have some distressing news. Would you please escort your daughter out of the sun, into the church? It is not for all ears."

Suffolk had grown red-faced as he spoke, looking as if he was about to burst with all the public attention focused on him. He was the first to look up when there was a clamor and a crash from the direction of the cathedral main door. Margaret saw an expression of deep relief come to Suffolk's face when Derry Brewer came out of the gloom and skidded to a stop. There were servants passing through the crowd with jugs and precious glasses of white wine. Derry snatched one as he passed and strolled on toward the carriages in their half circle.

"Master Brewer!" Suffolk said, wiping sweat from his brow with a cloth.

Margaret caught a glimpse of another tall lord turning sharply at the name and striding through the crowd toward them.

"What a beautiful day for a wedding," Derry said in English, emptying his glass in one long draft. He bowed to the French nobles watching him with suspicion. "Your Majesties, Lord Suffolk. And these flowers of France must be princesses Margaret and Yolande."

Derry bowed even deeper for them and kissed both hands with a smile that never left his face. He was sweating madly and looked as if he was trying to control his breathing, Margaret realized. Was he that excited to see them? It looked almost as if he had just been running. The nobles swirling around them were already whispering questions to each other.

Suffolk reached out and took Derry by the arm, growing even more flushed with strain and the heat.

"I was just explaining, Master Brewer, that we should move to a private place for a moment before the ceremony."

"Excellent," Derry replied. As a servant passed, he exchanged his empty glass for another and sank that as well in three gulps. "It's far too hot out here. Ah, Lord York! What a pleasure it is to see you so hale and hearty on such a day."

To Margaret's eyes, Lord York was much more the way she expected an English lord to look. He was tall and lithe, with a stern, square face and black hair cut short. His dark eyes flashed as he approached and all around them fell silent, sensing a threat like heat coming off the English nobleman. Once again, her father exchanged a glance with King Charles, growing more and more worried by the moment.

"Your Majesty, Lord René, Lord Suffolk," York said, bowing. "I am very pleased to see you here, Brewer. I would enjoy a chance to continue our last conversation later on."

"Oh, as you wish, my lord. But today is not about our grubby little concerns, now, is it? It is a day of celebration, with two great cultures joined in the promise of youth."

His face still shining with sweat, Derry beamed at them all, clearly delighted at something. Margaret had followed the English words with difficulty, and she looked from one to the other. Suffolk had spoken kindly enough, and she found herself liking him. Lord York had not even acknowledged her.

"This way, my lords, ladies. Let us take refuge from the sun in the cathedral."

Derry led the small group to the open doors, raising his glass to a cluster of panting English soldiers as he went. They glared at him, following his every step with cold eyes.

The inside of the church was like a cool breeze after the hot sun. Margaret breathed deeply, worried she might faint. She leaned on Yolande as the strange little assembly turned and waited to be enlightened.

Derry dabbed his forehead with a fine cloth before he spoke, very aware of the attention focused on him. He knew all the months of planning would come to nothing if he botched this one speech. He raised his head, tucking away the cloth.

"I'm afraid there is a small difficulty, my lords. King Henry was taken ill last night. It is nothing mortal, but even with purging it will not pass in time. Against his will, he has been forced to return to Calais and from thence to England. He is quite unable to attend and can only send his most abject apologies to Princess Margaret and her father."

"A *small* difficulty?" King Charles said in stupefaction. His English was excellent, Derry noted, though the accent was thick enough to carve. "Have you any concept of the work that has gone into this day? Now you tell me your king is ill? It is a catastrophe!"

"Your Majesty, all is not lost," Derry replied. "I have specific instructions from King Henry. This is a problem within the powers of men to solve."

"You have no bridegroom!" Lord René expostulated. "How will you solve *that*?"

"You cut straight to the heart of the matter, Lord Anjou," Derry said. His smile had not faltered. "Kings are not as other men, thank God. Lord Suffolk here has King Henry's permission to exchange the vows on his behalf. The wedding will go ahead in that form, with another ceremony in England at a later date. The truce and the exchange of lands will be secured."

"Exchange of lands?" York said suddenly.

Derry turned to him, raising his eyebrows in surprise.

"My lord York, I see the king has not told you every part of his plans, as is his right. Perhaps you should go outside rather than hear details that do not concern you."

York gritted his teeth, the muscles on his jaw standing out in lines.

"I will stay to hear the rest, Brewer. As commander of English forces in Normandy, I believe it does concern me."

Derry let a moment of silence stretch, as if he were considering having the man thrown out. York flushed further under the combined scrutiny of the French king and Lord Anjou.

"Very well, Lord York. Stay if you wish, but please allow me to discuss King Henry's plans without further interruption."

Margaret thought the thin English lord might explode with rage, but York mastered himself with a visible effort. She found herself drifting, her vision growing blurred with tears. Henry was not coming! Her

English wasn't good enough to follow all the quick conversation. Even as she was trying to understand the calamity, they seemed to be suggesting something else.

"Excuse me, my lords, Your Majesty," she murmured as Derry talked. No one seemed to hear her. "Pardon, Father," she went on, giving up on English when her heart was tearing in two in her chest. "Is there to be no wedding today?"

It was Suffolk who turned to Margaret then, his face registering sorrow and concern. He spoke in fluent French as he replied.

"My dear, I am very sorry. It is true King Henry cannot be here. I have his permission to exchange vows in his name. Such things can be done, and it will satisfy certain other parts of the union agreement. You will be betrothed today, at least, and you will marry formally in England. I would not be the one to bring such news to you, my dear, but we have come too far to lose it all now. If you will permit me, I will stand in place of King Henry this day."

Margaret stared, her mouth slightly open. She found the veil suddenly stifling and tugged it away from her face.

"Milord, tell me on your honor that this is a real thing? Am I to be married today or not?"

Suffolk hesitated, and Derry spoke for him.

"It will be a formal exchange of vows, Princess. Without a groom, it cannot properly be said to be a marriage, but it will be enough."

"But I see a ring on Lord Suffolk's finger!" Margaret said, shaking her head. "How can he stand in a church and make solemn vows when he is already married?"

"Kings make their own law, Princess. If Henry wants it so—and if King Charles agrees that it will do—well, it will do."

All eyes turned to the French king, who was listening in fascinated confusion.

"Your Majesty," Lord René said quietly. "We have come so far. This is but a step."

The king scratched his nose, thinking.

"I have certain sealed agreements with your King Henry," he said. "Agreements that become active as soon as Princess Margaret is married. You say you will honor this . . . betrothal as a true marriage in those terms?"

"I will," Suffolk and Derry said almost together.

The French king shrugged.

"Then I am satisfied." He changed to rapid French to speak again to Margaret. "The English are gauche and clumsy, my dear, but if their king is ill, it is God's plan and mere men can only bend. Will you accept these terms? It would honor your father."

Margaret curtsied.

"If it is your wish, Your Majesty."

Tension seemed to flow out of the small group as she spoke. Lord Suffolk patted her awkwardly on the hand.

"I think, then, that I should take my place at the altar, my dear. I see the bishop is waiting for the groom. He will surely believe I have led a terrible life to look so very old."

He smiled down at her, and Margaret's eyes filled with tears at his attempt to be kind. She saw the Englishman wrestle a gold band from his finger and place it carefully into a pocket. She could see a white line where it had been for many years.

Before he moved to take his place in the pews, she saw Lord York lean in close to Suffolk. Though the thin lord smiled as he spoke, whatever he said made Suffolk grow pale in the gloom.

Yolande reached up to dab away Margaret's tears before they could spoil the kohl on her lashes, then replaced the veil almost reverently. Margaret struggled to take a full breath. She was fourteen years old, and she told herself firmly that she would not wilt or faint on her wedding day, or whatever it had become. In her silent thoughts, she vowed to have words with her English king when she met him at last. Leaving her alone at their own wedding ought to be worth at least a castle.

The thought made her chuckle, and Yolande looked up in surprise. The rest of the men had dispersed to the pews and the crowd outside was coming in at last, looking nervously at her and whispering questions that could not be answered. At the end of the nave, William de la Pole had walked through the door in the black oak pulpitum that hid the mysteries of the altar and the choir from the congregation. Through that gap, she could see the Englishman's wide back as he stood and waited for a princess of France. Margaret shook her head in disbelief.

"This is a strange day," she muttered to her sister. "I find I am nothing more than a bauble, while they play games of power all around."

She set her jaw, refusing to look as her father came to her side and took her arm. Yolande and her cousins fell into step behind her, and the church filled with music as three harpists began to play. On her father's arm, Margaret walked slowly down the nave, her head held high. They passed through the pulpitum screen together, and the door was closed behind them. When Lord Suffolk looked back, he smiled to see such bravery in a girl so young. Whether by luck or God's blessing, or perhaps the sheer chicanery of Derry Brewer, Suffolk thought King Henry had found a rare one to be his bride.

THE BELLS of the St. Gatien Cathedral rang out over Tours, a joyous sound that rippled on and on in complicated patterns that never repeated for the course of a full peal.

Derry watched placidly as the French princess came out and was escorted back to her waiting carriage with the bells and roaring crowd echoing all around her. She was smiling and weeping at the same time, which made Derry chuckle. If his own daughter had lived, she would have been about that age. The thought brought the stab of an old pain to his chest.

The French king and his most powerful lords came out to see the bride leave for Saumur Castle, the monarch already deep in conversation and surrounded by messengers running to and from the army waiting outside the city.

Derry's thoughts were interrupted as a hand came down hard on his right shoulder. In the inns of east London, he'd have grabbed it and broken the small finger, but he resisted the impulse with an effort.

"What have you done, in the king's name, Derry Brewer?" York hissed at him. "Tell me this is not so. Tell me that we haven't just given up lands won back to good Englishmen by Henry of Monmouth."

"His son, our *king*, wanted a truce, Lord York, so yes, that is exactly what we have done," Derry replied. He removed the hand on his shoulder, deliberately squeezing the bones together as he did so. York grunted in pain, though he resisted the urge to rub his hand when he had it back.

"This *is* treason. You will swing for this, along with that fool Suffolk."

"And the king at our sides, I suppose? Lord York, is it possible you have failed to comprehend the arrangement? Maine and Anjou are the price for twenty years of truce. Will you gainsay your own king in this? It is what *he* wanted. We who are his humble servants can only give way to the royal will."

To his surprise, York stood back and smiled coldly at him.

"I think you will discover that there are consequences to these games, Derry Brewer. Whatever you think you have accomplished, the news is out now. As your secret deals are heard, the country will know only that King Henry has given away territories won by his father—

and by English blood, shed on the battlefields. They will say . . . Oh, I will leave you to work out what they will say. I wish you luck, but I want you to remember that I warned you." For a moment, York chuckled and shook his head. "Do you think they will go meekly, those Englishmen, just because a fat French lord points them back to Normandy? You have overreached yourself with your cleverness, Brewer. Men will die because of it."

"Are you selling lavender as well as prophecy? I ask because I would value a sprig of lavender and there are no gypsy women here."

He thought York would lose his temper then, but the man merely smiled once more.

"I have sight of you now, Derry Brewer. My men have sight of you. I wish you luck getting back to Calais, but I fear it is not with you today. All your bright magpie chatter will not serve you when we catch you up on the road."

"What an odd thing to say to me, Lord York! I will see you again in London or Calais, I'm certain. For the moment, though, the French king has invited me to accompany him on a hunt. I like him, Richard. He speaks English ever so well."

Derry raised a hand to catch the attention of the French noble party. One of the barons saw and gestured in reply, calling him over. With a last insouciant raise of the eyebrows for York's benefit, Derry strolled across to them.

Outside the town, the French army began to pack up its camp, ready to take command of more new land won in a morning than in the ten years before that day. Duke René was beaming as Derry reached the group. More than a dozen of his peers stood close around him, clapping him on the shoulders and calling their loud congratulations. To Derry's surprise, the Frenchman had tears running down his pale cheeks. He saw Derry's expression and laughed.

"Oh, you English, you are too cold. Do you not understand I have my family land back today? These are tears of joy, monsieur."

"Ah, the best kind," Derry replied. "There was talk of a hunt when His Majesty invited me to accompany him?"

Duke René's eyes changed subtly in the light.

"I suspect His Majesty King Charles was amusing himself at your expense, monsieur. There will be no hunting of boar or wolves, not today. Yet His Majesty will accompany his army as they move north through my land. Who can say what English deer we will find shivering in my family fields and vineyards?"

"I see," Derry said, his good humor vanishing. "I suspect I will not join you after all, Lord Anjou. If you don't mind, I will remain here for a time, while I make arrangements to return home."

He watched Richard of York striding away to give orders to the thousand men he had brought south. They, too, would withdraw to Normandy. The duke had no choice at all. For a moment, Derry had a sickening sense that York was not the fool he thought he was. There were many English settlers in Maine and Anjou, that much was true. Surely they would not be foolish enough to resist? The agreements King Henry had signed allowed for the peaceful uprooting of English families in the French provinces. Yet the mood of the nobles all around him was indeed that of a hunt. They showed their teeth, and he could sense a febrile excitement in the air that worried him. Derry could taste nervous acid in his throat. If the English in Maine and Anjou refused to go, it could yet mean a war. All the work he had put in, all the months of scheming, would be wasted. The hard-won truce would last no longer than frost in summer.

CHAPTER 8

For three days, the French army and York's soldiers shadowed each other, moving north through Anjou. Duke Richard's men pulled far ahead after that, in part because the French king stopped and held court in every town. The royal party made a grand tour of the Loire Valley, making camp whenever King Charles saw something of interest or wished to see a church with the bones of a particular saint. The rivers and vineyards stretching over many miles of land gave him especial pleasure.

Hundreds of Anjou families were evicted by rough French soldiers running ahead of the main army. In shock and despair, they took to the roads in carts or on foot, a great stream of suddenly beggared subjects that only grew each day. York pulled his men back to the new border of English land in France, picketing them on the outskirts of Normandy as the flood of evacuees kept coming, filling every village and town with their misery and complaints. Some of them called angrily for justice from King Henry for their losses, but most were too stunned and powerless to do more than weep and curse.

The evictions went on, and there were soon tales of rape and murder to add to the chaos and upheaval as the families came in. As the weeks passed, minor lords sent furious letters and messengers demanding that English forces protect their own, but York set them aside unread. Even if the evictions hadn't been by decree of an English king, he wanted them to come home with their tales of humiliation. It would fan flames in England, making a fire that would surely consume Derry Brewer and Lord Suffolk. He did not know if the unrest would reach as far as the king himself, but they had brought it about between them and they deserved to be shamed and vilified for what they had done.

Each evening, York went to the church tower of Jublains and looked south over the fields. As the sun set, he could see hundreds of English men, women, and children staggering toward the safe border, each with his own story of violence and cruelty. He only wished Derry Brewer or Suffolk, or even King Henry himself, could see what they had brought about.

He heard footsteps on the stone stairs as he stood there, watching the sun set on the forty-third day after the wedding. York looked round in surprise as he saw his wife ascending.

"What's this? You should be resting, not climbing cold steps. Where is Percival? I'll have his ears for it."

"Peace, Richard," Cecily replied, panting slightly. "I know my own strength, and I sent Percival away to fetch me cold, pressed juice. I just wanted to see the view that keeps you up here each evening."

York waved at the open window. In other circumstances, he might have appreciated the dark gold and rose of a French sunset, but as it was, he was oblivious to its beauty.

Cecily leaned on the wide sill after edging around a great bronze bell.

"Ah, I see," she said. "Those little people. Are they the English you mentioned?"

"Yes, all coming north into Normandy with their sorrows and petty rages, as if I do not have enough troubles. I don't come to watch them. I come because I'm expecting to see the French army marching up here before the year is out."

"Will they stop here?" Cecily asked, her eyes widening.

"Of course they will stop! Evicting families is more to their taste than English archers. We'll turn them round and send them south again if they put one foot on English land."

His wife relaxed visibly.

"Lord Derby's wife was saying it's all an awful mess. Her husband thinks we should tear up whatever agreement has been made and begin again. He says the king must not have been in his right mind . . ."

"Hush, my dear. Whatever the truth of it, we have no choice but to defend the new border. In a year or two, perhaps I will be given the chance to take it back in battle. We've lost Maine and Anjou before, under King John. Who knows what the future will hold?"

"But there *is* a truce, Richard? Lord Derby says there will be twenty years of peace."

"Lord Derby has a lot to say to his wife, it seems."

The tower was as private a place to be found in France, but even so, York stepped close to his wife, running his hand over the bulge of the child growing within her.

"The mood is ugly among the men, my dear. I have reports of unrest and it has only just begun to spread. I would prefer to know you are safe at home. King Henry has lost the faith of his lords. This will not end well, when enough of them learn it was his hand behind it—and Suffolk's name on the treaty. I'll have William de la Pole tried for treason, I swear it. By God, to think I am separated from the throne by the distance of one brother! If my grandfather Edmund had been born before John of Gaunt, *I* would be wearing the crown that sits so poorly on Henry's head. I tell you, Cecily, if I were king, I would not give back a single foot of land to the French, not till the last trumpet blast! This is *our* land, and I have to watch as it is given away by fools and schemers. Jesus wept! King Henry is a simpleton. I knew it when he was a boy. He spent too much time with monks and cardinals and not enough wielding a sword like his father. They ruined him, Cecily. They ruined the son of my king with their prayers and poetry."

"So let them fall, Richard," Cecily said, placing a hand against her husband's chest and feeling the heart beating strongly. "Let them reap the whirlwind, while you grow in strength. Who knows, but you may find yourself in reach of the crown in time? If Henry is as weak as you say?"

Paling, York put a hand tight over his wife's mouth.

"Not even here, my darling. Not aloud, not even whispered. It does not need to be said, do you understand?"

Her eyes were bright as he removed his hand. The last rays of the sun were shining into the tower, the entire sky darkening to claret and soft lilac.

"My dear, no matter what happens next year, this summer must come to an end first. While King Henry *prays*, good rivers and valleys are taken back by those French whores . . . I'm sorry, Cecily. My anger soars at the thought of it."

"It is forgotten, but you will not teach our child such terms, I hope."

"Never. You are as fertile as a vineyard, my fine Neville bride," he said, reaching out and touching her belly for good luck. "How is the Neville clan?"

Cecily laughed, a light tinkling sound.

"My nephew Richard is the one doing well, or so I've heard. He married the Beauchamp girl, if you remember? Shrewish little thing, but she seems to dote on him. Her brother is Earl Warwick, and I'm told he is failing faster than the doctors can bleed him."

"The one without a son? I know him. I hope your nephew will still come to visit, Cecily. What is he now, eighteen, nineteen? Half my age and almost an earl!"

"Oh, he worships you, you know that. Even if he does inherit the earldom, he'll still come to you for advice. My father always said Richard was the one with the wits, out of all the family."

"I'm sure he meant me," her husband said, smiling.

She tapped him on the forearm.

"He didn't mean you at all, Richard York. My brother's son is the one with the wits."

The duke looked out of the window. At thirty-four years old, he was strong and healthy, but he felt again the sense of creeping despair at the thought of a French army marching into view in the distance.

"Perhaps you're right, my dear. This Richard can hardly think his way past tomorrow, at least for the moment."

"You'll beat them all, I'm certain. If I know you at all, I know you don't lose easily—and you don't give up. It's a Neville trait as well. Our children will be terrors, I'm quite sure."

He placed a cool hand along her jaw, feeling a surge of affection. Outside, the evening had come in shades of purple and gray. He reached out to gather her cloak closer around her.

"I'll come down with you," he said. "I don't want you to fall on those steps."

"Thank you, Richard. I always feel safe with you."

MARGARET STOOD in the main yard of Saumur Castle, watching the man who had declared himself her protector teaching her brothers a thing or two about sword work. Her father was away to oversee the return of Anjou, busy with the thousand details of rents and land ownership he had won with the marriage of his daughter.

As she came back to Saumur on that first day, it had seemed at first as if nothing had really changed. She was not properly a queen after the odd ceremony, and England felt as far away as it had always been.

She watched Suffolk correcting little Louis as he overreached in a stroke.

"Guard, boy! Where is your guard?" Suffolk said, his voice booming back from the walls.

Margaret felt a wave of affection for the big English lord. Her father had returned briefly to Saumur after a week of riding with the king. Seeing his daughters, he'd told them gruffly to fetch their mother, giving orders with his old authority. The moment when Suffolk had stepped forward and cleared his throat had become one of the most cherished memories of her young life.

"Milord Anjou," Suffolk had said. "I must remind you that Queen Margaret is no longer at your command. As her husband's representative and champion, I must insist that she be treated with the dignity of her station."

René of Anjou had gaped at the Englishman standing so solidly between them in his own courtyard. He'd opened his mouth to reply, then thought better of it, glaring around him until his gaze fastened on the unfortunate Yolande.

"Fetch your mother, girl. I am weary and hungry and in no mood for such English games."

Yolande had scurried away with her skirts held in bunches. Her father's face had grown pink, his lower lip protruding like an offended mastiff as he walked on into his home. Duke René left again three days later, and in that time he had not said another word to her, or her English lord.

Margaret blushed at the memory. It had been a moment of pure joy to see the white slug forced to back down. She did not doubt Suffolk in his willingness to defend her honor. The man took his duty as her protector very seriously, and she suspected his sword training with her brothers had a similar aim in mind.

She looked up at the clash of swords. Her three brothers were all faster than the English earl, but he was a veteran fighter, a man who had suffered wounds at Harfleur and been commander at the siege of Orléans. He knew more about fighting than John, Nicholas, or Louis, and in fact he had fought them all together to demonstrate how armor could protect a man in a mêlée. Nonetheless, he was no longer young, and Margaret could hear him panting as he blocked and struck against Louis's shield.

The sword he carried was huge to Margaret's eyes, four feet of solid steel that he held with both hands. The weapon looked clumsy, but Suffolk made it come alive, moving it in complicated patterns as if it weighed nothing. With the blade, all sign of the kindly English lord vanished. He became simply terrifying. Margaret watched in fascination as Suffolk made Louis defend stroke after stroke until her brother's blade fell from nerveless fingers.

"Ha! Work on your grip, lad," Suffolk said.

They were wearing thickly padded tunics and leggings under light armor segments for the practice. As Louis massaged his numb fingers, Suffolk pulled off his helmet and revealed a bright red face, streaming with sweat.

"There is no better way to build your sword arm than by using the blade itself," Suffolk told her panting brother. "It has to feel light to you, as speed comes from strength. In some battles, the winning edge will come if you can break the two-handed grip at a crucial moment. John, step up for me to show your brother."

Her brother John was fresh, and he looked confident as he took his position, holding a blade upright while he waited for Suffolk to put his training helmet back on. It was a heavy thing in itself, of iron lined with thick horsehair padding. The wearer had to breathe through a perforated grille, while his field of sight was reduced to a narrow strip trimmed in polished brass. Already overheated, Suffolk eyed the sweat-stained lining with distaste. He placed it carefully on the stones behind him.

"Turn your right foot out a fraction more," he said to John. "You have to be in balance at every step, with your feet planted solidly. That's it. Right foot to lunge. Ready?"

"Ready, my lord," John replied.

He and Suffolk had fought a dozen times already, with the Englishman taking the honors. Yet John was improving, and at seventeen he had great speed, even if he lacked the strength built by decades of swordplay.

John struck fast and Suffolk batted the blade away, chuckling. The blades clashed twice more, and Margaret saw how Suffolk was always moving, his feet never still. John had a tendency to root himself to the ground and hack away, which meant Suffolk could increase the gap between them and draw him off balance.

"There! Hold!" Suffolk barked suddenly.

John's sword had arced round at head height, and Suffolk held it steady with an upright blade. For an instant, John was exposed across his chest. Her brother froze at the order, remaining in place.

"You see, Louis? He is open. If I have the strength to take his blow with one hand, I can remove my left gauntlet from the hilt and strike with it. A punch will do." He demonstrated by touching his mailed fist to John's helmet. "That will ring his bell for him, eh? Better still is a punch dagger, held in the fist with the blade between your knuckles. A punch blade will break his gorget if you hit it hard enough." To John's discomfort, Suffolk showed Louis another blow to the exposed throat. "Or even the eye slit of a helmet, though it's hard to hit if he's moving. It all comes back to the strength of your arm—and you must beware of him doing the same to you. Break your grip, John, and I'll show you some defenses against those strikes."

Suffolk stood back as he spoke and saw that Margaret was watching. He took a pace toward her and dropped to one knee with his sword in front of him like an upright cross. Margaret felt herself flush even more deeply as her brothers witnessed it, but she could not escape a feeling of pride that this big man was hers to command.

"My lady, I did not see you there," Suffolk said. "I hope I have not been neglecting my duties. I wanted to show your brothers some of the new techniques that have become popular in England."

"I'm sure they have learned a great deal, Lord Suffolk."

"William, please, my lady. I am your servant."

Margaret spent a moment considering the satisfaction it would bring if she ordered William to stuff her brother John into a cauldron in the castle kitchen. She did not doubt he would do it. With regret, she denied herself the pleasure. She was a married woman now, or half married, or at least betrothed.

"My mother asked me to tell you a friend of yours has arrived from England. A Monsieur Brewer."

"Ah, yes. I was wondering when he would show his face. Thank you, my lady. With your permission, I will withdraw."

Margaret allowed Suffolk to kiss her hand. He strode into the castle, leaving her alone with her three brothers.

"No hunting today, John?" Margaret asked sweetly. "No chasing your sister? I imagine Lord Suffolk would take his sword to you in earnest if I asked him to; what do you think?"

"He's an English lord, Margaret. Don't put too much trust in him," John said. "Our father says they are all vipers, for cunning. He said the snake in the Garden of Eden would surely have spoken in English."

"*Pfui!* Our father? He is so consumed with greed I'm surprised he says anything."

"Don't insult him, Margaret! You have no right. You're still my sister and a member of this house, and by God—"

"I'm not, John. I am Margaret of England now. Shall I call William back to make my case for me?"

John's brows lowered in anger, but he could not allow her to recall her protector.

"Your marriage has brought Anjou and Maine back to the family. That is what matters—that was your only purpose. Beyond that, you can do as you please."

John turned on the spot and stalked away from his sister. Nicholas followed him, and little Louis stayed only a moment longer, exchanging a wink and a smile with her over their brother's pompous manner. Margaret was left alone. As she looked around at the empty yard, she felt the pleasure of victory.

SUFFOLK WAS AMUSED to find himself taken to the great hall of Saumur Castle. Since the wedding, the servants had been at something of a loss where he was concerned. England was an avowed enemy, but then the families had been joined in marriage. The reality of the truce between nations would take time to sink in, he thought. For the moment, only a small group of lords on both sides of the Channel were privy to the details.

Suffolk suppressed a snort of amusement as the steward bowed with the utmost reluctance at the door. Perhaps the status of an English lord had already risen a little, at least in Saumur.

Derry rose from a stuffed and padded chair to greet him.

"You seem to have become part of the family, William. I suppose you did marry one of the daughters, so it's only right."

Suffolk smiled at the jest, looking up automatically to see if the children were listening on the balcony above. He saw nothing, but guessed Margaret at least was quite capable of eavesdropping on a conversation that surely concerned her. Was that a moving shadow in the gloom?

Derry followed his glance.

"Odd construction. Is it a minstrel gallery?"

"I have no idea. So, Derry, what brings you to Saumur?"

"No greetings? No inquiring after my health? Mine is a lonely business, William Pole. I'll tell you that. No one is ever pleased to see me. Come, sit with me by the fire. It makes me nervous having you standing there in pads like you're about to charge off to battle."

Suffolk shrugged, but he seated himself on the arm of a huge chair, where he could feel warmth from the hearth prickle his skin. After a moment's thought, he jerked his head up at the gallery.

"We may not be completely private here, Derry," he murmured.

"Ah, I see. Very well, I'll use my famous subtlety and craft. Are you ready?" Derry leaned forward. "The biggest frog, the *royal* frog, if you understand me, is making a right meal of Anjou."

"Derry, for God's sake. You haven't come here to play games."

"All right, Lord Suffolk, if you don't like codes, I'll speak it straight. King Charles is taking his time in Anjou. There have been some very nasty tales coming back to England, but for the most part, he's going by the law and our agreement over the evictions. The one thing that has slowed him down is distributing the wealth to his favorites. Old René may own the province again, but the businesses can be passed to anyone King Charles wants to favor. He seems to be enjoying himself, sending English merchants on their way. Half a dozen have already petitioned Henry's chancellor for the king to intervene. A dozen more are calling for soldiers to defend their property, but Lord York is sitting tight and warm in Normandy, and he isn't moving a step to help them. That's to the good."

"If it's as you expected, why come here?" Suffolk said, frowning.

For the first time, Derry looked uncomfortable. Wary of the balcony, he leaned closer and dropped his voice to a murmur that was almost lost in the crackle of the fire.

"One of my men sent me a warning about Maine. With all their king's trips back to court, the French forces are moving so slowly they may not even get there until next year. Either way, the word is that Maine won't roll over with its paws in the air. As close to Normandy as it is, there are a lot of old war wolves living out their retirement in Maine. They have yeomen and farmhands by the hundred, and they're not the sort to bend a knee just because some French lord waves a treaty in their face."

"So King Henry must order York to do the work with an English army," Suffolk replied. "We've come too far on this road to see it broken apart now."

"I did think of that, William, as I still have a spoonful of wit in my head. York isn't answering letters or commands. I've sent him orders under the king's seal, and it's like dropping them into a pit. He's letting this run its course while he keeps his hands clean. It's a clever move, I'll give him that. I have plans for Duke Richard, don't you worry, but it doesn't solve the problem of Maine. If fighting breaks out, your new French wife will be a hostage, and we can't let that happen."

Suffolk thought for a long moment, staring into the flames.

"You want her in England."

"I want her in England, yes. I want her properly married to Henry before it all falls apart. In time, I can send another man to take command of the Normandy army, maybe Lord Somerset, maybe even you, William. If the king sends York to some other place—somewhere like Ireland, say—he'll have to go. We'll manage the evictions in Maine next year without any French lord getting his nose bent. I'll arrange the wedding in England, don't worry about that, but I need a bride for it. We can't let them keep a valuable piece like Margaret while the evictions go on."

"The older sister is to be married in a month. Margaret will want to be here for that, I'm certain. Will they even let her leave?"

"They should," Derry replied. "She's already married, after all. It's just a matter of etiquette now, and they love all that. Henry will send an honor guard and a fleet of ships to bring his French bride home. We'll make a great celebration of it. It just has to happen before they stop for winter." For a moment, Derry rubbed his temples, and Suffolk realized how weary the man was. "This is just me thinking of everything, William, that's all. It may be that King Henry will send York to Ireland and you'll be the one putting our army into Maine to make the evictions run smoothly. It may be there'll be no trouble at all and all my reports are wrong. But I'd be a fool not to plan for the worst."

"*All* your reports?" William said suddenly, his voice back to a normal level. "I thought you said *one* of your men? How many reports have you had about Maine?"

"So far, eight," Derry admitted, holding the bridge of his nose and rubbing away tiredness. "I don't need to see the glow to know my house is on fire, William Pole. I can juggle the balls, I think, as long as you get your little princess back to England."

"How long do I have?" Suffolk asked.

Derry waved a hand airily.

"As long as five months, as little as three. Go to the sister's wedding, drink wine, and smile at the French—but be ready to jump after that, the moment I send word. In truth, it all depends how quickly the French move north—and how many of our own people we can persuade to leave homes and lands they bought in good faith in that time."

"I'll see to it, Derry. You don't have to worry about this part."

"I'll worry anyway, if you don't mind, William Pole. I always do."

CHAPTER 9

The road led up a small rise, cresting through a copse of gnarled oaks. From his poacher's spot, halfway up a nearby hill in the bracken, Thomas Woodchurch could see where the trees cast a shadow on the gray stones running through them. It was a perfect place for an ambush, the result of telling sullen English soldiers to cut turf and lay dressed stones from one town to another. Local roads were formed naturally, over centuries. They meandered past obstacles, detouring around old hills and ancient oaks. Not the English ones. Like the Romans before them, those forgotten teams of laborers had cut their routes in a straight line and dug up or burned anything in the way.

Thomas settled deeper into his crouch, knowing he was close to invisible on the hillside in his dark brown wool and hunter's leathers, while commanding a good view of the valley for miles around. The road crest could well be empty, but he'd spotted fresh hoofprints by a gate that morning and followed them for half a day. The marks of iron horseshoes suggested the riders were not local men, few of whom owned even a small pony.

Thomas had his suspicions about the group crossing his land. He also had a longbow at his side, wrapped in oiled leather. He had no idea if the baron's men knew he'd been a soldier before he became a wool merchant. Either way, if they showed themselves, someone was going to die. At the thought, he dropped his hand to the length of the bow and patted it. He'd stood at Harfleur and sent arrow after arrow into French ranks, calm and deadly. From a young age, he'd been told there were only three kinds of people in the world. There were those who fought: the earls themselves and their knights and armies. There were those who prayed: a group Thomas didn't know well, but who seemed to be the younger brothers of powerful houses on the whole. Finally, there were those who worked. He smiled at the thought. He'd already been two of the three estates of men. He'd fought and he'd worked. If he surprised half a dozen horsemen come to raid his flocks, he might find himself trying a desperate prayer or two as well, to complete the set.

Lying utterly still in the bracken, Thomas was alert for any movement. When he saw it, he didn't turn his head sharply. That kind of rashness could get a man killed. As something shifted on his right, he eased his gaze over. His heart sank and his eyes flickered back to the crest of the hill and the dark passage under the oaks, which had taken on an ominous look to his eye.

His son Rowan was on foot, dogtrotting, with his head turning back and forth as he looked for his father. The man in question groaned softly to himself, seeing his lad was blindly following the road toward the copse.

Thomas stood up sharply, raising the covered bow above his head to show himself. Down below, Rowan spotted him, and even at a distance Thomas could see him grin and change direction to come up the hill.

Thomas saw shadows move in the copse. His stomach clenched in fear as a rider came hard out of the gloom. Two more followed on his tail, and Thomas spent a sick moment trying to judge the distances.

"Run!" he yelled to his son, pointing back up the hill.

To his horror, the boy stopped and stared at the horsemen barreling down from the trees. They had drawn swords, Thomas saw, holding them low and straight over their horses' ears and pointing at his son. To his relief, Rowan broke into a sprint, seeming almost to fly over the rough ground. Thomas found himself breathing hard. The boy could run, at least. Rowan had grown up half wild on the estate and spent more time in the hills than even his father.

"Jesus keep him safe," Thomas muttered.

As he spoke, he slid the length of heartwood and sapwood yew out of the leather wrappings and fitted cow-horn tips to each end. The movements were second nature to him, and as he worked he watched Rowan climb the steepening hill and the horsemen accelerate to full gallop.

Six riders had come out of the stand of trees. Thomas knew all the baron's soldiers, and he could probably have named each man. In silent concentration, he fitted the linen string and tested the draw, then unrolled the soft leather tube, revealing a quiver full of shafts. He had fletched each one himself in the evenings at home, cutting the feathers before gluing and tying them. The arrowheads had come from his own smithy in the village, sharp as knives and containing the iron barb that made them impossible to pull out of flesh without ripping a man open.

Below him, the riders slowed to cut across the bracken. They'd seen the lone man standing high on the hillside, but they were confident in their numbers and their armor, and focused only on the climbing boy. Thomas showed his teeth, though it was not a pleasant expression. He'd shot arrows for two hours or more every Sunday after church since the age of seven. His local football team had been banned so the village boys would not neglect their bow work. Thomas's shoulders were a mass of ridged muscle, and if the baron's men thought of him as a wool merchant, that was fine with him. He'd been an English archer first. He dropped the long strap over one shoulder, so that the quiver sat low, almost at the level of his knee. The arrows leaned out to one side so he could grasp them with just a small movement. Two colors of thread told him which type he would find. He had broadheads for deer, but half his stock was bodkin-head shafts, with square-sided points as long as his thumb. Thomas knew very well what they could do with the power of a yew bow behind them. He selected a bodkin arrow and placed it on the string.

"Dropping ground," he whispered to himself. "Gusting wind from the east."

The draw was so natural that he did not need to look down the shaft. Instead, he watched the targets, the horsemen plunging up the hill and trying to catch his son.

The first arrow passed over Rowan's head, snapping through the air. It struck the lead rider neatly in the chest, and Thomas already had another on the string. As a much younger man, he'd stood in ranks of archers and poured thousands of shafts into a French advance until it collapsed. Today he was alone, but the body still remembered. He sent shaft after shaft with pitiless accuracy, punching them out into the air.

The horsemen behind may have thought the first man had simply fallen as his mount stumbled, Thomas didn't know. They kept coming. Rowan finally had the sense to jink out of his aiming path, and Thomas let the riders close on him. His next shot thumped high into a horse's neck, making it rear and whinny in pain.

He could hear Rowan panting as he reached his father and stood with his hands on his knees, watching the riders coming. The young man's eyes were wide. He had seen Thomas take deer before, but those had been measured shots in the stillness of a hunt. He had never seen his father stroke out arrow after arrow, as if the massive draw was nothing to him.

The shafts plunged into men with a sound like a thick carpet being beaten. Two of them had fallen. The riders were choking and yelling, and Thomas began to breathe hard as he felt the old burn across his back. It had been a good few years since he'd last shot in anger, but the rhythms were still there to be called upon. He fitted and drew in just a few heartbeats, implacable and without mercy. Four riders were down, with two of the horses stumbling with loose reins, having lost their riders. The final two men had realized the folly of going on, and they were shouting in panic to those dying on the ground.

Thomas ran forward suddenly. Twenty quick paces brought him to a range where he could not possibly miss. His grasping fingers found three arrows still in the quiver. A glance at the threads showed him two bodkins and a broadhead remaining. He shot two and held the final piercer ready on the string.

All six of the baron's men had been unhorsed. Four of them lay still and unblinking, with stiff feathers standing out on their chests. The last two were groaning in agony and trying to rise. Thomas had shot eleven goose-feathered shafts in all. He felt a touch of pride as he looked over the crumpled mass of men and armor he'd created, even as he began to consider the consequences.

"Look away now, Rowan," he called over his shoulder. "This is ugly work."

He turned to make sure his son was staring out over the valley.

"Keep your eyes on the hills, lad, all right?"

Rowan nodded, though he watched as soon as his father walked in among the men. At sixteen, Rowan was fascinated by the power he had seen. For the first time, he understood why his father made him practice until his fingers swelled purple and the muscles of his back and shoulders were like bands of hot rope. Rowan shuddered as his father drew a heavy seax knife and walked warily to the pair still alive. They had both been struck by broadhead arrows. One had pulled his helmet away to reveal a copper-colored beard made wet with blood from his open mouth.

"You'll hang for this," the man wheezed.

Thomas glared down at him.

"You're on *my* land, Edwin Bennett. And that was my *son* you were chasing like a deer."

The man tried to reply, but Thomas reached down and gripped his long, greasy hair. He ignored the mailed hand clutching at him and cut the man's throat, pushing the body away before turning to the last.

Of all of them, the remaining horseman was the least wounded. He had one of Thomas's arrows standing proud from his armor, but high, passing through a point that ruined his right shoulder.

"Truce, Woodchurch! Have mercy, man. Truce!"

"You'll get no truce," Thomas said grimly as he approached.

The man stumbled to his feet and raised a knife in his left hand, slicing the air in loops as he tried to stagger clear.

Thomas stalked after him, following closely as the man fell and rose again, trying to put distance between them. Blood was running out of his armor at the waist, and his face was white and desperate. Fear lent him speed, and Thomas was weary. With a soft curse, he reached for the last shaft. The man saw the action and turned to run.

The shaft struck below the flailing arm, the needle bodkin punching through the segments of mail as if they were soft wool at such close range. The man collapsed, and Thomas watched until he lay still.

He heard the crunching of bracken behind him as his son came up to stand at his shoulder.

"What will you do now?" Rowan asked.

For all his life, he'd known his father as an amiable man, a patient and honest merchant who bought and sold bales of wool in the town and had made a fortune doing it. In the brown cloth, with his left wrist bound in leather and a longbow in his hand, his father was a frightening figure. As Rowan watched, the breeze increased, and Thomas closed his eyes for a moment, taking a deep breath of it. When he opened them, the anger had almost gone.

"I'll cut my shafts out, for a start, if I can. And I'll bury the bodies. You run back to the house for me and fetch Jamison and Wilbur . . . and Christian as well. Tell them to bring shovels."

Thomas looked thoughtfully at the horses. He'd hit one of them, and it made him wince to see the animal standing and cropping at the grass with a shaft high in its neck. The whites of its eyes were showing. The horse knew it had been hurt, and the great flanks shuddered in pain, rippling along the brown flesh. Thomas shook his head. He could hide the bodies of men, but horses were a different matter entirely. For a moment, he was tempted to fetch a butcher to the spot, but it would take half a dozen boys and two or three carts to carry away the meat. The baron would be bound to hear of it eventually. Horses were valuable, and Thomas doubted there was a market in France that could take six trained mounts without news getting back to unwelcome ears.

"God, I don't *know* what to do, Rowan. I can hide them in the stables, but if the baron comes searching, it'll look like guilt. He'll have me up before the magistrate, and that man is too close a friend of his to listen to a word I have to say."

Thomas stood and thought for what seemed an age as the breeze grew stronger and gray clouds swelled over their heads. Rain began to fall in heavy drops, and the wounded horse shuddered and trotted some way off down the hill.

"Catch that one for me, would you, lad? I don't want it wandering back to its stable, looking to be fed. Go gentle and you won't spook it.

We'll put them in the old barn tonight. I know one man who might find a way out of this, if I can reach him. Derry Brewer might just keep my neck out of a noose."

He watched relief come into Rowan's face before the boy went jogging down the hill, calling softly to the wandering horse. It raised its head and looked at him with ears pricked, then went right back to cropping the turf, unconcerned. The boy had a way with horses that made Thomas proud.

"How did I get myself into this?" Thomas murmured.

He suspected Baron Strange wasn't even a real noble—at least that was the rumor. There was something about a title fallen into disuse and a distaff branch of the family, but Thomas had never been able to pin down the details of the claim. Either way, Strange was not going to ignore the willful murder of six of his soldiers, no matter whose land they'd been on or what mischief they'd been up to. The dispute between the adjacent landholdings had been simmering for months, ever since the baron's men had fenced off a pasture rightfully belonging to Thomas. That was how he saw it, at least. The baron's men told a different tale.

It had been small beer at first, with his servants and those of the baron coming to blows whenever they met in town. A month before, it had taken a bad turn when one of Thomas's men had been blinded in one eye. Some of the man's friends had gone out for revenge that night and burned one of the baron's barns, as well as killing some Welsh sheep in the fields. Thomas had raised welts on their backs for that, but it had grown into undeclared war from that night. He'd told his men never to travel alone—and then he'd spotted tracks leading through his land and done exactly what he'd warned them against. He cursed himself for a fool.

Rowan came back, leading two of the horses and patting their necks.

"These are big, strong boys," Rowan said. "Could we keep one, maybe?"

"Not a chance. I can't be found with them. A night or two is risk enough as it is. I'll wait for you to come back with the lads. We might get done before dark, if the rain doesn't get much worse."

A thought struck him, and he looked up.

"Why were you coming out, anyway? You knew I'd be away till dusk."

"Oh! There's a meeting in the town tonight. Something about the French. Mum sent me to let you know, so you don't miss it. She said it was important."

"Christ!" Thomas said bitterly. "How am I supposed to get back for that and clear this carrion at the same time? God, some days, I swear . . ."

"You could hobble the horses or tie their reins together. I can fetch Jamison and Wilbur and Christian. I can bury the bodies with them as well, while you go to the meeting."

Thomas looked at his son, seeing how much a man he'd become in the last year. He smiled despite his irritation, feeling pride enough to banish the black clouds overhead.

"Right, you do that. If you see anyone else on horseback, run like the Devil is after you, all right? If the baron's men come looking for their lost mates, I don't want you caught. Is that clear?"

"Course it is." Rowan still looked a little pale after what he had witnessed, but he was determined not to wilt in front of his father. He watched while Thomas gathered the leather wrap for his bow and loped off along the road to the town.

The rain fell harder, battering down as Rowan stood there on the exposed hill. The droplets seemed to roar across the open land, and he looked around unhappily, realizing he was alone with half a dozen dead men. He began to gather in the horses, trying not to look at the pale, staring faces slowly sinking into the bracken as it bent under their weight.

THE HALL smelled of damp wool, the air thick with it. In more normal times, it was the trading place for dozens of landowners. There, they brought sacks of oily fleeces to be judged and teased apart by experts from London and Paris before prices were set each shearing season. The bleating sheep were God's gift to farmers, the wool they produced as valuable as meat, and there was even cheese from ewe's milk, though that last was only popular in parts of the French south. The last flurry of orders had been completed a month before, at the beginning of summer. Perhaps because they had gold in their pockets, the men who had come were in bullish mood, their anger and dismay clear. In the twilight, they had dragged wooden benches into place that usually had their purpose making enclosures for the sales. The discussion was already loud when Thomas entered quietly at the back, a fresh shirt feeling stiff and itchy over the day's sweat.

He knew every man there, though some better than others. The one who called himself Baron Strange was addressing the rest as Thomas murmured a greeting to a neighbor and accepted a seat near the front. He felt the baron's gaze on him as he settled himself, but Thomas merely sat and listened for a time, gauging the temper of the room. He could feel fresh sweat starting on his skin at the growing heat in the wool hall. There were as many bodies packed in there as on a market day, and he shifted uncomfortably. He hated the press of men and always had. It was one of the joys of his life that he could walk free and alone in the hills of his own land.

"If anyone has better information, let them come forward with it," the baron was saying.

Thomas raised his head, feeling the man's gaze leave him. Baron

Strange had oiled his hair again, he noted, making a black slick of shining curls to frame a face weathered by sun and wind. The baron looked the part, at least, whether his claim to nobility was real or not. Thomas could see the hump of muscle on the man's neck and right shoulder shift as he gestured, the legacy of decades wielding a heavy sword. Baron Strange was not weak of body, and his arrogance was clear enough. Even so, Thomas had always sensed the man was a cracked bell, ringing a note that felt false. If they lived through the crisis, he vowed to pay for a search of the archives in London. He'd heard there was talk of founding a college of arms there, with all the family records brought to one place from around the entire country. It would be costly, but Thomas wanted to know if Strange was bluffing better men or really had a claim to his title. It gave Strange influence in their gathering of expatriates and explained why the baron stood to address the group, and why they listened to him.

"In normal times," Strange went on, "I employ a few men to pass information to me in exchange for a little coin. They've all fallen silent in Anjou. The last I heard was that the French king himself was riding through the Loire Valley. We've all seen the evicted families come through Maine! Now these black-coat English clerks are in every town hereabouts, telling us to pack up and move. I tell you, we've been bought and sold by our own lords."

A ripple of unrest went around the hall, and the baron held up his palms to quell it.

"I do not suggest King Henry has knowledge of this. There are men high in his court who could broker a deal, who could arrange treason without the king's knowledge." The noise grew to a clamor, and the baron raised his voice over them. "Well, what else would you call it but treason, when English landowners have their property stolen out from under them? I bought the rights to my holding in good faith, gentlemen. I pay my tithe to the king's men each year. Half of you here were soldiers with the good sense to use your bounties to buy land and sheep. Our land, gentlemen! Will you meekly hand your deeds to some poxed French soldier? Land and property you have sweated and bled for a hundred times over?"

A roar of anger was the response, and Thomas looked thoughtfully around him. Strange knew the right strings to pull, but the truth was a little more complex. It was King Henry who truly owned the land, from the smallest hamlet in England and Wales, to half of France. His earls and barons administered vast reaches, collecting tithes and taxes in return for providing the king with soldiers. The truth might sit like a stone in the throats of all the men there, but when the bluster was stripped away, they were all tenants of the king.

Thomas rubbed the bridge of his nose, feeling weary. He played no part in the politics of Maine, preferring to spend his time on his holding and returning to town only for the markets and supplies. He'd heard about the clerks infesting every market town with their warnings and threats of eviction. Like the others, Thomas felt a slow-burning anger at lords who had apparently betrayed him while he worked for his family. He'd heard the rumors from Anjou weeks before, but it seemed they'd all been confirmed.

"They could be here by Christmas, gentlemen," Baron Strange said as the noise began to ease. "If it's true that the price of this truce was Anjou and Maine, we'll be joining the evicted families on the road by the end of the year." He cracked his knuckles viciously, as if he wished for a throat to hold and crush between his hands. "Either we walk away from everything we have built here, or we defend it. I will tell you all, in this place, I *will* defend my land. I have—"

He had to stop as a bellow of agreement came from the farmers and landowners on the benches.

"I have sixty-eight family men working my fields: old soldiers who will stand with me. I can add another two dozen horsemen, and I have the coin to send for more from English Normandy. If you pool your gold with mine, it may be we can hire men-at-arms to come south and stand with us."

That idea brought a hush to the crowd, as they considered giving up their hard-earned gold for a cause that might already be lost.

Thomas rose to his feet, and Baron Strange frowned at him.

"You'll speak, Woodchurch? I thought you held yourself apart from the rest of us?"

"I have a holding, Baron, same as you. It's my right to speak."

He wondered how the baron would react when he discovered he had six fewer men-at-arms than he thought. Not for the first time, Thomas regretted his action earlier that day.

With ill grace, Strange gestured stiffly, and Thomas stepped forward and turned to face them. For all his love of solitude, he had come to know the English, Welsh, and Scots in that hall, and more than a few called a greeting or a welcome.

"Thank you," Thomas said. "Now, then. I've heard more rumors in the last week than in the year before it, and I need to know the solid truth of them. If the French are pushing north this year, where is our army to smack their heads and send them home? This talk of a truce is just wind. Why isn't York here, or Gloucester, or Suffolk? We have three high-ranking nobles in France who can send men into a battle line, and I don't see hide nor hair of any of them. Have we sent messengers into Normandy? Anyone?"

"I have," Strange replied for them. His mouth twisted in irritation at the memory. "I've heard nothing from the Duke of York, no word at all. They've abandoned us to fend for ourselves."

He would have gone on, but Thomas spoke again, his deep, slow voice rolling over the group. He'd already made his decision. It galled him to support the baron, but there was no choice, not for him. Everything he had was in his land. If he abandoned his holding, he and his family would be reduced to begging on the streets of Portsmouth or London.

"I'll send my girls back to England, while we take a measure of the trouble to come. I suggest you all do the same, if you have family there still. Even if you don't, you have funds enough to put them up in inns, in Normandy or England. We can't stay clearheaded with women to protect."

"You'll join me, then?" Baron Strange asked. "You'll put aside our differences and stand with me?"

"Jesus, Baron, I was going to ask you to stand with me," Thomas replied, a smile quirking the corners of his mouth. The men in the room laughed, and the baron flushed. "Either way, I won't give up my farm, I'll tell you that much. I'll add my gold to yours to hire soldiers, but we'll need a veteran officer or two as well. Better still would be to get a battle-seasoned lord to lend his name to our little rebellion."

The word stole away some of the humor in the room. Thomas looked around at them all, seeing solid farmers with rough, red hands from work.

"That's all it will be, if the French army comes hammering on our doors. Oh, I've seen Englishmen rout larger French forces. I've seen the backs of a few French soldiers running away from me in my time." He paused for a ripple of laughter to die down. "But we can't hold the land with what we have. All we can do is make them pay a price for it."

"What?" Baron Strange demanded incredulously. "You'd talk defeat before the fighting's even begun?"

"I talk as I see it," Thomas said with a shrug. "It doesn't make any difference to me. I'll still stand and send my arrows into them when they come. I'll fight, even if I'm on my own. I don't have any choices left but one, not the way I see it. But you know, I was an archer before I was a farmer—and an English archer at that. We don't run just because the odds are against us." He paused in thought. "It might be that if we hold them, if we knock them back, the English lords will *have* to support us. I know one man who'll tell me straight if we have a chance, if there'll be help from the north. He has the ear of the king himself, and he'll tell us what we need to know."

"Who is it?" Strange asked. He was accustomed to being the one with connections, or at least the claim of them. To hear Thomas Woodchurch talk of friends in high places was strangely unsettling to him.

"You won't know the name, Baron, and he wouldn't like me to use it. He and I fought side by side years ago. He'll tell me true, for the debt he owes me."

"Keep your secrets, then, Woodchurch. You'll bring me news if you hear from him?"

"I will. Give me a month at most. If I can't reach him by then, it's because he doesn't want to be reached and we're on our own."

Baron Strange chewed at his lower lip while he listened. He didn't like Thomas Woodchurch, not even a little. There was something in the way the man smiled whenever he heard his title that irked the baron like a cold key down his back. Yet he knew the man's word was good.

"I'll send letters to those I know as well," the baron replied. "Any of you with friends in the army should do the same. We'll come back here one month from today and we'll know by then where we stand."

Thomas felt a hand clap him on the shoulder and he looked round into the face of old Bernard, one of the few men there that he'd have called a friend.

"Will you join us in a drop, lad? I'm awful dry after all the talking, and it weren't even me doing it."

Thomas smiled wryly. He liked the old archer, though there was a good chance a few pints of ale would mean sitting through the Agincourt story once again. Thomas would have preferred to walk the eight miles to his home, but he paused before refusing. Most of the men would be wetting their throats before heading out. Thomas knew he might be asking them to fight for him before the end of the year or the following spring. It wouldn't hurt to hear what they had to say.

"I'll come, Bern," he said.

The old man's pleasure at his response went some way to ease the darkness plaguing Thomas's spirits.

"I should hope so, lad. You need to let them see you now. These boys need a leader, and that Strange is not the man for it, not as I see it. A title don't give him the right, though there's some as think it does. No, lad. They need an archer, with a sense of the land. Share a pint or three with me and I'll tell thee what I have in mind."

Thomas let himself be carried along in the group heading to the inn. He sent a silent prayer that Derry Brewer could be found quickly—and that he would answer an old friend.

CHAPTER 10

In the howling darkness Derry Brewer sat and waited, needing to know if it was a trap. He was convinced only an owl could have seen him move by then, but he still resisted the urge to wipe rain from his eyes. Though his sight blurred, he remained perfectly still, just blinking slowly as the heavens opened and drenched him. He wore a dark cloak of waxed linen, but he'd discovered it leaked and the rivulets running inside were freezing. He'd been in that spot for hours, with his back and knees growing slowly more painful.

There had been a little moonlight before the storm clouds boiled angrily above his head and the first fat drops pattered on the leaves. He'd seen that the land around the farmhouse had been cleared and laid out by a careful hand. The house looked normal enough at first glance, but the bushes and lane were planted so there was just one clear path to the door—a path a pair of archers could cover against an army. Derry smiled to himself, remembering different times, different places. He had spotted the pile of lumber left out in the open. It was in just the right place to use as a barricade and then fall back to the main house. Thomas Woodchurch was a careful man, just as Derry was. Being careful and taking time had saved both their lives more than once.

The rain was easing, but the wind still moaned through the trees, filling the air with leaves that spun and danced like wet coins. Still he waited, reduced to a bright point of awareness in a shivering body. In the cottage, he noted which rooms showed moving shadows and tried to guess how many people he might expect inside.

Without warning, a sudden sense of illness touched him, making his stomach clench and his testicles creep. He'd heard nothing, seen nothing, but in the darkness Derry realized he'd taken the *only* spot that gave him a good view of the front door and the main rooms of the cottage. His heart began to race in his chest and he wondered if he could run after so long in a crouch. He cursed himself in silence, thinking as fast as he ever had. He edged his hand to the heavy seax knife at his waist, the hilt slick under his grasping fingers. In the wind and rain, he knew no one could hear him taking a long, slow breath. His pride made him pitch his voice at a normal tone, trusting his instincts.

"How long will you wait out here with me?" Derry said loudly.

He was certain he'd guessed right, but he still almost jumped out of his skin when someone laughed softly behind him. Derry tensed to move, either to run or throw himself in that direction.

"I've been wondering the same thing, Derry," Thomas said. "It's damned cold and there's food and ale in the house. If you've finished playing your games now, why don't you come in?"

Derry swore to himself.

"There's a few men in France who'd love to know where I am to-night," he said. He stood, his knees and hips protesting. "I had to know you hadn't joined them."

"If I had, you'd be eating an arrow by now," Thomas said. "I had to know you were alone, for the same reasons. I have a few enemies my-self, Derry."

"Good men like us always do," Derry replied. Though he knew by then where Thomas was standing, it was still hard to make him out in the darkness.

"I'm not a good man, Brewer. And I *know* you're not. Peace, old son. Come down and break bread with me. I'll tell you what I'm after."

Thomas crunched through the dead leaves and clapped Derry on the shoulder, walking past him toward the house.

"How did you know I was there?" Thomas called over his shoulder.

"I remembered how you liked to hunt," Derry said, following him. "How did you get so close without me hearing you?"

He heard his old friend chuckle in the gloom.

"As you say, I'm a hunter, Derry. Stags or men, it's all the same."

"No, truly. How did you do it?"

The two men walked together across the open yard, passing the stack of lumber as they approached the house.

"I used the wind for cover, but there's a bit more to it than that. If you have twenty years, I'll teach you."

As they reached the door, the light from the lamplit windows let Derry see his friend's face for the first time. He watched as Thomas gave a low whistle out into the dark yard.

"Someone else?" Derry asked.

"My son, Rowan," Thomas replied, smiling as he saw the irritation in Derry's face. "This is my land, Derry—and his. You can't creep up on me here and not have me know it."

"You mustn't sleep much, then," Derry muttered.

As he spoke, a tall young man appeared out of the wind and rain, wearing a cloak similar to Derry's own. Without a word, Rowan took his father's bow and quiver. The weapons were better wrapped and protected than the men who owned them.

"Rub them down well with oil and check the shafts for warp," Thomas called as his son turned and walked away. He got a grunt in return, which made him smile.

"You're looking well," Derry said, meaning it. "Being a farmer has put a little meat on your bones."

"I'm well enough. Now come in out of the rain. I have a proposition for you."

THE FARMHOUSE KITCHEN was blessedly warm, with a small fire burning in the grate. Derry removed his waxed cloak before it made a puddle on the stone floor, dipping his head respectfully to the stern-looking woman sitting at the table. She ignored him as she took a cloth and removed a black iron kettle from where it hung over the flames.

"This is my wife, Joan," Thomas said. "A sweet little rookery girl who took a risk once and married an archer." He smiled at her, though her own expression remained wary. "Joan, this is Derry Brewer. We used to be friends once."

"We still are, or I wouldn't have risked my hide coming out here. You sent a message to John Gilpin at Calais and here I am, in the pouring rain."

"Why should we trust a man who sits out in the lane and watches us for hours?" Joan said. Despite the years in France, her accent was all London, as if she'd left the slums of the capital just the day before.

"All right, Joan, he's just a cautious man," Thomas replied as Derry blinked and fidgeted under her stare. "He always was."

She made a hard, snorting sound deep in her throat and set about pouring hot water into a dash of brandy in each cup. Derry noted that his measure was only half the size of her husband's, though he thought better of mentioning it.

"You can go to bed now, Joan, if you want," Thomas said. "There's no one else out there; I'd have seen them."

His wife frowned at her husband.

"I don't like to feel a prisoner in my own 'ome, Thomas Woodchurch. I'll take the girls away tomorrow. When I come back, I want this sorted out. I won't be looking over my shoulder no longer, I just won't do it. And you look after Rowan. He's just a boy, for all his size."

"I'll keep him safe, love. Don't worry about that."

Thomas kissed his wife on the cheek she offered him, though she still watched his guest with cold eyes.

When she had gone, Derry reached for the bottle of brandy and added another slosh to keep the cold out from his bones.

"You married a bit of a dragon there, Tom," he said, settling himself in a chair. It was well made, he noticed, taking his weight without a creak. The whole kitchen had the mark of a loved place, a home. It brought a pang of sadness to Derry that he had nowhere like it of his own.

"I'll thank you to keep your opinions about my wife to yourself, Derry. We've other things to talk about, and you'll want to be on your way before sunrise."

"You'd turn me out? I had hoped for a meal and a bed. I've been on the road for a week to get here."

"All right," Thomas said grudgingly. "There's a stew in that big pot. Horsemeat. As to whether you stay under my roof, maybe it depends on what you can tell me."

Derry sipped the hot drink, feeling it put a little fire back into his veins.

"Fair enough. So what was so important that you remembered your old friend? Gilpin nearly missed me, you know. I was at the docks on my way to England when he found me. It's a good thing the man knows my pubs or I wouldn't be here."

Thomas looked at the man he had not seen for fourteen years. Time and worry had weathered Derry Brewer. Yet he still looked strong and fit, even with wet hair plastered to his head and stuck with red-gold leaves.

"I heard you made good, Derry, over there in London."

"I do all right," Derry said warily. "What do you need?"

"Nothing for me. I just want to know what will happen if the men of Maine fight, Derry. Will King Henry send men to stand with us, or are we on our own?"

Derry choked on his drink and coughed until he was red in the face.

"There's a French army camped in Anjou, Tom. When they move next spring, will you have your wife wave her broom at them?"

He looked into the gray eyes of his old friend and sighed.

"Look, I wish it could be another way, but Maine and Anjou were the price for the truce. You understand? It's *done*, bought and sold. Your son won't have to go to war before he can grow a decent beard, the way we had to. This is the price."

"It's my land, Derry. *My* land that's been given away without so much as a word to me."

"What's that now? It's *not* your bleeding land, Tom! King *Henry* owns this farm and sixty thousand like it. He owns this house *and* this cup I'm holding. It sounds to me like you've forgotten that. You pay your tithe each year, though. Did you think it was voluntary? King Henry and the church are the only ones who own land, or are you one of those who think it should all be shared out? Is that it? Are you a firebrand, Tom? An agitator? Seems having a farm has changed you."

Thomas glared at the man he had once called a friend.

"Perhaps it *has* changed me, at that. It's *my* labor bringing in the fleeces, Derry. It's me and my son out there in all weathers, keeping the lambs alive. I don't work to fill a lord's purse, I'll tell you that. I work for my family and my holding, because a man must work or he isn't a man at all. If you'd ever tried it, you wouldn't mock me. You'd know I begrudge every coin I pay in tithe, every damned year. Every coin that *I* earned. My *work* makes this my land, Derry. My choices and my skills. Christ, it's not like this is some ancient Kent plot, with a lord's family ruling for generations. This isn't England, Derry! This is new land, with new people on it."

Derry sipped from his cup, shaking his head at the other man's anger.

"There's more at stake than a few hills, Tom. There'll be no help coming, trust me on that. The best thing you can do is cart away everything you can carry and head north before the roads get too crowded. If that's what you wanted to know, I'm doing you the courtesy of telling it to you straight."

Thomas didn't reply for a time, as he finished his drink and refilled both cups. He was more generous than his wife with the brandy, and Derry watched with interest as he crumbled a little cinnamon into the cups before handing one back.

"Then out of courtesy, Derry, I'll tell you we're going to fight," Thomas said. The words were not a boast. He spoke with quiet certainty, which was why Derry sat up straight, shrugging off tiredness and the effects of the brandy.

"You'll get yourself killed, then. There are two or three thousand Frenchmen coming here, Thomas Woodchurch. What do you have in Maine? A few dozen farmers and veterans? It will be a slaughter, and they'll *still* have your farm when it's over. Listen to me now. This is *done*, understand? I couldn't change it if my life depended on it. Yours does. You want to see your boy cut down by some French knight? How old is he? Seventeen, eighteen? Jesus. There are times when a man *has* to cut and run. I know you don't like to be pushed, Tom. But we ran when that cavalry troop spotted us, didn't we? Just three of us against fifty? We ran like fucking hares then, and there was no shame in it because we lived and we fought again. It's the same thing here. Kings rule. The rest of us just get by and hope to survive it."

"Are you finished? Good. Now *you* listen, Derry. You've said there won't be help coming, and I've heard you. I'm telling you we'll stand. This *is* my land, and I don't care if King Henry himself comes to order me off. I'd spit in his eye, too. I'm not running this time."

"Then you're *dead*," Derry snapped, "and God help you, because I can't."

Both men sat glaring at each other, no give in either of them. After a time, Derry drained his cup and went on.

"If you fight, you'll get your men killed. Worse, you'll break the truce I've worked for, before the damn thing has even properly begun. Do you understand that, Tom? If that's the way they're talking, I need you to go to your friends and tell them what I've told you. Tell them to let this one go. Tell them it's better to stay alive and start again than to throw it all away and end up another corpse in a ditch. There's more riding on this than you know. If you ruin it for a few scrub farms, I'll kill you myself."

Thomas laughed, though there was no mirth in it.

"You won't. You owe me your life, Derry. You owe me more than your old-woman warnings."

"I'm *saving* your life by telling you to get out!" Derry roared. "For once, why don't you just *listen*, you stubborn sod?"

"Our arrows had all gone, remember?"

"Tom, please . . ."

"You had a gash in your leg, and you couldn't run—and that French knight saw you in the long grass and turned back, do you remember?"

"I remember," Derry said miserably.

"And he didn't see me, so I jumped up at him and pulled him down before he could cut off your head with his fine French sword. I took my little knife and I stuck it into his eye slit, Derry, while you just stood and watched. Now that same man is sitting in my kitchen, on my land, and telling me he won't help? I thought better of you, I really did. We stood together once, and it *meant* something."

"The king can't fight, Tom. He's not his father, and he can't fight—or lead men who can. He's like a child, and it's my neck if you ever say it was me who told you. When my king asked me to get him a truce, I did it. Because it was the right thing to do. Because otherwise we'd lose the whole of France anyway. I'm sorry, because I know you and it's like a knife in me to sit in your kitchen and tell you it's hopeless, but it is."

Thomas stared at him over the rim of his cup.

"You're telling me this was all your idea?" he said in wonder. "Who the hell *are* you, Derry Brewer?"

"I'm a man you never want to cross, Tom. Never. I'm someone you should listen to, because I know what I'm talking about and I don't forgive easy. I've told you what I know. If you start a war over a few hills and some sheep . . . Just don't, that's all. I'll find you a stake to buy another place in the north, for old times' sake. I can do that much."

"Alms for the poor? I don't want your charity," Thomas said, almost spitting the word. "I earned my land here. I *earned* it in blood and pain and killing. It's all mine, Derry, no debts, nothing. You're sitting in my home, and these are the hands that built it."

"It's just another tenant farm," Derry growled at him, growing angry once more. "Let it go."

"No. *You* should go, Derry. You've said all there is to say."

"You're turning me out?" Derry asked incredulously. He closed his fists and Thomas lowered his head, so he looked back from under thunderous brows.

"I am. I'd hoped for more from you, but you've made yourself clear."

"Right."

Derry rose and Thomas stood with him, so that they faced each other in the small kitchen, their anger filling it. Derry reached for his waxed cloak and pulled it over himself with furious, sharp movements.

"The king wanted a truce, Tom," he said as he reached the door and flung it open. "He gave up some of his lands for it, and it's done. Don't stand in the road like a fool. Save your family."

The wind howled into the kitchen, making the fire flutter and spit. Derry left the door swinging and disappeared into the night. After a time, Thomas walked over and closed it against the gale.

THE SHIP PLUNGED, dropping into a wave with such suddenness that it seemed to leave Margaret's stomach behind. Spray spattered across the deck, adding to the crust of salt that sparkled on the railings and every exposed piece of timber. The sails creaked and billowed above her head, and Margaret could not remember when she had enjoyed herself as much. The second mate roared an order, and the sailors began heaving ropes as thick as her wrist, moving the wooden yards round to keep the sails full and tight. She saw William striding along the deck, one of his big hands hovering near the railing as he approached.

"One hand for the ship, one for yourself," she muttered, delighted at the English phrase and the sense of nautical knowledge it gave her. How could she have reached fourteen years of age and never been to sea? It was a long way from Saumur Castle in every possible sense. The captain treated her with blushing respect, bowing and listening as if every word she said was a gem to be treasured. She only wished her brothers could see it, or, better still, Yolande. The thought of her sister brought an ache to her chest, but she resisted, holding her head up and breathing in air so cold and fresh that it stung her lungs. Her father had refused to send even a maid with her, causing William to become so red-faced and angry that she'd thought he might strike Lord René of Anjou.

It had not been a pleasant parting, but William had given up his indignation and hired two maids in Calais to tend to her, using his own coins.

Margaret smiled as Suffolk staggered and grabbed the railing. The ship lurched on gray seas, with cold autumn winds battering from the west. Calais itself had contained so many new experiences that it had overwhelmed her. The fortress port had been crammed full of the English within its walls. She'd seen beggars and shopkeepers as well as hundreds of gruff sailors everywhere, bustling to and fro with their sea chests and cargoes. When they'd paid off the last carriage driver, William had hustled her past some painted women, as if Margaret had never heard of whores. She laughed to recall his very English embarrassment as he tried to protect her from a sight of them.

A seagull called overhead and, to her delight, settled on one of the spiderwebs of ropes that led everywhere, almost within reach of her hand. It watched her with beady little eyes, and Margaret was sorry she didn't have a crumb of cake or dry bread to feed the bird.

The gull startled and flew off with a harsh cry as William came up to her. He smiled to see her expression.

"My lady, I thought you might enjoy your first glimpse of England. If you'll keep a hand on the rail at all times, the captain says we can go to the prow—the front of the ship."

Margaret stumbled as she went eagerly, and he put a strong arm on hers to steady her.

"Forgive the impertinence, my lady. You're warm enough?" he asked her. "No sickness?"

"Not yet," Margaret replied. "A stomach of iron, Lord Suffolk!"

He chuckled at that, leading her along the pitching deck. Margaret could hear the hiss of the sea passing under them. Such speed! It was extraordinary and exhilarating. She resolved to return to sea when she was properly married in England. A queen could have her own ship, surely?

"Can a queen have her own ship?" she called, pitching her voice over the wind and screaming gulls.

"I'm sure a queen can have her own fleet, if she wants," William roared back, grinning over his shoulder.

The wind was freshening, and the mates were bellowing orders. The sailors moved busily once again, loosening shrouds and folding great wet sections of sails, then tying them off before making it all taut once again.

Margaret reached the bow of the ship, with William's hand steady on her shoulder. As well as the stays and the high jib sail, only the wooden bowsprit and some netting were farther out, crashing down almost to the waves and then up again, over and over. She gasped in delight as white cliffs loomed in the distance, bright and clean against the sea mist. Margaret took a breath and held it, knowing it was English air. She had never left France before. She had never even left Anjou. Her senses swam with so many new experiences and thoughts.

"They are beautiful, monsieur! *Magnifique!*"

The sailors heard her. They smiled and cheered, already affectionate toward the girl who would be queen and who loved the sea as much as they did.

"Look down, my lady," William said.

Margaret dropped her gaze and then gasped to see sleek gray dolphins racing along the surface of the sea, keeping perfect pace with the ship. They darted and leaped as if they played a game, daring each other to see how close they could come. As she watched, a pole and chain off the bowsprit dipped deep enough to touch one of them. In a sudden flurry, they all vanished into the deep as if they had never existed. Margaret was left with a sense of awe and wonder at what she had seen. William laughed, amused to be able to show her such things.

"That's why they call that part a dolphin striker," he said, smiling. "It doesn't hurt them." The wind howled, so that he had to lean close and shout into her ear. "Now, it will be a few hours yet before we make port. Shall I call your maids to prepare dry clothes for you?"

Margaret stared out at the white cliffs, at the land whose king she had never met but would marry twice. England, her England.

"Not yet, William," she said. "Let me stand here for a while first."

PART TWO

Mine heart is set, and all mine whole intent,

To serve this flower in my most humble wyse

As faithfully as can be thought or meant,

Without feigning or sloth in my servyse;

For know thee well, it is a paradyse

To see this flower when it begyn to sprede,

With colors fresh ennewyd, white and red.

WILLIAM DE LA POLE

(written about Margaret of Anjou)

CHAPTER 11

With warm furs on her hands and wrapped snugly around her neck, Margaret walked into the frost-covered gardens. Wetherby House was her first home in England, where she'd spent almost three months. The trees were still stark and bare, but there were snowdrops growing around their roots and spring was on its way. It could almost have been France, and walking the paths eased some of the homesickness in her.

All the local farms were slaughtering pigs and salting meat. Margaret could smell the smoke, and she knew the dead animals were being piled with straw, which was lit to burn off their bristles. The bitter odor brought a sudden memory, so vivid that she stood and stared. Her mouth recalled the taste when her mother had let the stable lads mix fresh blood with sugar into a paste, almost a mousse. Her sister, Yolande, and her brothers had shared a bowl of the rare treat, squabbling over the spoon until it fell into the dust, then dipping their fingers until their skin and teeth were stained red.

Margaret felt her eyes sting with tears. Saumur would be quieter without her that summer. It was hard not to miss her mother's stuffed sardines or fennel chicken when Margaret was presented with a solid pork joint sitting like a boulder in a sea of peas in heavy cream. It seemed the English liked to boil food. It was one more thing to get used to.

Lord William was a comfort, almost the only familiar face since leaving home. He had helped her improve her English, though he could rattle along in good French when he wanted, or when he had to explain a word. Yet he had been away more often than not, arriving back at the house every few days with more news of the wedding.

It was a strange hiatus in Margaret's life while great men and women arranged her second marriage. When she'd landed on the south coast by Portchester Castle, she'd hoped Henry would come to her. She'd had a vision of a handsome young king riding to the grand ruins from London, arriving perhaps that first night to sweep her into his arms. Instead, she'd been carried away to Wetherby and, apparently, forgotten. The days and weeks had slipped past with no sign of the king, only Suffolk or his friend Earl Somerset, a short, wiry man who had bowed so deeply that she feared he might never be able to rise again. She smiled to remember it. Before Somerset arrived, Derry Brewer had described him to her as "a right noble cockerel." She'd learned the phrase in delight, her amusement made deeper when she met the earl and found him dressed in bright blue and yellow. She liked all three men for different reasons. Derry was both charming and polite, and he'd slipped her a bag of tiny sweets when William wasn't looking. She'd been caught halfway between outrage at being treated as a child and delight at bitter lemon drops that made her mouth pucker as she sucked them.

Christmas had come and gone, with strange and gaudy presents arriving in her name from a hundred noble strangers, all taking the opportunity to introduce themselves. With William as her consort and chaperone, Margaret had gone to a ball she still remembered in a whirl of pungent apple cider and dancing. She'd hoped to see her husband there, her mind filled with romantic tales where the king would appear and the revelers would all fall silent. Yet Henry had not come. She was beginning to wonder if he ever would.

She looked up at the sound of a carriage crunching across the gravel drive on the other side of the house. William was away that day, and Margaret was filled with worry that it would be another of the English noblewomen come to inspect her or bargain for favors they clearly thought she could provide. She had sat in strained meetings with the wives of earls and barons, nibbling seed cake dipped into spiced wine and straining to find something to say in reply to their questions. Duchess Cecily of York had been the worst of them, a woman so very tall and assured that she made Margaret feel like a sticky child. Margaret's English was still less than fluent, and the duchess claimed to have no French, so it had been one of the hardest afternoons of her life, with far more silence than talk.

"I will be ill again," Margaret muttered to herself at the thought of another such meeting. "I will be . . . indisposed."

In fact, she had been truly sick for a time after arriving. The strange, heavy food, perhaps, or just the change of air, had reduced her to helpless vomiting, with learned doctors forbidding her to leave her bed for the best part of two weeks. She'd thought then that the exquisite boredom would kill her, but those days of quiet had become a strangely happy memory, already half forgotten.

She had a vague idea that a queen should support her husband by flattering and cajoling his supporters, but if Cecily of York was the standard, it would not be an easy thing to learn. Margaret recalled the woman's dry, sour smell and shuddered.

She looked up as a high voice called her name in the distance. Dear

God, they were looking for her again! She could see servants moving in the house, and she trotted a little farther down the garden paths to hide herself from the windows. William said the marriage would be in just a few days. He'd been red-faced and amused, his great mane of dark gray hair brushed and shining when he came to tell her. On his return, she'd travel to the abbey at Titchfield, not ten miles away. Henry would be there at last, waiting for her. She only wished she could picture the young king's face when she imagined the scene. In her mind, she'd married him a thousand times, with every detail vivid except for that one.

"Margaret!" someone called.

She looked up, suddenly more alert. When the voice called again, Margaret felt a great thump of excitement in her chest. She gathered her skirts and ran back toward the house.

Her sister, Yolande, was standing by the garden doors, looking out. When she caught sight of Margaret, her face lit and she ran forward. They embraced in the frozen garden, with white grass all around. Yolande poured out a torrent of rapid French, bouncing in place as she held her younger sister.

"It is such a joy to see you again! You are taller, I swear, and there are roses in your cheeks. It is agreeing with you to be in England, I think!"

When there was no sign of the chatter coming to an end, Margaret pressed her hand over her sister's mouth, making them both laugh.

"How are you here, Yolande? I am thrilled to see you. I can hardly breathe with it, but how did you arrive? You must tell me everything."

"For your marriage, Margaret, of course! I thought we would miss it for a time, but I am here even so. Your Lord William sent the most beautiful invitation to me at Saumur. Father objected, of course, but he was distracted with some new trip he is planning. Our dear mother said the family *must* be represented, and she *prevailed*, bless her saintly heart. Your English friend sent a ship for me, as you or I would send a carriage. Oh! And I am not alone! Frederick is with me. He's growing a set of ridiculous whiskers. You must tell him they look terrible, as they scratch me so and I won't have them on him."

Margaret looked away, suddenly aware of the strangeness of her situation. She had been married months before her sister, but had never yet seen her husband. With a quizzical eye, she looked more closely at Yolande.

"You look . . . blooming yourself, sister. Are you with child?"

Yolande blushed hot and pink.

"I hope so! We have been trying and, oh, Margaret, it is wonderful! The first time was a little unpleasant, but no worse than a beesting, perhaps. After that, well . . ."

"Yolande!" Margaret replied, blushing almost as deeply. "I don't want to hear." She stopped to consider, realizing she did want to hear, very much. "All right, I'm sure Frederick will be out here looking for you in just a little while. Tell me everything, so that I know what to expect. What do you mean 'a little unpleasant'?"

Yolande chuckled throatily as she took her younger sister by the arm and led her down the path away from the house.

EVERYTHING WAS DIFFERENT, yet everything was the same. The sense of déjà vu was intense as Margaret took her place in the carriage in the wedding dress she had worn at Tours. At least the day was cold, a blessing in a dress that crushed her.

Yolande sat across from her sister. To Margaret's eyes, she looked more adult, as if marriage had worked some strange alchemy, or perhaps because Yolande was now a countess in her own right. Her husband, Frederick, sat on the bench seat, looking stern in a dark tunic and with his sword across his knees. Margaret noticed he still wore the whiskers, stretching from his ears right down to his jawline. He'd said his father's set was much admired in their parish, and Margaret wondered if her sister would ever succeed in getting him to shave them off. Yet his sternness faded when he looked at Yolande. The affection between them was touching and obvious as they clasped hands and shifted with the coach on the potholed roads.

The morning had passed in a flurry of excitement, with William riding back and forth to the abbey on his own horse to see to the last details, then washing and changing into clean clothes in one of the upper rooms. Margaret had already been introduced to a dozen men and women she did not know as the wedding party filled Wetherby House, laughing and talking all the while. Her status was a delicate matter when it came to meeting noblemen and their wives. Not yet a queen, Margaret had curtsied to the Duchess of York even so, as she might have to any of her mother's generation. Perhaps she only imagined Cecily York's disdain as she complimented Margaret on her dress in return. Lord York was scrupulously polite and had bowed to her, saying how pleased he was to see her at her second marriage as well as her first. His wife had muttered a few words Margaret did not quite catch, but she saw it made York smile as he bent over her hand to kiss it. Something about their private amusement had irritated her.

With an effort, she put such thoughts aside. She would meet her husband today. She would see his face. As the cart rocked back and forth, she prayed silently that he would not be ugly or deformed. William had promised her that Henry was handsome, but she knew he could say nothing else. Fear and hope mingled in equal measures, and she could only watch the hedges pass and the black rooks flying. Her forehead itched where her maids had plucked it back, but she dared not scratch marks in the white powder and bit her lip against the irritation.

Flowers had been woven into her hair, and her face felt stiff with all the paints and perfumes that had been applied since she'd bathed at dawn. She tried not to breathe too hard against the confining panels of her dress in case she fainted.

Margaret knew when they were growing close to the abbey of St. Mary and St. John the Evangelist because the local families had come out to see her pass, gathering on the road that led into the vast farmland owned by the monks. Apprentices had been given the day off from their labors in her honor, and townsmen and -women had put on their church clothes just to stand and wait for the woman who would be Queen of England. Margaret had a view of a cheering, waving crowd before her carriage swept past onto a drive that led for miles through woodland and fields laid in dark furrows.

The well-wishers did not cross that invisible boundary, and as the road dipped, Margaret could see carriages ahead and behind, fourteen of them traveling together to the abbey church in the distance. Her heart hammered against the dress, and she touched her hand to her chest to feel it race. Henry would be there, a twenty-three-year-old king. She looked past her sister and Frederick to strain her eyes for the first glimpse of him. It was pointless, she knew. King Henry would be already inside, warned by the sight of the carriages on the drive. He could well be waiting at the altar, with William at his shoulder.

Margaret felt light-headed and feared she would faint before she could even arrive at the church. Seeing her distress, Yolande took out a fan and wafted cool air over her while Margaret sat back and breathed with her eyes closed.

The abbey church was part of a much larger complex of buildings. On that day, the monks were not working in the fields, but Margaret saw fishponds, walled gardens, and vineyards, as well as stables and a dozen other structures. She found herself getting out of the carriage, helped by Frederick, who raced round to take her hand.

The carriages ahead had emptied, and though many of the guests had gone inside, there was still a crowd at the church doors, smiling and talking among themselves. She saw Derry Brewer standing close to the Duke of York. Derry waved to her as Margaret swept forward with her sister and a gaggle of maids in tow. She saw him say something to York that made the man's expression harden. As Margaret approached the church door, they all went into the gloom beyond, like geese ushered in by a goose girl, so that she was alone with her sister and her maids.

"Bless you for being here, Yolande," she said with feeling. "I would not have liked to stand alone."

"*Pfui!* It should have been Father, but he is away searching for his foolish titles once again. He is never satisfied. My Frederick says—no, that does not matter today. I only wish Mama could have stood here with us, but Father insisted she stay and run Saumur. You are in her prayers, Margaret. You can be sure of that. Are you ready to see your king? Are you nervous?"

"I am . . . and I am, yes. I am dizzy with it. Just stay with me while I catch my breath, will you? This dress is too tight."

"You have grown since last summer, Margaret, that's what it is. It was not too tight before. I see a bosom developing, and I swear you are taller. Perhaps it's true that English meat is good for you."

She winked as she said it, and Margaret gasped and shook her head.

"You are shocking, sister. To make such jokes when I am waiting to be married!"

"Best time, I think," Yolande said cheerfully. She switched to English with a sparkle in her eyes. "Now will you bloody hell be married?"

"That's not how you say it," Margaret said, smiling. She took another breath as best she could and inclined her head to the monks standing at the door. Inside, bellows were pumped and the most complicated device in the world built up pressure. The first chords sounded across the church congregation, and they turned almost as one to see the bride enter.

Baron Jean de Roche was a happy man, though even brandy could not keep out the cold wind. Spring was coming, he could feel it. No one fought in winter. As well as being practically impossible to feed a marching army in the cold months, it was a brutal time to go to war. Hands went numb, rain soaked down, and there was always a chance that your men would simply up and vanish in the night. He looked around at his little band of ruffian knights and smiled widely, showing his pink upper gum where he'd had all the teeth pulled. He'd hated those teeth. They'd hurt him so badly that he hated them even when they were gone. The day he'd agreed to have the pincer man yank them all had been one of the happiest of his adult life. A mouthful of blood and having to dip his bread in milk was a small price to pay for release from agony. He was certain his life had begun to improve from that day on, as if his teeth had been holding him back with all their poisons and swellings. He sucked in his top lip as he trotted on, folding it back along the gum and chewing the bristles. He'd had a few taken out below as well, but just the big ones at the back, where they'd rotted. He still had the teeth at the lower front, and he had perfected a smile that revealed only that neat yellow row.

Life was good for a man with healthy teeth, he thought, complacently. He reached back and patted the saddlebags behind his hip, enjoying the fatness of them. Life was also good for a man with the initiative to ride ahead of the army into Maine. De Roche had been amazed at the results of looting homes in Anjou. It seemed the English did nothing but amass stores of coins, like the greedy little merchants they all were. De Roche had seen knights made rich in a single day, and the French lords had learned quickly that it was worth their while to search carts heading north away from them. Families tended to take their most valuable possessions and leave the rest. Why spend time smashing a house apart when those who knew had already taken the best pieces? The noblemen gave a portion of whatever they found to the king, of course, but that was exactly the problem, at least as far as de Roche was concerned. They could afford it. Those men were already rich and would be much richer by the time they finished taking back English farms and towns.

His expression soured as he considered his own estate compared to theirs. His men could almost be described as hedge knights if not for his house colors. Just a year before, he'd been considering turning them all out before he became known as a hedge baron. He sucked his lips again at bitter memories. His family farms had all gone to pay debts, sliced away year by year until he had almost nothing left. He'd discovered cards then, introduced by a friend of his who had long since had his throat cut. De Roche thought of the colorful boards and wondered if there was anyone in Maine who could be persuaded to gamble with him. He'd had a run of bad luck, it was true, but now he had gold again, and he knew he understood the games better than most people he came across. With just a little change of fortune, he could double what his men had won for him, or even triple it. He smiled, showing just his bottom teeth. He'd buy back his father's castle and turn the old boy out into the snow for all his sneering. That would be just the start.

The road under his little group changed from a dirt track to cut stone, a sure sign that those ahead were wealthy. De Roche let his mount amble along, wondering whether it would be worth the risk to enter a town. He had only a dozen men with him, enough to take whatever they wanted from a lonely farm or a small village. Towns could sometimes afford to employ a militia, and de Roche had no desire to get into a real fight. Yet he wasn't a criminal, he wasn't wanted for anything. He was merely the forward vanguard of the victorious French army. Some forty miles forward, before the rest of his countrymen could take all the best pieces. De Roche made a quick decision. He could at least glance around at the local English merchants and decide then whether they'd make it too hot for his men.

"Head into town," he called to the others. "We'll have a little look and, if it's quiet, see what we can find. If there's a guardhouse, or a militia, we'll find a good inn for the night like any other dusty travelers."

His men were weary after another day on the road, but they talked and laughed as they trotted along. Some of the gold and silver would make its way to them, and they'd found a farmhouse with three sisters the night before. De Roche scratched his crotch at the thought, hoping he hadn't picked up lice again. He hated having to get his groin shaved and singed. He'd gone first with the sisters, of course, as was his right. His men had stories from that encounter to last them for months, and he chuckled as they became wilder in the telling. De Roche had insisted on burning the place as they left that morning. Living witnesses could cause him a few difficulties, but another blackened shell would be ignored by the army coming up behind. God knew they'd created enough of them.

He saw Albert angle his mount closer. The old man had been with de Roche's family for as long as he could remember, as groundsman and horse trainer, usually, though de Roche could remember Albert running a few special errands for his father. Albert wore no armor, but he carried a long knife that was almost a sword, and, like his father before him, de Roche had found him a useful man in rough country.

"What is it, Albert?" he asked.

"I had an aunt near here when I was a boy. There's a castle a few miles west, with soldiers."

"Well?" de Roche said, glowering. It would not do to have a servant questioning his courage in front of the men.

"Begging your pardon, milord. I just thought you should know it might be a little tougher than farmhouses and women."

De Roche blinked at the old man. Had that been an insult? He could not believe it, but Albert was positively glaring at him.

"Do I have to remind you that this little trip is no more than the English will get from the king and his army? They could have left, Albert. Many of them already have, in fact. Those who remain are illegal, every man, woman, and child. No! Considering they have rebelled against their own king's wishes, they are *traitors*, Albert. We are doing God's work."

As he spoke, his troop passed a farmer standing with his head bowed. The man's cart was piled high with parsnips, and a few of the men reached down and took a couple at a time. The peasant looked angry, but he knew better than to say anything. Somehow the sight appeased de Roche's prickling outrage. He recalled that Albert had not taken his turn with the women the night before and decided the man *was* criticizing him.

"Ride at the back, Albert. I'm not a child for you to wag your fingers at."

Albert shrugged and pulled his horse to the side to let the others pass. De Roche settled himself, still furious at the man's insolence. That was one who would not be benefiting from the riches of Maine, he thought. When they turned back to the army, de Roche swore he'd leave Albert behind to beg for his food, with all the years he'd served the family to keep him warm.

They reached the outskirts of the town with the sun already low in the west, a short winter's day with a long night ahead before they saw it again. De Roche was tired and sweating by then, though his spirits rose at the sight of a painted inn sign swinging in the breeze. He and his men handed over their horses to stable lads, casting lots for which of their number would stay with the mounts while the others got a night's sleep. De Roche led them inside, calling for wine and food in a loud voice. He did not notice the inn owner's child leave a few minutes later, belting off down the street into the town as if the Devil himself was on his heels.

CHAPTER 12

Margaret released a breath she didn't know she'd been holding. Two little boys had taken up station in front of her as she walked into the church, the sons of some noble family. One of them kept looking back as they walked in time with the organ music through the crowd to the carved oak screen and hidden altar. The boys were dressed in red and wore sprigs of dried rosemary wound and tied around their arms. Margaret could smell the scent of the herb as she followed them. The entire standing crowd seemed to be carrying dried flowers, or golden wheat sheaves kept back from the harvest. They rustled as she passed through them, turning to watch and smile and whisper comments.

The boys and her maids stopped at the screen, so that only Yolande went through with her, giving her arm a squeeze as she, too, stepped aside and found her seat. Margaret saw Henry for the first time. Relief made her dizzy. Even through the haze of her veil, she could see he was not deformed, or even scarred. If anything, Henry was handsome, with an oval head, dark eyes, and black hair that curled over his ears. Henry wore a simple gold crown, and his wedding outfit was almost unadorned, a tunic of red that was belted at the waist and ended at his calves, where cream wool stockings covered his skin. Over it all was an embroidered cloak, patterned in gold thread and held with a heavy brooch on his shoulder. She saw that he wore a sword on his right hip, a polished line of silver chased in gold. The effect was one of understated simplicity—and then she saw him smile. She blushed, realizing she had been staring. Henry turned back to face the altar, and she kept walking, forcing herself to a slow pace.

The organ notes swelled, and the gathered crowd chattered to each other, letting out their own breaths as the great doors to the fields were shut behind them. Very few could see the altar, but they had witnessed her arrival and they were content.

Beyond the screen, the chancel was a much smaller space. Unlike the main church, there were chairs there, and Margaret passed rows of richly attired lords and ladies. One or two were fanning themselves from habit or custom, though the air was cold.

Margaret felt herself shivering as she reached Henry's shoulder. He was taller than she was, she noted with satisfaction. All the fears she had not even been able to admit to herself were washed away as the elderly abbot began to speak in sonorous Latin.

She almost jumped when Henry reached out and lifted her veil, folding it back onto her hair. Margaret looked up as he stared in turn, suddenly aware that he had not seen her face in life before that day. Her heart pounded. Her shivering worsened, but somehow it felt as if she gave off enough heat to take the chill from the entire church. The king smiled again, and some hidden part of her chest and stomach unclenched. Her eyes gleamed with tears so she could hardly see.

The abbot was a stern man, or at least seemed so to Margaret. His voice filled the church as he asked if there were impediments, whether prior betrothals or consanguinity. Margaret watched as William handed over a papal dispensation, bound in gold ribbon. The abbot took it with a bow, though he had read it long before and only glanced formally at it before handing it over to one of his monks. Though they were cousins, he knew there was no blood shared between them.

Margaret knelt when Henry knelt, rose when he rose. The Latin service was a peaceful, rhythmic drone that seemed to roll over and through her. When she looked up, she saw colored light come through a window of stained glass, patterning the floor by the altar in bright greens and red and blue. Her eyes opened wide as she heard her own name. Henry had turned to her and, as she looked at him in wonder, he took her hand, his voice both warm and calm.

"I take thee, Margaret of Anjou, to have and to hold, from this day forward, for better for worse, for richer for poorer, in sickness and in health, till death us depart, if Holy Church it will ordain. Thereto I plight thee my troth."

In something like panic, Margaret felt the eyes of the English lords and ladies fasten on her as she struggled to remember the words she had to say. Henry reached down to kiss her hand.

"It is your turn now, Margaret," he whispered.

The tension eased in her, and the words came.

"I take thee, Henry of England, to have and to hold, from this day forward, for better for worse, for richer for poorer, in sickness and in health, to be meek and obedient, in bed and at board, till death us depart, if Holy Church it will ordain. Thereto-I-plight-thee-my-troth." The last words came out in a rush, and she felt a great joy that she had managed it without a mistake. She heard William chuckle, and even the dour abbot smiled a little.

Margaret stood very still as her new husband took her left hand and placed a ruby ring on the fourth finger. She felt dizzy again, still struggling to take a full breath in the confines of the dress. When the abbot told them to kneel and prostrate themselves, she might have fallen, if not for Henry's arm on hers. A pure white cloth was placed over both their heads, draping itself down her back, so that for a moment she almost felt she was alone with her husband. As the Mass began, she sensed Henry turn toward her and looked back at him, tilting her head in silent question.

"You are very beautiful," he whispered. "William told me I should say so, but it is true anyway."

Margaret began to reply, but when he reached over and took her hand once more, she found herself weeping in reaction. Henry looked sideways at her in blank astonishment as the abbot performed the final part of the service over their bowed heads.

"IF WE DO THIS, we don't stop," Thomas said, leaning close to Baron Strange. "As soon as the French king hears there is fighting in Maine, he'll come in fast and rough, with his blood up. They won't dally in estates and vineyards any longer, sampling the wines and village girls. With spring on the way, there will be murder and destruction, and it won't end until we're all dead or we break the back of his men. Do you understand, milord Baron? It won't be enough to kill a few and vanish into the woods like Rob Hood or some outlaw. If we attack tonight, there'll be no going home for any of us, not till it's done."

"Thomas, I can't tell that to the men," Strange replied, rubbing his face wearily with his hand. "They'll have no hope at all. They're with me to pay back the French, perhaps to slit a few throats. You'd have them take on an army? Most of them are still hoping King Henry will relent, or Lord York. They still believe there'll be English soldiers coming to save us. If that doesn't happen, they'll break and they'll run."

Thomas Woodchurch shook his head, smiling wryly.

"They won't run, unless they see you riding away, or me dead maybe. I know these men, Baron. They're no stronger than the French. They can't fight longer without losing their wind. But they *are* killers,

Baron, every last one of them. They love to murder another man with a bit of good iron, standing with their friends. They scorn a coward like the devil—and they don't run."

A low whistle interrupted their conversation. Thomas contented himself with a meaningful last glance, then stood up in the shadows. The moon was out, and he had a good view of the road ahead.

He saw a bareheaded knight come staggering out of the inn with his helmet tucked under his arm and his free hand fumbling at his groin. Two more followed him, and Thomas understood they were looking for a place to empty their bladders. It took a while for a man to remove a metal codpiece. Thomas remembered the smell in battle, when knights just emptied their bladders and bowels down their legs, relying on their squires to clean up after the fighting had ended.

Thomas took his time placing an arrow on the string of his bow. He wanted them all to come out, and his mind seethed with the best way to do it. If he let the French company barricade themselves inside, they could be there for days, with food and drink and comfort. He turned back to the baron, sighing to himself.

"I'll get them out," he said. "You just call the attack when it's time. No one moves and no one comes to get me, no matter what happens. Understand? Pass the word. Oh, and tell the men not to shoot me in the back."

As Baron Strange vanished into the gloom, Thomas put his arrow back in the quiver and rested his bow against a wall. He tapped his hip to reassure himself he still had his hunting seax. With his heart beating hard and fast, he stepped out into the moonlight and approached the three French knights.

One of them was already groaning with relief as he released a stream of urine into the road. The others were laughing at him as Thomas came up behind, so that they didn't hear his approach until he was just a few steps away. The closest knight jumped and swore, then laughed at his own shock as he saw there was just one man standing there.

"Another peasant! I swear they breed like rabbits around here. On your way, monsieur, and stop bothering your betters."

Thomas saw the knight was standing unsteadily. He gave a whoop and pushed him over in a crash of metal on the road.

"You French bastards!" he shouted. "Go home!"

One of the others was blinking at him in amazement as Thomas rushed him and kicked hard at his leg. He, too, went over, flailing wildly as he tried to right himself.

"You've made a mistake tonight, son," a third knight said. He seemed a little steadier on his feet than the others, and Thomas backed away as the man drew a sword from his scabbard.

"Eh? You think you can attack a man of honor and not pay the consequences?"

The knight advanced.

"Help!" Thomas yelled, then in a moment of inspiration, switched to a French phrase he knew just as well. *"Aidez-moi!"*

The knight swung at him, but Thomas stayed out of range, moving quickly. He could hear the man puffing after a night of heavy drinking in the inn. If it all went wrong, Thomas thought he could still run for it.

The first knight he'd pushed over was clambering noisily to his feet when the inn door crashed open and a dozen armored men came out with swords ready. They saw one peasant dancing around an increasingly frustrated knight, and some of them laughed and called to him.

"Can you not catch the devil, Pierre? Try a lunge, man! Put his liver through!"

The knight in question didn't respond, focused as he was on killing the peasant who had infuriated him.

Thomas was beginning to sweat. He saw that another of the first three had drawn a narrow bollock dagger and was trying to get round to his side, either to attack or grab him for Pierre to spit with the larger blade. Thomas could hear the man chuckling blearily to himself, almost too drunk to stand, yet inching closer every moment.

He heard Strange shout an order, and Thomas threw himself to the ground.

"He's down!" he heard someone shout delightedly in French. "Did he fall over? Pierre?"

The voice choked off as the air filled with shafts, a rushing, meaty sound as the knights were struck, punched backward as arrows sent at full draw stopped in them. They roared and shouted, but the arrows kept coming, slotting through armor and mail links so that they spattered blood behind.

Thomas looked up to see the knight stalking him staring in shock at the feathered shafts standing out from his collarbone and through one of his thighs. The man made a sound of horror and tried to turn to face his unseen attackers. Thomas stood up behind him as the knight scrabbled round, dragging his damaged leg. Grimly, Thomas unsheathed his seax and stepped in close, taking a firm hold of the knight's helmet. He wrenched the head back as the man spasmed in panic, revealing the links of the metal gorget protecting his throat. Using the heavy blade like a hammer, Thomas rammed it down with all the strength of his bow arm, breaking the softer iron and cutting deep before wrenching the seax back and forth. The knight stiffened, choking and weeping as Thomas stepped away and let him fall.

Most of the knights were down, though some of the wounded had gathered around one who must have been their leader. De Roche watched in terror as he saw dozens of men wearing dark clothes and carrying longbows step out of the side streets and clamber like spiders down from roofs. As a group they walked in, silent.

The innkeeper had come to his door, crossing himself in the presence of death. Thomas made an angry gesture for him to go inside, and the man vanished back to the warmth and cheer of the inn.

"Monsieur!" de Roche called to him. "I can be held for ransom. You wish for gold?"

"I have gold," Thomas replied.

De Roche stared around him as he and four battered knights were surrounded.

"You understand the King of France is just a few miles away, monsieur? He and I are like brothers. Leave me alive and there will be no reprisals, not for this town."

"You make that promise? On your honor?" Thomas asked.

"Yes, on my honor! I swear it."

"And what about the rest of Maine? Will you leave that territory in peace? Will your king withdraw his men?"

De Roche hesitated. He wanted to agree, but it would be such an obvious lie that he could not speak. His voice lost its edge of desperation.

"Monsieur, if I could arrange such a thing, I would, but it is not possible."

"Very well. God be with you, my lord."

Thomas muttered an order to the archers around him even as the French baron cried out and raised his hands. One of the shafts went straight through his palm.

"Check the bodies now," Thomas said, feeling old and tired. "Cut their throats to be sure. There can't be witnesses."

The men set about the task as they would have slaughtered pigs or geese. One or two of the knights kicked as they were held down, but it did not take long.

Rowan walked back to his father with his longbow in his hand. He looked very pale in the moonlight. Thomas clapped him on the shoulder.

"Ugly work," he said.

Rowan looked out at the road full of dead men.

"Yes. They'll be angry when they hear," Rowan said.

"Good. I want them angry. I want them so furious they can hardly think, and I want them to charge at us the way they did at Agincourt. I was just a boy then, Rowan. Almost too young to carry the water casks for old Sir Hew. I remember it, though. That was the day I began to train with my bow, from then till now."

LONDON WAS simply overwhelming, too much to take in. Margaret had ridden with her new husband from the abbey at Titchfield to Blackheath, where she had seen the Thames for the first time and, in that moment, her first bloated body floating past on the surface.

The king's party had been blessed with a clear day, with the sky a washed-out blue and the air very cold. The mayor and his aldermen had met her there, dressed in blue gowns with scarlet hoods. There was an air of gaiety and festival to the procession as Margaret was led by hand to a large wheeled litter, pulled by horses in white satin cloth. From that point, she went where they took her, though she looked down at her new husband riding at her side at every spare moment. The procession choked the road to a standstill as they reached the single massive bridge that spanned the river, joining the capital city to the southern counties and the coast. Margaret tried not to gape like a country girl, but London Bridge was incredible, almost a town in its own right that stretched across the water on whitewashed brick arches. Her litter passed dozens of shops and homes built onto the bridge it-self. There were even public toilets, and she blushed as she glimpsed boards hanging above the river, set with circular seats. Her litter moved on, revealing strangeness after strangeness, then halted on the center of the bridge. Three-story buildings pressed in on both sides, but a small area had been set as a stage and the filth underfoot had been covered over with clean rushes. Two women waited there, painted and dressed as Greek goddesses. Margaret stared as they approached and pressed garlands of flowers over her shoulders.

One of them began to declaim lines of verse over the noise of the crowd, and Margaret had gathered only that it was in praise of peace before whips cracked and the scene was left behind. She craned round to see Yolande riding sidesaddle with her husband, Frederick. As their eyes met, both women were hard-pressed not to laugh in delight and wonder.

The mayor's men marched on with them through the streets, accompanied by more people than Margaret had even known existed. The entire city seemed to have come to a halt to see her. Surely there could not be any men and women beyond those she saw. The crowds struggled against each other, climbing up buildings and sitting on the shoulders of friends to catch a glimpse of Margaret of England. The noise of their cheering could be felt on her skin, and her ears ached.

Margaret had not eaten for hours, that small detail forgotten in the vast organization of her trip through her husband's capital city. The smell of the streets went some way to steal her appetite, but by the time she reached Westminster Abbey she was weak with hunger. The litter horses were allowed to rest, and Henry himself took her hand to guide her inside.

It was strange to feel the warmth of his hand on hers. She hadn't been sure what to expect after the wedding in Titchfield, but in the days that followed she had never been left alone with the young king. William and Lord Somerset in particular seemed determined to whisk the king away from her at every opportunity. At night she slept alone, and when she had asked and then demanded to know where the king was, she was told by sheepish servants that he had ridden to the nearest chapel to spend the night in prayer. She was beginning to wonder if what her father said about the English was true. Not many French-women remained virgins a full week after marriage. Margaret gripped Henry's hand tightly, so that he looked at her. She saw only happiness in his eyes as he walked her over the white stones into one of the oldest abbeys in England.

Margaret suppressed a gasp at an interior far grander even than the cathedral at Tours, with a vaulted ceiling stretching far above in spars of stone. Sparrows wheeled overhead in the cold air, and she thought she could surely feel the presence of God in the open space.

There were wooden benches filled with people stretching the length of the ancient church. At the sight of so many, her steps faltered, so that Henry had to put an arm around her waist.

"There isn't much more," he said, smiling.

A psalter of bishops carrying curled staffs of gold went before her, and Margaret let herself be guided to twin thrones, where she and Henry prostrated themselves before the altar and were blessed before seating themselves and facing thousands of strange faces. Margaret's sweeping gaze was arrested by the sight of her father in the front row, looking smugly self-satisfied. The day lost some of its glory then, but Margaret forced herself to nod primly to the slug. She supposed any father would want to see his daughter made a queen, but he had not been at the wedding, nor bothered to inform her he would interrupt his travels to cross to England.

Some of the congregation were eating and drinking, enjoying the holiday atmosphere. Margaret's stomach groaned at the sight of a cold roasted chicken being passed along a row. A great cloak of white and gold was placed around her shoulder, and the archbishop began the Latin ceremony.

An age passed as she sat there, trying not to fidget. At least she had no vow to remember, as a wife and queen. The safety of the realm was not her responsibility to protect. The archbishop rolled his words on and on, filling the space.

Margaret felt the weight of a crown pressed onto her head. Instinctively, she reached up and touched the chilled metal, just as the congregation began a crashing wave of applause and cheering. She bit her lip, refusing to faint as her senses swam. She was Queen of England, and Henry took her arm as he led her back down the aisle.

"I am so very pleased," he said over the noise of the clapping and calling voices. "We needed a truce, Margaret. I cannot spend every night in prayer. Sometimes I must sleep, and without a truce I feared the worst. Now you are queen, I can stop my vigil."

Margaret glanced at her husband in confusion, but he was smiling, so she merely bowed her head and continued out into the sunshine of London to be seen by the crowds.

THERE WERE green spring buds on the trees, swept back and forth in gusts as cold as midwinter. Thomas longed for warmer days, though he knew they would bring the French into Maine. It had been a month since he and his men had killed the French knights and their baron. Even Strange had been forced to admit their first taste of vengeance had worked well for recruitment. That single act had brought men into their group who had been ready to leave all France behind. They'd coalesced around his little force, doubling their numbers.

Thomas looked sideways at his son, lying on his stomach in the gorse. He felt pride for the man Rowan had become, before the thought soured in him. He didn't want to see the boy killed, but he could not send him away, not then. Too many others looked to Thomas for a slender reed of faith in what they had started. If he kept Rowan safe by sending him to England to join his mother and sisters, he knew how they would see it. Half of them would drift away again, choosing to save themselves.

Thomas saw movement in the distance, and he sat up, knowing his raised head would be all but invisible to whoever it was. He saw horsemen, walking their mounts at an easy pace so as not to leave behind the trudging men at their side.

"See them, Rowan? God smiles on us today, lad. I tell you that. God bloody smiles."

Rowan chuckled quietly, still hidden in the dark green scrub. Together, they watched the group moving slowly along the road. There were perhaps forty horsemen, but Thomas looked most closely at the walking men. They were the ones he had come to see, and they carried bows very much like his own. Twice as many as the men-at-arms they accompanied, the archers were worth their weight in gold as far as Thomas was concerned.

When the group was just a few hundred yards away, Thomas rose up and stood to wait for them. He made sure his bow was visible but unstrung, knowing they would be wary of an ambush so deep into Maine. He saw a ripple go through them as they noticed the pair of strangers by the road, and it was not hard for Thomas to spot the man giving orders to the rest. He'd left Baron Strange behind, but part of him wished he were there. Nobles had their own style and manners, and this one would be suspicious enough of strangers as it was.

"If this is a trap," Thomas murmured, "you're to run, Rowan, like a rabbit through the gorse. Understand?"

"I understand," Rowan said.

"Good lad. Stay here, then—and run if I'm taken."

Thomas strode closer to the group, which had halted on first sight of him. He felt the pressure of more than a hundred men staring his way, and he ignored them all, focusing on the one who led.

"Woodchurch?" the man called while he was still twenty paces away.

"I am," Thomas replied.

The lord looked relieved.

"Baron Highbury. These are my men. I was told you'd arrange a little hunting trip if I met you here."

"You were told correctly, my lord."

Thomas reached the man and took the gauntleted hand lowered to him in a firm grip. Highbury wore a huge black beard that ended in a flat line, cut wide like the blade of a shovel.

"The Duke of York was quite insistent there should be no private excursions into Maine, Master Woodchurch. My men and I are not here, if you follow me. However, if we are out hunting deer and we come across some French rapists and murderers, I cannot answer for the conduct of my men, not in those circumstances."

There was anger behind the man's smile, and Thomas wondered if he was one of those whose friends or family had suffered. He nodded, accepting the rules.

"Have you come far, my lord?" he said.

Highbury sniffed.

"From Normandy these last few weeks. Before that, my family had a little country place in Anjou. I hope perhaps to see it again one day."

"I cannot say as to that, my lord. But there will be good hunting in Maine, that much I can promise you."

"That will have to do for the moment, won't it? Lead on, then, Woodchurch. I presume you have a camp of some kind? My men need their rest."

Thomas chuckled, liking the man on instinct.

"I do, my lord. Let me show you."

He dogtrotted along the road with the English archers, noting the way they ran without sign of weariness. Rowan reached his side, and he introduced his son to the men around them. They had eyes more for Rowan's bow than the man himself, making Thomas chuckle.

"You can try your hand against my son at the archery butts, lads. I'll put a gold noble on him."

The dour archers looked more cheerful at that prospect as they jogged along.

"A betting man, is it?" Highbury called from behind them. "I'll wager two nobles on my men."

Thomas touched his forehead in acceptance. The day had started well, and it would get better. He tried to forget the French army marching across the fields and valleys into Maine.

CHAPTER 13

Surprise was a strange thing, Thomas thought to himself. He could feel it like coins in his hand: heavy and valuable, but something he could spend only once. He'd seen French armies before, but nothing like the neat ranks marching along a main road in southern Maine. The ones he'd known in his youth had been miserable beggars, half starved and dressed in whatever ragged coats they could steal. In the still air, he could hear French voices singing, and he shook his head in irritation. The sound offended some deep part of him.

The English found their soldiers from the poorest parts of cities like Newcastle, York, Liverpool, and London, from mines and fields and apprentices who had fallen out with their masters and had nowhere else to go. He'd been a volunteer himself, but there were many more who were too drunk to resist a tap on the head when the recruiters came through their villages. It didn't matter how it happened. Once you were in, you were in for good, no matter what you'd planned for your life. It was too much for some, of course, with terrible punishments meted out to those who tried to run. Even if a deserter made it clear on some moonless night, he'd be denounced at home by his own relatives, out for the reward for returning a king's man.

Thomas's thoughts were dark as he remembered his first months of training. He'd volunteered after giving his father a beating that was long overdue. It was either join up or risk the magistrates when the old sod woke up without his front teeth. So many years later, Thomas was only sorry he hadn't killed him. His father had died since, leaving him nothing beyond the same violent temper simmering beneath the surface.

He'd met Derry Brewer on his first day, when four hundred young men were being taught to march in time with each other. They hadn't even seen a weapon that month, just endless drills for fitness and wind. Derry had been able to run the legs off them all and still knock a man down with his fists at the end. Thomas shook his head, distressed at memories that had soured for him. He and Derry had been friends once, but it was Derry who'd given away the Woodchurch land, Derry who was responsible for the diabolical deal for Anjou and Maine. Whatever happened from that point, they weren't friends any longer.

Thomas looked over at his men waiting at the tree line. He'd laughed at the dyed green wool they'd used, saying it hadn't helped old Rob Hood. It had taken time away from archery practice to combine blue woad with a yellow dye that produced the rich color. Even so, Thomas had to admit Strange had been right about that, at least. Even when a man knew where they were, the bowmen were damned hard to see as they crouched and waited. Thomas tried to find Rowan among them. He'd seen no sign of his family anger in his son, perhaps the result of mother's milk compared to the vinegar and spit of his own line. Or perhaps he would see it come out in the killing as it had with him. That was another thing he and Derry had shared. They both had an anger that only grew with violence. No matter how hard they hit, it was still there behind the eyes, clawing away in a red room, scratching to be let out. It just had to be woken.

Slowly, Thomas turned back to the lines of fighting men striding or riding along the road as if they were heading to a saint's day celebration or a feast. The French had no scouts out, and he saw they were dressed warm and snug and carried decent pikes and swords. There was even a band of crossbowmen, strolling along with their weapons uncocked and resting on their shoulders. Thomas clenched his jaw, disgusted with all of them.

Farther back, he could just make out the French royal party, trotting on fine gray horses with bright headpieces of red or blue. It was spring and Anjou was behind them. Every man there had spent months getting drunk and slow on stolen wine. Thomas showed his teeth, knowing they could not see him. His two dozen arrows were ready, and he'd spent part of the gold he'd made from wool and mutton on having as many fletched as he could over the long winter. One thing was certain—his men wouldn't be able to get their arrows back afterward.

For a moment, he considered letting the French king come abreast of him before the attack. It could only help their cause if they slotted an arrow down a royal throat and it would sound across France like a struck bell, telling men everywhere that Maine would fight. Yet the king's personal guard could afford breastplates of thicker iron. Many of them wore extra layers of leather and padded cloth under their armor. It made a crushing weight, but then they were all big, powerful men, easily strong enough to fight under the added burden.

Thomas hesitated, feeling the responsibility and the advantage of surprise once more. When it was gone, when it was spent, he and his men would be facing an enraged army torn out of their comfort and ease. An army with hundreds of horsemen to run them down like foxes in the trees and fields. He'd seen it happen before, and he knew the bitter reality of seeing archers caught in the open, unable to defend themselves before they were cut down. He could not let that happen to Rowan, or Strange, or Highbury, or any of the others who depended on him. Thomas wasn't exactly certain when he'd become the leader of their motley group, but even Highbury accepted his right, especially after he and Strange had almost come to blows in a discussion of their mutual ancestors.

Thomas smiled to himself. That had been a good evening, with his men singing and laughing around a huge bonfire in the woods. Perhaps Robin of the Hood had known nights just like it, with his men dressed in Lincoln green.

He made his decision. The king had to be a target. Just one lucky arrow could end it as it began, and he could not give up the chance. The French army strolled on, just two hundred yards away across bushes and scrubland, before the trees opened out onto a vast forest. At Agincourt, England had fielded ten thousand men who could hit a target the size of a man's head at that distance, then do it again, ten or even twelve times a minute. He'd had Highbury's archers and his own veterans practicing each day until they could pass his personal test— when their right arms were strong enough and large enough to crack two walnuts held in the crook of their elbows.

Thomas stood up slowly in the dappled shade, breathing long and slow. For a quarter-mile, men rose with him, tapping nervous fingers on their bows and shafts for luck. He raised a hunting horn to his lips and blew a harsh note, then let it fall on the thong around his neck and sighted on his first man.

The closest French soldiers looked round in surprise as they heard the horn sound. Thomas stared down the shaft as a knight in armor rode up along the host of slanted pikes to see what was happening. Some of them pointed in the direction of the trees, and the man wheeled his horse, raising his visor and staring into the green.

Thomas could not read, even if he'd had the knowledge of it. Books blurred to his eyes up close, but at a distance he still had an archer's sight. He saw the knight jerk as he spotted or sensed something.

"Surprise," Thomas whispered. He loosed, and the knight took the arrow in the center of his face as he tried to shout, sending him backward over the haunches of his mount and falling into the pikemen around him.

All along the line, arrows punched out from the trees, then again in a rhythm Thomas knew as well as breathing. This was why he'd drilled and drilled them until their fingertips were swollen to fat grapes. His bowmen reached down to shafts they'd stuck into the black earth and pulled them free, slotting them on and drawing smoothly. The snap of bows was a clatter he loved to hear. A quarter of a mile and two hundred men loosing again and again into the crowded lines.

The French soldiers bunched up in their panic, yelling and helpless as shafts ripped into them. Hundreds fell or dropped to the ground, and Thomas shouted a wordless challenge as he saw the king's own guards reel as they were struck.

The knights around the king were battered and thumped as they raised shields over King Charles and yelled commands. Horns blew across the valley floor, and Thomas could see a thousand men or more come charging in. French knights and mounted men-at-arms spurred and kicked their horses hard, drawing swords and galloping toward the strip that had been torn out of their army, the bloody slash that looked as if a giant had crushed a footstep into them.

Thomas sent three of his precious bodkin arrows toward the king before he focused again on the men in front of him. The destruction was greater than even he had hoped, but it meant fewer targets and he saw dozens of shafts pass through scrambling men and miss completely.

"Aim for knights and horses!" he roared along the line.

He saw a hundred archers turn almost together, seeking out the same targets. More than one knight galloping to the rescue was struck by a dozen shafts, to fall broken and dead before he hit the ground. Thomas cursed to see the king flailing in his saddle, visibly alive though the noblemen around him showed red blood on their armor. They began to move the king back through the press of men riding in, and still the archers shot and shot, until they reached down and their fingers closed on empty air.

Thomas checked his own quiver as he always did, though he knew it was empty. Twenty-four arrows had gone in what seemed like a heartbeat, and by then the French army looked like some fool had knocked over a beehive. They formed up over the heaps of dead as the arrow storm began to falter.

It was time to run. Thomas had been staring in delight at the chaos, fixing the scene in his mind. Yet it was time, and he dragged his attention away from the enemy. A last glance confirmed the French king was still alive, being hustled back by his men. Thomas found he was panting, and he struggled to take a deep enough breath to sound the horn.

At the signal, his line of archers broke instantly, turning their backs on the French and racing off through the trees. More horns sounded behind them, and once again Thomas knew the sick terror of being hunted.

His breath was harsh and loud as he crashed through bushes and around trees, jarring his shoulder on a branch as he tried to duck under it and falling, only to scramble up again at full speed. He could hear the snorting of horses pounding the earth as armored knights reached the tree line and forced their way through.

Over on his left, he saw one of his men fall, and from nowhere a French knight appeared, aiming a lance into the man's back as he staggered to his feet. Thomas put on another burst of speed, appalled at how fast the French had gathered themselves. He hoped desperately that it was just one knight ahead of the rest. If they were that quick on the counter, he'd lose half his men before they reached the meadows beyond.

He heard hooves close behind him, with a jingle of harness. Thomas jinked from instinct, hearing a French voice curse as a knight missed his strike. The man's lance point dropped and wedged in the earth, though the knight was too canny to hold on to it. Thomas didn't dare look back, though he heard a sword drawn over the noise of his own racing steps. He cringed, expecting the strike as the forest brightened ahead of him and he realized he'd covered half a mile as fast as he'd ever run in his life.

Thomas broke out into spring sunshine, finding himself facing a line of archers with bows raised toward him. He threw himself down, and they sent quick shots over his head. He heard a horse scream, and, as he lay gasping, he looked back for the first time, seeing his pursuer crash to the ground at full speed as his horse collapsed with its lungs pierced.

Thomas forced himself up and on, red-faced and gasping as he staggered to the line and the second set of quivers they'd prepared. He thanked God the younger men had been faster than he was over rough ground. The fallen knight was beginning to rise when Thomas drew a new arrow and sent it through the man's neck.

The meadow was wider than it was deep, an open strip of ferns and heavy thornbushes, with a few stubborn oaks around a pond. It had been the obvious place for his men to fall back to, the fruit of local knowledge from boys who used to play and fish for newts there when they were young.

Thomas looked along the line for Rowan and breathed in relief when he saw him standing with the others. They'd lost a few men in the mad dash through the woods, but before he could call to his son, the trees erupted, mounted knights scattering small branches and leaves as they rode hard into the sunlight.

They died just as hard, hammered and battered as they entered the open space. The last of Thomas's archers staggered among them, some dying from their wounds. One or two of those were killed by their friends as they shot at anything they saw moving.

Thomas waited, trying to control his racing heart. He could hear crashing and horns blowing in the forest, but the numbers breaking through to them dwindled to nothing, and he stood there, waiting. Surprise. He had used it all. The French knew they were in a fight for Maine. He cursed aloud at the thought of the French king still among the living. Just one arrow in the right place and they would have won it all in a day, perhaps even saved his farm and his family.

He waited for a time, but no more knights came through, and Thomas reached for his horn, only to find it gone, with a painful stripe along his neck to show where it had lain. He could not remember it being torn free, and he rubbed in confusion at the red welt before raising his fingers to his lips and blowing a sharp tone.

"Away!" he called, gesturing with his aching right arm.

They turned immediately, trotting as fast as they could into the trees beyond. Thomas saw a couple of men bearing a friend, while others were left behind to bleed and cry out in vain. He closed his ears to the voices calling after him.

MARGARET LOVED the Tower of London. It wasn't just the way it made Saumur Castle look like a charcoal-burner's shack in comparison. The Tower was a complex of buildings as big as a village in its own right, girdled in huge walls and gatehouses. It was an ancient fortress protecting the most powerful city in England, and Margaret had begun to explore every part of it, making it hers in her mind as she had done with the Crow Room and the secret passages at Saumur.

London in the spring brought fresh breezes that were quite unable to carry away the stink of the city. Even where Roman sewers had survived, heavy rains summoned ancient filth to the surface, flowing as a tide of slurry down every hill. On most streets, pots of urine and feces were thrown out into a deep slop of animal and human dung, trodden down with the rotting guts of animals and the congealed blood of slaughtered pigs. The smell was indescribable, and Margaret had seen the wooden shoes Londoners wore over their boots, raising them up high so they could go about their business.

She had been told that if the planets were aligned in some way she did not understand, poisonous vapors arose and summer plagues would rip through the population. William said there had been even more people when his father was a child, with war and pestilence taking a terrible toll. Outside the city, whole villages had been left to grass and weeds, with their inhabitants all fled or boarded into their houses to die and be forgotten. Yet London survived. It was said that the people there were hardened to it, so they could breathe and eat almost anything and live.

Margaret shuddered delicately at the thought. On that spring day at the Tower, she could see pale blue skies and white clouds hanging like a painting above her head. Birds flew and the air seemed sweet enough up where she walked the crown of the walls, speaking to blushing soldiers as they found themselves under the scrutiny of a fifteen-year-old queen.

She stared south, imagining Saumur Castle across the sea. Her mother's letter had made their financial situation clear, but that was one thing Margaret had been able to put right. With just a word from her, Henry had agreed to send twelve hundred pounds in silver coins, enough to run the estate for two years or more. Margaret frowned to herself at the thought. Her husband was most amenable. He agreed to anything she wanted, but there was something wrong; she could sense that much. Yolande had returned to her husband's estate, and she dared not confide in anyone else. Margaret considered writing a letter, but she suspected they would be read, at least for the first few years. She wondered if she could find a way to ask questions about men that would not be understood by Derry Brewer. She shook her head as she stood there, doubting her ability to get anything past that infuriating man.

The subject of her thoughts broke in on them at that moment, clambering up to the highest point of the walls and smiling as he saw her.

"Your Royal Highness!" he cried. "I heard you were up here. I tell you my heart's in my mouth at the thought of you falling to your death. I think it would mean war within the year, all from a loose stone or a single slip. I'd be happier if you'd accompany me back to the ground. I think the guards would be as well."

He came up to her and took her arm gently, trying to steer her back to the closest set of steps heading down. Margaret felt a spike of irritation and refused to move.

"My lady?" Derry asked, looking wounded.

"I won't fall, Master Brewer. And I'm not a child to be shepherded to safety."

"I don't think the king would be happy at the thought of his new wife on these walls, my lady."

"Really? I think he would be perfectly happy. I think he would say, 'If Margaret wishes it, Derry, I am content,' don't you think?"

For a moment, they both glared at each other, then Derry dropped his hand from her arm with a shrug.

"As you say, then. We are all in God's hands, my lady. I did see your husband this morning, to discuss matters of state that cannot be ignored. I hesitate to suggest he misunderstood something you said to him, but he told me to seek you out. Is there something you would like to say to me?"

Margaret looked at the man, wishing William were there and wondering how far she could trust Derry Brewer.

"I am pleased he remembered, Master Brewer. It gives me hope."

"I have documents that he must seal, my lady—today, if possible. I cannot answer for the consequences if there is another delay."

Margaret controlled her anger with some difficulty.

"Master Brewer, I want you to listen. Do you understand? I want you to stop talking and just hear me."

Derry's eyes widened in surprise.

"Of course, my lady. I understand. I just—"

She held up a hand, and he fell silent.

"I have sat with my husband as he met noble lords and men from his council, this Parliament of yours. I have watched them present their petitions and discuss his finances in great detail. I have seen you come and go, Master Brewer, with your armfuls of documents. I have witnessed you guiding Henry's hand to place the wax and the royal seal."

"I don't understand, my lady. I was there when we arranged to send a fortune to your mother. Is that the source of your concern? The king and I—" Once more, Derry halted the torrent of words as she raised her hand.

"Yes, Master Brewer. I, too, have called on the king's purse. You do not need to bring it up. He is my husband, after all."

"And he is my king," Derry replied, his voice hardening subtly. "I have dealt with him and aided him for as long as you have lived."

Margaret felt her nerve begin to fail under the cold stare. Her breath seemed to catch in her throat, and her heart pounded. Yet it was too important to let go.

"Henry is a good man," she said. "He has no suspicions, no evil in him. Will you deny it? He does not read the petitions, or the laws he must sign, or if he does, he only glances at them. He *trusts*, Master

Brewer. He wants to please those who come to him with their tales of woe or terrible urgency. Men like you."

The words had been said, and for the first time Derry looked embarrassed, breaking her gaze and staring across the walls and moat to the Thames meandering past. Beyond the water gate under St. Thomas's Tower, there were boats out there, dredging the bottom with long hooked poles. Derry knew that another pregnant girl had drowned herself off London Bridge the night before. A crowd had seen her holding a swollen belly as she climbed over the edge. They'd cheered her on, of course, until she dropped and was swallowed by the dark waters. The boatmen were looking out for her corpse so they could sell it to the Guild of Surgeons. Those men paid particularly well for the pregnant ones.

"Your Highness, there is some truth in what you've said. The king is a trusting man, which is all the more reason to have good men around him! Believe me when I say I am a careful judge of those who are allowed into his presence."

"A guardian, then? Is that how you see yourself, Master Brewer?" Margaret found her nervousness disappearing and her voice strengthened. "If that is the case, *Quis custodiet ipsos custodes?* Do you know your Latin, Master Brewer? Who guards the guards?"

Derry closed his eyes for a moment, letting the breeze dry the sweat that had broken out on his forehead.

"I didn't hear much Latin round my way, my lady, not when I was a boy. Your Highness, you are just fifteen years old, whereas I have kept the kingdom safe for more than a decade. Do you not think I have proved my honor by now?"

"Perhaps," Margaret said, refusing to give way. "Though it would be a rare man who took *no* advantage from a king who trusts him so completely."

"I am that man, my lady; on my honor, I am. I have not sought titles or wealth. I have given all my strength to him, for his glory and the glory of his father."

The words seemed to have been dragged out of Derry as he stood with his hands splayed, resting on the stone wall. Margaret felt suddenly ashamed, though there was still a whisper of suspicion that Derry Brewer was not above manipulating her as easily as he did the king. She gathered her resolve.

"If what you say is true, you will not object to my reading the documents that come before Henry, will you, Master Brewer? If you have the honor you claim, there can be no harm in that. I asked Henry for his permission, and he granted it to me."

"Yes. Yes, of course he did," Derry said sourly. "You'll read it all? You'll submit the fate of a kingdom to the judgment of a fifteen-year-old girl with no training in the law and no experience of ruling more than a single castle, if even that? Do you understand what you are asking and the certain consequences of it?"

"I did not say I was asking, Master Brewer!" Margaret snapped. "I told you what the King of England said. Now, you may disobey his command or not, depending on whether you wish to continue in your role—or not! Either way, yes, I will read it all. I will see every document, *every* law that comes for my husband to seal in wax. I *will* read them all."

Derry turned to her, and she saw fury in his eyes. He had been reeling ever since King Henry had refused his request that morning. Refused! He had asked the king to look over a sheaf of documents and the man had shaken his head in what seemed like genuine regret, directing him to ask his wife. Derry could still hardly believe it. It seemed there had been no mistake, he thought grimly.

Margaret stared back, daring him to refuse her. After a time, Derry bowed his head.

"Very well, my lady. If you'll come with me, I'll show you what this means."

They went down the steps together to the main grounds, as busy with soldiers and staff as a market day in any large town. Derry led the way across the crowded sward, and Margaret followed, determined not to give up the least part of what she had won, whatever it turned out to be.

The White Tower was the oldest part of the fortress, built in pale Caen stone from France by William the Conqueror almost four centuries before. It loomed above them as Derry waved her up the wooden stairs that led to the only entrance. In time of war, the stairs could be removed, making the tower practically impregnable to assault. Inside the massive outer walls, she and Derry passed sentries and went up more stairs and through a dozen chambers and corridors before he halted at a thick oak door and turned the handle.

The room beyond was filled with scribes. High above the rest of the fortress, under the beams of a pitched roof marked in centuries of soot, they sat and scratched on vellum or bound scrolls in ribbons of different colors, passing them onward and downward to their superiors. Margaret's eyes widened as she saw piles of parchment stacked to the ceiling in a few places, or waiting to be moved on upright wooden trolleys.

"All of this amounts to just a few days, my lady," Derry said softly. "It is parchment that rules the kingdom, coming in and out of here to all the nobles and merchants and leaseholds and crofts—hundreds of ancient disputes and rents, my lady. Everything from the pay for a maid, to petitions for soldiers, to the debts on a great castle—it all comes through here. And this is just one room. There are others in the palaces of Westminster and Windsor that are at least as busy."

He turned to her, aware that all movement had ceased as the scribes understood that the queen herself had come into their cramped and stuffy domain.

"No one man can possibly read it all, my lady," Derry went on complacently. "No woman, either, if you'll forgive me. What small part reaches the king has already been checked and handed on to the most senior scribes, then passed again to the king's chamberlain and stewards. Men like Lord Suffolk will read some of it, as steward of the king's household. He will answer a few himself, or rule on them, but he, too, will pass on a part. Would you have it all stop, my lady? Would you clog the pipe that flows through this room with just your hands and eyes? You would not see daylight again for years. That would not be a fate I'd choose for myself, I'll tell you that much."

Margaret hesitated, awed by the room and the deathly silence her presence had created. She could feel the eyes of the scribes wandering over her like beetles on her skin, and she shuddered. She could sense Derry's triumph at the mountain he'd shown her, the impossibility of reading it all. Just the documents in that room alone would take a lifetime, and he said all that was the fruit of a few days? She was reluctant to give up the advantage she had won just by being up there, and she did not answer at first. The solution was clearly to read only the most important demands and petitions, the ones that found their way into Henry's own hands. Yet if she did that, Derry Brewer would still control the vast mass of communication in the king's purview. He was telling her as much, with the tableau of scribes to make his point. She began to appreciate what a dangerously powerful man he actually was.

She smiled, more for the benefit of the scribes than for Derry himself. With a hand laid on his arm, she spoke sweetly and calmly.

"I will see and read the parchments my husband must sign, Master Brewer. I will ask William, Lord Suffolk, to describe the rest, if he sees so many in his new role. I'm certain he can tell me which ones are important and which can be safely left to the king's chamberlain and others. Does that not sound like a fine solution to this mountain of work? I am grateful to be shown this room and those who labor here without reward. I will mention them to my husband, to their honor."

She sensed the scribes beaming at the words of praise, while Derry only cleared his throat.

"As you say, then, my lady."

He kept his smile in place, though he seethed inwardly. With anyone else, he knew he could persuade Henry to change his mind, but the king's own wife? The young woman who had him alone each evening in the royal rooms? He wondered if she was still a virgin, which might perhaps explain why she felt she needed to fill her time in such a way. Unfortunately, that was one subject he dared not raise.

Derry led her back down through the White Tower. At the final set of steps leading outside, he raised his hand to the small of her back to guide her, then thought better of it, so that she gathered her skirts and walked down without his aid.

CHAPTER 14

Jack Cade stumbled as he tried to dance a jig on the fine lawn. There was no moon, and the only light for miles was the house he had set on fire. As he waved his arms, he dropped the jug he was carrying and almost wept when it cracked into two neat pieces and its precious contents drained away. One half of the broken clay contained a mouthful of the fiery spirit, and he tipped it up and drank the last of it, never noticing how he cut his lips on the sharp edges.

Leaning back, he roared red-faced up at the windows already reflecting the flames creeping up to the roof.

"I *am* a drunken, Kentish man, you Welsh milk-liver! I am everything you said I was the last time you striped my back! I *am* a violent man and a whoreson! And now I've set your house on fire! Come out and see what I have for you! Are you in there, magistrate? Can you see me out here, waiting for you? Is it getting hot, you sheep-bothering craven?"

Jack threw his shard of pottery at the flames and staggered with the effort. Tears were running freely down his face, and when two men came running up behind him, he turned with a snarl, his fists bunching and his head dropping from a fighter's instinct.

The first man to reach him was around the same burly size, with pale, freckled skin and a mass of wild red hair and beard.

"Easy there, Jack!" he said, trying to take hold of an arm as it whirled by his head in a great missed blow. "It's Patrick—Paddy. I'm your friend, remember? For Christ's sake, come away now. You'll be hanged yourself, if you don't."

With a roar, Jack shook him off, turning back to the house.

"I'll be here when the craven is forced to come out." His voice rose to an almost incoherent bellow. "You *hear* me, you little Welsh prick? I'm out here, waiting for you."

The third man was thin, all knuckles and elbows, with hollow cheeks and long, bare arms. Robert Ecclestone was as ragged and pale as the other two, with black chemical stains marking the skin of his hands that looked like shifting shadows in the flamelight.

"You've shown him now, Jack," Ecclestone said. "By God, you've shown him well enough. This will burn all night. Paddy's right, though. You should take yourself away, before the bailiffs come."

Jack rounded on Ecclestone before he'd finished speaking, taking a bunched hand of his jerkin and lifting him. In response, Ecclestone's hand blurred, so that a long razor appeared at Jack's throat. Drunk as he was, the cold touch was enough to hold him still.

"You'd draw a knife on me, Rob Ecclestone? On your own mate?"

"You laid hands on me first, Jack. Let me down slow and I'll make it disappear. We're *friends*, Jack. Friends don't fight."

Jack unclenched the fist holding him, and, good as his word, Ecclestone folded the blade and slid it under his belt behind him. As Jack began to speak again, they all heard the same sound and turned as one to the house. Above the crackle and whoosh of the flames, they could hear the voices of children crying out.

"Ah shit, Jack. His boys are in there," Paddy said, rubbing his jaw. He took a more serious look at the house, seeing how the entire ground floor was in flames. The windows above were still whole, but no one could live who went in.

"I had a son yesterday," Jack growled, his eyes glittering. "Before he was hung by Alwyn bloody Judgment. Before the Welsh magistrate, who ain't even a Kentish man, hung him for practically nothing. If I'd been here, I'd have got him out."

Paddy shook his head at Robert Ecclestone.

"Time to go, Rob. Take one of his arms. We'll have to run now. They'll come looking tomorrow, if they aren't on the way here already."

Ecclestone rubbed his chin.

"If it were my lads in there, I'd have broken the windows by now and tossed 'em out. Why hasn't he done that?"

"Maybe because of the three of us standing here with knives, Rob," Paddy replied. "Maybe the magistrate would rather they died in the fire than see his little lads cut up; I don't know. Take an arm now. He won't come else."

Once again, Paddy grabbed Jack Cade by the arm and almost fell as the other man wrenched himself away. New tears were running through the soot and muck that covered his skin.

A window exploded above their heads, making them all duck away and cover themselves against flying glass. All three men could see the magistrate, dressed in a grubby sleeping shift, with his hair wild. The window was too small to escape, but he pushed his head out.

"I have three boys here," Alwyn Judgment called down to them. "They're innocents. Will you take them if I have them jump to you?"

None of them replied. Paddy looked away to the road, wishing he was already on it and running. Ecclestone watched Jack, who was breathing hard, a great bull of a man with his mind befuddled in drink. He glowered at the sight of his enemy above his head.

"Why don't you come down, you Welsh bastard?" Jack demanded, swaying as he stood there.

"Because my stairs are on fire, man! Now will you take my boys, in mercy?"

"They'll tell the bailiffs, Jack," Paddy muttered half under his breath. "If those boys live, they'll see us all hang."

Jack was almost panting as he stood with his fists clenched in rage.

"Throw them down!" he bellowed. "I'll give them more mercy than you showed my son, Alwyn bleeding Judgment."

"Your word on it?"

"You'll just have to trust a Kentish man, won't you, you Welsh pisspot?"

Whatever doubts the magistrate may have had were overcome by the torrent of black smoke that was already pouring out of the window around his head. He ducked back into the room, and they could hear him coughing.

"Are you sure, Jack?" Ecclestone said softly. "They're old enough to pick us out. Maybe Paddy and me should vanish."

"I didn't know there was bloody kids in there. The man lives alone, I was told, rattling around in that big house while better men have to poach a little just to eat. Men like my lad, my boy Stephen. God, my *boy*!"

Jack bent right over as a surge of grief hit him. He groaned at his boots and a long tendril of spit laced the grass from his lips. He only looked up when the first frightened child was shoved roughly out above his head, clinging to the broken window and crying.

"Jump, brat!" he shouted up. "Jack Cade will catch you."

"Christ, Jack!" Paddy swore. "*Names*, man. Stop using your bloody name!"

Above their heads, the little boy leaped out as far as he could, sailing through the air as a moving shadow with the light all behind him. Drunk as he was, Jack Cade caught him easily and set him down on the grass.

"Wait there," Jack said gruffly. "Don't move an inch, or I will rip your bleeding ears off."

Paddy caught the second boy, smaller than the first. He put him, still sniveling, by the first, and together they all stared up.

The eldest brother cried out in agony as he was forced past the broken glass. The window was almost too small for him, and his father was pushing him from inside, leaving skin and blood behind as he blocked the hole. With a lurch, the boy came out, tumbling down with a wail. Jack snatched him from the air as if his weight was nothing at all.

Once again, the three men saw the magistrate's head appear, looking down with an expression of mingled hope and rage.

"I thank you, Jack Cade, though you'll burn in hell for tonight's work, you drunken ass."

"What's that? What's that you say to me, you poxed Welsh—"

With a bellow like a dying bullock, Jack rushed toward the house. Both Paddy and Robert Ecclestone reached for him, but he slipped their clutching hands and threw his weight against the door, falling in on top of it. Flame gusted out above his head, driving his friends back. The two men looked at each other, then at the children sitting in wide-eyed misery on the grass.

"I ain't going in there," Paddy said. "Not for a pass to heaven and a bleeding fortune."

He and Rob backed away from the heat, staring into the inferno.

"Nothing's coming out of that," Paddy said. "By God, he always said he wanted a grand ending, and he found it, didn't he? He saved the boys and went back in to kill the magistrate."

They could hear Jack crashing about inside the house, lost to sight in the flames. After a time, the sounds grew quiet and Ecclestone shook his head.

"I've heard they're looking for workers up in Lincoln, to build some bridge. It'll be too hot for us around here now." He paused, knowing the words were the wrong choice as his friend died in the burning house.

"I might just walk north with you, at that," Paddy replied. He turned to the three boys staring at the fire consuming their home. "You three will tell the bailiffs about us, won't you? It won't matter a whit that we saved your lives, will it, lads?"

Two of them shook their heads in terrified confusion, but the oldest boy glared up at him and came to his feet.

"I'll tell them," he said. His eyes were bright with tears and a sort of madness as he heard his father crying out in terror above their heads. "I'll see you hanged for what you've done."

"Ah, Jesus, is that the way of it?" Paddy said, shaking his head. "If I was a harder man, lad, I'd cut your throat for a foolish threat like that. I've done worse, believe me. Oh, sit down, son. I'm not going to kill you, not tonight. Not with my friend dying with his grief on him. Do you know why he came here, boy? Because your father hanged his son this morning. Did you know that? For stealing a couple of lambs from a herd six hundred strong. How does that sit with your fine righteous anger, eh? His boy is dead, but he still caught you when you came falling."

The oldest boy looked away, unable to meet the fierce gaze of the Irishman any longer. A thumping crash sounded above them, and they all looked up as an entire section of burning wall fell out. Paddy lunged to protect the children, knocking the eldest to the ground in the impact. Ecclestone just stepped away, letting the section of brick and lime and ancient straw fall without him under it. He looked round to where the big Irishman's body was sheltering the magistrate's sons.

"You're soft, Paddy, that's your trouble. Jesus, you couldn't—"

He broke off, his jaw dropping as Jack Cade threw himself out of the hole above them, a body in his arms.

The pair landed hard, with a great shout of pain coming from Jack. He rolled as soon as he struck, and, in the light of the fire, they could all see smoke rising from his hair and clothes. The magistrate lay like a broken doll, completely senseless, while Jack turned onto his back and bellowed up at the stars.

Robert Ecclestone walked over to him, staring down in wonder. He could see his friend's hands were seared raw and marked in soot. Every exposed part of him seemed to have blistered or been torn. Cade coughed and wheezed and spat weakly as he lay there.

"Christ, it *hurts*!" he said. "My throat . . ."

He tried to sit up and gasped at the pain of his burned skin. His eyes turned as he remembered the pond across the garden, and he dragged himself up and wandered away.

Paddy stood and looked at the three children, though they only had eyes for their father.

"Is he . . . ?" the oldest boy whispered.

"You can see him breathing, though he might not wake after all that smoke. I've seen a few go like that in my time."

In the distance, they all heard the great splash as Jack Cade either fell or flung himself into the cold waters of the pond. The boys clustered around their father, pinching his cheeks and slapping his hands. The two youngest began to weep again as he groaned and opened his eyes.

"What?" he said.

The magistrate began to cough before he could speak again, a violent paroxysm that went on and on until he was close to passing out again and his face had gone purple. He could only whisper at his sons, rubbing his throat with a blistered hand that oozed blood over the soot.

"How . . . ?"

He became aware that there were still two men standing over his sons. With a massive effort, Alwyn Judgment heaved himself to his feet. He could not stand fully, and rested with his hands on his knees.

"Where's Jack Cade?" he wheezed at them.

"In your pond," Ecclestone replied. "He saved you, Your Honor. And he caught your sons and kept his word. And it won't matter a damn, will it? You'll send your bailiffs and we'll all be taken and have our heads on a spike."

The burning house still huffed and spat, but they all heard the noise of hooves on the road, drifting to them on the night air. Alwyn Judgment heard it at the same time as Jack Cade heaved himself out of the pond with a moaning sound that carried almost as far.

"Take the boys away, Paddy," Rob Ecclestone said suddenly. "Take them toward the road and leave them there for his men to find."

"We should run now, Rob. Only chance is to run like buggery."

Ecclestone turned to his old friend and shook his head.

"Just take them away."

The big Irishman chose not to argue with that look. He gathered them all up, taking the oldest by the scruff of the neck when he began to struggle and shout. Paddy cuffed him hard to keep him silent and half carried, half dragged them away across the garden.

The magistrate watched him uneasily.

"I could promise to let you go," he said.

Ecclestone shook his head, his eyes glittering in the light of the flames.

"I wouldn't believe a word, Your Honor. I've met too many of you,

you see? My mates and me will hang anyway, so I might as well do some good first."

Alwyn Judgment was opening his mouth to reply when Ecclestone stepped forward with a razor held just right in his hand. With one slash, he opened a gushing line in the man's throat and waited only a heartbeat to be sure before he walked away.

Jack Cade was staggering across the garden when he saw his friend kill the magistrate. He tried to shout, but his throat was so raw and swollen that only a hiss of breath came out. Ecclestone reached him then, and Jack was able to rest some of his sodden weight on the man as they headed away from the burning house.

"Paddy?" Jack grunted at him, shivering.

"He'll find his own way, Jack; don't worry about that big sod. He's almost as hard to kill as you are. God, Jack! I thought you were finished then."

"So . . . did I . . ." Jack Cade groaned at him. "Glad . . . you killed him. Good man."

"I am not a good man, Jack, as you well know. But I am an angry one. He should not've taken your boy, and he's paid for it. Where to now?"

Jack Cade heaved in a great constricted breath to give his answer.

"Hangman's . . . house. Going to set it . . . on fire."

The two men staggered and stumbled their way into the darkness, leaving the burning house and the dead magistrate behind.

THE MORNING was cold and gray, with a light drizzle that did nothing to wash the oily soot from their hands. As the three men came back to town, Jack would have walked right into the crowd gathered in the town square. It took Paddy's big hand pushing him against a wall to stop him.

"There'll be bailiffs in that crowd, Jack, looking for you. I have a coin or two. We'll find an inn or a stable and wait out this meeting, whatever it is. You can come back when it's dark again, to cut your boy down."

The man who looked back at him had sobered up somewhere during the long night. Jack's skin was swollen pink, and his eyes were deeply bloodshot around the blue. His black hair had crisped and gone light brown in patches, while his clothes were in such a state of filth that even a beggar would have thought twice before trying them.

He still wheezed a little as he took a breath and rolled his shoulders. He removed the hand from his chest almost gently.

"Listen to me close, Paddy. I've got nothing now, understand? They took my boy. It's in my mind to cut him down and put him safe in the ground up at the church. If they raise a hand to me, I'll make them regret it. I ha'n't got nothing else, but I'd like to do that last thing this morning before I fall down. If you don't like it, you know what you can do, don't you?"

They glared at each other, and Ecclestone cleared his throat loudly to interrupt them.

"I reckon I saved your life getting you away last night," Ecclestone said, rubbing his eyes and yawning. "I don't know how you're still standing, Jack, old son. Either way, that means you owe me, so come and sink a pint, then sleep. There are stables nearby, and I know the head lad. He'll turn a blind eye for a bent penny; he's done it before. We've no business walking into a crowd that has probably gathered to talk about the houses on fire last night. I don't want to state the bleeding obvious, Jack, but you stink of smoke. We all do. You might as well hang yourself now and save them the trouble."

"I didn't ask you to come with me, did I?" Jack grumbled back.

His gaze searched past them, out of the alleyway to the light of the square. The crowd was noisy, and there were enough people to hide the body creaking on the rope. Even so, Jack could see it. He could see every detail of the face he had raised, the boy who'd run from the bailiffs with him a hundred times, with pheasants hidden in their coats.

"No. No, it won't do, Rob. You stay here if you want, but I have my knife and I'm cutting him down."

He stuck out his jaw, his red eyes gleaming like the woken Devil. Slowly Jack Cade raised one meaty fist, a great hairy lump that had all the knuckles pushed in, so it seemed a hammer as he waved it in Ecclestone's face.

"Don't stop me, I warn you now."

"Christ," Ecclestone muttered. "Will you walk with us, Paddy?"

"Have you lost your wits along with him? Ever seen a crowd in a rage, Rob Ecclestone? They'll tear us to rags, from fear. By God, we look like the dangerous vagrants they say we are!"

"So? Are you coming or not?" Ecclestone said.

"I am. Did I say I wasn't? I can't trust you two to do this on your own. Jesus protect all fools like us, on fools' errands."

Jack smiled like a boy to hear them. He patted their shoulders and beamed.

"You're good mates when a man is down, lads. Come on then. This needs doing."

He straightened his shoulders and walked toward the crowd, trying not to limp.

THOMAS WATCHED in something like awe as Baron Highbury blew a horn and his troop of horsemen charged down a slope. In the cold of the morning, the horses steamed and came fast, like molten silver pouring out of the trees. The French knights chasing his group of archers were caught flat, their flank smashed apart by Highbury's lances. In just a moment, they went from hunters intent on their fleeing quarry to desperate men, hemmed in by the land and crushed by Highbury's hammer blow. Thomas yelled in savage pleasure to see them fall, men and horses spitted on sharp points. Yet Highbury's men were outnumbered even as they charged, and Thomas could see more and more French knights thundering in. The charge slowed and became a vicious mêlée of swords and swinging axes.

"Strike and away," Thomas whispered. "Come on, Highbury. Strike and away."

Those three words had kept them going for two weeks of almost constant fighting, taking a terrible toll on both sides. There were no songs sung in the French lines anymore. The king's column moved with scouts and merciless purpose through Maine, burning as they went. They left behind them villages and towns wreathed in black smoke, but they paid a price for every single one. Thomas and his men saw to that. The reprisals had grown more brutal every day and there was true rage on both sides.

Highbury had bought him time to get clear, and Thomas thanked God for a man who acted as he thought a lord should act. The bearded noble was driven by something, Thomas had learned that much. Whatever crime or atrocity he was repaying, Highbury fought with manic courage, punishing anyone foolish enough to come in range of his great sword. The men loved him for his fearlessness, and Baron Strange hated him with a fierce intensity Thomas could not understand.

As Thomas climbed the path through the trees his men had marked, he stopped and touched the scrap of cloth tied to a branch, then looked back. He knew the land around him. It was no more than a dozen miles from his own farm, and he'd walked every lane and riverbank with his wife and children at some point. That local knowledge made it even harder for the French army to pin them down, but still they pushed forward a few miles each day, enduring the ambushes and killing anyone they could catch. For a moment, Thomas felt despair. He and his men had watered the ground with French blood for forty miles, but there was no end to them.

"Get away now," Thomas said, knowing Highbury couldn't hear him.

The noble's men were defending their position as the French grew bold, more and more of them riding in hard and trying to surround the small English force. The only way clear was back up the hill, and Highbury gave no sign of even seeing the line of retreat. His sword swung tirelessly, his armor red with other men's blood or his own.

The fighting became a knot of swarming knights around Highbury, maces swinging to crush skulls in their helmets. They were just three hundred yards away, and Thomas saw Highbury's face bared as his helmet was smashed off in a single, ringing blow. His nose was running red, and his long hair fell free, whipping around in sweat-soaked strands. Thomas thought he could hear Highbury laugh as he spat blood and lunged at the man who had struck him.

"Shit. Get away *now*!" Thomas yelled.

He thought he saw Highbury jerk and turn at his roar. It jolted him out of whatever murderous trance he'd been in and the baron began to look round him. A dozen of his forty were unhorsed, some of them still moving and lashing out at any French knight they could reach.

Thomas swore softly. He could see flashes of silver movement in all the trees he faced across the valley. The French king had committed a massive force of knights to this action. It meant the archers Thomas had set to ambush the French in the closest town would face fewer men, but sheer numbers would carry the scrambling fight in the valley. Thomas gripped his bow, checking his remaining shafts without looking at them. He knew if he went down again, he would be slaughtered.

He turned at the sound of running steps, fearing some enemy had come up around his men. Thomas breathed in relief to see Rowan skidding to a halt with an odd smile. A dozen more stood waiting for Thomas to lead them over the hill and away.

Rowan saw his father's expression as both men watched Highbury smashing out his hurt and anger, laying about him with powerful sweeps of his sword. The man was grinning at something, his eyes wild.

"You can't save him," Rowan said. "If you go down to help him now, you'll be killed for nothing."

Thomas turned to look at his son, but only shook his head.

"There are too many, Dad," Rowan said. He saw his father running his fingers over the shafts left in his quiver, the motion like a twitch. It made a rough, dry sound. Six bodkin points and a broadhead, that was all.

Thomas cursed in anger, spitting out words that his son had never heard from him before. He liked Highbury. The man deserved better.

"Take the others clear, Rowan. Pass me your arrows and take the lads over the hill. Look to Strange for your orders, but use your own wits as well." Without looking back, he held out his hand for spare arrows.

"I won't," Rowan said. He reached out and took a grip on his father's right arm, feeling the muscle there that made it like a branch. "Come on with me, Dad. You can't save him."

Thomas turned and lunged at his son, grabbing the front of his green jerkin and pushing him back a pace. Though they were almost the same size, he dragged the younger man up, so that his feet dangled in the wet leaves.

"You'll *obey* me when I tell you to," Thomas growled at him. "Give me your shafts and go!"

Rowan flushed in anger. His big hands reached up to grip his father's where they held him. The two men stood, locked together for a moment, testing each other's strength, while the others looked on with wide eyes. They both let go at the same moment, standing with clenched fists. Thomas didn't look away, and Rowan removed the strap of his quiver, throwing it to the ground.

"*Take* them, then, for all the good they'll do."

Thomas took a handful of the feathered shafts and added them to his own.

"I'll find you at the farm, if I can. Don't worry." He grew still for a time under his son's glare. "Give me your word you won't follow me down."

"No," Rowan said.

"Damn you, boy. Give me your word! I won't see you killed today."

Rowan dipped his head, caught between sullen anger and fear for his father. Thomas breathed deeply, relieved.

"Look for me at the farm."

CHAPTER 15

Thomas Woodchurch stepped out on the green slope, his bow ready. He had a dozen shafts in the quiver and one on the string as he stalked toward the knights locked in their own form of battle. Every step seemed to double the noise until the crashes and squeals of metal on metal battered against his ears. It was an old music to him, a song he'd known from his earliest memories, like the half-remembered crooning of a nurse. He smiled at the thought, amused at his own fancies as he walked down the hill. The mind was a strange thing.

The French knights were intent on Highbury and his small, besieged force. It was violence as they knew it best, against men who understood honor. Each one barreling out of the trees roared a challenge as they saw the fighting mêlée, forcing tired horses into a last gallop to bring them against the edges and the armored English horsemen. They splintered lances on Highbury's men-at-arms if they could reach them, then raised axes or drew wide-bladed swords for the first crushing blow.

Two hundred yards across the green, Thomas stood alone, watching the vicious struggle as he placed his shafts into the soft earth, spacing them out. He stood for a moment more, rolling his shoulders and feeling the tiredness of his muscles.

"Well, then," he muttered. "See what I have for you."

He took care to sight down the first long shaft as he drew. Highbury's men were among the French knights, and with their armor spattered in mud and blood, it was hard to be sure who was who.

Thomas took a long, slow breath as he drew, reveling in the strength of his arm and shoulder as his knuckle touched the same point on his cheekbone. Some men favored a split grip, with the arrow between two fingers. Thomas had always found a low grip felt more natural, so that the feathered shaft sat touching his uppermost finger. All he had to do then was open his hand, easy as breathing. At two hundred paces, he could pick his shots well enough.

The bow creaked and he let go, sending a shaft whirring into the back of a knight lunging at Highbury. The rear plates were never as thick as the armor on a knight's chest. Thomas knew it was a matter of honor almost, so that if a knight ever turned to run he would be more vulnerable, not less. The hardened arrowhead punched straight through, stripping the feathers so that they erupted with a small puff of white.

The knight screamed and fell sideways, leaving a gap so that Highbury saw through the mêlée to where Thomas was standing. The bearded lord laughed. Thomas could hear the sound clearly as he bent the bow again and began the murderous rhythm he had known all his life.

He had only twelve heavy arrows, counting those Rowan had handed over. Thomas had to force himself to slow down, to make sure of every shot. With the first four, he killed men around Highbury, winning the nobleman a breathing space. Thomas could hear enraged shouts going up from the French knights farther out as they jerked round in their saddles, peering through slots in their helmets to see where the arrows were coming from. He felt his mouth grow dry and he sucked his teeth as he sent another two arrows in, watching them hammer knights who never saw the threat or the man who killed them.

From the corner of his eye, Thomas could glimpse silver armor surging toward him. He knew they would be coming fast, lances lowered to take him off his feet. He set his legs, standing in balance, placing his shots, sending them out. More men fell, and Highbury was reacting, using the gift he'd been given to bellow orders to his remaining men. One of the French knights galloped toward Highbury with a studded mace raised to smash the nobleman's bare head. Thomas took him with a snap shot, hardly aiming. The arrow sank in under the knight's raised arm, and the mace fell from suddenly nerveless fingers. Highbury brought his sword across, smashing the man's neck with ferocious glee.

From the height of his saddle, Highbury could see the lonely figure standing on the green grass, with just a few shafts remaining. Though Thomas looked small at a distance, for an instant Highbury had the sense of facing that grim archer himself. He swallowed drily. Just one man had taken a terrible toll, but Highbury could see a line of knights thundering toward the archer. They *hated* English bowmen, hated them like the devil. They despised the fact that common men could wield such weapons of power and dared to use them without honor on the battlefield. More than any other group, the French had long memories for those thumping bows that had slaughtered them on different battlefields. Some of them even pulled away from Highbury's knights in their rage and desire to murder the archer first.

Highbury turned his horse with a jerk on the reins, suddenly feeling the wounds and bruises that had been hidden to him before. The tree line was up the hill, and he dug in his spurs, making fresh blood run down his horse's flanks.

"Back, lads! Back to the trees now!" he shouted.

He went hard up the hill, trying to look back, to witness the end of it. His men came with him, panting and wild, lolling in their armor. Some of them were too tired, too slow. They were surrounded by the French and they could not defend themselves against so many. The maces hammered their armor into great dents, breaking bones beneath. Axes left puckered slots running red in the metal, lives pouring out over the steaming horses.

Away across the green, Thomas reached for an arrow and his fingers twitched on empty air. He looked up to see two French knights galloping at him, their lances aimed at his chest. He did not know if he'd done enough. He raised his head in sullen anger, trying to swallow fear as the sound of their thunder poured over him and filled the world.

The sun seemed to brighten as he stood there, so that he could see every detail of the horses and men coming so very fast to kill him. He considered throwing his bow at the first one to reach him, perhaps making the horse rear and turn. His hand refused to let go of the weapon, and he stood there in the open, knowing that whether he ran or stayed, it was all the same.

Rowan stood alone in the shadow of oaks, watching the scene unfold below him. The others had gone, but he was still there, staring through the green leaves at distant, struggling men. Rowan had seen bleak acceptance in his father's eyes and he couldn't leave, nor look away. He watched with fierce pride as his father dropped half a dozen knights, striking them down. Fear swelled in him then as he saw them spot the lone archer and begin to wheel away to butcher him. Rowan breathed hard as he saw his father shoot the last of his arrows, using them to save Highbury rather than himself.

"Run now, Dad!" he said.

His father just stood there as they accelerated toward him and the lance tips began to come down.

Rowan raised his right fist, counting widths down from the horizontal by turning it over three times. He shook his head, trying to remember how he was meant to adjust for a dropping shot. In desperation, he bent his bow. The other archers had passed him just one shaft each until he had a dozen. Wishing him luck, they'd gone running off over the hill, leaving him alone with the sound of his breath just a little louder than the crashes and yells below.

The range was more than four hundred paces, somewhere less than five. It was longer than Rowan had shot before, that much was certain. There was a light breeze, enough for him to adjust a fraction as the goose-feathered shaft tickled his cheek and the power of the bow coiled in his chest and shoulder. He leaned back from the waist, adding the width of two hands to the angle.

He almost lost the arrow straight up in the air when he heard running footsteps coming closer. Easing off the draw, Rowan turned, his stomach and bladder clenching at the thought of confronting armed pikemen. He sagged when he saw it was the same group of archers, chuckling as they saw the terror they had caused in him. The first one to reach him clapped Rowan on the shoulder and peered down into the valley.

"We have a couple dozen shafts between us and then we're done. Old Bert here has only one."

There was no time to thank them for risking their lives one more time when they could be sprinting clear. Rowan bent his bow again, his hands steady.

"Four hundred and fifty yards, or thereabouts. Three hands of falling ground."

As he spoke, he sent the first shaft soaring, knowing as soon as it went that it would miss. They all watched the flight with the eyes of experienced men.

In the months before, Thomas had tried to explain triangles and falling shots to Highbury's archers. Rowan's father had learned his trade from an army instructor with an interest in mathematics. In the evening camps, Thomas had drawn shapes in the dirt to pass on his knowledge: curves and lines and angles with Greek letters. Highbury's archers had been polite enough, but only a few listened closely. They were all men in their prime, carefully chosen to accompany the baron. They'd shot bows every day including Sundays, for two or even three decades. Their skill and power had been shaped past competence or calculation, back to something like a child's ability to point at a fast-flying bird. Rowan loosed his second shaft, and they drew their bows to match him, so that ten or twelve arrows soared out a fraction of a second later.

Rowan had to adjust quickly to get the feel of it. His second arrow felt wrong, but he sent four more that flew close to the path he could see in his head. Highbury's archers shot their second dozen, and Rowan stroked out each shaft as fast as he could, feeling his aim improve. On flat ground, he could not have reached the men charging at his father. On dropping ground, he could aim higher, reach them and snatch them down. As his last shaft went, he watched it fly, suddenly helpless.

"Now *run*, Dad! Just run," he whispered, staring.

THOMAS HEARD the arrows before he saw them. They hummed in the air, the shafts vibrating as they whirred in. He glanced up out of instinct, in time to see a group of them coming down as a dark streak.

With thumps, the first two sank to the feathers in the ground in front of the knights charging at him. The following group was well placed at that range, glancing off an armored shoulder and hitting one horse, so that it stood stiffly from the animal's haunch. In a few heart-beats, three more landed. One struck a saddle horn and ricocheted clear, while the final two struck horseflesh, dropping almost straight down onto them. The heavy steel heads sank deep, making the animals squeal and stagger. Thomas saw a spray of fine red mist as one horse reared, its lungs torn.

Two of the knights coming at him reined in sharply, staring up at the trees. The cold feeling of peace was torn away as Thomas came to himself. He took a quick glance around and his heart pounded.

"Sod this!" he shouted. He was off, jinking as he ran up the slope. He expected to feel the agony of a lance between his shoulders at any moment, but when he looked back the French knights had drawn up and were looking balefully after him. They thought it was another ambush, he realized gleefully, with himself as bait. He had no breath left to laugh as he ran on.

As GRAY EVENING stole upon the valley, King Charles came to see the brutal tally of the day's fighting. His foot soldiers had scouted the area and declared it safe enough for his royal presence, though his guards still watched and rode all around him. They had been ambushed too many times over the previous weeks. Close to the king, only bodies and still-screaming wounded remained, until they were silenced. The English were cut or strangled on the spot, while maimed French knights were borne away to be tended by the army doctors. In the darkening air, their wails could be heard in miserable chorus.

The king looked pale and irritable as he walked the field, stopping first where Highbury had made his charge, then striding farther out, to see where a single archer had been allowed to shoot from a safe distance. The king scratched his head as he imagined the scene, convinced he had picked up lice again. The damned things leaped off dead men, he had heard. There were enough of those.

"Tell me, Le Farges," he said. "Tell me once more how few men they have. How it will be nothing more than a boar hunt through the valleys and fields of Maine for my brave knights."

The lord in question did not meet his eye. Fearing punishment, he went down on one knee and spoke with his head bowed.

"They have first-rate archers, Your Majesty, much better than I expected to see here. I can only imagine they came out from Normandy, breaking the terms of the truce."

"That would explain it," Charles replied, rubbing his chin. "Yes, that would explain how I have lost hundreds of knights and seen my expensive crossbow troop slaughtered almost to a man. Yet no matter who they are, these men, no matter where they have come from, I have reports of no more than a few hundred, at most. We have captured and killed, what, sixty of them? Do you know how many of mine have lost their lives for that small number?"

"I can have the lists brought, Your Majesty. I . . . I'm . . ."

"My father fought these archers at Agincourt, Le Farges. With my own eyes, I have seen them slaughter nobles and knights like cattle, until those still alive were crushed by the weight of their own dead. I have seen their drummer boys run among armored men to stab at them, while archers laughed. So tell me, how is it that we have no archers of our own?"

"Your Majesty?" Le Farges asked in confusion.

"Always I am told how lacking in honor they are, what weak and spineless specimens of men they are, yet still they kill, Le Farges. When I send crossbowmen against them, they pick them off at a distance too great for them to reply. When I send knights, a single archer can murder four or five before being cut down—unless he is allowed to escape to return and kill again! So enlighten your king, Le Farges. By all the saints, *why do we not have archers of our own?*"

"Your Majesty, no knight would use such a weapon. It would be . . . *peu viril*, dishonorable."

"Peasants, then! What do I care who stands, as long as I have men to stand!"

The king reached down to pick up a fallen longbow. With a disgusted expression, he tried to pull back the string and failed. He grunted with the strain, but the thick yew weapon bent only a few inches before he gave up.

"I am not an ox, for such work, Le Farges. Yet I have seen peasants of great strength, great size. Why do we not train them for such slaughter, the way the English do?"

"Your Majesty, I believe it takes years to build the strength for such a bow. It is not possible simply to pick one up and shoot. But, Your Majesty, will you stoop to such a course? It does not suit a chivalrous man to use such a tool."

With a curse, the king threw the weapon away with a great heave, sending it whirring over his head.

"Perhaps. The answer may lie in better armor. My own guards are able to come through a storm of these archers. Good French iron is proof against them."

To make his point, he rapped his knuckles proudly against his own breastplate, making it ring. Le Farges kept silent rather than point out the king's ornate armor was nowhere near thick enough to stop an English arrow.

"The crossbowmen use mantlets and wicker shields, Le Farges. Yet that is no answer for knights who must wield sword and lance. Better armor and stronger men. That is what we need. Then my knights can go in deep among them, reaping heads."

King Charles stopped, wiping a drop of spittle from his mouth. Taking a deep breath, he looked into the sunset.

"Either way, they *have* broken the truce. I have sent the call to my lords, Le Farges. Every knight and man-at-arms in France is coming north even now."

Baron Le Farges looked pleased as he rose from his kneeling position.

"I would be honored to lead them, Your Majesty, with your blessing. With the noble regiments and your order, I will destroy these last stragglers and take all of Maine in a month."

King Charles looked at him, his eyes cold.

"Not Maine, you cloth-headed fool. They have broken the truce, have they not? I will have it all. I will take back Normandy and push the last English rags into the sea. I have eleven thousand men marching north. They have mantlets and shields, Le Farges! I will not see them cut down. Yet archers or no archers, I will not stop now. I will have France back before the year is out. On the Blessed Virgin, I swear it."

There were tears in the lord's eyes as he knelt again, overcome. The king placed his hand briefly on the man's matted head. For an instant, a surge of spite made him consider cutting the fool's throat. His hand tightened in the hair, making Le Farges grunt in surprise, but then the king released him.

"I need you yet, Le Farges. I need you at my side when we drive the English out of France for the last time. I have seen enough here. The truce is broken, and I will visit destruction on them that will stand for a generation. My land, Le Farges. *My* land and my vengeance. Mine!"

Jack Cade had to push hard against the crowd to force his way through. His two companions came with him in the space he created with his elbows and broad shoulders. More than one elbow poked back in time to catch Paddy or Rob Ecclestone as they went, making them curse. The crowd was already angry, and the three men earned furious glares and shoves as they made their way to the front. Only those who recognized Ecclestone or his Irish friend stopped short. The ones who knew them well edged away to the outskirts, ready to run. Their reputation made as much space as their elbows and helped to deposit Jack Cade into the open air.

He stood facing the crowd, panting, black with soot and raw as a winter gale. The man who had been shouting to the gathering broke off as if at an apparition. The rest of them slowly fell silent at the sight of the newcomers.

"Is that you, Cade?" the speaker asked. "God's bones, what happened to *you*?"

The man was tall and made taller by a brown hat that stood six inches off his forehead. Jack knew Ben Cornish well, and he'd never liked him. He stayed silent, his red-rimmed gaze drawn to the swinging figure off to one side of the square. They'd taken no notice of the body while they'd stamped and laughed and had their meeting. Jack had no idea what Cornish and the others were there for, but the sight of their blank stares made his anger rise again. He wished he had a full jug in his hand to drown it.

"I've come to cut my lad down," he said gruffly. "You won't stop me, not today."

"By God, Jack, there are greater matters here," Cornish blustered. "The magistrate . . ."

Jack's eyes blazed.

"Is a dead man, Cornish. As you'll be if you cross me. I'm about sick to my guts of magistrates and bailiffs—and sheriff's men like you. Bootlicking pox-boys is all you are. You understand me, Cornish? Get out of here now before I take my belt to you. No, stay. I've a mind to do it anyway."

To the surprise of Jack and his two friends, his speech was met with a growling cheer from the crowd. Cornish turned a deep red, his mouth working with no sound coming out. Jack reached down to the wide leather strap that held his trousers, and Cornish bolted, pushing through the crowd and disappearing at speed along the street away from the square.

Under the scrutiny of the crowd, Jack flushed almost as deeply.

"By hell, what gathering *is* this?" he demanded. "Did someone raise the tax on candles or beer? What brought all of you out to block the street?"

"You'll remember me, Jack!" a voice called. A burly figure in a leather apron pushed forward. "I know you."

Jack peered at the man.

"Dunbar, aye, I know you. I thought you were in France, making your fortune."

"So I was, till they stole my land from under me."

Jack raised his eyebrows, privately pleased to hear of the man's failure.

"Well, I ain't never had land, Dunbar, so I wouldn't know how that feels."

The smith glowered, but he raised his chin.

"It's coming back to me why I didn't like you, Jack Cade." For an instant, both men bristled with rising anger. With an effort, the smith forced himself to be pleasant. "Mind you, Cade, if you killed the magistrate, I'll call you friend and see no shame in it. He got what he was due and nothing more."

"I didn't . . ." Jack began to reply, but the crowd roared their approval and he blinked at them.

"We need a man to take our grievances to Maidstone, Jack," Dunbar said, taking him by the shoulder. "Someone who'll hold those county bastards by the throat and shake them until they remember what justice is."

"Well, I ain't him," Jack replied, pulling himself free. "I came for my boy and that's all. Now step out of my way, Dunbar, or, by God, I'll make you."

With a firm hand, he pushed the smith to one side and went to stand under the swaying body of his son, looking up with a terrible expression.

"We'll be going anyway, Jack," Dunbar said, raising his voice. "There's sixty men here, but there's thousands coming back from France. We're going to show them that they can't ride roughshod over Kentish men, not here."

The crowd cheered the words, but they were all watching Jack as he took his old seax knife and sawed at the rope holding his son. Paddy and Ecclestone stepped in to take the body as it fell, lowering it gently to the stones. Jack looked at the swollen face and knuckled tears from his eyes before he looked up.

"Ain't never been to Maidstone," he said softly. "There'll be soldiers there. You'll get yourself killed, Dunbar, you and the rest of them. Kentish men or not, you'll be cut down. They'll set their dogs and bully boys on you—and you'll tug your forelock and beg their pardon, I don't doubt it."

"Not with a thousand, they won't, Jack. They'll hear us. We'll *make* them hear."

"No, mate, they'll send out men just like you, is what they'll do. They'll sit in their fancy houses, and hard, London men will come out and crack your pates for you. Take the warning, Dunbar. Take it from one who knows."

The smith rubbed the back of his neck, thinking.

"Maybe they will. Or maybe we'll find justice. Will you walk with us?"

"I won't, didn't I just say? You can ask me that with my son lying here? I've given enough of my own to the bailiffs and judges, haven't I? Go on your way, Dunbar. Your troubles ain't mine." He knelt by his son, his head sagging from exhaustion and grief.

"You've paid enough, Jack. The good Lord himself can see that. Maybe it isn't in you to walk with Kentish lads, to demand of our king's men a little of the fine justice they only give out to the rich."

The smith watched as Jack straightened, very aware that the burned and blackened man before him was still carrying an ugly great seax with a blade as long as his forearm.

"Steady there, Jack," he said, raising his palms. "We need men with experience. You were a soldier, weren't you?"

"I've seen my share."

Jack looked thoughtfully at the crowd, noting how many of them were fit and strong. They were not city men, those refugees. He could see they'd lived lives of hard work. He felt their eyes on him as he scratched the back of his neck. His throat was dry, and his thoughts seemed to move like slow boats drifting on a wide river.

"A thousand men?" he said at last.

"Or more, Jack, or more!" Dunbar said. "Enough to set a few fires and break a few heads, eh? Are you in, Jack? It might be your only chance to take a good thick stick to the king's bailiffs."

Jack glanced at Ecclestone, who looked steadily back, giving nothing away. Paddy was grinning like the Irishman he was, delighted at the prospect of chaos that had descended on them from a clear morning. Jack felt his own mouth twist in reply.

"I suppose I could be the man for that kind of work, Dunbar. I burned two houses last night. It may be I've got an itch for it now."

"That's good, Jack!" Dunbar said, beaming. "We'll march through the villages first and gather up all those back from France—and anyone else who feels the same."

The smith broke off as he felt Jack's big hand press against his chest for the second time that morning.

"Hold up there, Dunbar. I ain't taking orders from you. You wanted a man with experience? You ain't even Kentish yet. You may live here now, Dunbar, but you were born some other place, one of those villages where sheep run from sight of man." He took a breath and the locals chuckled. "No, lads. I'll get you to Maidstone, and I'll break heads as called upon. My word on it, Dunbar."

The smith turned a deeper color, though he dipped his head.

"Right, Jack, of course."

Cade let his gaze drift over the crowd, picking out the faces he knew.

"I see you there, Ronald Pincher, you old bastard. Is your inn shut this morning, with a big gasping crowd like this one? I've a thirst on me, and you're the man to quench it, even with the piss-poor beer you serve." He raised his eyebrows as a thought struck him. "Free drink to Kentish men on a day like today, I'm thinking?"

The innkeeper in question looked less than pleased but raised his eyes and blew air from puffed cheeks, accepting his lot. The men roared and laughed, already smacking their lips at the prospect. As they moved off, Dunbar looked back to see Jack and his two friends still standing by the gibbet.

"Are you coming?" Dunbar called.

"Go ahead. I'll find you," Jack replied without looking. His voice was hoarse.

As the crowd moved away, his shoulders slumped in grief. Dunbar watched for a moment as the big man lifted his son's body onto his shoulder, patting it gently as he took the weight. With Paddy and Ecclestone walking on either side of him, Jack began the long trudge up to the churchyard to bury his boy.

CHAPTER 16

Illiam de la Pole walked up spiraling wooden stairs to the room above. It was a spartan place for a man with authority over the prestigious Calais garrison. One small table looked over a leaden sea through narrow slots in the stone walls. William could see white-flecked waves in the distance and heard the ever-present calls of gulls wheeling and hovering in the wind over the coast. The room was very cold, despite the fire burning in the hearth.

The Duke of York rose from his seat as William entered, and the two men shook hands briefly before York waved him to a seat and settled himself. His expression was sardonic as he folded his hands on his belt and leaned back.

"How should I address you now, William? You have so many new titles, by the king's hand. Admiral of the fleet, is it? The king's steward? Earl of Pembroke? Or perhaps *Duke* of Suffolk now, my equal? How you have risen! Like fresh bread. I can hardly comprehend what service to the Crown could have been so valuable as to earn such rewards."

William stared back calmly, ignoring the mocking tone.

"I suspect you know I have been sent here to relieve you, Richard. Would you like to see the royal order?"

York waved a hand dismissively.

"Something else Derry Brewer put together, is it? I'm sure it is all correct. Leave it with my servant on the way out, William, if that's all you have to say."

With ponderous care, William removed the scroll from a battered leather satchel and pushed it across the table. Despite himself, Richard of York eyed the massive seal with a dour expression.

"King Henry sealed it with his own hand, in my presence, my lord. Active upon my arrival in Calais. Whether you choose to read it now or not, you are hereby relieved of your post here."

William frowned at his own tone. The Duke of York was losing his most prized possession. It was surely a moment to be gracious. He looked out of the window at the gulls and the sea, the waves of slate and white, with England just twenty miles away. On a clear day, William knew the coast was visible from Calais, a constant reminder of home to the man who sat in the tower and ruled in the king's name.

"I regret . . . that I must be the bearer of such news, Richard," he said.

To his surprise, York broke into harsh laughter, patting the table with his outstretched palm as he shook and gasped.

"Oh, William, I'm sorry, it's just your grave expression, your funereal manner! Do you think this is the end of me?"

"I don't know what to think, Richard!" William retorted. "The army sits in Calais and doesn't move a step, while the king's subjects are forced on to the road across Anjou and Maine. What did you expect, if not to be relieved from this post? God knows I would rather not see you shamed in such a way, but the king commands and so I am here. I do not understand your mirth. And still you laugh! Have you lost your wits?"

York controlled himself with difficulty.

"Oh, William. You will always be a cat's-paw to other men, do you know that? If ever there was a poisoned cup, this is it. What will you do with my soldiers in Calais? Send them out? Will you have them play nursemaid to all the English stragglers coming home? They won't thank you for it. Have you even heard of the riots in England, or are your ears stopped up by all your new titles? I tell you this scroll is no favor to you, no matter what it says. I wish you luck in Calais, William. You will need it, and more."

With a sharp gesture, York broke the wax seal and unrolled the sheet, looking it over. He shrugged as he read.

"Lieutenant of Ireland, the king's man? As good a place as any to watch this fall apart, William, don't you think? I could have wished for somewhere warm, I suppose, but I have a small estate in the north there. Yes, it will do well enough."

He rose, tucking the scroll into his tunic and putting out his right hand.

"I have heard there is fighting in Maine, William. You'll find I have a good man here in Jenkins. He passes out coin so that I am kept informed. I'll tell him you are his new master in France. Well, then. My regards to your lady wife. I wish you luck."

William rose slowly, taking the hand offered to him and shaking it. York's grip was good and his palm dry. William shook his head, nonplussed at the man's mercurial moods.

"My regards to Duchess Cecily, Richard. I believe she is enceinte?"

Richard smiled.

"Any day now. She has taken to sucking on pieces of coal—does it not amaze you? Perhaps the child will be born on the Channel, now that we are leaving. Or the Irish Sea, who knows? Salt and soot in its veins, with Plantagenet blood. It would be a good omen, William. God willing they both survive."

William bowed his head at the brief prayer, only to be startled as York clapped him on the shoulder.

"You'll want to be about your work now, William. It's been my practice to have a ship and crew ready at all hours for the commander of the Calais garrison. I trust you won't object to me taking her home?" He waited while William de la Pole shook his head. "Good man. Well, I won't disturb you further."

The duke strode over to the steps leading down, and William was left alone in the high tower, with the gulls calling overhead.

BARON HIGHBURY panted as he drew rein, his lungs feeling cored out and raw with the cold. Every breath hurt as if he bled inside. Above the wedge of his beard, his pale skin was spattered by mud thrown up from the hooves of his mount. He'd halted in a field of green, growing crops, with a cold wind blowing straight through his men. He could see they were as bedraggled and weary as he was, with their chargers in an even worse state. Highbury worked his dry tongue around his mouth, feeling spit glue his jaws. The water flasks were all empty, and though they'd ridden over two streams that morning, they hadn't dared stop. The French were relentless in their pursuit, and a drink was a high price to pay for being caught and slaughtered.

Highbury's mood was somber at how few had made it through with him. He'd brought forty horsemen south into Maine the previous winter, the best of those retained by his family. They'd known the odds against them and volunteered even so. Just sixteen remained, while the rest had been left to rot on French fields. There had been twenty men just that morning, but four of the mounts had been lame, and when the French horns blew, they were run down.

At the thought, Highbury dismounted with a groan, standing with his head pressed against his saddle for a moment while his legs un-cramped. He walked quickly around his brown gelding, running his hands up and down the legs, checking for heat. The trouble was, it was there, in every swollen joint. His horse reached back to nuzzle him at his touch and he wished he had an apple, or anything at all. As he heaved himself up into the saddle once more, Highbury scratched his beard, pulling a fat louse from the black depths and crushing it be-tween his teeth.

"Right, lads," he said. "I think that's it for us. We've bloodied their noses and lost good men in turn."

His men-at-arms were listening intently, knowing that their lives depended on whether the baron saw his family honor as satisfied or not. They'd all seen the massive numbers flooding into the area over the previous few days. It seemed the French king had summoned every peasant, knight, and lord in France to Maine, an army to dwarf his original force.

"Anyone seen Woodchurch? Or that coxcomb Strange? No one?"

Highbury scratched at his beard roughly, almost angrily. He'd rid-den miles that morning, pursued by French forces doggedly on their tracks. He wasn't even sure where Woodchurch had gone to ground or whether he was still alive. Yet Highbury didn't like the idea of leaving without a word. Honor demanded he return, even if it was only to say he was leaving. Woodchurch was no fool, he told himself. If he lived, he'd surely be finding his own way north, now that the towns and fields of Maine were full of French soldiers.

Highbury smiled tiredly to himself. He'd repaid his nephew's mur-der, many times over. He'd disobeyed orders from Lord York to come south into Maine, and he suspected there would be a reckoning for that. Even so, he had forced the French king to run from archers and English horsemen. He had seen the man's soldiers cut down by the hundred, and Highbury had taken a personal tally of six knights to add to his slate. It was not enough, but it was something—and far better than sitting safe in Calais while the world fell apart.

"We're thirty miles south of the Normandy border, perhaps a little less. Our horses are blown, and if any of you feel the way I do, you'll be about ready to lie down and die right here." A few of his men chuckled at that as he went on. "There's a good road about four miles to the east. If we cut across to it, we'll have a straight run north."

Some of the small group turned sharply as they heard a horn blowing. Highbury cursed under his breath. He couldn't see over the closest hedge from the height of his saddle, so he pulled his feet from the stirrups and clambered up to kneel on it, feeling his hips and knees creak. He heard the horn blow again, sounding close. Highbury swore softly at the sight of eighty or ninety horsemen streaming along a path across the nearest hill. As he stared, they began to cut across the plowed land in his direction, their horses making hard work of the clogging mud.

"Christ, they've seen us," he said bitterly. "Ride, lads, and the devil take the hindmost—or the French will."

THOMAS WOODCHURCH lay flat. His hand was on Rowan's arm, keeping him still but also bringing some comfort to the father.

"Now," he said.

The two men staggered up from the ditch and crossed the road. Thomas checked both ways as they ran and dropped down on the other side. They waited breathlessly for a shout to go up, or the horn call that would bring French horsemen galloping in search of them. Seconds passed before Thomas released his breath.

"Help me up, lad," he said, accepting an arm and limping on through the trees.

Thomas kept the sun on his right hand as best he could, heading north to stay ahead of the men hunting for them. He could feel the wound he'd taken stretch and pull with every step. Leaking blood had made his trousers sodden on the right side, and the pain was unceasing. He knew he had a needle and thread pressed into a seam somewhere, if he could find a place to rest out the day. If he'd been alone, he would have hidden himself in some deep bracken and set strangling traps for rabbits with a few pieces of twine. His stomach grumbled at the thought, but he had Rowan to keep safe and he stumbled on.

He reached the boundary of a plowed field and looked out from the trees and bushes along the edge over open ground, with all its possibilities for being spotted and run down. Thomas took his bearings once again. He could see horsemen in the distance, thankfully heading away from them.

"Stay low, Rowan. There's cover enough, so we'll wait here awhile."

His son nodded wearily, his eyes large and bruised-looking. Neither man had slept since the attack the day before. A massive force of pikemen had charged the archers. Dozens of the French had died, but it seemed their lords had put more of a scare into them than even English bowmen could. If there had been a way to get new arrows, Thomas thought they would have stopped them cold, but bows were no more use than sticks when the quivers were empty.

They'd scattered, sprinting away through fields and farms Thomas knew well. At one point, he'd even crossed his own land at the western field, causing him a different kind of pain. The French had fired his home, perhaps for no other reason than delight in destruction. The smell of smoke seemed to stay with him for miles.

He lay back and looked up at gray clouds, gasping. Rowan remained in a crouch, his eyes sweeping back and forth for the enemy. They'd both seen Baron Strange killed, though neither had mentioned it. Thomas had to admit the man had died well, fighting to the end as he was surrounded and hacked off his horse with axes. Thomas had felt his fingers itch then, but his arrows had all gone and he'd forced himself to run again as they removed the baron's head.

"Can you stitch a gash?" Thomas said quietly, without looking at his son. "It's on my right side, toward the back. I don't think I can reach it. There's a needle in my collar, if you feel for it."

His arms and legs were leaden, and he only wished he could lie there and sleep. He felt Rowan tugging at his shirt, pulling out the valuable steel and thread.

"Not yet, lad. Let me rest for a time first."

Thomas was exhausted, he knew it. Just the thought of examining the wound was too much. His son ignored him, and Thomas was too weary to raise the will to sit up.

Rowan hissed to himself as he revealed the deep gash on his father's hip.

"How's it look?" Thomas said.

"Not good. There's a lot of blood. I can close it, I think. I've practiced on dogs before."

"That is . . . a great comfort. Thank you for telling me," Thomas replied, closing his eyes for a moment. His side felt like it was on fire, and he thought a couple of his ribs were cracked. He hadn't even seen the French soldier until the sod had leaped up and almost disemboweled him. If the blade hadn't turned on his hipbone, he'd be dead already.

He felt a wave of sick dizziness sweep over him as he lay there, panting.

"Son, I may pass out for a time. If I do . . ."

His voice trailed away, and Rowan sat by his side, waiting to see if his father would speak again. He looked through the bushes and took a sharp breath. Just across the field there were soldiers marching. He could see a host of their pikes above the hedges. With an expression of fierce concentration, Rowan began to stitch his father's wound.

HIGHBURY KNEW he was no more than a few miles from the border of English Normandy. The roads were filled with families of refugees, and it was an odd contrast to be running for his life while he passed wagons and carts piled high with personal possessions, their owners trudging along the same roads. Some of them called out for his aid, but he was close to collapse and ignored them. Behind him, French horsemen followed, getting closer with every step.

His sixteen men were down to eight after a long day. With so many soldiers following in his steps, he knew he couldn't turn to fight, but he was equally unwilling to run to complete exhaustion and be taken as easily as a child. His beard was wet with sweat and his horse stumbled and skidded at intervals, a warning that the animal would drop soon.

Highbury reined in at a crossroads, looking back at the shining armor of the men following. They wouldn't know who he was, he was almost sure, only that he was running from them toward English territory. That was enough for them to give chase.

He could see a stone marker giving the distance to Rouen. It was just six miles or so, but too far. He was finished, his hands frozen and numb, his body reduced to a hacking cough and pain that seemed to have reached even his beard, so that the very roots of it ached.

"I think they have me, lads," he said, gasping for breath. "You should go on, if you have the wind. It's just an hour's ride, no more and maybe less. I'll slow them as best I can. You've made me proud and I wouldn't change a day."

Three of his men hadn't stopped with him. Weak from their wounds, they rode with their heads lolling, the big warhorses ambling along. The remaining five were only slightly more alert, and they looked at each other and then back down the road. The closest removed a mailed gauntlet and wiped his face.

"My horse is finished, my lord. I'll stay, if it's all right."

"I can surrender, Rummage," Highbury said. "You they'll just cut down. Go on now! I'll hold them as long as I can. Give me the satisfaction of knowing I saved a few of my men."

Rummage dipped his head. He'd done his duty with the offer, but English territory was tantalizingly close. He dug in his spurs once more, and his weary horse broke into a trot past a wagon and a miserable family staggering along.

"Go with God, my lord," one of the others called as they moved away, leaving Highbury alone at the crossroads.

He raised a hand to them in farewell, then turned and waited for their pursuers.

It didn't take long for them to reach the lone English lord. The French knights filled the little lane and spread out around him, cursing another family who pressed back into hedges to let them pass, terror clear on their faces.

"Pax! I am Lord Highbury. To whom am I surrendering?"

The French knights pulled up their visors to get a good look at the big, bearded lord. The nearest had his sword ready as he brought his horse in close and laid a hand on Highbury's shoulder, claiming him.

"Sieur André de Maintagnes. You are my prisoner, milord. Can you pay a ransom?"

Highbury sighed.

"I can."

The French knight beamed at such a windfall. He continued in halting English.

"And your men?"

"No. They are soldiers only."

The knight shrugged.

"Then it falls to me to accept your surrender, milord. If you will hand over your sword and give your parole, you may ride at my side until I find a place to keep you. Can you write, to have the money sent?"

"Of course I can write," Highbury replied. With a muttered epithet, he unstrapped his great sword and handed it over. As the knight's hand closed on it, Highbury held on.

"You will let my men go, in exchange for my parole?"

Sieur André de Maintagnes laughed.

"Milord, there is nowhere for them to run, not anymore. Have you not heard? The king is coming, and he will not stop until he has pushed you English into the sea."

With a jerk, he took the scabbard out of Highbury's hands.

"Stay close to me, milord," he said, turning his horse.

His companions were cheerful enough at the thought of a fine ransom to share among them.

Highbury briefly considered asking for food and water. As his captor, the French knight had a responsibility to provide such things, but for the moment, Highbury's pride kept him silent.

They rode back down the road Highbury had followed all afternoon, and as they went, he saw more and more knights and marching men, until he was staring around in confusion and dismay. He'd ridden so far and fast that he'd failed to understand that the entire French army was coming north behind him. The fields were filled with them, all heading to the new border of English territory in France.

CHAPTER 17

William de la Pole paced up and down, his hands shaking as he gripped them together behind his back. The gulls screeched around the fortress, a noise that had begun to sound like mockery. He'd spent the morning roaring orders at his hapless staff, but as the afternoon wore on, his voice had grown quieter and a dangerous calm had settled on him.

The last messenger to reach him was kneeling on the wooden floor, his head bowed out of a sense of self-preservation.

"My lord, I was not given a verbal message to accompany the package."

"Then use your wits," William growled at him. "Tell me why there are no reinforcements ready to cross to Calais, when my forces are outnumbered and a French army is charging across English Normandy."

"You wish me to speculate, my lord?" the servant replied in confusion. William only glared at him, and the young man swallowed and stammered on. "I believe they are being gathered, my lord, ready to be brought south. I saw a fleet of ships in harbor when I left Dover. I heard some of the Crown soldiers have been sent to quell unrest, my lord. There have been murders and riots in Maidstone. It may be that—"

"*Enough*, enough," William said, rubbing at his temples with a splayed hand. "You've said nothing more than I can hear in any ale-house. I have letters to be taken home immediately. Take those and go, in God's name."

The young messenger was grateful to be dismissed, scuttling out of the duke's presence as fast as he could go. William sat at York's table and seethed. He understood his predecessor's words a little better after a few bare weeks in command. France was falling apart, and it was small wonder that Richard of York had been so cheerful and enigmatic at being relieved.

William wished Derry were there. For all the man's sarcasm and acid, he would still have had suggestions, or at least better information than the servants. Without his counsel, William felt completely adrift, lost under the weight of expectations on him. As commander of English forces in France, he was required to turn back any and all interference by the French court. His gaze strayed to the maps on the table, littered with small lead pieces. It was an incomplete picture, he knew. Soldiers and cavalry moved faster than the reports that reached him, so the stubby metal tokens were always in the wrong places. Yet if only half of the reports were true, the French king had crossed into Normandy, the fragile and hard-won truce ripped apart as if it had never been agreed.

William clenched his fists as he continued to pace. He had no more than three thousand men-at-arms in Normandy, with perhaps another thousand archers. It was a massive and expensive force for peacetime, but in war? Given a battle king to lead them, they might still have been enough. With an Edward of Crécy, or a Henry of Agincourt, William was almost certain the French could be sent running in humiliation and defeat. He stared hungrily at the maps as if they might contain the secret to life itself. He had to take the field; there was no help for it. He *had* to fight. His only chance lay in stopping the French advance before they were knocking on the doors of Rouen or, God forgive him, Calais itself.

He hesitated, biting his lip. He could evacuate Rouen and save hundreds of English lives before the French assault. If he accepted the impossibility of taking the field against so many, he could devote himself instead to defending Calais. He might at least win time and space enough to allow his king's subjects to escape the closing net. He swallowed nervously at the thought. All his choices were appalling. Every one seemed to lead to disaster.

"Damn it all to hell," he muttered to himself. "I need six thousand men."

He barked a short laugh and puffed out his cheeks. If he were wishing for armies he did not have, he might as well ask for sixty thousand as six. He'd sent his pleas to both Derry Brewer and King Henry, but it seemed the refugees coming home from Anjou and Maine had brought their contagious fear with them. The king's forces had been deployed to keep the peace at home. Back in France, William was left with too few. It was infuriating. By the time the English court even understood the magnitude of the threat, he thought Normandy would be lost.

William wiped sweat from his forehead. Calais was a superb fortress on the coast, with a double moat and massive walls that were eighteen feet thick at the base. Set on the coast and supplied by sea, it could never be starved into surrender. Yet King Edward had broken it once, a century before. It could be taken again, with enough men and massive siege weapons brought in to hammer it.

"How can I stop them?" William said aloud.

Hearing his voice, two servants came scurrying in to see if the commander had fresh orders. He began to wave them away, then changed his mind.

"Send orders to Baron Alton. He is to make the garrison ready to march."

The servants disappeared at the run, and William turned to stare out at the sea.

"Christ save us all," he whispered. "It's been done before. It can be done again."

Numbers were not everything, he knew. English kings had commanded a smaller force against the French almost every time they'd met in battle. He shook his head, his thick hair sweeping back and forth on his neck. That was the difficulty that faced him. The people of England expected their armies to win against the French, regardless of numbers or where the battles were fought. If he failed to protect Normandy, after the chaos of Maine and Anjou . . . William shuddered. There was only one other piece of English territory in France—Gascony in the southwest. It would be swallowed up in a season if the French triumphed in their campaign. He clenched his fist, hammering it on the table so that the lead pieces scattered and fell. He had lost his own father and brother to the French. Every noble house had taken losses, yet they had kept and enlarged the French territories. They would all despise a man who could not hold what their blood had won.

William understood the "poisoned cup" York had described in their brief meeting. Yet he did not think even York had foreseen the sudden advance of French forces into Normandy. He sighed miserably, rubbing his face with both hands. He had no choice but to meet the French king in battle and trust to God for the outcome. He could not choose disaster, only have it forced upon him.

He summoned his personal servants, three young men devoted to his service.

"Bring me my armor, lads," William said, without looking up from the maps. "It seems I am riding to war."

They cheered delightedly at that, bolting out of the room and heading to the armory for his personal equipment. It would be well oiled and maintained, ready to encase him in iron. Staring after them, William found himself smiling as they shouted the news to others and a ragged cheer began to spread across the fortress of Calais. Despite his black mood, he was pleased at their enthusiasm and confidence in him. He did not share it, but he could not refuse the cup he had been given either.

THOMAS GROANED and then began choking when a big hand was pressed over his mouth and nose. He struggled against the weight, bending fingers back until whoever it was hissed in pain. Just before the finger bones cracked, the pressure vanished and Thomas was left panting for breath in the dawn light. His mind cleared and he felt a wave of shame as he made out his son sitting in the dim light next to him. Rowan's eyes were furious as he rubbed his bruised hand.

Thomas was alert enough by then not to speak. He watched his son's eyes slide over as he tilted his head, indicating someone close by. In panic, Thomas felt his gorge rise, some last symptom of the fever that had gripped him cruelly and made his body as weak as rotted cloth. The last thing he remembered was being dragged through a field by his son, under moonlight.

The fever had broken, Thomas understood that much. The terrible heat that dried his mouth and made every joint ache had gone. He tasted vomit rising in his throat and had to use his own hands to close his jaw, pressing as hard as he could as the world wavered and he came close to passing out. His hands felt like slabs of cold meat against his face.

Rowan tensed at the grunting, choking noises coming from his father. The young man peered through the slats of the barn at whoever was walking around out there, but he could see very little. In more peaceful times, it would have been nothing more sinister than the farmer's lads roused for a day of work, but it had been days since the two archers had found a farm that wasn't abandoned. The roads heading north had clogged with a new wave of refugees, but this time there was no excuse at all, no fine talk of a truce and deals struck in private. Rowan knew he and his father were over the Normandy border, though it had been a while since they'd dared to cross a main road and scrape the moss from a milestone. Rouen lay somewhere to the north, that was all Rowan knew. Beyond that city, Calais would still be there, the busiest port in France.

In the dust and crumbling chicken muck, Thomas could not prevent the spasms as his empty stomach heaved. He tried to smother the noise with hands black with dirt, but he could not be completely silent. Rowan froze as a board creaked nearby. He hadn't heard anyone enter the barn, and caution made little sense. The French soldiers marching north were loudly confident in the strength of their own army. Yet there was a chance Thomas and Rowan were still hunted by their original pursuers. They'd learned enough about those stubborn, dogged men to fear them, men who had followed the two archers for sixty miles of night treks and daylight collapse.

In his imagination, Rowan had fleshed out the dim moving shadows he'd seen in the distance more than once. His mind made vengeful devils of them, relentless creatures who would not stop, no matter how far they had to follow. He looked helplessly at his father's battered body, far thinner now than when they had fought and lost. They had thrown their bows away days before, a gesture of survival that felt more like yanking healthy teeth from a jaw. Apart from losing the weight of the weapons, it would not save them if they were taken. The French were known to look hard for the peculiar build of archers, reserving a special hatred and appalling punishments for those they caught. There was no hiding the calluses of an archer's hands.

Rowan's hand still ached for the weapon he'd lost, clutching for it whenever he was afraid. God, he could not bear it! He still had his seax with a horn hilt. He almost wished he could just launch himself from the shadowed stall at whoever was creeping around the barn. The tension was making his heart pound so fast it made lights flash across his vision.

He jerked his head round at a rustle, almost cursing aloud. There was always something moving in a barn among the bales of straw. Rats, of course, and no doubt cats to chase them; insects and birds making their nests in the spring. Rowan told himself he was probably surrounded by creeping, living things. He doubted any of them were heavy enough to make the floorboards creak.

Outside, he heard a crash of plates, shattering and spinning on the ground with a noise that could be nothing else. Rowan stood up from his crouch to peer through the slats once again. As he did so, he heard a footstep in the gloom. He glanced quickly into the yard, catching sight of a French soldier laughing as he tried to pick whole plates out of the pile he'd dropped. They were not the dark pursuers he'd feared, just looting French pikemen.

Yet there was still that step, inside the barn. Rowan looked down at his father, at the clothes wet with sweat and mired in his own filth. When Rowan looked up again, it was into the face of a startled young man wearing rough blue cloth. They gaped at each other for an instant of pounding hearts and then Rowan leaped forward, thrusting his knife into the other's chest and crying out as he did it.

His weight took the stranger down onto his back and the seax sank in farther, pressing through him until Rowan felt ribs crack under his hand. The young Frenchman blew out a great rush of air. Whatever he had been trying to say was lost in the agony of the knife in his chest. Rowan stared down in terror at the scrabbling figure he had pinned to the ground. He could only lean on him with his full weight, smothering the kicking legs with his own.

In the yard, a voice called a question or a name. Rowan's face crumpled in something like weeping as he pressed his forehead against the cheek of the man he held down, just hanging on and waiting for the twitches and scuffles and gasping moans to come to an end. Rowan was shaking when he finally raised his head, looking down into eyes that were smeared with dust from his tunic, yet did not close.

The voice called once more, closer. Rowan sank into a crouch, baring his teeth like a dog defending its kill. He slid the big knife out from between the ribs and held it up, ready to be attacked again. There could be a dozen soldiers nearby, or a hundred, or just one or two. He had no way of knowing, and terror and disgust overwhelmed him. He wanted nothing more than to run, just *run* from the scrabbling horror he had felt as another man's life was stolen. What he'd felt had been sickeningly intimate, and he wanted to get away from that place.

He heard a soft sound at his feet and glared down, understanding that the young man's bowels had emptied themselves, along with his bladder. The soldier's penis was clearly erect, visible in his darkening trousers. Rowan felt his stomach heave and his eyes fill with unwanted tears. He'd heard of such things, but the reality was far, far worse. It was nothing like striking a man from a distance with a cloth-yard arrow and a good yew bow.

A shout from outside made him start and scramble back to the wooden stall. The voice was growing louder and more irritable, as the man outside lost patience with his missing companion. Rowan peered through tiny cracks and nail holes, looking for others. He could not see them, though he had the sense that they were all around the ramshackle barn in the dawn. He shuddered, muscles twitching all along his side and back. He needed to get away into the fields, but his father was too heavy to carry farther.

On impulse, Rowan crouched by Thomas and slapped lightly at his face. The eyes opened, the dark irises tinged in yellow as his father pushed his hands away.

"Can you walk?" Rowan whispered.

"I think so," Thomas said, though he did not know. A childhood story of Samson losing his hair came to his mind, and he smiled weakly to himself, using the handle of an old plow to heave himself up. He rested then, fat drops of sweat pouring from his face to strike the dust and darken it.

Rowan crossed the lines of golden sunlight streaming into the barn. He stood by the door, looking out on the morning as he gestured for his father to come over. Thomas gathered himself, feeling as if he'd been beaten the night before. He needed to sleep, or perhaps just to die. The promise of rest called to him with enough force to make black shapes swim across his vision. He shuffled across the dusty floor, trying not to gasp as his mind swam and sank in waves of sickness.

Rowan almost threw himself back as a voice spoke a torrent of French right by his head.

"Are you hiding from me, Jacques? If I catch you asleep, I swear . . ."

The door came open and Rowan narrowed his eyes, seeing the man's astonishment slide into terror at the sight of his knife and bulk in the gloom.

The man bolted, slipping and falling as he turned in panic. His voice was already rising in a shout as he scrambled up, but Rowan was on him in one great lunge, stabbing wildly through the coat. With savage strength, he reached his left arm around the man's neck and crushed it close. The desperate noises became creaks of sound and Rowan found himself sobbing as he struck and struck, seeing red blood spatter around them. He let the body fall onto its face, standing up and panting, with senses suddenly dull in the morning sun.

The farmyard was empty, with rich green grass growing between the cracked stones. He saw a tumbledown cottage that had been invisible the night before, the door hanging open from a broken leather hinge. Rowan looked around him, then down at the vivid red drops in the dust and smeared on his knife. Just two men looking for something worth stealing while their officers slept. Rowan knew he should have dragged the second body back into the barn, but instead he stood there in the yard, with his eyes closed and his face raised to the sun.

He heard his father come out and stand at his shoulder. Rowan didn't look at him, preferring to let the warmth ease into his skin. He'd slaughtered animals with his father on the farm, he reminded himself. They'd killed deer while hunting, then dressed the flopping bodies on hillsides until they were covered in gore and laughing.

Thomas took a long breath, unsure if his son would want him to speak or not. Hunger pangs bit at his stomach, and he found himself wondering if the two soldiers had any food with them. It was another sign that his body had fought through the illness that had struck him down.

"Did you enjoy it?" he asked.

Rowan opened his eyes and looked at him.

"What?"

"Killing. I've known men who enjoy it. I never did, myself. It always seemed like an odd thing to *want* to do. Too much like work, I've always thought. In a pinch, all right, but I wouldn't seek out another man for killing, not for pleasure. I've just known men who did, that's all."

Rowan shook his head in dull astonishment.

"No . . . I didn't . . . God, no . . . enjoy it."

To his surprise, his father clapped him on his back.

"Good. There's that. Now I find I have an appetite. I'm still weak enough to be frightened by a small boy with a stick, so would you search the house for food? We need to find a place to rest and hide for the day, and I can't do it starving, not after the sickness."

"What about staying in the barn?" Rowan asked, looking back fearfully to the dark doorway.

"Not with the bodies of soldiers and blood on the ground, son. Wake up! We'll need to move a few miles in cover, and my stomach is hurting something terrible. I need a little food, and I'm not eating a Frenchman—not today, anyway."

Rowan chuckled weakly, but his eyes were still troubled. Thomas gave up on his smile, which was taking too much out of him to maintain.

"What is it?" He saw his son's skin twitch like a horse beset with flies, then roughen as the hairs stood up.

"The one in the barn . . . his . . . manhood was stiff . . . God, Dad, it was horrible."

"Ah," Thomas replied. He stood there, letting the sun warm them both. "Perhaps he liked you?"

"Dad! Jesus!" Rowan shivered in memory, rubbing his arms. His father laughed.

"I had to keep watch once, after a battle," he said. "I was about twelve years old, I think. I sat all night, surrounded by dead soldiers. After a while, I heard them start to belch and fart like living men. Twice, one of them sat up, just jerked right up like a man surprised by a thought. Sudden death is a strange thing, sunshine. The body doesn't always know it's dead, not at first. I've seen . . . what you saw on a hanged man before, when I was a boy. There was some old woman at the gibbet when everyone else had gone, scratching the ground by his feet. I asked her what she was doing and she said a mandrake root grows from the seed of a hanged man. I ran then, Rowan, I don't mind telling you. I ran all the way home."

Both men grew still as a rustling sound carried to them on the still air. They turned slowly to see an elderly goose come out of the trees by the cottage, where a rope swing hung from a branch. The bird pecked the ground and peered at the two men standing in its yard.

"Rowan?" Thomas murmured. "If you can see a stone, move slowly and pick it up. Try to break a wing."

The goose ignored them as Rowan found a rock the size of his fist and hefted it.

"It's not afraid of us, I think," he said, walking toward the bird. It started to hiss, spreading its wings. The stone flew out, knocking the bird over with a squawk and revealing a matted underside of feathers and dirt. Rowan had it by the neck in a moment and dragged the flapping, protesting bird back to his father before silencing it with a sharp tug.

"You may just have saved my life again this morning," Thomas said. "We can't risk a fire, so cut it and drink while it's warm. Well done, lad. I think I'd have wept like a child if she'd got away from us."

His son smiled, beginning to feel his strange, fey mood pass. He took care to wipe his knife on the man lying facedown in the yard before he used it on the bird.

"I ONLY WISH your grandfather could be here," York said, sipping at his wine. "The old man took such joy in the birth of children—as you might expect, with twenty-two of his own! Still, the omens are excellent, I've been told. A boy, surely."

He stood in an internal courtyard, roofed in oak and tile, with cream-colored stone on all sides. The white rose of the house of York was much in evidence, as a painted crest on the beams or carved into the stone itself. In the rooms above his head, an unearthly cry rang out, making his companion wince.

Richard Neville was as tall as his uncle, though he had yet to grow a beard. Through two marriages, it was true his grandfather had sired so many that Richard was used to aunts who were children, or nephews of his own age. The elder Neville had been a potent man and the number of his living descendants was a source of envy to many.

Before Richard could reply, York spoke again.

"But I am forgetting! I must congratulate you on your new title, well won. Your father must surely be pleased to see you made Earl of Warwick."

"You are too kind, my lord. I am still learning what it entails. My father is delighted to have the title and the lands come to the family, as I think you know. I'm afraid I never knew my grandfather."

York chuckled, draining his cup and raising it for a servant to refill.

"If you are half the man Ralph Neville was, you will still be twice blessed. He raised me when ill fortune made me an orphan, at the mercy of all men. Old Neville kept my estates and titles intact until I was grown. He asked for nothing in return, though I knew he wanted me to marry Cecily. Even then, he left the final choice to me. He was . . . a man of great personal honor. I have no higher praise than that. I just hope you understand. I owe him more than I could ever say, Richard, no—Earl Warwick!"

York smiled at his nephew. Another screech came from the birthing room, making both men wince.

"You are not worried?" Richard of Warwick said, fiddling with his goblet and looking up as if he could see through the walls to the feminine mysteries within that chamber.

York made an elaborate shrug.

"Five dead true, but six alive! If I were a gambling man, I would not bet against another healthy York boy. The twelfth birth is the number of apostles, so my learned doctor is fond of saying. He believes it is a powerful number."

York fell silent then, considering for a moment that the twelfth apostle had been Judas. The younger man's eyes were shadowed as he had the same thought, but chose not to voice it.

"The seventh alive, then," Warwick said to break the silence. "A number of great fortune, I'm certain."

York relaxed visibly as he spoke. He had been drinking heavily during the confinement, for all his semblance of being unworried. He called for the cups to be refilled once more, and Warwick had to drain his own quickly, feeling the wine heat his blood. It was necessary, he'd found. Fotheringhay Castle may have been well fortified, but even in the shelter of the covered courtyard it was very cold. A fire burned in a nearby hearth, ready to consume the newborn's caul and birth cord. The warmth seemed to disappear before it could reach the men waiting.

"I am not sure, my lord, if I should congratulate you in turn," Warwick said. York looked at him with a questioning air as he went on. "On Ireland, my lord. My father tells me you have been appointed king's lieutenant there."

York waved dismissively.

"I have enemies who would prefer me to be far away from England for the next few years, Richard. I will go where I am sent—eventually! For the moment, I am content to remain, as they climb over each other like drowning rats. I have taken my seat with the Lords Temporal more than once, just to watch and listen. I recommend you do the same, to see what fools scramble and bluster in London." He considered his words before continuing. "For those with an eye to see, this will be a year of storms, Richard. Those who survive it, well, they can only rise."

"My lord York!" a voice called.

Both men leaned back to look up to the small walkway overhead, separated by a generation but joined in concern for Cecily Neville and the child. As they waited, wine forgotten in their hands, a midwife came out through thick curtains, using a cloth to wipe any remaining traces of blood from the face of a baby. The infant was tight-wrapped in swaddling bands of dark blue. It did not cry as she held it out for the father and young uncle to see.

"It is a boy, my lord, a son," she said.

York breathed out through his nose, utterly delighted.

"Have you a name for the child?" Warwick asked, smiling. He could see the pride in Richard of York. For once, the man was almost boyish in his pleasure.

"I have a ten-year-old named Edward, one named Edmund, and a sweet little lad named George. I won't risk offending the poor souls who perished, so not Henry, John, William, or Thomas. No. I think . . . Yes, I think this one will be Richard."

Richard, Earl of Warwick, barked a laugh of surprise and honest pleasure.

"Three Richards then, between us. Richard like the Lionheart king. No, three lions, my lord! A fine omen."

York looked a little taken aback as he followed the path taken by Warwick's quick mind. Two centuries before, King Richard the Lionheart had adopted three lions as his royal seal. More recently, that royal emblem had been carried at Agincourt, by the house of Lancaster and the father of King Henry. It was an association that did not fill York with joy.

"It is a good name," he said grudgingly, raising his cup in toast. "It will do."

CHAPTER 18

The city of Rouen lay around a hundred miles south and west of Calais. In normal times, William would have counted it a stronghold. As the capital of English Normandy, it had witnessed English victories, including the execution of Joan of Arc after her rebellion. William had ridden south to the city with the army, through lands that could have been English farms in Kent or Sussex for their familiarity. He'd crossed the Seine and reached Rouen on a chilly morning three days before, with dawn frost crunching under the hooves of his mount.

The city had been a silent witness to his arrival, the great gates solidly shut. William had stared up at dozens of bodies in the breeze, hanging by their necks from the walls. Almost a hundred swung and creaked, many of them still bearing the marks of violence or stained dark brown with dried blood. William had crossed himself at the sight, saying a brief prayer for the souls of good men guilty of no crime but their place of birth.

The people of Rouen knew the French king was on the march and they had taken courage from that knowledge. Consumed by fury, William could hardly bear to think of the rape and slaughter that must have gone on within those walls. There had been hundreds of English families in Rouen. He had seen cities fall before, and the memories were among the ugliest things he had ever witnessed. He thought the hanged men were the lucky ones.

Denied the resources of the city, he had been forced to open lines of supply right back to Calais, guarding the roads and losing vital men just to keep the carts coming. At least there was water. Rouen was girdled by the Seine, almost enclosed by a great curve of the river as it cut through the rich soil of the province. His army crossed the river on stone bridges, then made their camp in open fields to the south of the city. They turned their backs on Rouen and began the work of pounding sharp wooden stakes into the ground to defend the position against a cavalry charge. Still more of his men used the protection of heavy wooden mantlets to approach the silent city and spike the gates with massive beams and iron nails as long as a man's forearm. There would be no sudden attack from the rear. William only hoped he would have the chance to visit retribution on those within for what they had done.

The scouts brought in reports every day, all worse than the ones before. William was certain the French king could not have hidden the existence of so many trained men. Half the army he would face had to be peasants drafted for the task, and such men had not fared well in the past against English armies. It was a slender thread of hope, but there was not much else to raise his spirits with Rouen at his back.

The open landscape dwarfed even armies, so that it was almost a month after his arrival before William caught his first glimpse of soldiers moving in the distance. He rode closer with a dozen of his senior barons to observe the enemy. What they saw did not please any of them.

It seemed the scouts had not exaggerated. Thousands upon thousands marched north toward the city and the river. William could see blocks of cavalry and armored knights, as well as the expected host of pikemen so favored by the French king. From the height of a small hill, William watched them come, all the while counting and assessing, seeing how they moved. Before long, he glimpsed a second group of colorful shields and banners snapping in the breeze. The king's party of lords had come to the front. From a distance of more than a mile, William watched as one young fool made his horse rear, the hooves kicking air. He reviewed his own position, unpleasantly aware that he had to keep the bridges open across the Seine or his men could be trapped against the city that had left them to stand alone.

William turned in the saddle to see Baron Alton glaring across the shrinking distance.

"What do you think, David?" William asked.

His senior commander shrugged eloquently.

"I think there are a lot of them," he replied. "We may run out of arrows before they're all dead."

William chuckled as he was expected to do, though the jest moved him not at all. He had not seen so many French soldiers since the Battle of Patay twenty years before. It made him feel old to realize how much time had passed, but he could still remember that disaster—and the slaughter of English archers that had followed. He told himself he would not make the same mistakes and could not help looking back over his shoulder to where his bowmen had prepared their killing ground. Nothing alive could reach them as long as his swordsmen held the center. He shook his head, wishing for greater confidence in his own abilities. He would fight a strong defense, because he knew how to do it. He could at least thank the French king for not halting and forcing him to attack. King Charles would be confident, but then with such numbers he had every right to be.

"I've seen enough here," William said firmly. "I think we should rejoin the men. My lords, gentlemen. With me." As he spoke, he turned his horse and they trotted back toward the English lines. William forced himself to ride without looking back, though he felt the enemy coming up behind.

As they crossed the lines of pointed stakes, William waved two earls and half a dozen barons off to their positions. Each of them commanded hundreds of men-at-arms, hard men sheathed in heavy mail under their tunics. They had left their horses beyond the river, though William still fretted over what looked like an escape route. Such things did not sit well with the archers, he knew. They had no horses. William remembered again how mounted knights had fled at Patay, leaving the hapless bowmen to be slaughtered. He swore it would not happen again, but still, there were the horses, a great herd of thousands ready to race away if the battle went badly.

As the French army approached, William rode up and down the lines once more, exchanging a few words with senior men and commenting on their positions. In defending the river plain, there was nothing to do but wait, and William sipped water from a flask as the French came closer and closer. After a time, he took his place in the center, one of the few mounted men there among those with swords and shields. His cavalry held the right wing, but they would not charge unless the French king himself was exposed or the French were routed. Swallowing drily at the size of the army coming to kill him, William doubted he would see such a thing, not that day.

As the distances shrank, William could see the bulk of mantlets being brought up by the French king's crossbowmen. The heavy wooden shields took three men apiece to move them on their wheels, but they would provide shelter even against the arrow storm he could bring down. William frowned at the sight of the columns trudging onward with the mantlets at the front like an armored helmet. He could see French lords riding alongside the columns, roaring orders. They moved with solid purpose, he thought, though he would still wager on his longbows against them. His archers had their own heavy wooden barriers that they could raise or drop to protect them from barrages of bolts or sling stones. William thanked God there were no siege engines or cannon in the French army. Everything he had heard made it unlikely, but he was still relieved. The French were moving quickly, rushing to take Normandy before the summer ended. The heavy machines of war would be coming up behind them, ready for sieges to come. Until then, the most powerful weapons on the field were English longbows.

In the French center, their cavalry trotted together as a mass. William almost smiled to see it, as one who had ridden to battle more times than he could remember. It was easy to imagine the banter and overloud, nervous laughter as they closed on the English position. He said a short prayer to his patron saint and the Virgin, then dropped his helmet visor down, reducing what he could see to a slit of light.

"Ready archers!" he bellowed across the field.

William watched as the French crossbowmen wheeled their mantlets into a staggered line, giving the best cover they could. Yet to reach the English lines, the enemy knights would have to leave their shadow. He bared his teeth, hearing his own breath sound loudly inside the helmet. He would stop the French king before Rouen. He had to.

He could hear orders shouted in the distance, thin sounds borne away on the wind. The mass of enemy pikemen came to halt and the center cavalry reined in. The two armies faced each other, the French force almost five times the size of his own, a veritable sea of iron and shields. William crossed himself as the crossbow ranks marched on. It was a blessing that they didn't have the reach of his archers. To get close enough to kill, they had to come within the range of the yew bows. His archers, in loose tunics and leggings, were in high spirits as they waited for them to do just that.

The last two hundred yards were known as the "Devil's hand" to

French soldiers. William had heard the term years before, and he re-called it now as the crossbowmen walked with their weapons on their shoulders, still too far off to reach the English lines. They could not run, with the heavy mantlets being wheeled along with them. Those who rushed in had paid for it in battles of the past. Instead, they had to walk the last eighth of a mile, knowing all the time that they were in range.

William raised his hand and dropped it suddenly, answered by thousands of arrows soaring out as one, then again and again. He had never lost his awe at the accuracy of men who trained for twenty years at their craft. He knew they were despised by his armored knights, seen as men who killed like cowards. Yet those bowmen gave as much of their lives to building skill and strength as any professional soldier. Welsh and English in the main, with a few Scots and Irish sprinkled among them, they could aim and strike a man down at four hundred yards. There was nothing in the world like them, and William felt a rush of joy as the crossbowmen began to fall.

The mantlets protected many of the enemy, creeping ever closer in their columns. The longbows shot over the wooden shields, letting their arrows drop onto the bunched men behind, a hundred shafts at a time, spearing into the packed ranks. William could hear screaming and he saw a ripple go through the French cavalry. There were proud men there, knights and noble lords unwilling to see the hated English archers wreaking havoc.

"Let them charge," William whispered to himself. He had seen it before, as knights driven to frenzy tried to face down the arrow storm. They knew fear against the rushing, whining shafts—and they were men who reacted to fear with rage.

"Please," William whispered again. "Jesus and St. Sebastian, let them charge."

The Devil's hand had been passed, and the crossbowmen had

forced their mantlets close enough to form up and reply. For the first time, the air filled with black bolts, no longer than a man's finger but deadly. All along the English line, shields were raised and locked together. The sound of the bolts striking was like hail, a roaring rattle that claimed men in the gaps, so that they cried out.

William raised his own shield, though he knew the iron bolts would not pierce his armor beyond the luckiest of shots. He had seen battles where the exchange of bolts and arrows could go on for days before the armies met, but he was counting on the French confidence in superior numbers. He was sure there were already voices calling for a sudden attack, beseeching the French king to let them catch his archers by surprise. He had planned for it.

White, goose-feathered shafts stood out like a mat of some strange weed around the French mantlets. The crossbowmen had suffered for their lack of accuracy and power. Hundreds of them were down, or limping back through their lines with terrible wounds. William saw the ripple pass through the French knights yet again as they shuffled forward, the horses stamping and snorting.

He shouted the order he had discussed with Baron Alton. It was passed on to the archers, who looked predictably scornful. Some of them spat on the ground in his direction, but William didn't care what they thought of the tactic, as long as they obeyed.

As the next volley of iron bolts came over, hundreds of archers dropped flat, as if they had been struck. A great cheer went up from the crossbowmen, and it was answered by their center. William's heart raced as he saw the knights kick in and canter down the middle, ignoring all orders to halt in their delight at seeing archers in disarray. They had a vast and overwhelming advantage in numbers, and they fought with their king on the field, determined to impress him and make their names.

William waited as they came in, waited while his heart thumped, until they were fully committed and within the range of the bows. Despite their misgivings, his archers were enjoying the subterfuge, sending a few desultory arrows out as if the great storm had been reduced to nothing.

"Wait! Hold!" William roared.

The men lying on the ground were smiling like idiots, he could see them. Baron Alton wore a savage expression, his eyes wide as he watched William for the order.

"Up! Archers up!" William shouted.

He watched as the "dead" men leaped to their feet and slotted new arrows on to the bows. The French charge could not turn by then. It could not halt. The knights had passed the mantlets, streaming around them in their desire to close and slaughter the enemy. They had swallowed up their own crossbow positions, just as they had done at Agincourt. William clenched his mailed fist, making the metal and leather creak.

The charging knights were staring ahead at the massed swordsmen facing them. Those men-at-arms raised their weapons, jeering and gesturing for them to come on. With a rippling crack, hundreds of arrows were loosed from the wing, cutting through the French with buzzing terror.

The first few ranks crumpled, collapsing as the closest men and horses were struck over and over. It was as if a blackened twine had been stretched across a lonely road, with the French knights the ones who caught it in the throat. They died in droves until the rising mass of broken men and corpses forced the charge to a furious halt.

William called an order and the entire center of his army moved in. He rode with the sword and axemen, weapons raised to kill as they ran as fast as they could. They reached the lines of the dead in a hundred heartbeats, clambering over still-kicking horses and into the crush of mounted knights behind them. All the time, the arrows soared over their heads, killing men who never even saw what hit them.

William watched as a group of burly English axemen cut their way into a dozen knights, hammering them from their saddles. The great advantage of a horse was its speed and agility, but the lines had compressed and the French knights could hardly move to fight back.

William saw lances thrown away in disgust and swords drawn to hack down as the roaring English butchers killed their way deeper into the French lines. He exulted at the damage they were doing, but from the height of his own saddle, he could see farther than the men on the ground. As he looked up, his heart sank. The brutal action had not touched the bulk of the French army. They were shifting and moving under new orders to come round and hit his flanks. There were so many of them! It made his triumphant ruse and sudden attack look no more dangerous than a minor skirmish.

He turned to the messengers running at his side.

"Find Baron Alton and give him my regards. Tell him I would appreciate our mounted knights being used to prevent the enemy horse flanking us."

One of them raced off and time seemed to stand still for William while his men hacked and killed for him. He waited for Alton to respond. The French cavalry were pulling back at last from the impossible crush of the center. William could see fresh pike regiments marching stolidly into where the killing was going on. It was an impressive maneuver under pressure, and he assumed the order for it had come from the king himself, the only man on that field with the authority to order his knights to withdraw.

The English sword line surged forward, killing anyone they could reach. They'd gone too far for support from the archers by then, and it was that which made William hesitate. His men-at-arms had pushed on into a long column of their own while pursuing the enemy. They were not only exposed along the flanks, but also in real danger of being cut off. He looked into the distance again and shook his head at the numbers still untouched by the battle. He had hoped against hope for a rout, to fold the French lines into themselves in the sudden terror of the attack. It had not happened, and he knew he should fall back. Yet Alton's heavy cavalry was moving up on the wings, and when he glanced behind, he saw hundreds of archers stalking forward, trying to keep up with the moving battlefront, where they could still do damage.

William found himself sweating. He was still vastly outnumbered, but moving forward at a good pace against enemy pike regiments. Those cruel weapons were nearly impossible to charge with cavalry, but his sword and axemen would go through them, dodging past the outer points and then wreaking havoc on the untrained men holding the long weapons. He knew he should pull back in good order, but not yet, not quite yet.

The ranks of pikemen lowered the heavy iron heads and broke into a charge of their own, a line of sharp metal and pounding feet that was terrifying to stand against. The English men-at-arms readied their shields, knowing they had to turn the closest pike head with a blade and then slip in with a straight thrust to kill the wielder. It was a difficult move to pull off with hearts racing and hands slippery from sweat and blood. Many of them missed the deft touch and were impaled, the heavy pikes driven as much by the running men behind as those who held them. Hundreds more slipped the pikes and stabbed past, but the rush and press was so great that they too were swallowed, knocked off their feet by the weight of the charge. William cursed aloud, calling for his men to fall back and re-form. He turned his mount and trotted a hundred paces to the rear before facing the enemy again. Still they came on, roaring in excitement despite their losses.

"Archers!" William shouted, hoping to God that they could hear him over the noise of the battle.

He heard the snap of bows release behind him and holes appeared in the line of pikes. Those men needed both hands to balance the heavy poles. The peasants carried no shields, and boiled leather jackets were no protection at all against the shafts that tore into them. The foot charge wavered as yew bows punched out volley after volley.

Despite the carnage of the assault, it was the sight of the hated archers that kept the French pikemen coming. Standing in wide-spaced rows, wearing simple brown cloth like farmers, the archers were the monsters of a thousand tales and disasters. The pike ranks pushed on, desperate to reach the men calmly killing their friends. It was all they knew—the one weakness of a bowman. If he could be rushed, he could be killed.

William was forced to retreat once more. His ranks of swordsmen came back with him as the pike lines re-formed and left their dead behind. Step by step, the English forces lost the ground they had gained in the first advance, until they were back in their original positions. There, they dug in and stood with raised swords and shields, panting and waiting.

Some of the archers had been too slow to retreat with them, so that they vanished in a moving tide of men and rage. Yet around eight hundred made it back to their own mantlets and stakes. They turned once more with blood in their eyes for the pikemen.

Those volleys of arrows did not soar. As the pike regiments continued to charge, the shafts punched out in short, chopping blows, cutting off battle cries and sending men to their knees. Gaping holes appeared in the lines and pikes dropped or wavered upward to the sky. The entire French line tried to slow down rather than rush into withering fire. Those behind compressed, their pikes as dense as spines on a hedge pig, a forest of wood and iron.

The pikemen came to a staggering, bloodied halt and the archers took fresh quivers from arrow baskets and shot until their hands were blistered and their shoulders and backs ached and tore with every shaft sent out. Against a standing enemy, it was a savage slaughter, and they delighted in it.

The French regiments retreated at last, unable to force themselves any closer. They jogged away, turning their backs and then feeling the surge of terror that lent wings to their feet. Behind them, archers cheered and howled like wolves.

William felt a surge of pleasure that lasted as long as it took him to look over his forces. He'd lost a great number of men in just the first action, perhaps six hundred or a little more. He closed his eyes, suddenly feeling sick. Ahead of him, French knights were massing again and their king had even sent small groups forward to manhandle the mantlets into better positions. His archers responded with a dozen boys who sprinted out and gathered arrows into their arms, plucking them from the ground into great sheaves. As William watched, a lone crossbowman took careful aim and shot one of the boys as he turned to come back. He fell with his arrows spilling like a white wing and the archers roared in anger.

The French were going to charge again, William was certain. He could see more than eight thousand of the enemy who had not yet fought that day. His soldiers had wreaked bloody destruction, but the cost had been high and there were simply too many of the enemy still fresh and ready to attack.

"Second charge coming, Alton!" William bellowed across the field.

As he spoke, his horse made a huffing sound and sank to its knees, almost sending him over the animal's head. In his heavy armor, William dismounted slowly and clumsily. He found two bloody holes in the horse's chest, where it had been struck by bolts. He could see red droplets around the muzzle and he patted the powerful neck in distress, already looking for another mount to carry him.

"A horse here!" he called, standing patiently while his messengers found one of the reserve mounts and brought it to him. It was the first time that morning that he had seen the battlefield from the height of his men-at-arms and he drooped at the width of the ranks still facing him. The French had lost a crippling number, perhaps two thousand against hundreds of his own. In any other circumstances, the victory would be his. Yet the king still lived and he would only have grown in fury and bile.

"One more charge," William muttered, as he was helped to mount. In the privacy of his own thoughts, he knew he would surely have to retreat after that. He'd tell the surviving archers to run for the bridges, while his knights and men-at-arms fought the rear. He could do that much, he told himself, redeem that much honor. Until then, he had to survive another massed charge by an enemy who sensed their weakness.

"Ready archers!" he bellowed.

Few of the crossbowmen had survived the mêlée around the mantlets. If the French wanted a victory that day, they were damn well going to have to charge the yew bows they hated. With an effort, William pulled off his helmet, wanting to breathe and see clearly. They were coming, and the archers were already bending their bows, waiting for them. He kept a spark of hope alive because of those men—and those men alone.

CHAPTER 19

I don't understand what you are saying!" Margaret retorted, driven
to fury. "Why this talk of degrees and arcs and shadows? Is it illness or not? *Listen* to me. There are times when Henry speaks
clearly, as if there is nothing wrong. There are other times when he
talks without sense, like a child. Then something changes and his eyes
grow dull. Do you understand? It lasts for minutes, or hours, or even
days, then he revives and *my husband* looks back at me! *Those* are your
symptoms, Master Allworthy! What herb do you have in your bag for
those? This talk of fluxes and the . . . *planets* does you no credit at all.
Should I have my husband moved from London, if the air carries such
a taint here? Can you answer that at least, if you can't treat whatever
ails him?"

The king's physician had drawn himself up, his face reddening further with every word she spoke.

"Your Royal Highness," Master Allworthy began stiffly. "I have
dosed and purged the king. I have administered sulfur and a tincture
of opium in alcohol I have found to be most effective. I have bled His
Grace repeatedly and applied my best leeches to his tongue. Yet his

humors remain out of balance! I was trying to explain that I have feared the conjunction of Mars and Jupiter for days, knowing what it might bring. It is an evil time, my lady. His Grace suffers as the *representative* of his people, do you follow?" The doctor rubbed the small beard he allowed himself, winding his fingers into the knots of hair as he thought. "It may even be his nobility, his holiness, that is his undoing. Royal blood is not as that of other men, my lady. It is a beacon in the darkness, a bonfire on a hill that calls to dark forces. In such a time of unrest and chaos in the heavens, well . . . if God is ready to clasp His Royal Highness to His embrace, no mere man can stand in the way of that divine will."

"Oh, stand aside, then, Master Allworthy," Margaret said, "if that is all you have to say. I will not listen to your mealymouthed talk of planets any longer, while my husband is in such distress. *Stay* here and consider your precious Mars and Jupiter. I wish you joy of them."

The doctor opened his mouth, growing even redder. Whatever he might have replied was lost as Margaret pushed past him and entered the king's chambers.

Henry was sitting up in bed as she entered. The room was gloomy, and as she crossed to him, Margaret's foot caught on some part of the learned doctor's equipment. It fell with a crash and made her stumble, then kick out in a temper. A complex contraption of brass, iron, and glass went spinning across the floor. In her fury with the doctor, she was tempted to follow it like a fleeing rat and stamp it to pieces.

Her husband turned his head slowly at the clatter, blinking. He held up bandaged hands and Margaret swallowed as she saw fresh blood on the bindings. She had cleaned and dressed them many times, but she knew he bit at the wounds whenever he was left alone, worrying at them like a child.

With care, she sat on the bed, looking deeply into her husband's eyes and seeing only grief and pain reflected. There were scabs on her husband's bare arms, where the doctor's narrow knives had opened his veins. He looked thin, with dark circles under his eyes and blue lines showing on his pale skin.

"Are you well, Henry?" she said. "Can you rise? I think this place carries illness on the very air. Would you prefer to be moved along the river to Windsor, perhaps? The air is sweeter there, away from the stinks of London. You can ride to the hunt, eat good red meat and grow strong."

To her dismay, her husband began to weep, fighting it, his face crumpling. As she moved to embrace him, he held up his hands between them, as if warding her off. His fingers shook as if he had an ague, a chill, though the room was hot and sweat shone on his face.

"The soups and doses make my senses swim, Margaret, yet I cannot sleep! I have been awake now for . . . for longer than I can recall. I must not rest until I am certain the kingdom is safe."

"It *is* safe!" Margaret said, desperate to reassure him.

Henry shook his head in sad reproof.

"My people stir restlessly, knowing not what I do for them. They have taken arms against anointed men and murdered them! Has my army remained? Can you tell me that, or will you bring me news I cannot bear to hear? Have they all deserted me, Margaret?"

"No one has deserted you! *No one*, do you understand? Your soldiers would stand at your side on the Day of Judgment if you asked them to. London is safe, Henry, I swear it. England is safe. Be at peace and please, *please* try to sleep."

"I cannot, Margaret. Even if I wished it, I go on, I go on, burning down like a candle until the snuffer comes." He looked vaguely around the shadowed room. "Where are my clothes? I should dress and be about my duties."

He began to rise, and Margaret pressed a hand to his chest, almost recoiling from the heat of his skin as her bare palm touched him. She felt a different ache then, for the man she had married but who had not yet pressed her down. He didn't struggle against her touch, and she caressed his face, soothing him even as it stoked fires inside her. He closed his eyes and lay back against the bolsters and pillows. She grew bolder, uncaring that his doctor still stood outside.

Margaret leaned forward and kissed her husband on the neck, where his throat was revealed by the open nightshirt. His chest was white and hairless like a boy's, the arms slender. He smelled of pungent powders, of sulfur and bitter lime. His skin seemed hot to her lips, almost as if she had taken a burn.

Holding her breath, she let her hand fall to his lap and shifted closer on the bed, so that she leaned over him and was able to kiss him more firmly on the mouth. She felt his lips tremble and his eyes opened, staring into hers with wonder. He gasped into her mouth as she stroked him. She saw muscles twitch, and she gentled them with her hands.

"Lie still and let me tend you," Margaret whispered into his ear. "Let me bring what peace I can."

She felt her voice grow hoarse as her throat tightened and a flush stole its way across her face and neck. Her touch seemed to bring him calm, so that she dared not step away to undress. Instead, she kept her lips on his as her hands worried at ties and fastenings, yanking cloth away from her shoulders, baring them. It was impossible. She was terrified he would speak to forbid her, or rise and throw her off. Yet her dress would not come undone! She pressed her head against his neck as she wrestled with it, so that her hair draped across his face.

"I . . ." he began, the word smothered instantly as she kissed him again. She could taste the blood that rimed his lips from the leech wounds, like iron in her mouth.

With one hand she pulled her dress up and tore at the cloth beneath, so that her buttocks were revealed. A stray thought came to her mind of the learned doctor opening the door at that moment, and she stifled a giggle as she put one bare leg across her husband and tried to bring about a joining beneath the mass of garments. When she dared to look at Henry, he had his eyes closed once again, but she could feel the proof that his body at least was willing. By God, she'd seen enough animals do this small thing over the years! The ludicrousness of her situation made her want to laugh as she shifted and pressed down, trying to find a position that would work.

It happened suddenly and unexpectedly, so that they both gasped and Henry's eyes snapped open. He seemed vague even then, as if he thought it was a dream. Margaret found herself panting as she held his head in her hands and felt his hand reach down to grasp her bare thigh. She could feel the roughness of the bandages touch her skin, making her shudder. She closed her eyes and blushed as an image of William surged into her mind. William, who was so very old! She tried to banish the picture, but she could see him in the yard at Saumur, strong and laughing, his hands rough and powerful.

With her eyes tight shut, she moved on her husband as Yolande had described in the garden of Wetherby House, sharing breath and heat and sweat and forgetting about the doctor's impatience behind the door. When Henry cried out, Margaret felt her body shiver in response, thin tremors of pleasure amid the discomfort that somehow promised much more. She felt her husband rise away from the pillows, his arms and back growing hard as he held her, then going suddenly limp, so that he fell back like a dead man. He breathed shallowly as he lay there and Margaret felt warmth flood her loins.

She rested her head on her husband's chest until her breathing eased and she felt the soreness that was no worse than she had expected. The frantic images of William faded with vague stirrings of guilt.

She smiled as she heard Henry begin to snore lightly, and when the door opened and the doctor looked in, she did not open her eyes until he went away, not even to see his appalled expression.

Jack Cade looked around at the men who waited on his orders. Paddy and Rob Ecclestone were there, of course, his trusted lieutenants, who could hardly hide their delight at the way things were going. He'd realized early on that a mere rabble of angry farmers would have no chance at all when the sheriff of Kent sent out professional soldiers. The answer had been to train the refugees from France until they could stand and kill in a line, and march, and do as they were damn well told by those who knew.

"Will someone fetch me a flagon of black, or do I have to talk dry?" Jack said.

He'd learned it was a good idea to get his drink early in the taverns they used each night. His men had a thirst, and the barrels were always dry by the time they moved on. Every morning had them groaning and complaining about their splitting skulls, but Jack didn't mind that. If he'd learned anything fighting in France years before, it was that Kentish men fight better with a little ale inside them—better still with a skinful.

The widow behind the bar was not at all happy about men drinking for free. Flora kept a good house, Jack had to admit. There were clean rushes on the floor, and the planks and barrels were worn smooth with years of scrubbing. It was true she was no kind of beauty, yet she had the sort of square-jawed stubbornness Jack had always liked. In happier times, he might even have considered courting her. After all, she hadn't run, not even when two thousand men came marching up the road toward her tavern. That was Kentish, right there. Jack waited patiently while she filled a pewter cup and passed it to him to blow off the froth.

"Thank you, my love," he called appreciatively.

She looked sourly at him, folding her arms in a way he knew from every boardinghouse and tavern he'd been turned away from over the years. The thought made his spirits rise. They couldn't turn old Jack Cade out into the night any longer, not now. With huge gulps, he sank the beer to the dregs and gasped, wiping away a thick line from the bristles around his mouth.

The inn was packed with around eighty of those he'd singled out in the previous few weeks. For the most part, they were men like himself: heavy in the shoulders, with good strong legs and big hands. Every one of them had been born in Kent, it went without saying. With the exception of Paddy himself, Jack was more comfortable with those. He knew how their minds worked, how they thought and how they spoke. As a result, he could speak to them, something he was not accustomed to doing, at least not in crowds.

Jack looked round at them appreciatively, all waiting on his word.

"Now, I know some of you buggers don't know me well, so you're perhaps wondering why Jack Cade tapped you on the shoulder. You'll know I don't like to talk the way some do, either, so you'll know it's not just froth."

They stared back at him, and Paddy chuckled in the silence. The big Irishman was wearing new clothes and boots, taken fresh from one of the towns they'd passed and better than anything he had ever owned before. Jack let his eyes drift until he found Rob Ecclestone at the back. That was one more suited to standing in the shadows, where he could keep an eye on the rest. Ecclestone seemed to make the men uncomfortable when he was seen stropping his razor each morning— and that was a good thing, as far as Jack was concerned.

"Fetch me another, would you, Flora?" Jack called, passing the cup. "All right?"

He turned back to the crowd, enjoying himself.

"I've had you buggers running and marching to mend your wind.

I've made you sweat with pruning hooks and axes, whatever we could find for you. I've done all that because when the sheriff of Kent comes against us, he'll have soldiers with him, as many as he can find. And I ha'n't come so far to lose it now."

A murmur came from the crowd as those who knew each other bent their heads and muttered comments. Jack flushed slightly.

"I've heard your tales, lads. I've heard about what those bastards did in France, how they gave away your land and then stood back while French soldiers put hands on your women and killed your old men. I've heard about the taxes, so a man can work hard all his life and still have nothing when they've done taking their share of *your* money. Well, lads, you've got a chance now to make them listen, if you want. You'll stand in a muddy field with the men you see around you—and the ones outside. You'll watch the sheriff's soldiers marching up with their swords and bows, and you'll want to forget how bleeding angry you are at them. You'll want to run and let them win, with your piss running down your legs as you go."

The packed tavern seemed almost to shake as the men inside it growled and shouted that they would do no such thing. Jack's lips curled in amusement as he took his second ale and sank it as fast as the first.

"I've known that fear, lads, so don't go telling me about how brave you are when you're standing safe in the warm. Your guts will tighten and your heart will jump and you'll want to be *anywhere* else." His voice hardened and his eyes glittered, the old anger rising in him with the drink. "But if you do, you won't be Kentish men. You won't even be men. You'll get *one* chance to knock their teeth back into their head, just one fight where they'll expect you to run and piss yourself. If you stand, they won't know what's hit them and we'll go through them like wheat, I swear to God. We'll put that sheriff's head on a stick and carry it like a fucking banner! We'll march on London, boys, if you can stand. Just *once*, and then you'll know you have the stomach for it."

He looked around the room, satisfied at what he saw in their expressions.

"When you go out, I want each of you to pick a dozen men. They'll be yours, so learn their names and have them learn each other's. I want them to know that if they run, their mates will be the ones they leave behind, understand? Not strangers, their *mates*. Have them drink together and train together every day until they're as close to brothers as you can make them. That way we have a chance."

He lowered his head for a moment, almost as if he were praying. When he spoke again, his voice was hoarse.

"Then, when you hear me shout, or Paddy or Rob, you follow. You do as you're told and you watch the sheriff's soldiers fall. I'll point you in the right direction. I know how. You take your one chance and you take heads. You'll walk right over the men who stand against us."

Paddy and Rob cheered, and the rest of them joined in. Jack waved a hand to Flora and she spat on the floor in disgust but began passing out more flagons of ale. Over the noise, Jack raised his voice once again, though his sight was blurring. The black ale was good enough to pay for, if he'd been paying.

"There's more and more Kentish men coming in to join us every day, lads. The whole county knows what we're about by now, and there's more from France every day as well. They say Normandy is falling and that our fine king has betrayed us all again. Well, I have an answer to that!"

He raised a hatchet from where it had been lying by his boots and slammed the blade into the wooden bar. In an instant of silence, Flora swore. The word she used made them all laugh as they cheered and drank. Jack raised his cup to them.

THOMAS WALKED with a slight limp, the remnant of the injury he'd taken. The stitches had puckered into a swollen line that ran across his hip and stretched painfully with every step. After a week of crossing fields and hiding in ditches, it was strange to use the roads again. He and Rowan blended well into the miserable, straggling crowd of refugees heading toward Calais. There was no room on most of the carts, already creaking under the weight of anyone with a few coins to spend. Thomas and Rowan had nothing between them, so they trudged on with lowered heads, just putting as many miles under their boots as they could each day. Thomas tried to stay alert, but hunger and thirst made him listless and he sometimes came to evening with very little memory of the roads he'd taken. It grated on his nerves to travel in the open, but neither he nor his son had seen a French soldier for days. They were off somewhere else, perhaps with better things to do than harass and rob the flood of English families leaving France.

The twilight was shading into darkness when Thomas dropped. With a grunt, he simply crumpled and lay flat in the road, with refugees stepping over him. Rowan heaved him up and then gave his horn-handled seax to a carter willing to shove two more into the back. The man even shared a thin soup with them that night, which Rowan spooned into his father's mouth. They were in no worse a state than many of those around them, but it helped to be carried along.

Another day passed with the world reduced to a square of sky visible through the back of the cart. Rowan stopped looking out when he saw three men battering and robbing some helpless soul. No one went to the man's aid, and the cart trundled on, leaving the scene behind.

They were not asleep when the cart came to a halt, just in a state of dazed stupor that made the days a blur. Rowan sat up with a start when the carter thumped loudly on the flat sides of his wagon. There were three others pressed in with the archers, two old men and a woman Rowan understood was married to one of them, though he wasn't sure which. The old folks stirred sluggishly as the carter continued to thump and rouse them all.

"Why have we stopped?" Thomas murmured, without getting up from his place against the wooden side.

Rowan clambered down and stood, looking into the distance. After so long, it was strange to see the fortress walls of Calais, no more than a mile off. The roads were so packed that the cart could only move with the flow of people, at the speed of the slowest. Rowan leaned back in and shook his father by the shoulder.

"Time to get off, I think," he said. "I can smell the sea at last."

Gulls called in the distance, and Rowan felt his spirits lift, though he had no more coins than a beggar and not even a knife to defend himself. He helped his father down to the road and thanked the carter, who bade them farewell with his attention on his parents and the uncle in the back.

"God be with you, lads," he said.

Rowan put an arm around his father, feeling the bones stand out sharply where the flesh had wasted away.

The walls of Calais seemed to grow as they pushed and shoved their way through the mass of people. The archers were at least unencumbered, with no possessions to guard. More than once they heard a cry of outrage as someone stole something and tried to vanish. Rowan shook his head as he saw two men kicking another on the ground. They were intent on the task, and as Rowan passed, one of them looked up and stared a challenge. Rowan looked away, and the man resumed stamping on the prone figure.

Thomas groaned, his head hanging as Rowan struggled with him. There were so many people! For a man raised on an isolated sheep farm, it made Rowan sweat to be in such a crush, all heading to the docks. They were almost carried along, unable to stop or turn aside from the movement of people.

If anything, the press grew even thicker as Rowan staggered with his father through the massive town gates and along the main street toward the sea. He could see the tall masts of ships there and lifted his head in hope.

It took all morning and the best part of the afternoon before they reached the docks themselves. Rowan had been forced to rest more than once, when he saw an open step or even a wall to sag against. He was dizzy and weary, but the sight of the ships drew him on. His father drifted in and out of alertness, sometimes completely aware and talking, only to sink back into his drowsing state.

The sun was setting on another day without a decent meal. There had been some monks giving out rounds of hard bread and ladles of water to the crowd. Rowan had blessed them for their kindness, though that had been hours ago. He felt his tongue had thickened in his mouth, and his father hadn't said a word since then. With the sun creeping toward the horizon, they'd joined a queue that bustled and wound through the moving crowds, heading always to a group of burly men guarding the entranceway to a ship. As the light was turning red and gold, Rowan helped his father along the last few steps, knowing they must look like beggars or the damned, even in that company.

One of the men looked up and winced visibly at the two gaunt scarecrows standing and swaying before him.

"Names?" he said.

"Rowan and Thomas Woodchurch," Rowan replied. "Have you a spot for us?"

"Do you have coin?" the man asked. His voice was dull with endlessly asking the same questions.

"My mother has, in England," Rowan said, his heart sinking in him.

His father stirred in his arms, raising his head. The sailor shrugged, already looking beyond them to the next in line.

"Can't help you today, son. There'll be other ships tomorrow or the day after. One of them will take you."

Thomas Woodchurch leaned forward, almost toppling his son.

"Derry Brewer," he muttered, though it scorched him to use the name. "Derry Brewer or John Gilpin. They'll vouch for me. They'll vouch for an archer."

The sailor stopped in the act of waving the next group forward. He looked uncomfortable as he checked his wooden tally board.

"Right, sir. On you go. There's space still on the deck. You'll be all right as long as the wind stays gentle. We'll be leaving soon."

As Rowan watched in astonishment, the man used his knife to mark two more souls on the wooden block.

"Thank you," he said as he helped his father up the gangplank. The sailor touched his forelock in brief salute. Rowan shoved and argued his way into a bare spot on the deck near the prow. In relief, he and his father lay down and waited to be taken to England.

CHAPTER 20

Derry looked out of the window of the Jewel Tower, rather than face the forbidding expression of Speaker William Tresham. He could see the vast Palace of Westminster across the road, with its clock tower and its famous bell, the Edward. Four parliamentary guards had kept him cooling his heels in the tower for an entire morning, unable to leave until the great man graced him with his presence.

Derry sighed to himself, staring out through thick glass with a green tinge that made the world beyond swim and blur. He knew Westminster Hall would be at its busiest, with all the shops inside doing a roaring trade in wigs, pens, paper: anything and everything that might be required by the Commons or the courts to administer the king's lands. On the whole, Derry wished he could be out there instead. The Jewel Tower was surrounded by its own walls and moat, originally to protect the personal valuables of King Edward. With just a few guards, it worked equally well to keep a man prisoner.

Having seated himself comfortably at an enormous oak desk, Tresham cleared his throat with deliberate emphasis. Reluctantly, Derry turned from the window to face him, and the two men stared at each other with mutual suspicion. The Speaker of the Commons was not yet fifty, though he had served a dozen parliaments since his first election at the age of nineteen. At forty-six, Tresham was said to be at the height of his powers, with a reputation for intelligence that made Derry more than a little wary of him. Tresham looked him over in silence, the cold gaze taking in every detail, from Derry's mud-spattered boots to the frayed lining of his cloak. It was hard to remain still with those eyes noticing everything.

"Master Brewer," Tresham said after a time. "I feel I must apologize for keeping you waiting for so long. Parliament is a harsh mistress, as they say. Still, I will not keep you much longer, now that we are settled. I remind you that your presence is a courtesy to me, for which you have my thanks. I can only hope to impress you with the seriousness of my purpose, so that you do not feel I have wasted the time of a king's man."

Tresham smiled as he spoke, knowing full well that Derry had been brought to him by the same armed soldiers who now guarded the door of the tower two floors below. The king's spymaster had not been given a choice, or a warning, perhaps because Tresham knew very well that he would have quietly disappeared at the first whisper of a summons.

Derry continued to glower at the man seated before him. Before the career in politics, he knew Sir William Tresham had trained first as a lawyer. In the privacy of his own thoughts, Derry told himself to tread carefully around the horse-faced old devil, with his small, square teeth.

"You have no answer for me, Master Brewer?" Tresham went on. "I have it on good authority that you are not a mute, yet I have not heard a word from you since I arrived. Is there nothing you would say to me?"

Derry smiled but took refuge in silence rather than give the man anything he could use. It was said Tresham could spin a web thick enough to hang a man from nothing more than a knife and a dropped glove. Derry only watched as Tresham harrumphed to himself and sifted through a pile of papers he had arranged across the desk.

"Your name appears on none of these papers, Master Brewer. This is not an inquisition, at least as it pertains to you. Instead, I had rather hoped you would be willing to aid the Speaker of the House in his inquiries. The charges that will be laid are in the realm of high treason, after all. I believe a case can be made that it is your *duty*, sir, to aid me in any way I see fit."

Tresham paused, raising his enormous eyebrows in the hope of a comment. Derry ground his teeth but kept silent, preferring to let the older man reveal whatever he knew. When Tresham merely stared back at him, Derry felt his patience fray in the most irritating manner.

"If that is all, Sir William, I must be about the king's business. I am, as you say, his man. I should not be detained here, not with that greater call."

"Master Brewer! You are free to leave here at any moment, of course—"

Derry turned instantly toward the door, and Tresham held up a single bony finger in warning.

"But . . . ah, yes, Master Brewer, there is always a 'but,' is there not? I have summoned you here to aid my lawful inquiries. If you choose to leave, I will be forced to assume you are one of the very men I seek! No innocent man would run from me, Master Brewer. Not when I pursue justice in the king's name."

Despite himself, Derry's temper rose and he spoke again, perhaps taking comfort from the doorway so close to hand. It was no more than an illusion of escape, with guardsmen below to stop him. Even so, it freed his tongue against his better judgment.

"You seek a scapegoat, Sir William. God knows you cannot involve King Henry in these false charges of treason, so you wish to find some lesser man to hang and disembowel for the pleasure of the London crowds. You do not deceive me, Sir William. I know what you are about!"

The older man settled back, confident that Derry would not, or rather could not, leave. He rested his clasped hands on the buttons of his tired old coat and looked up at the ceiling.

"I see I can be candid with you. It does not surprise me, given what I have been led to understand about your influence at court. It is true that your name appears on no papers, though it is certainly *spoken* by many. I did not lie when I said you were in no danger, Master Brewer. You are but a servant of the king, though your service is wide and astonishingly varied, I believe. However, let me be blunt, as one man to another. The disasters in France must be laid at the feet of whoever is responsible. Maine, Anjou, and now Normandy have been lost—no, torn—from their rightful owners in murder, fire, and blood! Are you so surprised that there is a cost to be paid for such chaos and bad dealing?"

With a sick sense of inevitability, Derry saw where the man was prodding him. He spoke quickly to head him off.

"The marriage in France was at the king's own request, the terms agreed by His Royal Highness to the last drop of ink. The royal seal sits secure upon it all, Sir William. Will you be the man to lay your accusations at the king's feet? I wish you luck. Royal approval is immunity enough, I think, for the disasters you mention. I do not deny the lost territories, and I regret the loss of every farm and holding there, but this scrabbling around for a culprit, a scapegoat, is beneath the dignity of Parliament or its Speaker. Sir William, there are times when England triumphs, and others where . . . she fails. We endure and we go on. It behooves us ill to look back and point fingers, saying, 'Ah, *that* should not have happened. *That* should not have been allowed.' Such a perspective is granted only to men staring backward, Sir William. For those of us with the will to go *forward*, it is as if we walk blindfolded into a dark room. Not every false step or stumble can be judged after the moment has passed, nor should it be."

Sir William Tresham looked amused as Derry spoke. The old lawyer brought his gaze down from on high, and Derry felt pierced by eyes that saw and understood too much.

"By your reasoning, Master Brewer, there would never be punishment for any misdeeds! You would have us shrug our shoulders and put all failures down to luck or fate. It is an intriguing vision and, I must say, an interesting insight into your mind. I almost wish the world *could* work like that, Master Brewer. Sadly, it does *not*. Those who have brought about the ruination and deaths of thousands must in turn be brought to justice! There must *be* justice and it must be *seen* to be done!"

Derry found himself breathing heavily, his fists curling and uncurling in frustration at his sides.

"And the king's protection?" he demanded.

"Why, it extends only so far, Master Brewer! When riots and vile murders spread across the country, I suspect even the king's protection has its limits. Would you have those responsible for such destruction go unpunished? The loss of Crown lands in France? The butchery of men of high estate? If so, you and I must differ."

Derry narrowed his eyes, wondering again at the peculiar timing of the summons that had snatched him up and borne him across London to Westminster.

"If my name is nowhere mentioned, why am I here?" he demanded.

To his irritation, Tresham chuckled in what looked like genuine pleasure.

"I am surprised you did not ask that question at the start, Master Brewer. A suspicious man might find fault in you taking so long to reach this point."

Tresham stood up and looked out of the window himself. Close by the river, the great bell chimed at that moment, struck twice within to let all men know that it was two hours past noon. Tresham clasped his hands behind his back as if he was lecturing students of the law, and Derry's heart sank at the man's unnerving confidence.

"You are an intriguing fellow, Master Brewer. You fought as a king's man in France some sixteen years ago, with some distinction, I am told. You found service as a runner and an informant for old Saul Bertleman after that. Risky occupations both, Master Brewer! I have even heard talk of you fighting in the rookeries, as if both violence and peril are things you crave. I knew Saul Bertleman for many years, are you aware? I would not say we were friends, exactly, just that I learned to admire the quality of information he could provide. Yet the aspect of him that remains in my mind was perhaps his greatest virtue: caution. Your predecessor was a cautious man, Master Brewer. Why such a man would choose *you* to follow him is beyond me."

Tresham paused to observe the effect of his words. His delight at having a captive audience was vastly irritating, but there was nothing Derry could do but endure it.

"I expect he saw things you don't," Derry replied. "Or perhaps you didn't know him as well as you thought."

"Yes, I suppose that is possible," Tresham said, his doubts clear. "From the first moment I began looking into this farrago, this unspeakable mess of vanity and truces and *arrogance*, your name has been whispered to me. Honest men will breathe it from behind their hands, Master Brewer, as if they fear you would learn they have spoken to me, or to my men. Whatever the truth of your own involvement, it seems but the merest common sense to keep you under my eye while I send men to arrest a friend of yours."

Derry felt a cold hand clutch his innards. His mouth worked but no words came. Tresham could hardly contain his satisfaction as he smiled in the direction of the clock tower.

"Lord Suffolk should be arriving at Portsmouth today, Master

Brewer, while the ragged survivors of his army lick their wounds in Calais. The reports are not good, though I daresay I do not have to tell *you* that."

Tresham gestured to the papers on the desk, the corners of his mouth turning down in something like regret.

"*Your* name may not be mentioned here, Master Brewer, but that of William de la Pole, Lord Suffolk, is on almost every one. You ask why you are here? It was the message of those whispering voices, Master Brewer. They warned me that if I were to set out nets, I should first be sure you were not there to cut them. I believe that task has been accomplished by now. You may leave, unless, of course, you have any further questions. No? Then speak the word 'fisherman' to the guards below." Tresham chuckled. "A foolish conceit, I know, but if you give them the word, they will let you pass."

He spoke the last words to empty air as Derry clattered down the steps. He'd lost the best part of a day being held at Tresham's pleasure. His thoughts were wild as he ran across the road and hard along the outer edge of the palace, heading down to the ferryboats on the river. The Tower of London was three miles off, right round the bend of the Thames. He had men there who could be sent to the coast on fast horses. As he ran, he laughed nervously to himself, his eyes bright. Sir William bloody Tresham was a dangerous enemy to have, there was no doubt about it. Yet for all his cleverness, Tresham had been wrong in just one thing. William de la Pole wasn't coming to Portsmouth, two days' ride and southwest of the city of London. He was coming to Folkestone in Kent, and Derry was the only one who knew it.

He was out of breath by the time he reached the landing stage, where ferries for members of Parliament waited at all times of the day and night. Derry pushed past an elderly gentleman as he was being helped down, leaping aboard the narrow scull and making its owner curse as the vessel lurched and almost went over.

"Take me to the Tower," he said over the ferryman's protest. "A gold noble if you row like your house is on fire."

The man's mouth shut fast then. He abandoned the old man he'd been helping and touched his forehead briefly before jumping down and sweeping them out onto the dark waters.

"I BLOODY *hate* fighting in mist and rain," Jack Cade said as he walked. "Your hands slip, your feet slip, bowstrings rot, and you can't see the enemy worth a damn before he's on you."

Paddy grunted at his shoulder, hunched and shivering as they walked in line. Despite Jack's irritation at the downpour, he supposed it was some sort of a blessing. He doubted the sheriff of Kent had many archers at his disposal. It was a valuable talent, and those who had it were all in France for better pay, getting themselves slaughtered. If the king's officers in Kent had even a dozen crossbows between them, they'd be lucky, but in heavy rain the strings stretched and the range was reduced. If Jack hadn't been miserable, sodden, and frozen, he might have thanked God for the rain. He didn't, though.

Paddy's outlook was, if anything, slightly worse. He had always been suspicious of good luck in any form. It didn't seem to be the natural order of things, and he was usually happier when his fortunes were bad. Yet they'd marched through Kent almost without incident, from Maidstone on. The king's sheriff hadn't been in the county seat when they came looking for him. Cade's army had caught a few of his bailiffs around the jail and amused themselves hanging them before freeing the prisoners and burning the place down. Since then, they'd walked like children in the Garden of Eden, with neither sight nor sound of the king's soldiers. With every day of peace, Paddy's mood sank farther into his boots. It was all very well spending the daylight practicing with farm tools in place of weapons, but there would come a reckoning and a retribution, he was certain. The king and his fine lords couldn't allow them to roam the countryside at will, taking and burning whatever they wanted. Only the thought that they were not alone kept Paddy's spirits up. They'd heard reports of riots in London and the shires, all sparked off by the righteous grievances of families coming home from France. Paddy prayed each night that the king's soldiers would be kept busy somewhere else, but in his heart of hearts, he knew they were coming. He'd had a grand few weeks in the Kentish Freemen, but he expected tears and the weather suited his gloom.

The rain had lessened to a constant drizzle, but there was mist thick around them when they heard a high voice shouting nearby. Jack had insisted on scouts, though they had only stolen plow horses for them to ride. One of the volunteers was a short, wiry Scot by the name of James Tanter. The sight of the little man perched on the enormous great horse had reduced Paddy almost to tears of laughter when he'd seen it. They all recognized Tanter's thick brogue yelling a warning through the rain.

Jack roared orders on the instant to ready weapons. Tanter may have been a bitter little haggis-sucker, as Jack called him, but he wasn't a man to waste breath on nothing, either.

They marched on, holding pruning hooks and scythes, shovels and even old swords if they'd come across them or taken them from unfortunate bailiffs. Every man there stared through the gray, looking for shapes that could be an enemy. All noises were muffled, but they heard Tanter shout a curse and his horse whinny somewhere up ahead. Paddy turned back and forth as he walked, straining to hear. He made out small sounds and swallowed nervously.

"Christ save us, there they are!" Jack said, raising his voice to a bellow. "You see them? Now kill them. Pay a little back of what you're owed. Attack!"

The lines of men broke into a lurching run through the thick mud, the ones at the rear watching their mates disappear into the swirling mist. They could see no farther than thirty paces, but for Jack Cade and Paddy, that small space was filling with soldiers with good swords and chain mail. They, too, had been warned by Tanter's desperate shouts, but there was still confusion in the sheriff's ranks. Some of them stopped dead on seeing Cade's men drift like ghosts out of the land in front of them.

With a roar, Cade charged, raising a woodcutter's ax above his head as he went. He was among the first to reach the sheriff's soldiers, and he buried the wide blade in the neck of the first man he faced. The blow cut deep through mail links and wedged, so that he had to wrench it back and forth to free the blade, spattering himself with gore. Around him, his men were surging forward. Rob Ecclestone wore no armor and held only his razor, but he did bloody work with it, stepping past armored men with a quick flick that left them gasping and holding their throats. Paddy had a pruning hook with a crescent blade that he held out flat. He hooked men's heads with it, pulling them in as the blade bit. The rest were Kentish men for the most part, and they'd been angry ever since the French had evicted them. They were angrier still at the English lords who'd connived in it. In that boggy field near Sevenoaks, there was a chance for them to act at last, and all Jack's speeches were as nothing next to that. They were furious men holding sharp iron and they poured forward into the soldiers.

Jack staggered, swearing at a dull pain from his leg. He didn't dare look down and risk getting his head split at the wrong moment. He wasn't even sure he'd been cut and had no memory of a wound, but the damned thing buckled under him and he limped and hopped with the line, swinging his ax as he went. He fell behind despite his best efforts, staggering on while the noises of battle receded away from him.

He stepped over dead men and took a careful route around the screaming wounded. It seemed an age of limping along, lost in hissing rain that made the blood on his ax run down his arm and chest. In the mists, it took him a little time to understand no one else was coming against him. The sheriff had sent four hundred men-at-arms, a veritable army in the circumstances. It was easily enough men to quell a rebellion of farmers—unless there were five thousand of them, armed and raging. The soldiers had made bloody slaughter on some of Cade's Freemen, but in the drizzle and fog, neither side had seen the numbers they faced until there were no more soldiers left to kill.

Jack stood with his boots so clogged he thought it made him a foot taller. He was panting and sweat poured off him, adding to his stink. Still no one came. Slowly, a smile spread across Jack's face.

"Is that *it*?" he shouted. "Can anyone see any more of them? Jesus, they can't all be dead already? Rob?"

"No one alive here," his friend shouted from over on his right.

Jack turned to the voice and through the mist he saw Ecclestone standing alone, with even the Kentish Freemen shying away from him. He was covered in other men's blood, a red figure in the swirling vapor. Jack shuddered, feeling cold hands run down his back at the sight.

"Didn't the sheriff have a white horse on his shield?" Paddy called from somewhere on Jack's left.

"He'd no right to it, but I heard that."

"He's here, then."

"Alive?" Jack demanded hopefully.

"He'd be screaming if he was, with a wound like this one. He's gone, Jack."

"Take his head. We'll put it on a pole."

"I'm not cutting his head off, Jack!" Paddy replied. "Take his shield for your bloody pole. It's the horse of Kent, isn't it? It'll do just as well."

Jack sighed, reminded once again that the Irishman had some odd qualms for a man with his history.

"A head sends a better message, Paddy. I'll do it. You fetch a good pole and sharpen the end. We'll take his shield as well, mind."

The lack of an enemy was slowly being understood by his ragged army, so that cheering erupted in patches from them, echoing oddly across the fields and sounding thin and exhausted, despite their numbers. Jack stepped over dozens of bodies to reach Paddy. He looked down onto the white face of a man he'd never met and raised his ax with satisfaction, bringing it down hard.

"Where next, Jack?" Paddy said in wonder, looking at the corpses all around. Blood squelched around his boots, mingling with the rainwater and mud.

"I'm thinking we have a proper army here," Jack said thoughtfully. "One that's been blooded and come through. There's swords for the taking, as well as mail and shields."

Paddy looked up from the headless figure that had been the sheriff of Kent. Just the day before, the sheriff had been a man to be feared across the county. The Irishman looked at Jack in dawning astonishment, his eyes widening.

"You aren't thinking o' London? I thought that was just fighting talk before. It's one thing to take down a few hundred sheriff's men, Jack!"

"Well, we did it, didn't we? Why not London, Paddy? We're thirty or forty miles away, with an *army*. We'll send a few lads to get the lay of the land, to see how many brave soldiers they have to man the barricades. I tell you we'll never have a chance like this again. We can make them clean out the courts, maybe, or give us the judges to hang, like they hung my son. My boy, Paddy! You think I'm done yet? With an ax at their throats, we can force them to change the laws that took him from me. I'll make you free, Paddy Moran. No, sod that. I'll make you a bleedin' earl."

WILLIAM DE LA POLE stepped gingerly onto the docks, feeling his bruises and his years. Everything ached, though he had taken no wound. He still remembered a time when he could fight all day and then sleep like the dead, just to rise and fight again. There hadn't been the pains in his joints then, or a right arm that felt as if he had something sharp digging into the shoulder, so that every movement sent shudders through him. He remembered too that a victory washed it all away, even minor wounds. Somehow, seeing your enemies dead or fleeing made the body heal faster, the pain less vicious. He shook his head as he stood on the dock and looked out over the fishing town of Folkestone, gray and cold in the wind off the sea. It was harder when you lost. Everything was.

The arrival of his ship had not gone unnoticed or unremarked by the fishing crews of the town. They'd gathered in their dozens on the muddy streets, and it wasn't long before his name was being shouted among them. William saw their anger and he understood it. They held him responsible for the disasters across the narrow Channel. He didn't blame them; he felt the same way.

There was mist on the sea in the cold morning light. He couldn't see France, though he felt Calais looming at his back as if the fortress town was just a step away across the brine. It was all that remained, the last English possession in France beyond some scrubland in Gascony that wouldn't survive a year. He'd come home to arrange ships to take his wounded, as well as for the miserable task of reporting a French victory to his king. William rubbed his face hard at the thought, feeling the bristles and the cold. Gulls dipped and wheeled in the air all around, and the wind bit through him as he stood there. He could see fishermen pointing in his direction, and he turned to the small group of six guards he'd brought home, all as battered and tired as he was.

"Three of you bring the horses out of the hold. The rest of you keep your hands on your swords. I'm in no mood to talk to angry men, not today."

Even as he spoke, the small crowds of locals were growing as others came out of the inns and chandlery shops along the seafront, responding to the news that Lord Suffolk himself was there in the town. There were more than a few present who had come home from France in the previous few months, then stayed on the coast with no coin to take them farther. They looked like the beggars they'd become, ragged and filthy. Their thin arms jabbed the air, and the mood was growing uglier by the minute. William's guards shifted uneasily, glancing at each other. One of them shouted to the others to look brisk in the hold, while the other two gripped their sword hilts and hoped to God that they wouldn't be rushed in an English port after surviving war in France.

It took time to break apart the wooden stalls in the bowels of the ship, then blindfold each of the mounts and bring them safely over the narrow walkway to the stone dock. The tension eased in William's men as each animal was saddled and made ready.

Beyond the gulls and fishermen, one man came running out of a tavern, passing quickly through the crowds and making straight for the docks. Two of William's guards drew swords on him as he approached, and the man skidded to a stop on the cobbles, holding empty hands up.

"Pax, lads, pax! I'm not armed. Lord Suffolk?"

"I am," William replied warily.

The man breathed in relief.

"I expected you two days back, my lord."

"I've been delayed," William said irritably.

His retreat to Calais had been one of the worst experiences of his life, with baying French pikemen at their heels the whole way. Half his army had been slaughtered, but he hadn't abandoned his archers, not even when it looked as if they'd never make it to the fortress. Some of them had taken riderless horses, or run alongside, holding loose stirrups. It was a small point of pride among the failure, but William hadn't left them to be tortured and torn apart by the triumphant French knights.

"I bear a message, my lord, from Derihew Brewer."

William closed his eyes for a moment and massaged the bridge of his nose with one hand.

"Give it to me, then." When the man remained silent, William opened his bloodshot eyes and glared at him. "Well?"

"My lord, I think it is a private message."

"Just . . . tell me," he said, weary beyond belief.

"I am to warn you there are charges of treason waiting in London, my lord. Sir William Tresham has sent men to Portsmouth to arrest you. I am to say, 'It's time to run, William Pole.' I'm sorry, my lord, those are the exact words."

William turned to his horse and checked the belly strap with a dour expression, slapping the animal on the haunch and then tightening it carefully. The servant and his guards all waited for him to say something, but he put a foot in a stirrup and mounted, casting a glance at the crowd, who had not yet dared to approach and truly threaten him. He placed his scabbard carefully alongside his leg and took up the reins before looking down at his guards.

"What is it?" he demanded.

The guards looked helplessly up at him. The closest cleared his throat.

"We were wondering what you intended, my lord Suffolk. It's grave news."

"I intend to honor my commission!" William said curtly. "I intend to return to London. Now mount up, before these fishermen find their nerve."

The messenger was gaping, but William ignored the man. The news had sickened him, but in truth it changed nothing, whatever Derry might have thought. William tensed his jaw as his men mounted their horses. He would not be a coward. He kept his back stiff as he walked his horse, *walked* it, by God, past the fishermen. Some stones were thrown, but they didn't touch him.

THOMAS WOODCHURCH watched the Duke of Suffolk ride by. He'd seen William de la Pole before at a distance, and he knew that iron hair and upright carriage, though the nobleman had lost a great deal of weight since then. Thomas scowled as some fool threw a stone. His angry expression was noticed by some fishermen nearby, watching the proceedings.

"Don't worry, lad," one of them called. "Old Jack Cade'll get 'im, God's as witness."

Thomas turned sharply to the speaker, a grizzled old man with wiry hands and arms that were marked in white net scars.

"Jack *Cade*?" he demanded incredulously, taking a step closer.

"Him who 'as an army of free men. They'll settle yon fancy gen'lman, with his nose in the air while better men starve."

"Who's Jack Cade?" Rowan asked.

His father ignored him, reaching out and taking the boatman by the shoulder.

"What do you mean, an army? Jack Cade from Kent? I knew a man by that name once."

The boatman raised thick eyebrows and smiled, revealing just a couple of teeth in an expanse of brown gum.

"We've seen a few come through to join 'im, last month or so.

Some of us 'as to fish, lad, but if you're of a mind to break heads, Cade'll take you."

"Where is he?" Thomas demanded, tightening his grip on the arm as the man tried to pull away and failed.

"'E's a ghost, lad. You won't find 'im if 'e don't want it. Go west and north, that's what I heard. He's up the woods there somewhere, killing bailiffs and sheriff's men."

Thomas swallowed. The wound on his hip still hurt, the healing slowed by starvation and sleeping each night on the shore in the wind and rain. He and Rowan had been eating fish guts on fires of driftwood, whatever they could find. He hadn't even a coin to send a letter to his wife and daughters—and if he had, he'd have bought a meal with it. His eyes brightened as if his fever had returned.

"That messenger, Rowan. He came on a horse, didn't he?"

Rowan opened his mouth to reply, but his father was already walking to the tavern where they'd seen the man arrive. Thomas had to thump a stable boy to get the horse, but he and his son were thin and the animal was grain-fed, able to carry them both. They passed the dumbfounded messenger as he walked back just a little while later. The fishermen hooted with laughter at the man's appalled expression as he watched his horse ridden away, slapping their knees and holding on to each other to stay upright.

CHAPTER 21

In his rooms in the White Tower, Derry came awake by grabbing the hand that had touched him on the shoulder. Before he was even fully aware, he had a blade against the shocked face of his servant, pressing a line in the cheek below the eye. As quick as he had moved, he took a moment longer to understand he was not under attack, and he put the blade away with a muttered apology. His servant's hands were shaking as the man lit a candle and placed it under a glass funnel to spread the light.

"I'm sorry, Hallerton, I'm . . . not in my right mind at the moment. I see assassins everywhere."

"I understand, sir," Hallerton replied, still pale with fear. "I would not have woken you, but you said to come if there was news of Lord Suffolk."

The older man broke off as Derry swung his legs over the bed and stood up. He was fully dressed, having collapsed on to the blankets just a few hours before.

"Well? Spit it out, then, man. What news?"

"He's taken, sir. Arrested by Cardinal Beaufort's men as he tried to report to Parliament."

Derry blinked, his mind still foggy from sleep.

"Oh, for Christ's *sake*. I sent him a warning, Hallerton! What on earth was he thinking to come to London now?" He rubbed his face, staring into nothing while he thought. "Do we know where they took him?"

His servant shook his head, and Derry frowned, thinking hard.

"Fetch me a bowl of water and the pot, would you?"

"Yes, sir. Will you be needing me to shave you this morning?"

"The way your hands are shaking? No, not today. I'll shave myself, make myself neat for Speaker Tresham. Send a runner to his offices in Westminster announcing me. No doubt the old spider is already up and doing this morning. It is still morning?"

"It is, sir," Hallerton replied, searching under the bed for the porcelain pot waiting there, already quarter-full with dark urine. Derry groaned to himself. He'd gone to bed with the first light of the sun in the sky. It felt as if he'd hardly slept at all, yet he had to be alert, or Tresham and Beaufort would have their scapegoat. What *had* William been thinking to come meekly into their hands? The trouble was that Derry knew the man's pride well enough. Suffolk wouldn't run, even from charges of high treason. In his own way, William was as much an innocent lamb as the king himself, but he was surrounded now by wolves. Derry had no illusions as to the seriousness of the charges. His friend would be torn apart unless Derry could save him.

"Stop fiddling around with the damned pot, Hallerton! And forget Tresham. Where is the king this morning?"

"In his chambers here, sir," his servant replied, worried at the wooly dullness of his master. "He remains abed and his servants say he is still suffering with an ague. I believe his wife is with him, or close by."

"Good. Announce me there instead. I will need the fountainhead if I'm to find a way through for William. Go, man! I don't need you to watch me piss."

Derry placed the pot on the blankets and sighed in relief as he urinated into it. Hallerton left quickly, calling for other servants to attend the spymaster. He raced down the steps of the White Tower and out across the open sward beyond, slowing only a fraction as he passed marching files of heavily armed soldiers. The Tower of London was a maze of buildings and paths, and Hallerton was sweating by the time he reached the king's personal chambers and announced the imminent arrival of his master to the servants there. He was still arguing with the steward of the royal bedchamber when Derry came up panting behind him.

"Master Brewer!" the king's steward said loudly. "I have been explaining to your servant that His Royal Highness King Henry is unwell and cannot be disturbed."

Derry went past them both, simply pressing a hand onto the steward's chest to hold him back against the wall. Two stern-looking soldiers watched his approach and stepped deliberately into his way. Derry had a sudden thought of Lord York attempting to reach the king in Windsor and he almost laughed.

"Step aside, lads. I have standing orders to be allowed to reach the king, day or night. You know me, and you know that is true."

The soldiers shifted uncomfortably. They looked past Derry to the king's steward, who folded his arms in clear refusal. It was an impasse, and Derry turned in relief at the sound of a woman's voice on the floor above.

"What goes on? Is that Master Brewer?" Margaret called as she came halfway down a set of oak stairs, peering at the group of men gathered there. She was barefoot, dressed in a long white sleeping robe with her hair tousled. After a moment of dull shock, all the men looked at their boots rather than stare at the queen in such a state of undress.

"Your Highness, I don't . . ." the king's steward began, still looking down.

Derry spoke over him, suddenly feeling that time pressed on them all.

"Suffolk has been arrested, my lady. I need to speak to the king."

Margaret's mouth opened in surprise, and the king's steward stopped talking. The queen saw the worry in Derry and made a quick decision.

"Thank you, gentlemen," Margaret said in clear dismissal. "Come, Master Brewer. I will wake my husband."

Derry was too concerned even to enjoy his small victory over the steward and clattered up the steps behind Margaret. As they walked down a long corridor, he passed rooms that stank of bitter chemicals. Derry shuddered as the air seemed to thicken. The king's chambers smelled of sickness, and he sipped his breath to avoid drawing in too much of the bad air.

"Wait here, Master Brewer," Margaret said. "I will see if he is awake."

She stepped into the king's personal rooms, and Derry was left to kick his heels in the corridor. He noticed two more soldiers watching him suspiciously from one end of it, but Margaret's permission put him beyond their reach in all ways. He ignored them while he waited.

By the time the door opened again, Derry had readied his arguments. They died in his throat as he saw the pale figure of the king sitting up in bed, his thin white chest wrapped in a cloak. Derry could still remember the bull-like frame of the boy's father, and sadness came in a surge as he closed the door and faced King Henry.

Derry knelt, with his head bowed. Margaret stood watching him, her hands writhing together as she waited for Henry to acknowledge his spymaster. When the silence stretched unbroken, it was she who spoke at last.

"Please stand, Master Brewer. You said Lord William has been arrested. On what charge?"

Derry rose slowly and dared to step closer. Without looking away from the king, he replied, searching for some spark of life that would show Henry was aware and understood.

"For high treason, my lady. Cardinal Beaufort's men arrested him when he came back from Kent last night. I'm certain Tresham is behind it. He said as much to me a few days ago. I told him then that it was a charge that could lead only to disaster." He stepped closer still, within arm's reach of the king. "Your Grace? We cannot let William de la Pole go to trial. I feel York's hand in this. Tresham and Beaufort will put Lord Suffolk to the question. On such a charge, there are no protections. They will insist on proving the truth with hot irons."

He waited a beat, but Henry's eyes remained blank and guileless. For an instant, Derry believed he saw something like compassion, though he could equally have imagined it.

"Your Grace?" he said again. "I fear this is a plot aimed at the royal line itself. If they force Lord Suffolk to reveal the details of the truce in France, he will say the truth, that it was by royal order. After the losses there, such an admission will aid their cause, Your Grace." He took a slow breath, forcing himself to ask a question that shamed him. "Do you understand, Your Grace?"

For a time, he thought the king would not respond, but then Henry sighed and spoke, his voice slurred.

"William would not betray me, Master Brewer. If the charge is false, he should be released. Is that the truth?"

"It *is*, Your Grace! They seek to blame and kill Lord Suffolk, to placate the mobs of London. Please. You know William cannot be put to trial."

"No trial? Very well, Master Brewer. I know . . ."

The king's voice faded, and he stared with dull eyes. Derry cleared his throat, but the face remained utterly still and slack, as if its guiding spirit had been snuffed.

"Your Grace?" Derry said, glancing up at Margaret in confusion.

She shook her head, tears filling her eyes so that they shone.

The moment passed, and Henry seemed to return, blinking and smiling as if nothing had happened.

"I am weary now, Master Brewer. I would like to sleep. The learned doctor says I must sleep if I am to be well again."

Derry looked at Margaret and saw her anguish as she gazed down on her husband. It was a moment of shocking intimacy, and it surprised him to see something like love there as well. For a moment, their eyes met.

"What do you need from your king, Master Brewer?" Margaret asked softly. "Can he order William's release?"

"He could, if they would honor it," Derry said, rubbing his eyes. "I don't doubt the order will be delayed, or William taken to some dark place where I can't reach him. In Westminster, Tresham and Beaufort have a great deal of power, if only because Parliament pays the guards. Please, my lady, let me think for a moment. It is not enough to send a written order to free him."

He hated to speak of Henry while the man himself sat there and watched him like a trusting child, but there was no help for it.

"Is His Royal Highness well enough to travel? If the king took a barge to Westminster, he could walk into the cells and no one would dare to stop him. We could free William today, before they have done too much harm."

To his sorrow, Margaret shook her head, reaching down to touch Derry's shoulder, then drawing him aside. Henry's head turned to watch them, smiling innocently.

"He has . . . suffered this . . . vagueness for days now. He is as well as I have seen him, at this moment," Margaret whispered. "There has to be some other way to get William out of their clutches. What about Lord Somerset? Is he not in London? He and William are friends. Somerset would not allow William to be tortured, no matter what charges they have brought."

"I wish it were that simple. They have him, Your Majesty! I can hardly believe he was such a fool as to give himself up to them, but you know William. You know his sense of honor and his pride. I gave him the chance to run, but instead he came meekly, trusting that his captors were men of honor themselves. They are not, my lady. They will either bring down a powerful lord who supports the king, or . . . the king himself. I don't know yet exactly what they intend, but William . . ."

His voice trailed off as a fresh thought struck him.

"There *is* a way to avoid a trial, I think! Wait . . . yes. They cannot put him to the question if he admits guilt immediately, to all the charges."

Margaret's brow furrowed as she listened.

"But does that not play into their hands, Master Brewer? That is surely what this Tresham and Cardinal Beaufort want!"

To her confusion, she saw Derry smile, his eyes glittering. It was not a pleasant expression.

"It will do for now. It will give me a little more time and that is what I lack most. I have to find where they have put him. I have to reach him. Your Highness, thank you. I will fetch Lord Somerset from his home. I know he will help me and he has his own men-at-arms. Only pray that William has not been tortured already, for his honor and his damned pride."

He knelt again at the bedside of his sovereign, bowing his head to address Henry once more.

"Your Grace? Your palace at Westminster is but a short boat's journey away. It would help William if you were there. It would help me."

Henry blinked at him.

"No beer from you, Brewer! Eh? Doctor Allworthy says I must sleep."

Derry closed his eyes in frustration.

"As you say, Your Grace. If it pleases you, I will leave now."

King Henry waved a hand, and Margaret saw Derry's face had grown pale and strained as he bowed slowly to her and then clattered out of the room at a run.

IN THE JEWEL TOWER, across the road from the Palace of Westminster, William paced the room, making the thick oak boards creak with every step. The room was cold and bare beyond a table and chair placed for the light to fall across it. Some perverse part of him felt it was only right that he should be confined in such a way. He had been unable to stop the French army. Though his men had butchered or maimed thousands of them, they'd still been forced back to Calais, step by bloody step. Before he'd left, he'd seen his men winching up the Calais gates, closing the ancient portcullis and lining the walls with archers. William smiled wearily to himself. At least he'd saved the archers. The rest fell on his head. He had not resisted when Tresham's men came to arrest him. His guards had touched their swords in question, but he'd shaken his head and gone quietly. A duke had protections from the king himself, and William knew he would have the chance to deny the charges against him.

Staring out of the window, he could see both the king's palace and the ancient abbey, with its octagonal Chapter House. The Commons met there, or in the Painted Chamber in the palace. William had heard talk of giving them some permanent place for their debates, but there were always more pressing issues than warm seats for men from the shires. He rubbed his temples, feeling tension and not a little fear. Only a blind man would have missed the anger and threat of violence he'd seen ever since touching the land of his birth. He'd ridden fast through Kent, at times in the same tracks as large bodies of soldiers. When he'd stopped for the night at a crossroads inn, he'd heard nothing but stories of Jack Cade and his army. The owners had thrown hostile glances William's way all evening, but whether he'd been recognized or not, no one had dared to interrupt his progress back to the capital.

Turning away from the view, William resumed his pacing, clasping his hands tightly behind his back. The charges were a farce to anyone who knew what had truly gone on that year and the one before. He was certain they would not stand, not once the king was informed. William wondered if Derry Brewer had heard of his confinement. After the warning he'd sent, it amused William to think of Derry's disgust at his decision to come home anyway, but there had been no real choice. William straightened his back. He was the commander of English soldiers in France and a duke of the Crown. For all the disasters he'd witnessed, nothing changed that. He found himself thinking of his wife, Alice. She would know nothing except the worst rumors. He wondered if his captors would let him write to her as well as to his son, John. He did not want them to worry.

William paused in his slow tread as he heard men's voices on the floors below. His mouth firmed into a hard line and the knuckles showed white on his clasped hands. He stood waiting at the top of the stairs, almost as if he were guarding the room. Without conscious thought, his right hand moved to clutch at the empty space where his sword would usually sit.

Richard of York led two other men up the stairs with boyish energy. He paused with his hand on the railing at the sight of Suffolk standing to face them as if he might attack at any moment.

"Calm yourself, William," York said softly as he came into the room. "I told you in France you'd been given a poisoned cup. Did you think I would vanish quietly to Ireland while great events played themselves out in my absence? Hardly. I've been busy these last few months. I believe you have been busier still, though not perhaps with such good results."

York crossed the room to stare out at the rising sun and the mists burning off around Westminster. Behind him, Sir William Tresham and Cardinal Beaufort stepped into the tower space. York waved two fingers in their direction without looking round.

"You know Tresham and Beaufort, of course. I suggest you listen to what they have to say, William. That is my best advice to you."

York smiled thinly, enjoying the view. There was something about high places that had always pleased him, as if God were closer than to men on the ground below.

William had noticed York's sword, of course, as well as the bollock dagger he wore thrust through his belt, with a polished pair of carved wooden testicles holding it steady. It was a stabbing blade, long and thin. William doubted York was fool enough to let him come within reach of either weapon, but he judged the distances even so. Neither Tresham nor Cardinal Beaufort was armed, as far as he could see, but William knew he was as much a prisoner as any wretch in the cells of Westminster or the Tower. The thought made him look up from his musing.

"Why have I not been taken to the Tower of London? On charges of high treason? I wonder, Richard, if it is because you know these accusations sit on weak foundations. I have done nothing on my own. It was never possible for *one* man to arrange a truce with France, however it turned out." His mind flashed to Derry Brewer and he shook his head, sick of all the games and promises.

No one answered him. The three men stood patiently until two heavyset soldiers trudged up the stairs. They wore mail and grubby tabards, as if they had been called from other duties. William noticed that they carried a stained canvas sack between them. It clinked as they rested it on the wooden floor and then stood to attention.

Cardinal Beaufort cleared his throat, and William turned to the man, hiding his distaste. The king's great-uncle looked the part, with his shaven pate and long, white fingers held together as if in prayer. Yet the man had been lord chancellor to two kings and was descended himself from Edward the Third, through John of Gaunt. Beaufort had been the one who sentenced Joan of Arc to death by fire, and William knew there was no kindness in the old man. He suspected that of the three, Beaufort was his true captor. The presence of York was a clear statement of the cardinal's loyalties. William could not keep a sneer from his face as Beaufort spoke in a voice made soft by decades of prayer and honey wine.

"You stand accused of the most serious crimes, Lord William. I would have thought an aspect of humility and penance would suit you more than this feigned blustering. If you are brought to trial, I am sorry to say I do not doubt the outcome. There are too many witnesses willing to speak against you."

William frowned as the three men exchanged glances before Beaufort went on. They'd discussed his fate before—that much was obvious. He tensed his jaw, determined to resist their conspiracy.

"Your name appears on all the papers of state, my lord," Beaufort said. "The failed truce, the original marriage papers from Tours, the orders to defend Normandy against French incursion. The people of England cry out for justice, Lord Suffolk—and your life must answer for your treasons."

The cardinal had that white softness of flesh William had seen before, from a life of cloisters and the Mass. Yet the black eyes were hard as they weighed him and found him wanting. He stared back, letting his contempt show. Beaufort shook his head sadly.

"What a bad year it has been, William! I know you for a good man, a pious man. I wish it had not come to this. Yet the forms must be observed. I will ask you to confess to your crimes. You will no doubt refuse and then, I am afraid, my colleagues and I will retire. You will be secured to that chair and these two men will persuade you to sign your name to the mortal sin of treason."

Listening to the soft voice drone on, William swallowed painfully, his heart pounding. His certainties were crumbling. York was smiling wryly, not looking at him. Tresham at least looked uncomfortable, but there was no doubting their resolve. William could not help looking over to the canvas sack as it sat there, dreading his first sight of the tools within.

"I demand to speak to the king," William said, pleased that his voice came out calm and apparently unafraid.

When Tresham replied, the old lawyer's voice was as dry as if he was discussing a difficult point from the statutes.

"I'm afraid a charge of high treason does not allow that, my lord," he said. "You will appreciate that a man who has conspired *against* the Crown can hardly be allowed to approach the Crown. You must first be put to the question. When every detail . . . and all your confederates have been named, you will sign the confession. You will then be bound over for trial, though as you know it will be no more than a formality. The king will not be involved at any stage, my lord, unless, of course, he chooses to attend your execution."

"Unless . . ." York said. He paused as he stood staring out of the window over Westminster. "Unless the loss of France can be laid at the feet of the king himself, William. You and I both know the truth of it.

Tell me, how many men came at your request to bolster your forces in Normandy? How many stood with you against the French king? Yet there are eight *thousand* soldiers in the counties around London, William, all to ease a king's terror of rebellion. If those men had been allowed to cross to France when you needed them, do you think you would be here now? Would we have lost Normandy if you'd had twelve thousand in the field?"

William glowered at York, anger building in him as he saw where the man was aiming his thrust.

"Henry is my *anointed* king, my lord York," he said slowly and with force. "You will not have petty accusations from me, if that is what you're after. It is not my place to judge the actions of the King of England, nor yours, nor this cardinal, his *uncle*, nor Tresham, for all his lawyer's tricks. Do you understand?"

"Yes, I do," York said, turning to him with an odd smile. "I understand that there are only two paths, William. Either the king loses you, his most powerful supporter, or . . . he loses *everything*. Either way, the kingdom and my cause will be strengthened immeasurably. Face the truth, Suffolk! The king is a boy too weak and sickly to rule. I am not the first to say it, and, believe *me*, it is being muttered now in every hamlet, town, and city across England. The losses in France have only confirmed what some of us knew since he was a child. We waited, William! Out of respect and loyalty to his father and the Crown, we waited. And look where that has brought us!" York paused, finding calm once again. "To this room, William, and to you. Bear the guilt on your own and die, or name your king as the architect of this failure. It is your choice, and it matters not to me."

In the face of York's poisonous triumph, William sagged, resting one hand on the table to support his weight.

"I see," William said, his voice bleak. For all York's words, he had no choice at all. He seated himself at the table. His hands trembled as they rested on the polished wood.

"I will not confess to treasons I have not committed. I will not name my king, or any other man. Torture me if you must; it will make no difference. And may God forgive you, because *I* will not."

In exasperation, York gestured to the two soldiers. One of them crouched by his bag and began unrolling it, revealing the neat lines of pincers, awls, and saws within.

CHAPTER 22

More than thirty of the fifty-five lords of England had property around the center of London, Derry knew. Given an hour or two, he could have listed each house, as well as the men and women he had working for him. Yet Somerset was William's personal friend. More importantly, Derry knew he was in London that day, rather than his estates in the southwest. He'd had another Thames boatman come close to bursting his lungs to reach Somerset's town house along the river, drawing up on the wide water landing. Derry had almost got himself killed by Somerset's guards there before he'd identified himself and raced with them through the gardens. Somerset had been writing letters and stood to listen with a quill held in his fingers. Though every passing moment was an agony, Derry had forced himself to explain clearly what he needed. Halfway through, the diminutive earl clapped him on the back and shouted for his stewards.

"Tell me the rest on the way, Brewer," Somerset said briskly, walking down to the water landing.

The earl was forty-four years of age, with no spare flesh on his frame and the energy of a man twenty years younger. Derry had to scurry to keep up with him, and despite the earl's lack of height and amiable look, he noted how Somerset's guards still jumped when he gave orders. The earl's personal barge was being poled along the river barely an hour after Derry had arrived.

They grounded it at Westminster dock and Derry found himself breathing hard as he counted the men Somerset had summoned. It looked like his entire personal guard. There were six men on the barge with them, while another dozen had been told to make their best speed to Westminster on the roads. They had run a good two miles around the bend of the river that flowed through London, plunging through filthy streets to arrive spattered and panting only a brief time after their master's barge drew up.

Derry was impressed, despite himself. Somerset was in a froth of indignation at the thought of a threat to his friend, and yet he turned to Derry with a questioning look as they strode toward the river gate of the palace.

"Stay close, my lord, if you would," Derry said. "I will need your authority for this."

Having eighteen armed men at his back was satisfying and worrying at the same time. It was not beyond possibility that Parliament would react badly to an armed invasion of their sanctum. Derry felt his heart thump in anticipation as he approached the first guards, already yelling for their superiors and fumbling their pikes and swords. Somerset cracked his neck with a sharp gesture, his expression both confident and eager. The two men were from very different worlds, but with William de la Pole in danger, both of them were spoiling for a fight.

MARGARET HEARD her name called when she was in the middle of another furious conversation with the king's physician. She broke off on the instant, rushing back to her husband's rooms. She gaped as she saw Henry with his legs on the floor and two boots waiting to be put on. He had pulled a long white shirt over his bony chest and found woolen leggings.

"Margaret? Can you help me with these? I can't pull them on myself."

She knelt quickly, yanking the thick wool up his legs before taking up one of the boots and working his foot into it.

"Are you feeling better?" she said, looking up at him. There were dark circles under his eyes, but he seemed more alert than she had seen him in days.

"A little, I think. Derry was here, Margaret. He wanted me to come to Westminster."

Her face crumpled, and she hid her expression by bowing her head and concentrating on the second boot.

"I know, Henry. I was with you when he came. Are you well enough to rise?"

"I think so. I can take a boat and that will not be much of a trial, though the river is cold. Would you ask my servants to bring blankets for me? I will need to be well wrapped against the wind."

Margaret finished pulling on the second boot and rubbed her eyes clear. Her husband put out an arm and she helped to raise him to his feet, tugging the leggings higher and fastening his belt. He looked thin and pale, but his eyes were clear, and she could have wept just to see him standing. She saw a robe hanging on a hook across the room and fetched it for him, placing it around his shoulders. He patted her hand as it touched him.

"Thank you, Margaret. You are very kind to me."

"You honor me. I know you are not well. To see you rise for your friend—"

She broke off before the mingled sadness and joy overwhelmed her.

Taking her husband's arm, she went out into the corridor, surprising the guards as they came to attention.

Master Allworthy heard the noise and came out of the next room along, holding some twisted piece of the contraption Margaret had kicked earlier on. His thunderous expression cleared into amazement as he saw the king. The doctor lowered himself to kneel on the stone floor.

"Your Grace! I am so very pleased to see this improvement in you. Have you moved your bowels, Your Grace, if I may make so bold with such a question? Such an event will sometimes clear a confused mind. It was the green liquor, I am certain, as well as the wormwood tapers. Are you to take a turn in the gardens? I would not like you to exert yourself too much. Your Grace's health is balanced on a hair. If I may suggest—"

Henry seemed willing to listen to the babbling doctor forever, but Margaret's patience wore thin. She spoke over him.

"King Henry is going to the river gate, Master Allworthy. If you'd step out of the way instead of blocking the entire corridor, we might get past you."

In response, the doctor tried to bow and press himself against the wall at the same time. He could not help staring at the king as Margaret helped her husband along the corridor, and she shuddered under that professional inspection. Perhaps her glare kept the man quiet; she neither knew nor cared. She and Henry descended the stairs and the king's chamber steward came rushing to greet them.

"Have the barge made ready," Margaret said firmly, before he could object. "And have blankets brought, as many as you can find."

For once, the steward did not reply, only bowing and retreating at speed. The news spread quickly that the king was about and the wing of the Tower seemed to fill with bustling servants carrying armfuls of thick cloth. Henry stared glassily as his wife brought him into the breeze. She felt him shiver and she took a blanket from a young woman heading for the royal barge, draping it over Henry's shoulders. He clutched it to his chest, looking sick and frail.

Margaret held his hand as he stepped onto the rocking barge and lowered himself onto the ornate bench seat on the open deck, unaware or uncaring as crowds began to gather on the banks all around. Margaret could see men waving their hats and the sound of cheering began to grow as the locals realized the royal family were coming out and could be seen. Servants piled more blankets around the king to keep him warm, and Margaret found she too was shivering, so that she was grateful for the thick wool coverings. The bargemen cast off, and the sweeps dipped into the current, taking them out onto the fast-flowing waters of the Thames.

The journey was strangely peaceful, with just the sound of the oars and shouts from the banks as urchins and young men and women ran along with them, keeping pace as best they could. As they rounded the great bend in the river and sighted the Palace of Westminster and the docks there, Margaret felt Henry's grip tighten on her small hand. He turned to her, wrapped in the layers of wool.

"I am sorry I have been . . . unwell, Margaret. There are times when I feel as if I have fallen, am still falling. I cannot describe it. I wish I could. I will try to be strong for you, but if it comes on me again . . . I cannot hold it back."

Margaret found herself weeping once more and rubbed her eyes, angry at herself. Her husband was a good man, she knew. She raised the bandaged hand and kissed it gently, weaving the fingers into hers. It seemed to comfort him.

DERRY MOVED as fast as he could, using his lamp to peer into the dark spaces. He had an idea that Tresham would summon men to stop his search as soon as he was told. Even the presence of the Earl of Somerset might not be enough to prevent Derry's arrest if he refused to obey the Speaker, or perhaps Cardinal Beaufort. It didn't help that he'd left Somerset behind some dozen rooms ago.

Derry was still finding it hard to believe the size of the warren under the Palace of Westminster. He'd searched the main cells easily enough, but William wasn't there to be found. The line of iron-barred rooms was just one small part of the floors and basements beneath the palace, some so far beneath the level of the river that they stank of mildew and the walls seeped black spores and dribbling green liquid. Derry expected to hear shouts telling him to stop at any moment and he'd begun to think he'd set himself an impossible task. Given a hundred men and a week, he could have searched every part of the storerooms and the openings to sewers that gusted fetid vapors when he yanked at the doors. William could be anywhere and Derry was beginning to wonder if Tresham hadn't guessed he would try to find him and moved the duke to some other location.

Derry shook his head as he ran, arguing with himself in silence. The Commons Parliament had little power outside the Palace of Westminster, even less outside London. Away from the Painted Chamber, or the Chapter House, they had no real authority beyond business in the king's name. In a conflict with the king himself, they would hardly dare to use a royal property. Derry skidded to a stop, raising his iron lamp to illuminate a long, low vault that stretched away into the distance, far beyond the range of his small light.

Tresham was clever, Derry knew. If he kept William long enough to secure his confession, it didn't really matter where they'd put him. Derry had no illusions about William's ability to resist. The duke was a strong man in every sense, too strong perhaps. Derry had seen torture before. His fear was that his friend would be permanently crippled or driven insane by the time his will failed at last.

He was halfway through the vaulted room, ducking his head to miss an ancient arch, when he stopped again and turned to two of Somerset's guards.

"Come away, lads. I want to try another place."

He began to run back along the way he'd come, weighing his chances. He wouldn't be allowed back into Parliament, once he left the main palace. Tresham would surely see to that. The old spider was probably organizing men to arrest him as he came out, with Derry rushing right into their arms.

Derry headed up a rickety stairwell, slipping as a step cracked and fell to the floor below. God, the whole place was damp and rotten! One of the men with him swore and yelped as he put his foot through the hole. Derry didn't stop to help him out and instead rushed through the floor above and up another half flight to the better-lit corridors by the cells. He heard angry voices before he could see who was making the noise, though his heart sank.

Tresham caught sight of Derry first, as he'd been staring in that direction. The lawyer's face was brick-red with fury and he raised a hand to point.

"There he is! Arrest that man!" Tresham shouted.

Soldiers began to move, and Derry looked desperately to Somerset. He could have blessed the earl when he spoke with only an instant's hesitation, though his reputation and life were at stake.

"Stand back from him!" Somerset roared at the parliamentary guards. "Master Brewer is in my custody. I am on the king's business, and you are not to impede or hinder him."

Tresham's guards hesitated, unable to decide who had the authority. Derry had not stopped moving, and he sauntered past the guards and right up to Tresham in the moment of stillness.

"William, Lord Suffolk," Derry said, watching the other man closely. "Is he in the Chapter House? Shall I search the abbey itself, or would it be sacrilege to torture a man on consecrated ground?" He was watching Tresham closely as the man relaxed, lines smoothing around his eyes. "Or the Jewel Tower? Would you have had the gall to put him where you held me?"

"You have no authority here, Brewer! How *dare* you put questions to me!" Tresham sputtered indignantly.

Derry smiled, satisfied.

"I think that's where he is, Lord Somerset. I'll run across the road and see."

"Guards!" Tresham roared. "Arrest him now or, by *God*, I'll see you all swing."

It was enough of a threat to decide the impasse. They reached for Derry, but Somerset's men blocked the passage with their swords drawn. Derry ran, leaving them all behind.

As he came out into the main halls and the light of the afternoon, he heard horns blow down by the river. The heralds sounded only on state occasions or to announce a royal visit. Derry stopped, unable to believe it could be Henry. Could Margaret have come alone? She had almost no formal authority, but there were few men who would risk offending the Queen of England and, through her, the king. Derry shook his head, caught in indecision. He stood and practically quivered, pulled in two directions. No. He *had* to keep moving.

He pelted on toward sunlight, sprinting the length of the palace and passing into the vast beamed space of Westminster Hall. Derry didn't pause for the bustling crowds there, threading through them all, then across the road with the abbey shadow falling on him as he went. He passed hawkers and rich men enjoying the sun, carriages and walkers both, leaving the smell of the river far behind.

As he went, he fretted. He was on his own. Even if he was right, he knew William would surely be guarded. Derry's mind raced as fast as his feet, panting hard as he came to the moat of the Jewel Tower. The drawbridge was down, at least. At the sight of it, he almost doubted his initial certainty that William was inside. Yet Tresham was too canny to give away the location of his prisoner by making the place a fortress. Derry shot past a single guard and then came to a halt.

Two men faced him at the main door. Two solid soldiers who had watched him run across the road from the palace and had their swords drawn and ready. Seeing their expressions, Derry knew he was done, at least for a moment. He'd have to run back and fetch Somerset. No doubt Tresham would have summoned more soldiers by then, enough to turf them all out of the palace or straight into the cells. Speed and surprise had brought him only so far—and not far enough. Derry swore and one of the guards raised his head in a scornful jerk, agreeing with his assessment.

Derry filled his lungs, cupping his hands around his mouth.

"William Pole!" he bellowed at the top of his lungs. "Confess! Throw yourself on the king's mercy. Give me time, you stupid *sod*!"

The guards gaped at him as Derry panted and then repeated himself, over and over. The Jewel Tower was only three floors high and he was certain he could be heard, if William was being held inside.

Derry sagged as a troop of guards came jogging into view from over the road. They were not Somerset's men, and he made no protest as they took him into custody and half dragged him back to the palace over the road.

WILLIAM HAD BITTEN his lower lip right through. It bled freely, leaving trails of blood on the wooden table that one of the two men mopped up at intervals, his face blank of anything except a slight irritation. Tresham, Beaufort, and York had waited until William was tied securely to a chair, then left him alone with the pair of men. York had left last, raising his hand in farewell with something like regret on his face.

William had been horrified to see the two soldiers set about their work with a relaxed and casual air he still found hard to believe. They were not silent, and they made no threats. Instead, they chatted idly as they brought various devices into view, each one designed to rip away a man's dignity and will. He'd learned that the older man was Ted and the younger, James. James was something of an apprentice to Ted, it seemed, still learning the trade. The older man often paused to explain what he was doing and why it worked, while William only wanted to scream. In a strange way, he was almost an observer, a thing to be worked upon rather than another man.

At the start, they'd asked him only if he was right- or left-handed. William had told them the truth and Ted laid out a set of nasty-looking vices that could be screwed down until his fingers broke. They cut his wedding ring off with a pair of clippers, tucking it into his pocket for him. They'd chosen that finger to attach the first screw and wound it down, ignoring his hissing breath.

William had begun to pray in Latin as the finger burst all along its length, looking as if a seam had ripped. He'd thought that was agony enough until the bone cracked with another two turns, bringing the plates together with the broken flesh crushed between. The two men took their time attaching the others, winding each one farther shut at intervals as they discussed some whore down at the docks and what she would do for a few pennies. James claimed to have shown her things she'd never known before and Ted told him not to waste his breath lying, or his money on getting the pox. It touched off a furious argument, with William the unwilling witness, bound and helpless between them.

His left hand throbbed in time with his heart; he could feel it.

They'd sat him at the table with his hands free on the wood, passing the ropes around his chest. He had tried to jerk his hands away at first, but they'd held him too firmly. He looked down now at the swollen, purpling flesh, seeing a spur of bone sticking out of his smallest finger. He'd chewed the marrow from chicken bones in his life and the picture of his hand with the dreadful little contraptions attached was somehow unreal, not his hand at all.

William shook his head, breathing the Pater Noster, the Ave Maria, the Nicene Creed, mumbling lines he had learned as a boy, with his tutor taking a whip to him if he stumbled over a single syllable.

"Credo in unum Deum!" he said, gasping. *"Patrem omni . . . potentem! Factorem caeli . . . et terrae."*

He'd taken wounds in battle that hadn't hurt as much. He tried to list them in his mind, as well as how they'd occurred. He'd once had a gash branded shut with a hot iron and, though he could not understand it, his nose filled with the same smell of burning flesh that he thought he'd forgotten, making him retch weakly against the ropes.

The two men paused, with Ted holding a hand up to interrupt his companion when he asked a question. William's senses swam in pain, but he thought he heard a voice he knew. He'd seen dying men suffer terrifying visions in the past and he tried to close his ears against the sound at first, believing in his terror that he was hearing the first whispers of an angel, come to take him.

"Confess!" he heard clearly, the voice muffled by the stones all around.

William raised his head, tempted crazily to ask his torturers if they had heard it as well. The words were being shouted at the top of someone's voice and with each repetition, different parts were lost. William pieced it together, crying out in surprise and pain as Ted lost his vague look of incomprehension and remembered to tighten the screws once more. Another bone cracked, sending a spray of blood across the wooden surface. William felt tears come from his eyes, though it only increased his anger at the thought of such men thinking they saw him weep.

He took a deep, shuddering breath. He knew Derry's voice. No one else called him William Pole. It broke his heart to consider giving in to the two men, but the thought of it opened the door and his resolve vanished like wax in a furnace.

"Very well . . . *gentlemen*," he said, panting. "I confess to it all. Bring me your parchment and I will sign my name."

The younger man looked astonished, but Ted shrugged and began to unwind the screws, wiping each one down with great care and applying oil to the mechanisms so that they would not rust in the bag. William glanced down at the open roll of thick cloth and shuddered at the things he saw there. They had only begun his torment.

Ted cleared his throat, wiping the table clean of blood and lifting William's crushed hand onto a cloth to one side. With care, the man placed a sheet of calfskin vellum where William could reach it. From his bag of equipment, he brought an inkpot and quill, dipping the nib for him when he saw William's right hand was shaking too violently and might upset the ink.

William read the accusations of high treason with a feeling of nausea. His son John would hear. His wife would live the rest of her life in the shadow of such a shameful admission. It was a lot to ask to trust Derry Brewer with his honor, but he did, and he signed.

"I told you he would!" James said triumphantly. "You said a duke would hold out for a day or two, maybe more!"

Ted looked disgusted, but he handed over a silver groat to his young companion.

"I had money on you, old son," he told William, shaking his head.

"Remove these ropes," William replied.

Ted chuckled.

"Not yet, my lord. We had a fellow once who threw his own confession on the very fire we'd heated for him. Had to start it all again! No, mate. You'll abide while James takes it to the men who asked for it. After that, you're no concern of mine."

With mocking ceremony, he handed over the signed sheet to James, who rolled it up and placed it in a tube, tying the ends with a clean black ribbon.

"Don't dawdle now, lad!" Ted called after him as he left. "There's daylight still, and I'm dry—and you're buying!"

TAKEN BY FORCE at a slower pace, Derry was struck once more at the sheer size of the Palace of Westminster. The guards who marched him back into the building were determined to bring him straight through, but it was still a different route from the one he had taken before. Derry passed courtrooms and chambers with vaulted ceilings like cathedrals. By the time they'd passed the echoing chamber where the Lords met, he was deeply glum. His search for Suffolk had never had a chance of succeeding in the time he'd been given. All he had was what he'd read in Tresham's furious face and he was not certain, could not be certain. An army could search the vast palace and never find a single man.

Ahead of his small group of guards, Derry saw another cluster of people swirling in something like agitation. He'd been taken right through to the other side of the palace, and as he was shoved closer, he saw to his astonishment that the river gate was open, a bright bar of sunlight gleaming like heaven. Derry stumbled on the uneven floor, his attention drawn to the two figures entering the palace. One of his guards cursed as they heaved him onward, then a mutter of awe went through them.

They brought Derry to the rear of a group facing the outer gate.

Every man there was down on one knee, or bowing deeply as the King and Queen of England entered their domain. Derry began to smile, looking round to see Tresham and Cardinal Beaufort among them. His moving gaze sharpened at the sight of Lord York to one side. It was no surprise to find the duke had not yet gone to Ireland, but it confirmed some of Derry's suspicions about the plot against William Pole.

King Henry looked thin and white. Derry saw him pass a thick blanket from his shoulders to a servant, revealing simple clothes with no ornament. The queen seemed to be holding his arm in support and Derry's heart went out to her, blessing Margaret for bringing her husband. His mind began to race again, weighing his chances.

Derry turned to the guard who held him. The man was trying to bow in the king's presence without removing his grip from the felon he'd been charged with capturing.

"There are no cardinals on a chessboard, but a king takes your bishop, if you follow me. Now, then. I'm on the king's business, so *take* your hand off my arm."

The guard stood back, unnerved by the presence of the king and simply wanting to remain unnoticed by so many men of power. Derry cracked his neck and stretched his back, the only one standing up straight. Other men were beginning to rise, Tresham and Cardinal Beaufort among them.

"Your Royal Highness, it is a great honor to see you well," Tresham said.

Henry blinked in his direction, and Derry was sure he saw Margaret tighten her grip.

"Where is William de la Pole, Lord Suffolk?" Henry said clearly.

Derry could have kissed him as a ripple went around the group. Some of them were clearly puzzled, but the expressions of Beaufort, York, and Tresham told Derry all he needed to know.

"Your Grace!" Derry called.

Dozens of men turned to see who was speaking, and Derry used the opportunity to walk through the crowd. His guards were left grasping air behind him, furious that he had brought such attention on them.

"Your Grace, Lord Suffolk has been accused of treason against the Crown," Derry said.

Tresham was hissing instructions to another man and Derry went on quickly before the Speaker could regain the initiative. In his mind, he could see how it had to go, if he could find the words.

"Lord Suffolk has thrown himself on your mercy, Your Grace. He submits to the king's will, in this and all things." Derry saw only blankness in Henry's face and had the sickening sense that the man hadn't heard him. He looked desperately to Margaret, silently pleading for her help as he kept speaking. "If you summoned his peers, Your Grace, you could decide his fate yourself."

Cardinal Beaufort raised himself up then, his voice ringing out.

"Lord Suffolk will be brought to trial, Your Grace. It is a matter for the courts of Parliament."

As he spoke, Derry saw a grubby young man come racing through the crowd from the back. He carried a tube tied with a black ribbon and whispered to Tresham before bowing and backing away. Tresham shot a triumphant glance in Derry's direction, raising what he had been given.

"Lord Suffolk has confessed, Your Grace. He must—"

"He has thrown himself on your mercy! He submits to the royal will!" Derry said firmly and clearly, his voice ringing out across them all.

The phrases he used were as old as the building around them, a call for the king himself to rule on the fate of one of his lords. Derry was desperate, but he could not let Tresham and Beaufort assert their authority. The king was on the board. The *queen* was on the board as well, he realized, as Margaret began to speak.

MARGARET SHOOK with the effort of holding back tears. She had never been so terrified in her life as she was facing that array of powerful men. She'd seen the light fade in her husband's eyes. The river trip had exhausted him, his body and mind as weak as a child. He had struggled against it, with thin muscles twisting in his arms and back as he left the barge and walked into the palace. He had called for William with the last whispers of his will, and she could feel him stagger against her as the men shouted and gamed for position. She listened closely to Derry's words, knowing that at least he would be protecting William.

For an age, Margaret waited for Henry to speak again. He said nothing, just blinking slowly. Her throat was dry, her heart hammering against her dress, but she could feel his coldness through the cloth, and there was no one else.

"My husband . . ." she began. Her voice came out like a creaking door, and she stopped and cleared her throat to try again. At one time or another, half the men there had tried to manipulate her husband. God forgive her, but she had to do the same.

"King Henry will retire to his chambers now," she said clearly. "It is his command that William, Lord Suffolk, be brought to him. Lord Suffolk has submitted to the king's will. The king alone bears the responsibility."

She waited while the men stared at her, unsure how to take such a statement from the young Frenchwoman. No one seemed able to respond and her patience wore thin.

"Steward! His Royal Highness is still recovering from his illness. Help him."

The king's servants were more used to her authority, and they bustled around on the instant, leading Henry away from the chamber in the direction of the king's personal rooms in the palace. A great tension left the group of men, and Derry released a held breath in a long sigh. He winked at Tresham. The horse-faced lawyer could only glower as Derry strolled after the royal party. No one dared to stop him. The king's presence had changed the entire game and they were still reeling.

CHAPTER 23

Through a narrow window, Derry stared out over a cloister in the Palace of Westminster. It was cold outside, dark beyond the glass. He could see little except his bulging reflection staring back at him in gold and shadow. He sniffed and rubbed his nose, suspecting he had a cold coming on. Giving orders on behalf of the king, it had taken him two days to bring every lord in reach of London to Henry's royal chambers. At Derry's back, even the largest of the private rooms was uncomfortably crowded and warm. Fat white candles lit the stateroom from the walls, adding oily smoke to the fug of heat and sweat. In all, twenty-four men of great estate had come to witness the king's judgment on one of their own. Derry had slept for just a few hours while they rode in and he hurt with tiredness. He had done all he could. When he'd finally seen William's broken hand, he'd vowed to keep going until his heart gave out.

Lord York was there, of course, standing with six other noblemen with connections to the Neville family. Richard, Earl of Salisbury, stood at York's right shoulder, wearing a thick Scots twill that may have suited the far north, but was making him sweat profusely in the cramped confines of that room. Derry found he could watch the group in the reflection of the glass and he studied the man's son, Richard of Warwick. The young earl seemed to sense his scrutiny and suddenly looked over at him, pointing and muttering something to York. Derry didn't move, or reveal his awareness of them. Those six men continued to talk quietly among themselves, and Derry continued to watch them. Together, they represented a faction at least as powerful as the king himself. Three of them were Richards, he thought wryly: York, Salisbury, and Warwick. Married to a Neville, son and grandson of old Ralph Neville. It was a powerful little triumvirate, though the Neville clan had married its daughters and sons into every line from King Edward the Third. Derry smiled at the thought that York had given his youngest son the same name, with a shocking lack of imagination.

Against them—and he was no longer in doubt that he stood against them—Derry had Somerset among the king's allies, along with the lords Scales, Gray, Oxford, Dudley, and a dozen other men of power and influence. All who could be called in time were present that evening, some of them still travel-stained and tired from a breakneck ride to reach London. It was more than the fate of a duke that had brought them. The king's own powers had been called into question and the country was still going up in flames away from the streets around the capital.

Derry rubbed his eyes, thinking of the reports stacking up in the Tower for him to read. He recalled Margaret's promise that she would cast an eye over every vital document. It made him smile wearily. There were too many for him—and he knew how to sift the wheat from the chaff.

He turned to the room, wanting it to be over. The life of his friend was at stake, but while fine lords played at justice and vengeance, the country they ruled was falling into banditry and chaos. It galled Derry that he had known Jack Cade during his time in the army. If he could go back to that time and put a knife in the man's ribs, it would have eased his mind considerably.

"Bloody Jack Cade," he murmured to himself.

The man he remembered had been a weeping drunk, a terror with an ax and a natural bully, though he'd held no rank of note. Cade's tendency to thump his sergeants put paid to any chances of promotion from within, and as far as Derry recalled, the man had served his term and gone home with just a lattice of stripes on his back to show for it. It beggared belief to hear Cade had assembled an army for himself, roaring through hamlets and villages around London as they grew wild on success. They'd taken the head of the king's own sheriff, and Derry knew it had to be answered, hard and fast. It was almost sinful to have the king and his lords distracted at such a time. Derry vowed his own vengeance on all the men responsible, bringing calm to his disordered thoughts. Cade, York, Beaufort, the Nevilles, and bloody Tresham. He'd have them all for daring to attack the lamb.

The room fell silent as William, Lord Suffolk, was brought in. He walked upright, though his arms were manacled behind his back. Derry had been able to see him only once in the Jewel Tower and he still felt rage at the cruel injuries and indignities his friend had suffered. Suffolk was an innocent in many ways. He did not deserve the spite leveled against him. Much of the responsibility lay with Derry himself and the guilt was a heavy burden as he saw William suffer the scrutiny of the Neville lords. William's left forearm was like a leg of pork, fat and pink with splints on the fingers and all wrapped around in bandages. They'd had to find leg irons to get a set big enough to enclose his swollen flesh. Derry knew the sleeve of William's jacket had been cut along the seam just to pull it on.

The king's chancellor entered behind the prisoner, a short man with a wide forehead made larger by his receding hair. The chancellor looked around the room and pursed his lips in satisfaction as to how the lords were arrayed.

A lonely little space at the center of the room had been left for William to face his peers. As he took his place, they murmured, staring and commenting in fascination. Suffolk waited with dignity for the king, though his eyes rested briefly on Derry as they passed over the room. William's hair had been brushed by some anonymous maid. That small touch of kindness brought Derry a twinge of pain for some reason. In the midst of enemies and plots, some pot-girl had thought to take a cloth to the duke's stained clothes and a brush to his head.

There was no fanfare to announce the king, not in his private chambers. No horns sounded. Derry saw a servant come like a mouse into a cage of lions, whispering to the king's chancellor and then retiring at speed. The chancellor cleared his throat to announce the royal presence and Derry closed his eyes briefly, sending up a prayer. He'd seen King Henry often over the previous two days and found him just as vague and blank as he had the morning Derry had rushed off to find William. The surprise had been to see Margaret bear up so well under the strain. For William's sake, to save him, she'd put aside her fears. She'd given orders in her husband's name as Derry instructed, trusting him. For the task of keeping William off the executioner's block, they were allies to the end. He was only sorry Margaret could not attend the summoning. With the Neville lords and York watching, it would have been a sign of weakness to have the queen guide her husband. Yet the alternative was as bad, or worse. Derry bit his lip at the thought of Henry speaking to them. He'd risked treason himself in telling the king that he could *not* speak, not that night. Henry had agreed, of course, smiling and not seeming to understand a word. Yet there had been moments over the previous days when the king's eyes sharpened, as if some part of his soul still struggled to rise above the seas that swamped him. Derry crossed his fingers as the king came in, new sweat breaking out over the old.

A padded chair had been placed a few paces away from the right side of William, Lord Suffolk, so that Henry looked down the length of the room, seeing all those who had come at his royal command. Derry watched with his heart in his mouth as the king seated and settled himself, then looked up with amiable interest. The muttering and whispering lords fell silent at last and the king's chancellor made his voice ring out.

"His Excellent Grace: King Henry, by descent, title and grace of God, King of England and France, King of Ireland, Duke of Cornwall, and Duke of Lancaster."

Henry nodded peaceably to the man and the chancellor swelled like a bladder as he opened a scroll with a flourish and read.

"'My lords, you have gathered at the king's command to hear charges of high treason against William de la Pole, Duke of Suffolk.'"

He paused as William knelt on the stone floor with difficulty, bowing his head. Derry saw York smother a smile and would have given his eyeteeth to have that man alone to himself for an hour.

The chancellor read the list. Half the charges related to the failed truce and the responsibility for the loss of English possessions in France. Derry had tried to strike some of the wilder accusations from the record, but that was one area where he had little influence. The scroll had been prepared by Tresham and Beaufort, no doubt with York looking over their shoulders and making suggestions. It was a damning list, even before the chancellor recited charges of secret meetings with the French king and lords, with the intention of usurping the English throne.

Only the slow flush spreading across William's face as he knelt showed he was listening intently to every word. Derry clenched his jaw as the chancellor read amounts in gold that William had apparently taken in return for his support. Anyone who knew him would have scoffed at Suffolk taking bribes of any kind. Even the idea that such amounts would have become part of the record was ludicrous. Yet as Derry looked around the chamber, serious men were shaking their heads as each article, each vile calumny, was read.

"'Be it known that on the twentieth of July, in the year of our Lord fourteen hundred and forty-seven, the accused conspired in the parish of St. Sepulcher, in the ward of Farringdon, to facilitate a French invasion of these shores, with an aim to usurping the rightful throne of England. Be it also known . . .'"

It was not a trial. That was the only ray of light in the gloom, as far as Derry was concerned. He'd spent hours in argument with lawyers for Parliament and the Crown, but the king had the right to rule on a member of the peerage if the lord submitted to the king's mercy. Yet William's confession would stand, even when every man there knew how it had been obtained. The charges could not be completely revoked—that had been the deal hammered out in the small hours. To a degree, Derry had to accept Tresham's claim that the country would rise in rebellion without a scapegoat for the loss of France.

Cade's rough army was poised to enter London, no doubt waiting to hear Suffolk's fate with as much interest as any others in the kingdom. Many of Cade's recruits had known William in France. It grated like sand between Derry's teeth that none of them seemed to blame York for losing Maine and Anjou, though he had been in command at the time. Richard of York had been quick to accuse the king's supporters and, in doing so, had escaped criticism himself.

"Lord Suffolk has confessed to all charges," the chancellor finished, clearly enjoying his position at the heart of the drama that evening. He held up a scroll with a black ribbon in his other hand. Derry was only surprised the thing wasn't spotted with blood after the injuries he'd seen.

"I deny all charges, all treason!" William growled suddenly.

The silence was perfect in the chamber as all eyes fell on the kneeling man. Derry's mouth went dry. He'd discussed this with William. Having the man recant his confession was not part of it.

"You, er . . . you *deny* the charges?" the chancellor said faintly, floundering.

Even kneeling, even in manacles, William made an arresting figure as he raised his head and replied, "The charges are preposterous, the product of evil minds. I deny them utterly. I am innocent of treason. Yet I am brought low by scoundrels acting against my king and my country."

Derry wanted to shout for William to shut his mouth before he ruined them all. He saw York was smiling at the outburst, his eyes bright.

"My lord Suffolk, are you now claiming your right to trial?" the chancellor said.

Derry saw York lean forward in anticipation. He wanted to shout out, but Derry had no real right even to be in that room. He dared not speak and only closed his eyes, waiting for William to respond.

William glared round at them; then his massive head dipped and he sighed. "I do not. I submit to the king's will and judgment in this. I trust in God's grace and King Henry's honor."

The chancellor mopped sweat from his high brow with a large green cloth.

"Very well, my lord. It is then my duty to read the king's judgment."

Many of the lords turned in surprise toward Henry, understanding that he would not speak and that the judgment had been prepared beforehand. York scowled and Derry held his breath in terror that Henry would sense the scrutiny and respond.

The king looked around him, a faint smile playing at the corners of his mouth. At a loss, he inclined his head and the chancellor took it as a signal to go on, holding up the third of his scrolls and unrolling it with a flourish.

"'Be witness to the king's judgment against William de la Pole, Duke of Suffolk, in the year of our Lord fourteen hundred and fifty.'" He paused to take another breath and wipe his brow once more. "'For service past, the eight capital charges are dismissed by the king's order and the king's will.'"

There was a sudden barrage of sound from the gathered lords, led by York and Cardinal Beaufort as they barked angry responses. The chancellor wilted, but kept reading over the noise, his hands shaking visibly.

"'The remaining eleven charges, misprisions not criminal, are considered proven, insofar as the prisoner has confessed.'"

Another, greater growl came from the lords, and the chancellor looked helplessly at them, unable to go on. He did not have the authority to order silence and, though he looked to the king, Henry said nothing.

Seeing the impasse, it was Somerset who called out, the wiry little earl standing with his chest out and head raised aggressively.

"My lords, this is not a trial. This is certainly not a common taproom! Will you barrack the king in his own chambers? Cease your noise."

Led by York's furious whispering, some of them continued to shout and argue, though the majority accepted the rebuke and closed their mouths. The chancellor glanced in thanks to Lord Somerset, reaching once more for his cloth and wiping the shine from his face.

"'The sentence for these misprisions is banishment from these shores for the period of five years from today. You have our blessing for your patience. These papers signed and sealed in the year of our Lord fourteen hundred and fifty, Henry Rex.'"

The tumult died away at the speed of a candle being snuffed, falling to nothing as soon as the lords understood they had been listening to the words and orders of the king himself. In the moment of surprise, Derry stepped forward and used a heavy key to open the manacles around William's wrists. His friend looked ill with relief. He stood slowly, rubbing his swollen hand and reminding those closest to him that he was yet a man of prodigious strength. His sword arm was undamaged, and he flexed it in front of him, making a fist as he glared at York, Tresham, and Beaufort.

Derry reached out to take William's arm. Without warning, his friend turned to face King Henry and a sudden tension stole across the room, with even York looking up. For such crimes and accusations, there had been no punishment but execution in the past. Yet a man who had confessed to treason stood within reach of the king. William was unarmed, but again they became aware of the bearlike strength in him and the king's own frailty. Before anyone could move, William stepped forward, went down on one knee and bowed his head right to his chest.

"I am sorry to have brought you grief, Your Royal Highness. If it please God, I will return to serve you again."

Henry frowned vaguely. For an instant his hand half reached but then fell back. All the lords knelt as Henry rose from his seat, guided from their presence by the chancellor and his personal servants. He had not spoken a single word.

William remained kneeling until the door closed behind the king. When he stood once more, there were tears in his eyes, and he accepted Derry's hand on his shoulder to lead him out. As they walked away through the corridors, they were passed by messengers running with the news to all those who had paid a few coins for it. William looked as if he had been struck, pale and stunned at the sentence he had been given.

"I have horses waiting to take you through London to the coast,

William," Derry said, searching his friend's face as they walked. "There is a cog waiting at Dover, the *Bernice*. She'll take you to Burgundy, where Duke Philip has offered to give you sanctuary for the period of your banishment. Do you understand, William? You'll have a house of your own and you can bring Alice out there when you're settled. Your son can come to see you and I'll write each month to keep you informed of what goes on here. It's just five years."

Derry was struck by the look of despair William turned on him. He seemed dazed and Derry's hand remained on his shoulder to keep him upright, though he was careful not to touch the swollen hand and forearm.

"I'm sorry, William. If the king had dismissed all the charges, there would be riots, do you understand? This was the best deal I could broker for you. There was a vintner hanged just yesterday for threatening unrest if you were set free."

"I understand, Derry. Thank you for all you've done. Perhaps I should have run when you told me. Yet I didn't think they would go so far."

Derry felt the grief of his friend as if it were his own.

"I'll pay them what they're owed, William, I swear it. In five years, you'll return to England and we'll chase them like hares, if I haven't finished. You'll see."

They'd walked together through the vast space of Westminster Hall, ignoring the stares of merchants and members of Parliament. The news was spreading quickly, and some of them were daring to hiss and jeer at the sight of a condemned traitor walking among them. William raised his head at their noise, a touch of anger replacing the dead look in his eyes.

"As you say, Derry. It's just five years," he muttered, straightening his back and glaring around him.

They left the hall and walked to the two men waiting with pack-horses. Derry swallowed nervously as the crowd began to thicken, the sense of violence in the air growing with every passing moment.

"Go with God, my friend," Derry said softly.

With his damaged hand, William could not mount easily on his own, and Derry helped him into the saddle with a great heave, then passed a sword with belt and scabbard up to him. The sight of the long blade helped to quell the more raucous in the crowd, but more and more were pushing in, hissing and shouting insults. William looked down on them, his mouth a firm, pale line. He nodded to Derry, then clicked his mouth and dug in his heels, trotting close enough to a bawling collier to send the man lurching back into the arms of his mates. Derry had borrowed two good men from Lord Somerset to escort him. They drew swords as they kicked their mounts and rode, the threat clear.

Derry stood for a moment watching them go, until he sensed the spite of the crowd swing away from them, searching for another target. With a few quick steps, he disappeared back into the great hall and the gloom within. There in the shadows, away from their sight, he rested his head against cool plaster, wanting only to sleep.

THOUGH IT was dark outside, the Palace of Westminster was lit gold, every window gleaming with the light of hundreds of candles. The noble lords who had assembled to hear the king's judgment on William de la Pole did not depart quickly. Their servants scuttled back and forth, taking messages between them as they walked the corridors or called for wine and sat to discuss the night's events. Two clear factions emerged in just a short time after the king had retired. Around Lord Somerset and Lord Scales, a dozen other barons and earls gathered to discuss the evening and express their dismay at the fate of Suffolk.

York had strolled with the Neville lords to an empty room not far from the king's chambers. Tresham and Cardinal Beaufort went with them, deep in conversation. Servants scurried around the group of eight men, lighting candles and a fire in the hearth, while still more went to fetch wine and food. As the evening wore on, a number of noble lords found their way to the open door and raised a glass to York's health. They said nothing of importance, but they showed their support.

Tresham had been out and returned twice by the time he settled himself close to the fire, accepting a glass of hot wine with murmured thanks. He was frozen from walking outside and shivered as he sat back and picked up the thread of the conversation. The elder Richard Neville was speaking. Beyond his title as Earl of Salisbury, Tresham did not know the man well. Salisbury had estates and duties that kept him away on the border with Scotland and he was rarely seen in Parliament. Tresham sipped his wine gratefully, noting the number of men with connections to the Neville family. When York had married into that particular clan, he'd gained the support of one of the most powerful groups in the country. It had certainly not hurt the man to have the Nevilles behind him.

"I'm saying only that there must be an heir," Salisbury was saying. "You saw the queen, still as slender as a reed. I do not say a child will *not* come, only that if she is barren, in time it will plunge the country into chaos once again. With this army of Cade's threatening even London, it would not hurt to propose a named heir."

Tresham pricked up his ears, sitting forward and draining his cup. He'd seen the mood of York's friends go from delight to despair as he'd dropped in on them over the previous hours. They'd found a scapegoat for the disasters in France, though the king and Derry Brewer had saved Suffolk from the headsman's ax. The name of Brewer was spoken with particular disgust and anger in that room, though in truth he'd only partly dodged the blow York had arranged. Suffolk was gone for five years, removed from the king's side at the height of his strength. It was a partial victory, despite Brewer's quick feet and wits. Yet the talk of an heir was a new thing and Tresham listened closely as the Neville lords mumbled assent into their cups. They had their own loyalties and if the elder Richard Neville spoke, it would be for all of them, long before decided.

"We could ask Tresham here," Salisbury went on. "He'd know the papers and laws that need to be proposed. What do you think, Sir William? Can we name another heir, until such time as a child is born to the king and queen? Is there precedent?"

A servant refilled his cup, giving Tresham time to sip it and think.

"It would take a law, passed in Parliament, of course. Such a vote would be . . . contentious, I suspect."

"But possible?" Salisbury barked at him.

Tresham inclined his head.

"All things are possible, my lord . . . with enough votes."

They chuckled at his response, while York sat at the center of them and smiled to himself. There was no question who the heir would be, if such a vote could be called on the floor of Parliament. Richard of York was descended from a son of King Edward, as Henry was himself. Cecily York's grandfather had been John of Gaunt, another of those sons. Between them, the Yorks had a claim that was as good as the king's own—and they had six children. Tresham mentally corrected himself, recalling the recent birth of another son. Seven children, all descended from sons of the battle king.

"Such a proposal would be a declaration of intent, my lords," Tresham said, his voice low and firm. "There would be no disguising its purpose, nor the loyalties of those in support. I mention this to be sure you understand the possible consequences, should such a vote fail."

To his surprise, York laughed bitterly as he sat looking into the fire.

"Sir William, my father was executed for treason against *this* king's father. I was brought up an orphan, reliant on the kindness of old Ralph Neville. I think I know a little about the consequences—and the risks—of ambition. Though perhaps a man should not fear to talk of treason after what we all witnessed tonight. It seems it does not bear the sting it once had."

They smiled at his wry tone, watching him and each other closely.

"Yet I am not talking in whispers, Sir William! This is no plot, no secret cabal. Only a discussion. My blood is good, my line is good. The king has been married now for years yet filled no womb. In such a time of upheaval, I think the country needs to know it has a strong line in waiting, if his seed is weak. Yes, I think so, Tresham. Prepare your papers, your law. I will allow my name to go forward as heir to the throne. What I have seen tonight has convinced me it is the right thing to do."

Tresham saw from the satisfied smile on Salisbury that it was not the first time they had discussed the subject. He had a sense that all the men there had been waiting only for his arrival to spring the conversation on him and gauge his response.

"My lord York, I agree. For the good of the country, there must be an heir. Of course, any such agreement would be void if the queen conceives."

"Of course," York replied, showing his teeth. "Yet we must be prepared for all outcomes, Sir William. As I discovered tonight, it is good to have plans in place, no matter the weave of events."

CHAPTER 24

William, Lord Suffolk, stood on the white cliffs above the harbor of Dover. Somerset's men waited respectfully a little way off, understanding perhaps that an Englishman might like a moment of quiet reflection before he left his home for five years of banishment.

The air was clean after the stews and stenches of London. There was a touch of spring warmth to it, even at such a height. William was pleased he'd stopped. He could see the merchant ship waiting in the harbor, but he just stood, and looked out across the sea, and breathed. The massive fortification of Dover Castle could be seen over on his right. He knew William the Conqueror had burned it, then paid for its restoration, a mixture of terror and generosity that was typical of the man. The French had burned the entire town just a century before. Memories went a long way back on that piece of coast. William smiled at the thought, taking comfort from it. The locals had rebuilt after disasters far worse than the one that had befallen him. They had stood in ashes and set to, building homes once more. Perhaps he would do the same.

He was surprised to find his mood growing light as he drew in the soft air. So many years of responsibility had not seemed a weight. Yet losing it made him feel free for the first time in as long as he could remember. He could no longer change anything. King Henry had other men to support him and guide him through. While Derry Brewer lived and schemed, there was always hope.

William knew he was making the best of ill fate, a trait he shared with the phlegmatic people of the town below. Life was *not* a walk in the Garden of Eden. If it had been, William knew he was the sort to look around and build himself a damned house. He'd never been idle and the thought of how to fill his years in Burgundy was a prickling worry. Duke Philip was a good man to have made the offer, and was at least no friend of the French king. The irony of being accused of treason was that William had far more friends in France than England, at least at that moment. Traveling under papers granting Duke Philip's personal protection, he would pass through the heart of France, stopping for a time in Paris before heading on to his new home.

William worked the tip of his boot into the green turf, down to the chalk below. Yet his roots were *there*, his soul in the chalk. He brushed roughly at his eyes, hoping the men had not seen the strength of emotion that washed through him.

William released a breath, clearing his lungs.

"Come on, lads," he said, walking back to his horse. "The tide won't wait for us or any man."

He had found a way to mount without jarring his arm too badly, and he struggled into the saddle and took the reins in his good hand. They made their way down paths and a solid road to the dock front. Once again, William could feel hostile gazes on him as he heard his name whispered, though he thought he must have been a day ahead of the news. He kept his head high as he was introduced to the merchant captain and oversaw the unloading of the supplies Derry had provided. It was only enough to keep a man of his station for a few weeks at most. William knew he would have to send to his wife for both funds and clothes. Burgundy was part of the French mainland, a world away and yet painfully close to home. He dismissed Somerset's men, passing over a few silver coins and thanking them for their protection and courtesy. At least they treated him with the respect due to a lord, a fact not lost on the ship's captain.

William was used to naval vessels and the merchant cog seemed sloppily kept to his eye. Ropes were not curled in neat loops and the deck was in need of a good scrub with rough stones. He sighed to himself as he leaned on the rail and looked out at the townsfolk moving busily around. Derry had greased palms as necessary for his journey, achieving wonders in just a short time. As well as his wife and son, William knew he was leaving good friends behind. He stayed on deck as the ship cast off, the first and second mate shouting from bow and stern to each other. The crew heaved the mainsail yard up the mast, chanting in rhythm with each pull. William looked up as the sail billowed above his head and the ship gathered speed.

William saw the land recede from him and he drank in the sights, wanting to catch every last detail to sustain him. He knew he'd be almost sixty years of age by the time he saw those white cliffs again. His father had died at just forty-eight, killed in battle. It was a disturbing thought, and he wondered if it would be his last glimpse of home, shivering as the wind picked up past the harbor, making the great sail creak.

Out of the shelter of the coast, the open sea hissed under the prow and the cog rolled. William recalled his trip across the Channel with Margaret, when she had been little more than a girl. Her delight had been infectious and the memory of it made him smile.

He was lost in a reverie of better times and at first he did not understand the sudden flurry of barefooted sailors racing from one end of the deck to the other. The first mate was roaring new orders and the ship heeled over onto a different tack, ropes and yards shifted by men who knew their trade. In confusion, William looked first at the crew, then turned to see where they were all staring.

He gripped the rail hard at the sight of another ship surging out from a bay farther along the coast. It was a warship, built high on the bow and stern with a low middle deck for boarding—no merchant vessel. A wave of nausea swept over William as all his plans, all the peace he had gathered like sand, was suddenly washed away. Heavily laden cogs like the *Bernice* made fine prizes for pirates. The Channel between France and England was busy with traders at all times of year and pirates raided ships and coastal villages, slipping over from France, or even up from Cornwall to raid their own folk. If they were caught, the penalties were brutal, and it was rare to see the cages empty in the big seaports.

William's sense of sick dismay only intensified as the other ship came on with its one great sail bellied taut. Despite its unwieldy fore and aft castles, it was narrower in the beam than the *Bernice* and clearly faster. It lunged at them like a hawk stooping on prey, trying to snatch them up.

France was close enough to run for the coast. William could *see* it, though the wind was still rising and the continent was blurring in the distance. Of all of those on board, William knew there were few safe havens left in France. He grabbed a running sailor by the arm, almost sending the man tumbling.

"Make for Calais," William ordered. "Tell the captain. It's the only port with English ships."

The man gaped at him, then touched his forehead in acknowledgment before pulling away, racing back to his duties.

The sky began to darken overhead, the weather lowering. Through the mist and wet, William could still catch glimpses of France ahead and England behind, the white cliffs of Dover just a dim line. The *Bernice* heeled right over under the weight of sail and the wind, but he could see it was not going to be enough. Cogs were built wide to carry cargo, great lumbering vessels that were the life's blood of trade. The chasing ship was practically a greyhound compared to the *Bernice*, edging closer and closer as the waves grew rough and spray battered the decks of both vessels. William could taste salt on his lips as the *Bernice* hissed along and the captain roared orders to head for Calais.

A dozen crewmen heaved at thick ropes to turn the yards, while others put their weight against the long beam of the whipstaff, porting it over to force the ship on to the new course. The sail fluttered wildly as ropes were eased and the following ship seemed to leap closer. If they could have run on, it would have been a much longer chase, but one that ended with the *Bernice* crashing into the French coast. They *had* to try for Calais, though the turn stole almost all their speed.

William felt his heart thumping as the *Bernice* slowed and creaked. He could see every detail of the ship pursuing them by then, just half a mile away over the gray waves and closing. He squinted at it, reading a name marked out in enormous gold letters. The *Tower* was an exceptionally well-appointed vessel for a pirate to command.

The sail came taut once more in the wind, and the merchant sailors gave a ragged cheer as they tied off ropes and rested, panting. The senior men would all own shares in the ship and its cargo. Their livelihood as well as their lives depended on the *Bernice* escaping. The waves seethed again under the prow as they cut through the dark waters. France was just a few miles away and William dared to hope. The other ship was still astern of them, and there would surely be English ships closer to France, ready to fly out when they saw a valuable cog being chased down.

An hour crept by, then another, with the wind growing in strength the whole time and clouds sinking toward the rough sea below. White caps appeared on the waves and cold salt water was flung through the air as mist. William knew the Channel could be capricious, sending squalls from nowhere. Yet the *Bernice* was solid and he thought she could keep her great sail out longer than the *Tower.* He began to mutter a prayer for a storm, watching the captain closely as the man stood at the bottom of his mainmast and looked up, waiting for the first sign of a rip. The wind became a gale and darker clouds scudded overhead, matching the ships struggling on the sea below. The sunlight faded quickly and William felt the first drops of rain even as he heard them drumming on the deck. He shivered, seeing the chasing ship plunge deep and come up with white and green seawater streaming from its prow.

Their pursuers were no more than a few hundred yards off the stern by then. William could see men in chain mail and tabards standing on the open deck. There were perhaps two dozen of them, no more, though they carried swords and axes enough to board against a merchant crew. He swallowed as he saw archers come to the high wooden castle built up behind the prow. With both ships rising and falling and the wind blowing in gusts, he wished them luck, then watched in dismay as three longbows bent and sent arrows soaring to strike the deck of the *Bernice* with a noise like hammers.

William's good hand gripped the rail like a clamp, his frown deepening. Pirates found their crews in coastal towns, but there had never been a French bowman capable of that sort of accuracy. He knew he was watching English archers, traitors and scoundrels who preferred a life of thieving and murder to more honest work. The captain came past him at a run, heading to the stern to see this development. William tried to go with him, but with only one good hand, he staggered and almost fell as soon as he left the rail. From instinct, the captain grabbed at him before he went into the sea. It was bad luck that he fastened on the mangled hand, making William cry out in sudden pain.

The captain was shouting an apology over the wind when an arrow took him, sinking cleanly into his back and through, so that William could see the bodkin head standing clear, with white rib splinters around the dark iron. The two men gaped at each other and the captain tried to speak before his eyes dulled and rolled up in his head. William flailed at him, but the weight was too much and the captain vanished over the rail into the froth, slipping under in an instant.

More arrows thumped around them, and William heard a sailor shout in pain and surprise as another found its mark. The great sail above William's head began to flap. He could see the men at the whip-staff were lying flat, abandoning their duty in the face of arrow fire. The *Bernice* moved sloppily without their hands to guide her, wandering off course. Keeping as low as he could, William bellowed for them to take hold once again, but the damage was done. The pursuing warship crashed suddenly along the side, a rasping roar of splintering wood while the rain hammered down on them all.

William was thrown from his feet and was still struggling up as armed men leaped over, yelling their own fear as they crossed the strip of heaving leaden waves. William saw one man miss his catch and slip to be crushed or drowned, but there was another there in an instant, scrambling over to him with a sword held straight and sure.

"Pax!" William said, gasping as he tried to rise. "I'm Lord Suffolk! I can be ransomed."

The man looming over him put his foot down hard on William's broken hand, making the world go white for a second. He groaned and gave up any thought of standing as he lay there on the deck, drenched and frozen as the rain drummed the wood around him.

The boarders relied on shock and violence to secure the *Bernice*. Her hapless crew were either tossed overboard or cut down in the first wild flurry, most of them unarmed. William glared up at his captor, half surprised he had not already been killed. He knew they'd strip the cargo and probably sink the *Bernice*, taking all witnesses down with her. He'd seen bodies washed ashore enough times to know how they worked and even the prospect of a ransom might not be worth the added risk. He waited for the blow, sickened by the waves of agony coming from his crushed hand.

The wind continued to howl around the ropes and the strange beast of two ships wallowing together in a crashing sea.

JACK CADE glowered at the men who'd come to him daring to dispute his plans. It didn't help that they were all those he'd raised to command others. They were the originals from his meeting at the tavern, where he'd set them to training groups of a dozen men. Under his leadership, they'd fought and won against the sheriff of Kent. That man's gaping head still leaned at an odd angle on the top of a pole by Jack's fire, with the white-horse shield resting at its foot. The sheriff had been a short man in life, but, as Paddy pointed out, he was finally taller than all of them.

Although Jack could not have said exactly why, it bothered him more than anything that it was Ecclestone they'd asked to beard the lion in his tent, or whatever the phrase was. His friend stood at the head of a small group of men, talking calmly and slowly, as if to a lunatic.

"No one's saying they're afraid, Jack. That's not it. It's just that London . . . well, it's big, Jack. God knows how many people are there, all crushed up between the river and the old walls. The king doesn't even know, most likely, but there are a lot of them—and a lot more than we have."

"So you think we're done," Jack said, his eyes glinting dangerously beneath his dipped head. He sat and watched the fire they'd lit, feeling nicely warm outside and in, with a bottle of clear spirit to hand that he'd been given just that morning. "Is that it then, Rob Ecclestone? I'm surprised to hear it from you. You think you speak for the men?"

"I don't speak for any of them, Jack. This is just me talking now. But you know, they have thousands of soldiers and a hundred times as many seething in the city. Half of those are hard men, Jack. There'll be butchers and barbers to stand against us, men who know one end of a gutting knife from another. I'm just saying. It might be a step too far to go looking for the king himself. It might be the kind of step that will see us all swinging on the Tyburn gibbets. I hear they have three of them now, with room for eight on each one. They can hang two dozen at a time, Jack, that's all. It's a hard city."

Jack grunted in irritation, tipping his head back to empty the last of the fiery spirit down his throat. He stared a while longer and then clambered to his feet, looming over Ecclestone and the others.

"If we stop now," he said softly, "they'll still come for us. Did you think you could just go home? Boys, we've robbed and stolen. We've killed king's men. They're not going to let us walk away, not now, not since we started. We either throw the dice for London, or . . ." He shrugged his big shoulders. "Well, I suppose we could try for France. I don't think we'd be too welcome there, though."

"They'd hang you in Maine, Jack Cade. They know a Kentish scoundrel when they see one."

The voice had come from the back of the group. Jack stiffened, blinded by the firelight as he peered into the darkness.

"Who the hell was that? Show your face if you'd speak to me."

He squinted into the yellow and black flickers. Shadows moved across men turning nervously to see who had spoken. Jack made out the bulk of his Irish friend heaving two other men toward him.

"He said he knew you, Jack," Paddy said, panting. "He said you'd remember an archer. I didn't think he was a madman to taunt you."

"He's had worse from me in the past, you great Irish bullock," Thomas Woodchurch replied, struggling against an iron grip. "Christ, what do they feed you?"

With both his hands full of cloth, Paddy could only shake the two he held in exasperation. He did that until their heads were lolling dizzily.

"Had enough?" he said.

"Woodchurch?" Jack said in amazement, walking forward out of the firelight. "Tom?"

"I am. Now, will you tell this bog hound to put me back on my feet before I kick his balls up his throat!"

With a roar, Paddy let go of Rowan and raised his fist to hammer Thomas to his knees. Rowan saw what he was about and grappled the Irishman in a rush, toppling all three in a heap of kicking and swearing.

Jack Cade reached down and pulled the young man away with his fists still flailing.

"Who's this, then?" Jack asked.

Rowan could only glare at him, held by his own collar so tightly that he was choking and turning red.

"My son," Thomas said, sitting up and fending Paddy's kicks away.

Thomas got to his feet first and put out his hand to help the Irishman. Paddy was still ready to attack, but he settled down to an angry muttering as Jack held his palms up and dusted Rowan down with an odd smile flickering about his mouth.

"I remember him, Tom, when he was just a squalling brat, about as red in the face as he is now. Whatever happened to that girl from the rookeries? She was a right smart little piece, I always thought."

Jack sensed Paddy's temper was about to get the better of him and put a hand on his friend's shoulder.

"It's all right, Paddy. Tom and I go back a long, long way. I'll hear whatever he has to say, and if I don't like it, perhaps you can tempt him to try a bit of bare knuckle, to cheer the lads up."

"I'd like that," Paddy grumbled, still glaring.

Thomas squinted up at him, judging the Irishman's size and weight before chuckling.

"I couldn't take him if I was fit—and I was cut getting out of France. It's been a rough year for me and the boy. Then I heard Jack Cade had himself an army and I thought I'd trot over and see if it was the same man I remembered."

"Come to join the Kentish Freemen, have you? We can always use an archer, if you still have the arm for it."

"I was thinking about it, Jack, but your men are saying you have an eye on London and the king himself. What do you have, three thousand?"

"Five," Jack said instantly. "Almost six."

"With enough warning, they could put double that on the roads, Jack. That's a nasty old city. I should know."

Cade's eyes glinted as they assessed the man before him.

"How would you do it then, Tom? I remember you used to see clear enough once."

Thomas sighed, feeling his years and his body's weakness. He and Rowan had eaten a haunch of the horse they'd stolen, exchanging a few days of rich meat for walking the last part of the way. Even so, he knew it would be a while longer before he could empty a quiver at a decent speed. He did not reply for a moment, his eyes dim as he thought back to the farms he'd seen burned and the bodies of entire families he'd passed on the road. In all his life he'd been quick to anger, but this was not the same thing. He'd built this fury slowly, over months of loss and being hunted. He blamed King Henry and his lords for everything he'd seen; that was true enough. He blamed the French, though he'd made them bleed for every yard of his land. He also blamed Derry Brewer, and he knew London was where he'd find him.

"I'd go for the heart, Jack. The king will be in the Tower or the palace at Westminster. I'd send a few men in who know the city, long enough to find out where he is. My choice would be the Tower, for the Royal Mint and all the gold it holds. Then I'd make the run at night, fill my pockets and cut his black heart out. I'm done with kings and lords, Jack. They've taken too much from me. It's about time I took something back for my trouble."

Jack Cade laughed and clapped him on the shoulder.

"It's good to see you, Tom. Good to hear you as well. Sit with me and tell me what roads you'd take. These fainthearted girls are telling me it can't be done."

"Oh, it can be done, Jack. I don't know if we can beat London, but we can show those nobles the price of what they took from us. Maybe we can make ourselves rich at the same time. There are worse ideas—I've been on the wrong end of most of them."

WILLIAM'S STOMACH was rebelling, forcing acid into his mouth as he knelt on the heaving deck with his hands tied behind his back. His old wound was cramping one of his legs and the muscle was scream-ing, but whenever he tried to move, one of the pirates would kick out at him, or cuff his head back and forth until he spat blood. He was helpless and furious, unable to do anything but watch as the last of the crew were killed without ceremony and pushed over the side, to vanish into the sea.

He could hear his captors rummaging around below deck, hooting and shouting with glee at whatever they found there. His own bags had already been cut open, with men scrambling after the purse of coins Derry had placed in there for him. William had said nothing as they'd jeered and taunted him, waiting for whoever commanded them to show himself.

He knew the man was coming when the wild excitement in the pirate crew was suddenly snuffed out. They stared instead at the deck or their feet, like dogs in the presence of the pack leader. William craned his neck to see, then gave a shout of surprise and pain as he was suddenly dragged forward along the deck, his legs sprawling behind him. Two pirates had a hold on his armpits and they grunted with his weight as he sagged and stumbled. He guessed they would take him across to their ship like a trussed sheep and only hoped that they wouldn't drop him on the way, with the whitecaps tossing spume into the air and every step a challenge to remain upright.

He did not understand as they dragged him right to the prow of the *Bernice*, so that William looked out over the stays and the churning water below. The man the others obeyed came round into his sight, and William looked up in confusion.

The pirate captain was both scarred and sallow, a hard sort such as William had seen butchering pigs in the Shambles of London. The man's face bore old pox marks in great pits on the cheeks and when he smiled, his teeth were mostly dark brown and lined in black, as if he chewed charcoal. The captain leered down at his prisoner, his eyes alive with satisfaction.

"William de la Pole? Lord Suffolk?" he said with relish.

William's heart sank and his thoughts cleared and settled, the nausea in his gut becoming a distant annoyance. He had not given his family name and those were not the sort of men to know it, unless they had been looking for his ship from the beginning.

"You know my name, then," he said. "Who gave it to you?"

The captain smiled and tutted at him in reproof.

"Men who expected justice from a weak king, Lord Suffolk. Men who *demanded* it and were denied."

William watched in sick fascination as the man unsheathed a rusty-looking blade and ran his thumb across it.

"I have surrendered, to be held for ransom!" William said desperately, his voice cracking in fear. Despite his broken hand, he struggled against the ropes, but sailors knew how to tie a knot and there was no give in them. The captain smiled again.

"I do not accept your surrender. You are a convicted traitor, William de la Pole. There are some who feel you should not be allowed to walk free, not with treason around your neck."

William could feel himself growing pale as the blood drained from his face. His heart was beating strongly as he understood. He closed his eyes for a moment, struggling to find dignity as the deck climbed and fell beneath his feet.

His eyes opened as he felt a rough hand in his hair, gripping him and forcing his head forward.

"No!" he shouted. "I have been given parole!"

The captain ignored his protest, taking a great bunch of the gray hair and lifting it up to reveal the seamed neck beneath, paler than the rest. With grim purpose, the man began sawing into the muscle. William's outraged shout turned to a grunt of agony as blood spattered and greased the deck in all directions, whipped and carried by the spray. He jerked and shuddered, but he was held firmly until he slumped forward, thumping hard on the deck.

The captain ruined the blade chopping through the thick muscle and bone. He threw the weapon aside carelessly as he reached down and held up the severed head. His crew cheered the sight as it was put into a canvas bag and William's body was left in a crumpled heap on the deck.

The *Bernice* was freed from the ropes that bound her, left behind to buck and toss on the seas alone as the pirate ship headed back for the coast of England.

PART THREE

There shall be in England seven
halfpenny loaves sold for a penny; the three-
hooped pot shall have ten hoops; and I will make
it felony to drink small beer. All the realm shall
be in common, and in Cheapside shall
my palfrey go to grass.

SHAKESPEARE'S JACK CADE:
HENRY VI, PART 2, ACT 4, SCENE 2

The first thing we do, let's kill all the lawyers.

HENRY VI, PART 2, ACT 4, SCENE 2

CHAPTER 25

The London gates are closed at night, Jack," Thomas said,
pointing at the floor. The two men were alone on the upper
floor of an inn in the town of Southwark, just across the river
from the city. With a rug pulled back to reveal ancient floorboards,
Thomas had scratched a rough map, marking the Thames and the line
of Roman wall that enclosed the heart of the ancient city.

"What, *all* of them?" Jack replied. He'd never been to the capital
and he was still convinced Woodchurch had to be exaggerating. Talk
of sixty or eighty thousand people seemed impossible, and now he was
supposed to believe there were huge great gates all around it?

"That is the point of city gates, Jack, so yes. Either way, if we're
looking to reach the Tower, it's inside the wall. Cripplegate and Moor-
gate are out—we'd have to march right round the city and the villagers
there would be rushing off to fetch the king's soldiers while we did.
Aldgate to the east—you see it there? That one has its own garrison. I
used to walk the streets there when I was courting Joan. We could
cross the Fleet River to the west perhaps, and come in by the cathedral,

but no matter where we enter, we have to go over the Thames—and there's only one bridge."

Jack frowned at the chicken scratches on the floor, trying to make sense of them.

"I don't much like the idea of charging down a road they know we have to take, Tom. You mentioned ferries before. What about using those, maybe farther along, where it's quieter?"

"For a dozen men, that would be your answer. But how many do you have since Blackheath?"

Cade shrugged. "They keep coming in, Tom! Essex men, though, even some from London. Eight or nine thousand, maybe? No one's counting them."

"Too many to ferry over anyway. There aren't boats enough and it would take too long. We need to get in and out again 'fore the sun comes up. That's if you want to live to a ripe old age. Of course, there's still the chance the king and his lords will answer our petition, don't you think?"

The two men looked at each other and laughed cynically, raising the cups they both held in silent toast to their enemies. At Thomas's urging, Jack had allowed a list of demands to be taken to the London Guildhall on behalf of "The Captain of the Great Assembly in Kent." Some of the men had suggested virgins and crowns for their personal use, of course, but the discussion had eventually settled down to genuine grievances. They were all sick of high taxes and cruel laws that applied only to those who could not buy their way out. The petition they'd sent to the London mayor and his aldermen would change the country if the king agreed. Neither Jack nor Thomas expected King Henry even to see it.

"They won't answer us," Thomas said. "Not without crossing the interests of all those who take bribes and keep the common families under their bootheels. They've no interest in treating us fair, so we'll just have to knock sense into them. Look there—the Tower is close by London Bridge—no more than half a mile at most. If we take any other route in, we'll have to find our way through a maze of streets even local men don't know that well. You asked for my advice and that's it. We come up from Southwark and cross the bridge around sunset, then cut east for the Tower before the king's men even know we're there among them. We'll have to crack a few pates along the way, but if we keep moving, there aren't enough soldiers in London to stop us. As long as we don't get jammed into a small space, Jack."

"More people than I've ever seen, though," Jack muttered uncomfortably. He still couldn't imagine such a vast number of men, women, and children all crammed into the filthy streets. "Seems like they could stop us just by holding hands and standing still."

Thomas Woodchurch laughed at the image.

"Maybe they could, but they won't. You heard the men you sent scouting. If half of it is true, Londoners are about as angry with the king and his lords as we are. They can hardly move or shit without some fat fool demanding a fine that goes into his pockets or to the lord that employs him. If you can keep your men from looting, Jack, they'll *welcome* us in and cheer us all the way."

He saw the big Kentish man glare at his map through red-rimmed eyes. Cade was drinking hard each evening, and Thomas suspected he'd have stayed in Blackheath or the edge of Kent until doomsday. Cade was good enough in a stand-up fight against bailiffs or sheriff's men, but he'd been lost at the task of taking on London. He'd fallen on Woodchurch like a drowning man, ready to listen. After all the bad fortune Thomas had suffered, he felt he was due a little of the other sort. For once, he felt he was in the right place at the right time.

"You think we can do it?" Jack mumbled, slurring. "There are a lot of men looking to me to keep them alive, Tom. I won't see them all cut down. I'm not in this to fail."

"We won't," Woodchurch said softly. "The country's up in arms for a reason. This king of ours is a fool and a coward. I've lost enough to him and so have you—so have all the men with us. They'll stand when they need to; you've shown that. They'll stand and they'll walk right into London's Tower."

Jack shook his head. "It's a *fortress*, Tom," he said, without looking up. "We can't be outside it when the king's soldiers catch up with us."

"There are gates there and we have men with axes and hammers. I won't say it will be easy, but you have eight or nine thousand Englishmen and, with that many, there isn't much that will stand against us for long."

"Most of them are *Kentish* men, Tom Woodchurch," Jack said, his eyes glittering.

"Better still, Jack. Better still." He chuckled as Cade clapped him on the back, making him stagger.

The sun was coming up when the two men lurched out of the inn and stood in the doorway, blinking at the light. The band of Freemen had raided every farm and village for five miles and many of them were lying in a stupor on the ground, senseless on stolen barrels of spirits or wine. Jack nudged a man with his foot and watched him slump, groaning without waking up. The man was holding a great leg of pork, his arms wrapped around it like a lover. They'd marched hard over the previous few days and Jack didn't begrudge them the chance to rest.

"All right, Tom," he said. "The men can sober up today. I might sleep a while, myself. We'll go in tonight across the bridge."

Thomas Woodchurch looked north, imagining the morning fires of London being lit, creating their greasy fog and the smells he remembered so vividly from his youth. His wife had returned to her family home with his daughters and he wondered if they even knew he and Rowan were alive. The thought of his women brought his brows down in sudden thought.

"You'll have to tell the men there'll be no rape or looting, Jack. No drinking, either, not till it's done and we're safe back here. If we turn the people against us, we'll never get out of the city."

"I'll tell them," Jack said sourly, glaring at him.

Thomas realized he'd come close to giving the big man an order and spoke to smooth over the moment of tension.

"They'll listen to you, Jack. You're the one who brought them all here, every last one of them. They'll follow you."

"Get some sleep, Woodchurch," Jack replied. "It'll be a busy night for both of us."

DERRY BREWER was in a foul mood. With his boots clacking on the wooden floor, he paced the room above the water gate of the Tower, looking out on the slate-gray Thames rushing past. Margaret watched him from a bench seat, her hands held tightly in her lap.

"I'm not saying they'll ever get closer than they are now, my lady, but there's an army on the edge of London and the whole city is either terrified or wanting to join them. I have Lord Scales and Lord Gray at me every day to send out royal soldiers to scatter Cade's men, as if they're all peasants who'll run from the sight of a few horses."

"Are they not peasants, Derihew?" she said, awkwardly using his Christian name. Since they'd been thrown together as allies, she'd asked Derry to call her Margaret, but he resisted still. She looked up as he stopped and turned, wondering whether he saw strength or weakness.

"My lady, I have men strolling right through their camp. That fool Cade knows nothing about passwords or guards. In that drunken crowd, anyone can come or go as they please, and, yes, most of them are laborers, apprentices, hard men. There are gentlemen there, too, though, with friends in London. They have voices calling everywhere in their support and I smell York's coins behind them." He blew out a breath and rubbed the bridge of his nose. "And I knew Jack Cade once, when he was just another big . . . um . . . devil, standing in ranks against the French. I heard he even fought for the French once, when they were paying better than us. There's anger enough in him to burn London to the ground, my lady, if he gets the chance."

He stopped speaking, considering whether he could ask one of his spies to put a dagger in Cade's eye. It would mean the man's death, of course, but Derry had the king's purse available to him. He could pay a fortune to a widow and children, enough to tempt, at least.

"No matter who they are, or why they've gathered, there's a right horde of them, my lady, all shouting and giving speeches and working each other up to a fine lather. With a spark, London could be sacked. I'd be happier if I didn't have to plan for the king's safety, as well as everything else. If he was away from the city, I could act with a free hand."

Margaret dipped her gaze, rather than be caught staring at her husband's spymaster. She did not trust Derry Brewer completely, or understand him. She'd known he was on her side over the fate of William de la Pole, but it was weeks since a headless body had washed up with a dozen others at Dover. She closed her eyes briefly at a stab of pain for her friend. One of her hands clenched over the other.

Whether she trusted Derry Brewer or not, she knew she had few other allies at court. The riots seemed to be spreading and those lords who supported the Duke of York were not working too hard to put them down. It suited his faction of lords to have the country up in arms, roaring their discontent. She had learned to hate Richard of York, but hatred wouldn't jar him from his course. London and her husband had to be made safe before anything else.

As Derry turned back to the window, she ran a hand lightly over her womb, praying for life within. Henry didn't seem to remember their first stolen intimacy, as drugged and ill as he had been at the time. She had been bold enough to go to him half a dozen times since, and it was true her fluxes were late that month. She tried not to hope too desperately.

"My lady? Are you unwell?"

Her eyes came open and she blushed, unaware that it made her pretty. She looked away from Derry's searching gaze.

"I am a little weary, is all, Derry. I know my husband does not want to leave London. He says he must remain, to shame them for their treason."

"Whatever he wants, my lady, it will not help him if thousands of men tear London apart. I cannot say for certain that he is safe here; do you understand me? York has his whisperers in as many ears as I have—and a fat purse to bribe weak men. If Cade's army comes in, it would be too easy to stage an attack on the king—and too hard to protect him with the city under siege."

He stepped closer and his hand came up for a moment as if he might take hers in his grasp. He let it drop, thinking better of it.

"Please, Your Highness. I asked to see you for this reason. King Henry has a castle at Kenilworth, not eighty miles from London on good roads. If he is well enough to travel, he could be there in just a few days by carriage. I would know my king is safe, and it would be one less burden in defeating the rabble with Cade." He hesitated, then spoke again, his voice dropping. "Margaret, you should go with him. We have loyal soldiers, but with Cade so close, the people themselves are rioting and looting. They block roads and there are mobs gathering all over the city. Cade coming in will be the tipping point, the spark. This could go badly for us, and I do not doubt York's supporters have marked you well. After all, your fine and loyal members of Parliament have made York the royal heir 'in the event of misfortunes.'" Derry almost spat the words of the decree. "It would be madness to invite exactly what they want. To stay is to hold the knife to your own breast."

Margaret looked steadily into his eyes as he spoke, asking herself again how much she trusted his man. What advantage would he gain with the king and queen gone from London, beyond his claims and the ease of his fears? She knew by then that Derry Brewer was not a simple man. There was rarely *one* reason for him to do anything. Yet she had seen his grief and rage when he heard of William's murder. Derry had disappeared for two days, drinking himself into a stupor in one London tap house after another. That had been real enough. She made her decision.

"Very well, Derry. I will ask my husband to go to Kenilworth. I will stay in London."

"You'd be safer away," he said immediately.

Margaret didn't waver.

"There is *nowhere* safe for me, Derry, not as things stand. I am not a child any longer, to have the truth hidden from me. I am not safe while other men covet my husband's throne. I am not safe while my womb is empty! Well, a pox on all that! I will stay here and I will watch my husband's lords and soldiers defend the capital. Who knows, you may have need of me, before the end."

CADE ROLLED his shoulders, looking out over a host of men that stretched far beyond the light of the crackling torches. He was feeling strong, though his throat was dry and he would have liked another drink to warm his belly. The summer twilight had faded slowly, but darkness was truly upon them at last and an army waited on his word. God knew, he'd stood with smaller forces against the French! He looked around him in awe, sensing rather than seeing the extraordinary number of men who'd gathered. He knew at least half of them had come to him after some injustice. He'd heard a hundred angry stories, more. Men who had lost everything in France, or had their lives and families wrecked by some judgment of the courts. With everything taken away from them, they'd all come to walk with Jack Cade.

His original few thousand men of Kent had almost been swallowed by the mass of latecomers from Essex and London itself. He shook his head in wonder at that thought. There were scores there who lived within London's walls yet were willing to march with billhook and sword against their own city. He didn't understand them, but then they weren't Kentish men, so he didn't try.

His lieutenants had been busy all day, taking names and getting the army ready to march. Over the previous few weeks, the newcomers had arrived in such numbers it had been all he could do to assign them to a particular officer and leave them to find weapons for themselves. Paddy seemed to enjoy the work and Jack thought he'd have made a fine sergeant in the real army. With Ecclestone and Woodchurch, he'd worked to bring some order to the mass of men, especially those who had no training at all. The vast majority had some sort of iron in their hands, and there was only one way to point them. Jack had no idea how they'd fare against royal troops in mail and plate, but at least the narrow streets of London would take away the threat of horsemen at the charge. His men *walked*, foot soldiers all, but then that was the sort of army he understood and he didn't sweat too hard at the lack of mounts.

On his left, he could see the little Scot, Tanter, on the enormous beast of a plow horse he'd been given. Jack thought the man looked like a fly sitting on an ox, with his legs tucked up under him. Tanter was watching a pair of mistle thrushes, darting and soaring in an empty evening sky. The air was already thick, and a bank of dark clouds was massing to the west. Cade suddenly remembered his mother telling him the thrushes were the last birds in the air before a great storm. Country folk would see them flying alone on the wind and know a tempest was on its way. Jack smiled at the memory. He was *bringing* the storm to the city that night, walking with it all around him, in the faces and cold iron of angry men.

A dozen of the biggest Kent lads stood close to Cade, grinning wolfishly in the light of the torches held high in their hands. It made a ring of light around him, so that they could all see their leader, as well as the Kentish banner they followed. Jack looked down at the boy carrying the pole, just one of a hundred keen lads they'd picked up along the way. Some of them were sons of the men, others just home-less urchins who'd followed in their wake, fighting over scraps and staring with wide eyes at adults who looked so fierce with their blades and tools.

Jack saw the boy was watching him and he winked.

"What's your name, lad?"

"Jonas, Captain," the boy replied, awed at having Cade speak to him.

"Well, raise it up, Jonas," Jack said. "Both hands and steady, lad. It's a good Kentish sign—and a warning."

Jonas straightened, lifting the pole like a banner. The boy lacked the strength to hold it steady and it swayed in the golden light under the weight of the white-horse shield and the sheriff's head.

"You keep that high while we march. The men need to see it and know where I am, all right?"

"Yes, Captain," Jonas said proudly, staring in concentration at the wavering point above him.

"Ready, Captain!" Paddy bellowed from over on his right.

"Ready, Jack!" Woodchurch shouted, farther back.

Cade smiled as the calls were echoed all around him, until there were hundreds, then thousands repeating it in a growl of sound. They were ready.

Jack inflated his chest to give the order to march, but he saw a fel-low pushing through the ranks toward him and waited to see what he was after. Heads turned to follow as the man grunted and slipped through, arriving panting at Jack's side. He was a small man, with the sallow skin, thin arms, and hollow cheeks that only decades of poverty could produce. Jack beckoned him closer.

"What is it? Lost your nerve?" he said, making his voice kind as he saw the man's worry and fear written into every line of him.

"I . . . I'm sorry, Jack," the man said, almost stammering. He looked around him at the glowering axemen and briefly up to the Kentish banner. To Jack's surprise, he crossed himself as if he saw a holy relic.

"Do I know you, son?" Jack said, confused. "What brings you to me?"

Cade was leaning close to hear the reply when the man lunged toward his neck, a dagger in his hand. With a curse, Jack smacked it away with a raised arm, hissing in pain as the blade cut the back of his hand. The knife flew out of the man's grip, clattering against metal and vanishing. Jack clenched his jaw and reached out with both hands, grabbing the man's head and twisting hard. The man screeched and struggled until a snap sounded and he went limp. Jack let the body fall bonelessly to the ground.

"*Fuck* you, boy, whoever the hell you were," he said to the corpse. He found he was breathing hard as he looked up into the shocked faces of the men around him.

"Well? Did you think we didn't have enemies? London's sly, and don't you forget it. Whatever they promised him, I'm still standing and he's done."

At a sudden flurry of movement, Cade spun round, convinced he was about to be attacked again. He saw Ecclestone barge through the crowd, with his razor held high, ready to kill. Jack faced him, raising his shoulders bullishly as rage filled him with strength.

"You, too?" he growled, readying himself.

Ecclestone looked down at the body, then up into Jack's eyes.

"*What?* Christ, no, Jack. I was following him. He looked nervous and he kept creeping closer to you."

Jack watched as his friend folded the narrow blade and made it vanish.

"You were a bit late then, weren't you?" he said.

Ecclestone gestured uncomfortably to where blood dripped from Jack's hands.

"He cut you?" he asked.

"It's not bad."

"I'll stay close, Jack, if you don't mind. We don't know half of the men now. There could be others."

Jack waved away the idea, his good mood already returning.

"They've shot their bolt, but stay if it makes you happy. Are you ready, lads?"

The men around him were still pale and shocked at what they had witnessed, but they mumbled assent.

"Watch my back while we march, then, if it pleases you," Jack said. "I'm for London. They know we're coming and they're frightened. So they should be. Raise that pole high, Jonas! I bloody told you once! Let them see us coming."

They cheered him as he set off, thousands of men walking in the darkness toward the capital. Fat drops of warm summer rain began to fall, making the torches sizzle and spit. The men talked and laughed as they went, as if they were strolling to a market day or a county fair.

CRIPPLEGATE REMAINED OPEN, lit by braziers on iron poles. The king's carriage was enclosed against the cold, with Henry well wrapped inside. Around the king, sixty mounted knights were his escort north, taking him away from the capital city. Henry looked out at the lighted gate, trying to turn in his seat to see it shut behind him. The ancient Roman wall stretched away in both directions, enclosing his city and his wife. His hands trembled and he shook his head in confusion, reaching for the door and opening it part of the way. The movement brought the instant attention of Lord Gray, who turned his horse toward the king's carriage.

Henry gathered his thoughts, feeling the process like grasping threads. He recalled speaking to Margaret, asking her to come with him to Kenilworth, where she would be safe. Yet she was not there. She'd said Master Brewer had asked her to stay.

"Where is my wife, Lord Gray?" he asked. "Is she coming soon?"

To Henry's surprise, the man did not respond. Lord Gray colored as he dismounted and came to the carriage side. Henry blinked at him in confusion.

"Lord Gray? Did you hear me? Where is my wife, Margaret . . . ?"

He broke off, suddenly sensing it was a question he had asked many times before. He knew he'd been dreaming for a time. The physician's drafts made false things seem real and dreams as vivid as reality. He could no longer tell the difference. Henry felt a gentle pressure on the carriage door as Lord Gray pushed on it, looking away at the same time so he would not have to see his king's wide eyes and grief-stricken expression.

The door shut with a soft click, leaving Henry peering out of the small square of glass. When it misted with his breath he rubbed at it, in time to see Gray shake his head at one of the knights.

"I'm afraid the king is unwell, Sir Rolfe, not quite in his right mind."

The knight looked uncomfortable as he glanced back at the pale face watching him. His head dipped.

"I understand, my lord."

"I hope so. It would be unwise of you to suggest I ever closed a door on my sovereign, Sir Rolfe. If we understand each other . . . ?"

"We do, Lord Gray, of course. I saw nothing of note."

"Very good. Driver! Ride on."

A long whip snapped in the air, and the carriage began to move away, bouncing and shuddering on the potholed road. As it went, the wind blew harder and it began to rain, the heavy drops drumming on the carriage roof and the dusty ground.

CHAPTER 26

Derry held his temper in check with a huge effort. Midnight was not far off and he was weary and fed up.

"My lord Warwick, if you withdraw your men-at-arms from the north of the city, we will have no one there to contain the rioting."

Richard Neville was tall and slender, too young still for a beard. Yet he was an earl himself and the son and grandson of powerful men. He stared back with the sort of arrogance that took generations to perfect.

"Who are *you* to tell me where to place *my* men, Master Brewer? I see you have Lord Somerset's soldiers racing hither and thither at your word, but you'd have me stay away from the army approaching London? Have you lost your wits? Let me be clear. You don't give orders here, Brewer. Don't forget that."

Derry felt his instincts bristle, but provoking a confrontation with a Neville while London was in real danger would serve no one.

"My lord, I agree Cade's mob is the worst of the threats facing the city. Yet when he comes, we will still have to keep the streets in order. The presence of an army on the doorstep of the city has riled and excited every troublemaker in London. There are riots tonight by St. Paul's, calling for the king to be dragged out and put to trial. Smithfield by the Tower has a gathering of hundreds with some damned Sussex orator firing their blood. Those places need an armed presence, my lord. We need soldiers to be seen on *every* street, from the Shambles to the markets, from Aldgate to Cripplegate. I only ask that you . . ."

"I believe I have answered, Brewer," Richard Neville said coldly, talking over him. "My men and I will defend London Bridge and the Tower. That is the post where I have chosen to stand. Or will you tell me the king has other orders? *Written* orders I may read for myself? No? I should think not, as His Majesty has left the city! You overreach yourself, Brewer. I'm sure you would prefer a Neville to guard street corners while the true fight goes on without me. Yet you have no authority here! I suggest you remove yourself, or at least remain silent while your betters plan for the worst."

Something about the dangerous stillness in Derry Brewer made Warwick stop talking. There were five men in the room at the newly built Guildhall, the seat of all civic authority in London. Lord Somerset had been listening closely to the conversation, making his own assessment of those present. Observing that Derry was about to speak in anger, he cleared his throat.

"This is no time to argue, gentlemen," he said drily. "Lord Scales? You mentioned guarding the other gates?"

Scales was in his fifties, a veteran of the French conflict who had remained in London ever since the trial of William, Lord Suffolk. He accepted the olive branch Somerset held out, speaking in a smooth baritone to break the tension in the room.

"We know this chap Cade has a large number of followers. It is only the merest sense to reinforce the gates of London."

"*Seven* gates, Lord Scales!" Derry said, frustrated into letting his irritation show. "If we put even forty more men on each, we'll have lost a vital number who can keep order on the *streets*. My lord, I have men in villages around the city, watching for an attack. Cade hasn't moved out of Southwark. If he's coming at all, he's coming like a bull at a gate. If he was the only factor, I'd agree with the young earl here that we should gather like a knot at London Bridge. But there are tens of thousands in London who will take advantage of this unrest to burn, murder, rape, and settle old scores. We may be spread too thin as it is, but Cade is only one part. Cade's attack is no more or less than the horn signal that will destroy the city."

Derry stopped, looking round at the men who would defend London when Cade came, assuming he ever did. At least Derry trusted Somerset, though the older man was just as prickly as Richard Neville when it came to being denied the honor of a prominent position. Scales had subsided into flushed silence for the same reason. Baron Rivers he knew hardly at all, beyond the fact that he had brought two hundred men down to London on orders Derry had written and sealed for the king. In comparison, the young Earl of Warwick was as hostile as any rioter, the face the Neville clan had chosen to represent their power. Derry regarded him sourly, knowing that York stood behind him, though of course the man himself was nowhere to be seen. The Neville faction could only gain from an attack on London, and Derry despaired at the thought of such men seizing their chances in the chaos that would follow. He needed more soldiers!

Margaret was safe enough in the Tower, Derry thought. He'd rather not have left four hundred men to guard her, but when she'd refused to leave, he'd had little choice. Derry knew the sins of men better than most. If London was saved but Margaret lost, Derry knew the Yorkist cause would be immeasurably strengthened. The Duke of

York would then be king within the year, he was certain. Just once, he would have liked a single enemy facing him, like the old days. Instead, he felt as if he trod through a room of snakes, never knowing which one would strike at him.

One of the mayor's staff came puffing up the stairs to the room, a great fat alderman in silks and velvet. He was pink-faced and sweating as he entered, though the stairs were few. The four lords and Derry turned to him with dark expressions, making him stare.

"My lords," he panted. "Cade's men are coming. Now, my lords. *Tonight.*"

Warwick cursed under his breath.

"I am for the bridge," Warwick said. "The rest of you see to your own."

The alderman stood back to let him pass, trying to bow and breathe hard at the same time. Warwick vanished down the steps at a run. Derry glared after him, turning quickly to Lord Scales.

"My lord, I have the king's authority in this. Please give a part of your men to guard the city from within."

Lord Scales looked down on the shorter man, weighing his words.

"No, Master Brewer. My answer is no. I too will defend the bridge."

"*Christ*, Scales," Somerset said. "We're on the same side. I'll send sixty men into the streets for you, Derry. I'll have them report to the Guildhall for you to send where they're needed, all right? That is all I can spare."

"It's not enough," Derry said. "If Cade's men get into the city, we'll need hundreds to take them on, whichever way they turn."

His fists were clenched, and Somerset shrugged regretfully.

"Then pray they do not get into the city," he said. He indicated the steps leading down. Outside, they could hear the hiss and roar of the rainstorm beginning to spread across London. "It looks to be a wet night. Shall we, gentlemen?"

There were torches on London Bridge, wide spitting bowls of flaming oil on pillars at the entrance and all along its length. The bridge shone gold in the darkness and could be seen from far to the south. Bowed down under the rain, Jack Cade marched toward that gleaming spot with his Freemen, wrapping a cloth around the wound he'd taken as he went and pulling the knot tight with his teeth. Behind the fingers of black cloud scudding across the sky, the moon was almost full. He could see the silvery mass of his men as they trudged on, moving closer to the city.

The Thames was a glittering strip across his path as he approached the bridge. Jack could hear Woodchurch yelling at the men behind to form a column. The bridge was wide, but most of that width was taken up with the buildings along each edge. The central road could take no more than four or six men abreast—and Jack could see it wasn't empty. London Bridge seethed with people, animals, and carts, with more and more of them staring out at the armed men. Jack felt like a wolf approaching a flock of lambs, and he smiled at the thought, hefting his ax and letting it rest on his shoulder like any woodsman out for a stroll. Ecclestone chuckled with something like the same thought, though it was not a pleasant sound.

"No killing the lambs!" Jack growled at the men around him. "No stealing or touching the women! Understand? If you see a man with a blade or a shield, you can cut his damned head off. No one else."

His guards grumbled their assent.

It was probably Jack's imagination when he felt the stones tremble underfoot as he crossed from solid ground to the first steps of the bridge itself. His men went before him, but he had insisted on being in the first few ranks, to call orders as necessary. Despite Woodchurch's efforts, they had formed too wide a line on the open road and had to funnel in behind him, with thousands just standing with their heads bowed in the pouring rain, unable to go forward. Yet the snake of armed Kentish men pushed farther and farther in, driving the crowds before them like animals on market day. To Jack's surprise, many of the Londoners were cheering and shouting his name, pointing him out as if he were coming to break a siege. They didn't seem to be afraid and Jack Cade couldn't understand them at all.

He swallowed nervously as he began to pass buildings on either side, hanging so far out above his head that they blocked the falling rain from all but the track down the center. He didn't like being over-looked, and he glared up at the open windows.

"Watch for archers!" Woodchurch shouted behind them.

Jack could see Ecclestone jerking his head around, wiping his eyes of rain and trying to see in all directions. If the windows filled, Jack knew his men would seek the shadow of the buildings themselves, crowding the pavements for the false promise of cover. They'd be vul-nerable to anyone with a bow on the other side then, like chickens in a pen. Jack crossed his fingers, but he could hear the jingling tramp of soldiers up ahead, moving to block the far end of the bridge. He shifted his ax to his other shoulder, forcing himself to keep walking, steady and strong behind the Kentish banner that little Jonas held high.

Jack looked back over his shoulder, trying to judge how many had come on to the bridge. Woodchurch had been like an old woman all day, worrying about being bottled up. In the light of the crackling bridge lamps, Jack could see the man and his son, both archers staring up at the windows. They were empty, dark spaces with no lamps lit inside. Something about that bothered Jack, but he couldn't put a name to it.

Ahead of him, the crowds had thickened into a great mass, so that it began to look as if the marching men would have to stop.

"Show them your iron, lads!" Jack bellowed. "Keep the lambs moving!"

Ecclestone held his razor a little higher, steady against his thumb. On all sides, Cade's men raised axes and swords, while those with shields used them roughly, shoving and pushing anyone too slow to get out of the way. They marched on and as they passed the midpoint, Jack could see flashes of polished armor on the far side, with the fleeing crowd streaming through lines of waiting men. It came to his mind that the king's soldiers were as hampered by the crowds as he was himself. They could not form solid shield walls while innocents still struggled to get away.

He raised his head and gave a great bellow, trusting the men with him to obey.

"For Kent! Forward and attack!"

He could only jog rather than sprint forward as the men ahead of him lurched on through slippery mud. Jack saw Ecclestone shove a cheering Londoner in the chest, knocking him aside as they began to run. Each man roared so that it became a wall of sound over the hiss of rain, echoing back in the enclosed space. It was wordless, a rising snarl from hundreds of throats.

Jack slipped on something underfoot, staggering. At least he could see. The bridge lamps lit the whole length, their light filled with glittering flecks driven by the rising wind. He was no more than two hundred yards from the hard men waiting for him.

Some of the crowd flattened themselves against the walls of the houses rather than try to outrun a charging army. Others were not fast enough and screamed as they fell, quickly trampled. Jack had glimpses of shocked and tumbling bodies as he went faster and faster, trusting to speed and his own weight to break through.

The windows ahead and above filled with men leaning out from the dark spaces. Jack swore in horror at the sight of crossbows. With such weapons, the narrow bridge was a brutal trap, the slaughter limited only by how fast the soldiers could reload and how many of them there were. Jack dared not turn to see how far along the bridge they stretched, but his heart pounded in terror with the desire to seek cover. Their only chance to survive lay ahead: through the soldiers, off the bridge and into the city proper.

"Rush 'em!" he yelled.

He went faster as the men with him surged forward in panic. The boy Jonas could not keep up, and when he staggered, one of Jack's guards reached out and grabbed the banner pole in one hand, lowering it almost like a lance as he sprinted.

The first bolts thumped down into the running men from just a few feet above their heads. Jack ducked under a raised shield held by the man closest to him, flinching as he ran on. He heard screams of shock and pain all along the bridge and he knew he was the prime target, standing almost directly behind the banner. Jack looked up in time to see the boy Jonas shudder and skid forward on his chest as he was struck. Another bolt smacked into the man who had grabbed the falling banner and he too crashed down. The shield of Kent and the sheriff's head dropped into the mud and filth and no one tried to raise them up once more as they ran in mindless terror.

THOMAS HAD FELT the same unease as Jack at the empty windows—dark when every man and woman in London wanted to see Cade's Freemen coming in. He'd sensed the trap and shouted to anyone with an ax to peel off at every door they passed. Even as the first bolts flew, those doors were being kicked in. Some of the crossbowmen had thought to block the floor below and it took heavy blows to smash down their doors and barricades.

Thomas jogged slowly, with Rowan on his left, down the center of the bridge. They carried longbows that were still green and lacked the power and workmanship of the ones they'd lost in France. Half the skill of a longbow archer came from knowing his own weapon, with all its quirks and strengths. Thomas would have given a year of his life then for the bows he and Rowan had left behind.

The Freemen shoved and bustled around them, panicking men in rain-sodden clothes who knew that to stop was to die, that they *had* to reach the end of the bridge. It was impossible to aim in the bustle of elbows and pushing. All Thomas and his son could do was send out snap shots, relying on instinct and training to guide them. The range was practically nothing at first, but then Thomas saw Jack roar and race ahead, forced on by the bolts streaking down to tear holes in his men. There were no axemen to kick in doors beyond that front rank and the crowd had run for it, leaving the last hundred yards clear all the way to a line of king's soldiers. Thomas thought furiously. It was a killing ground and he knew Jack would not survive it. He glanced up as a crossbowman above his head was jerked back with a strangled shriek. Someone had reached him inside.

"Christ!" Thomas growled aloud. "The windows ahead, Rowan! Pick your shots; we've only a few shafts."

He grabbed two men trying to run past him, placing them with main strength in the path behind and yelling orders to give him space. They stared wide-eyed as they recognized him, but they took up the positions a few paces back, perhaps grateful to walk in his shadow while bolts buzzed and hissed through the air. Their presence allowed father and son the space to aim as they stalked forward along the bridge.

Thomas felt his hip pull in agony, as if someone had cut him. Instinct made him drop a palm to his side and check it for blood, but it was just the scars stretching. He showed his teeth then, anger engulfing him. He was strong again. Strong enough for this.

He bent the longbow and sent a shot into a window up ahead. The range was no more than fifty yards and he knew it was good before the man fell out onto those passing below. Rowan's first shot missed by inches, making its target flinch back. The young man sent another on almost the same path, staring ahead and up as he strummed the bow. A soldier sighting down a crossbow took the second shaft in the neck, twisting in agony as it nailed him to the wooden window frame.

Father and son walked on together, eyes focused through the drizzle on the low windows ahead. Those who had thought to shoot down into helpless men did not know they were vulnerable until an arrow tore through them. As the two archers walked, they killed farther and farther ahead, keeping Cade safe as he ran to see what else the London lords had ready for their arrival.

JACK HEARD the thump of longbows behind him, and his first reaction was to flinch. He'd known that sound on battlefields and he was filled with horror at the thought of English archers being part of the ambush on the bridge. Yet the crossbowmen leaning out of windows began to lurch and fall out of their dark slots. The barrage of bolts lessened overhead and the dead and dying fell behind.

Jack was panting hard as he saw he'd come almost to the end of the bridge. His clothes were heavy and plastered to him, chilling his flesh. There were soldiers waiting there in mail, ready for his attack. Despite the cold, his eyes gleamed at the sight, the distance closing too fast for him to take in more than a blur. He could only thank God they had chosen to place their crossbowmen along the bridge rather than making a fighting line. His front ranks had a few shields, but there was nothing in the world as terrifying as running into a massed volley of bolts or shafts.

All thought stopped as he ran full tilt at two of the king's men, his ax held high for a butcher's chopping blow. The Kentish men around him raised their own weapons in blind fury, driven almost to madness by their run under the bolts, by seeing their friends killed. They fell on the front ranks of soldiers like a pack of baying hounds, cutting in a frenzy and not feeling the wounds they took in return.

Jack struck as hard a first blow as he'd ever landed in his life, giving no thought to defense. He was lost in rage and near mindless as he smashed a smaller man out of his path, hitting with the heavy blade edge, or striking with the haft, all the time roaring at those standing in his way. He did not feel alone as he went over the first rank and into the second. Some of his guards had fallen to bolts, but the survivors, even the wounded ones, were swinging with abandon, as much a danger to the ones around them as the men in front. It was savage and terrible and they lurched on the slippery ground as they pushed on, pressured in turn by the men at their backs who wanted just to get off the damned bridge.

Jack could see beyond the soldiers into the darker streets. He had a sense that there were only few hundred men waiting there for him. It might have been enough to hold the Freemen on the bridge forever, unless they could be forced back into the wider roads beyond. Jack acted as soon as he saw the need, pushing forward with his ax shaft held across his chest like a bar. With a burst of strength, he shoved two men onto their backs when they raised shields against him. He shuddered as he stamped over them, imagining a blade licking up from below. The pair of fallen soldiers were too busy in their panic as the Freemen trampled after him. One moment, there had been neat lines of sword and shield men; the next, they were down and the Freemen were rushing over the fallen and wounded, knocking the next rank apart with great blows and crushing the rest underfoot.

Those still on the bridge felt the blockage of men give way. They shouted wildly as they were given space to push forward, cheering as they surged out into the streets of rain-swept London. Nothing lived in their wake, and they only stopped to make sure of helpless soldiers, stabbing and kicking down with hard boots until the king's men were a bloody mess on the stones and wet straw.

A hundred yards past the bridge, Jack came to a halt and stood panting, with his hands resting on the haft of his ax and the blade half buried in the thick mud of the street. The storm was right over the city and the rain was striking hard enough to sting exposed skin. He was puffing and dizzy as he looked back, his face showing wild triumph. The bridge had not held them. He exulted as he stood there, with men clapping him on the back and laughing breathlessly. They were in.

"Soldiers coming," Ecclestone shouted nearby.

Jack raised his head, but he couldn't tell the direction over the rain and rumbling clouds overhead.

"Which way?" Jack yelled back.

Ecclestone pointed east toward the Tower as Paddy appeared at Jack's shoulder. Half their army was either on the bridge or still across the river, waiting impatiently to join them in the city.

"We need to go farther in, Jack," Paddy said. "To make room for the rest."

"I know," Cade said. "Let me take a breath to think."

He wished he had a drink in him to keep out the cold. Beyond that thought, he wondered what the hell he was stepping in that could suck at his feet in such a sickening way. Streams had begun to run along the streets, shining where the moon reached through the clouds. Some of his men had come to a gasping stop with him, while others shoved and cursed each other to stand at his side. Though his hearing wasn't as good as Ecclestone's, Cade fancied he could indeed hear the jingle of armored men coming closer by then. He had a sudden vision of the London Guildhall that Woodchurch had described and he made his decision. He needed to get all his followers into the city and God knew the Tower would wait a while longer.

"Woodchurch! Where are you?"

"Here, Jack! Watching your back, as usual," Thomas replied cheerfully. He too was giddy with their success.

"Show me the way to the Guildhall, then. I'll have a word with that mayor. I have a grievance or two for him! On now, Freemen! On, with me!" Jack bawled, suddenly enjoying himself again.

The men laughed, still dazed at having survived the brutal run across the bridge. Good plans changed, Jack reminded himself. The guildhouse would do as a base to plan the rest of the evening.

As he marched away, Jack gave thanks for the dim light of the moon. The houses seemed to close in on all sides when it passed behind rushing clouds. In those moments, he could see almost nothing of the city all around him. It was dark and endless, a labyrinth of streets and alleyways in all directions. He shuddered at the thought, feeling as if he'd been swallowed.

It was with relief that he reached a small crossroads, a quarter of a mile from the bridge. Like a blessing, the moon struggled free of the clouds and he could see. There was a stone at the center of it, a great boulder that seemed to have no purpose beyond marking the spot between roads. Jack rested his arms on it and looked back down the street to the men coming on behind him. He had a thought of gathering them in some open square and making them cheer for what they'd achieved. There just wasn't the room for that and he shook his head. Every door around the crossroads was barred, every house filled with whispering heads watching from the upper floors. He ignored the frightened people as they stared down.

Rowan had found himself a torch from somewhere, a bundle of rags tied to the end of a wooden pole and dipped in oil—perhaps from the oil lamps of London Bridge, Jack didn't know. He welcomed the yellow light as Woodchurch and his son caught up.

Thomas chuckled at the sight of Jack Cade resting on the stone.

"Do you know what that is, Jack?" he said.

His voice was strange, and Jack looked again at the rock under his hands. It seemed ordinary enough, though he was struck again at finding such a massive natural thing marking a city crossroads.

"It's the London Stone, Jack," Thomas went on, his voice awed. There had to be some fate at work that had led Jack Cade along roads he didn't know to that very spot.

"Well, I can see that, Tom. It's a stone and it's in London. What of it?"

Woodchurch laughed, reaching out himself and patting the stone for luck.

"It's older than the city, Jack. Some say it was a piece of King Arthur's stone, the one that split when he pulled a sword out of it. Or they say it was brought over from Troy to found a city here by the river." He shook his head in amusement. "Or it could just be the stone they measure the mile markers from, all over England. Either way, you have your hand on the cold stone heart of London, Jack."

"I do, do I?" Jack said, looking down at the boulder with new appreciation. On impulse, he stood back and swung his ax, making the blade skip and spark across the surface. "Then it's a good place to declare Jack Cade has entered London with his Freemen!" He laughed aloud then. "The man who will be king!"

The men around him looked serious, and their voices stilled.

"Well, all right, Jack," Woodchurch murmured. "If we survive till morning, why not?"

"Christ, such fancies," Jack said, shaking his big head. "Show me which road leads quickest to the Guildhall, Tom. That's what matters."

CHAPTER 27

Richard Neville was beginning to appreciate the accuracy of
Brewer's warnings. His headlong rush across the city had
been hampered by crowds of drunken, violent men and even
women, screeching and jeering at his soldiers. Entire streets had
been blocked by makeshift barricades so that he had to divert again
and again, guided by his London-born captains toward the Kentish
Freemen.

He could not understand the mood on the streets, beyond a cold
contempt for opportunists and wrongheaded fools. Cade's army was a
threat to London, and there Warwick was, rushing to their defense,
only to be pelted with cold slop, stones and tiles whenever a mob gathered in his way. It was infuriating, but there were not yet enough of
them to block his path completely. He was ready to give the order to
draw swords on any rioters and ne'er-do-wells, but for the moment, his
captains led him on a twisting path through the heart, heading south
with six hundred men.

The knights and men-at-arms he had brought to London were not
enough to take on Cade directly, he knew that much. Yet his captains

assured him Cade's mob would be spread out along miles of streets and tracks. The young earl knew his best chance would be to cut the line at any one of a dozen places, then withdraw quickly to strike again somewhere else. He knew he should avoid a major clash—the numbers invading the city were just too high.

His first chance came as he had imagined it, as Warwick turned a corner and looked down a slight hill to a junction, skidding to a stop at the sight of armed men streaming past in a great hurry. He stood under the downpour in relative safety, not twenty yards from Cade's main forces as they headed unaware across his route. Some of them even looked left as they passed the mouth of the road, catching a glimpse of Warwick's soldiers in the dark side street, watching them. Caught up in the snake of angry men, they were carried on past before they could stop.

"Keep a line of retreat," Warwick ordered. To his disgust, his voice trembled, and he cleared his throat loudly before going on with his orders. "They are traitors all. We go in, kill as many as we can in the surprise, then pull back into . . ." He looked around, seeing a small wooden signpost. He leaned closer to read it and for an instant raised his eyes to heaven. "Back into Shiteburn Lane."

It helped to explain what he had sunk ankle-deep into, at least. He spent a moment longing for wooden overshoes to raise him up above the slop, though he could hardly have fought in those. His boots would just have to be burned afterward.

He drew his sword, the hilt still new, with the Warwick coat of arms enameled on silver. Rain streamed down it, joining a slurry of filth at his feet. He settled his shield against his left forearm and briefly touched the iron visor across his brow. Unconsciously, he shook his head, almost shuddering at the thought of disappearing into that mass of armed men with just a slit of light to see through. He left the visor up and turned to his men.

"Cut the line, gentlemen. Let's see if we can hold a single street. With me now."

Raising his sword, Warwick strode forward to the road crossing, his men forming up around him for the first strike.

THOMAS DOGTROTTED along roads he kept remembering from his youth, so that moments of nostalgia would strike him, set against the insane reality of following Jack Cade and his bloodstained followers through the heart of London. He kept Rowan close as they went and both of them wore the longbows strung on their shoulders, useless now with rain-stretched strings and all the arrows gone on the bridge. Swords were in short supply, and Thomas had only a stout oak club he'd wrestled from a dying man. Rowan was armed with a stabbing dagger he'd picked up from one of the soldiers foolish enough to stand in their way.

Jack's men took better weapons from each group they came across, overwhelming lines of soldiers and then robbing the bodies, replacing daggers with swords, bucklers with full shields, regardless of whose colors they carried. Even then, there were not enough for all those behind still clamoring for a good length of sharp iron.

The storm squalls were growing weaker and the moon had risen overhead, lending its light to the streets running directly beneath. The violence Thomas had seen in the previous hour had been simply breathtaking as Cade's men cut anyone in front of them to pieces and then walked on over the dead. The soldiers defending the city were in disarray, appearing in side streets or standing in panic as they realized they had maneuvered themselves into Cade's path. The king's men simply had too much ground to cover. Even if they guessed Cade's intentions from his path toward the Guildhall, they couldn't communicate to the individual forces in the streets. Roaming troops of soldiers either manned barricades in the wrong places, or followed the sounds of fighting as best they could in the maze.

Cade's front ranks had come across one group of around eighty men in mail just standing in an empty street under the moonlight, with their heads cocked as they listened to the night noise of the city. They had been cut apart, then suffered the indignity of having their greasy mail shirts wrenched from still-warm bodies.

The snake of Kent and Essex men had spread out as the streets diverged, adding new tails and routes as men lost track of each other in the darkness. The general direction was north, into the city, with Cannon Street and the London Stone far behind.

Thomas stretched his memory back, checking every crossroads for some sign that he was on the right path. He knew Jack looked to him to know the way, but the truth was he hadn't been in the city for twenty years and the streets always looked different at night. He chuckled at the thought of Jack's reaction if he led them round in a great circle and they saw the Thames again.

One street wider than the rest allowed Thomas to check his bearings on the moon and as soon as he was sure, he urged the others on. He sensed they had to keep moving, that the king's forces would be massing somewhere close. Thomas wanted to see the Guildhall, that symbol of the city's wealth and strength. He wanted the king and his lords to know they'd been in a real fight, not just some petty squabble with angry traders giving speeches and stamping their feet.

Ecclestone jerked and stumbled ahead of him. Thomas looked up in time to see a dark shape rush past Ecclestone's feet, squealing in terror before anyone could stab it.

"A pig! Just a bleeding, *fucking* pig," Ecclestone muttered to himself, lowering his razor.

No one laughed at the way he'd jumped and cursed. There was

something terrible and frightening about Ecclestone and his bloody short blade. He was not the sort of man to invite rough humor at his expense, not at all. Thomas noted how Ecclestone kept an eye on Jack at all times, watching his back. The thought made him look for the big Irishman, but for once, Paddy was nowhere to be seen.

As they passed a side street, Thomas looked into it automatically, almost coming to a shocked halt at the sight of ranks of armed men waiting there, just twenty paces away. He had a glimpse of iron and dark-bearded soldiers before he was carried past.

"Ware left!" he shouted to those behind, trying to hold himself back against the rush of moving men for a moment before he was shoved on. Thomas moved faster to catch up with Rowan and the group around Jack.

"Soldiers behind, Jack!" Thomas called.

He saw the big man look over his shoulder, but he too was deep in the press and they were all moving forward, unable to slow or stop. They heard the crash and shouting begin, but by then it was a hundred yards to the rear and they could only go on.

The streets were just as thick with clotted mud underfoot as they'd been since first entering London, but Thomas could see some of the houses had changed to stone, with better gutters running along the edges of the main road, so that men lurched as they put their feet into them. A wisp of memory told him where he was and he had time to shout a warning before the front lines staggered out into a wider stone yard.

London's Guildhall lay ahead of them under the rain, deliberately imposing, though it was less than a dozen years old. Thomas saw Jack raise his head from rebellious instinct as he caught sight of it, knowing only that it represented wealth and power and everything he had never known. The pace increased, and Thomas could see king's men scurrying around the great oak doors, screaming orders at each other in desperation as they saw hundreds of men come pouring out of the night streets at them.

On the other side, ranks of marching men appeared, their neat lines faltering as they saw Cade's army swelling into the open like a burst blister. At both ends of the small square, captains yelled orders and men began to run toward each other, raising weapons and howling. The rain drummed hard across the wide flagstones and the sound echoed back on all sides from the buildings, magnified and frightening in the moonlight.

DERRY WAS four streets east of the Guildhall when he heard the sounds of fresh fighting. He was still groggy from a blow taken from some swearing great farmer in a side alley as he raced through the city. Derry shook his head, feeling his eye and cheek swell until he could hardly see from his right side. He'd chopped the bastard, but left him wailing in pain when more of Cade's men had appeared.

Derry could hear Lord Scales panting over on his right. The baron had stopped his bristling resentment some time before, after Derry had led the soldiers out of an ambush, taking alleyways that were little wider than the shoulders of a single man with unerring accuracy. They'd run through reeking filth that was almost knee-deep in places, darting along turns and pushing aside damp washing when it slapped into their faces. They'd come out on the other side of a makeshift barricade and killed a dozen rioting men before they even knew they'd been flanked.

It should have been more of an advantage, Derry told himself. He knew the city as well as any urchin used to escaping from shopkeepers and the gangs. The king's defenders should have been able to use that knowledge to run rings around Cade's mob. The problem was that most of them had been summoned to London from the shires or even farther. Very few knew the streets they were running down. More than once that night, Derry and Scales had been brought up short by armored men, only to discover they were on the same side. It was cold and messy and chaotic, and Derry didn't doubt Cade was taking full advantage of the feeble defenses. If they'd had one man in command, it would have been easier, but with the king out of the city, eleven or twelve lords were their own authority over the forces they led. Derry cursed, feeling his lungs burn. Even if King Henry had been there in person, he doubted the Yorkist lords would have put themselves under anyone else's command. Not that night.

"Next left!" Scales shouted to those around him. "Head toward the Guildhall!"

Derry counted in his head. He'd just run past two side streets and was certain it hadn't been more.

"The Guildhall is two streets up from here," Derry said, his voice little more than a croak.

He could not see the baron's expression clearly, but the soldiers running with them knew better than to question their lord's orders. They swung left in good order, tramping around abandoned carts and a pile of bodies from some previous encounter that night. Derry thought his lungs were going to burst as he staggered over a dark mass of dead men, wincing as he heard bones creak and snap under his boots.

"God forgive me," he whispered, suddenly certain he'd felt one of them move and groan under his weight.

There were moving torches ahead and the sound of a woman screaming. Derry's face was burning and the spittle in his mouth was like thick pease pudding, but he set his jaw and stayed with the others. He told himself he'd be damned if he'd let young soldiers run the legs off him, but he was out of condition and it was beginning to show.

"Anyone looting or raping is fair game, lads," Derry called.

He sensed Lord Scales jerk his head around, but it hadn't been a true order. The growl of agreement from the soldiers made their feelings plain, but Scales took a moment to reply over his weariness and frustration.

"Cade's men are the priority," he said firmly. "Anything else, *anything*, can wait till morning."

Derry wondered what Scales thought their fourscore could do against thousands, but he kept his silence as the light ahead grew and they saw men streaming past. Whatever else Scales may have been, the man had no sense of fear at all. He didn't slow at all as he reached the junction. Derry could only heave for breath as the rest of them went with him, smacking against the bellowing crowd with a crash, followed instantly by the first screams. Scales's soldiers wore breastplates and mail shirts. They cut into the crowd like a spear thrust, striking down anything in their path. Around them, Cade's men fell back, scrambling to get away from soldiers who used their armor as its own weapon, smashing metal-clad elbows into the teeth of men with every swing.

Derry found himself plunging into the flow as if he'd leaped into a river. He blocked a swinging staff and stabbed out with a good bit of sharp iron that had seen service for a century or more. Scales's men swung swords and long-handled hammers as if they'd gone berserk in a great slaughter, cutting right across the torchlit procession. They held a place in the center of the road, blocking the onward movement as they faced those still coming up behind.

Derry glanced left and right, seeing the line stretched to the Guildhall in one direction and back around a corner on the other side. There seemed no end to the red-faced Kentish men, and he realized Scales had found the wellspring. For all Derry knew, this mob stretched the whole way back to the river. In the first mad rush, Scales and his men had carried all before them and blocked the road. They now stood together, bristling with weapons, daring the heaving crowd to try to regain the ground.

Derry chuckled as he saw the lack of desire in Cade's men. They'd been cheerfully following those in front, not quite ready to lead on their own, at least not then. The head of the snake traveled on, with the rearmost ranks looking back and calling jeers and insults, but still choosing to march on rather than turn and fight. With just eighty men, Scales had stopped the mob cold, but Derry saw them moving into side streets even as he had the thought.

"Watch the flanks!" he called.

There was no single route to the Guildhall, and by instinct or local knowledge, Cade's men were already working their way around, taking their torches with them so that the light in the street began to fade. Derry looked to Scales, but the lord was hesitating, indecision writ clearly on his face. They could hold the spot, or chase down the moving streams of men. Derry tried to think. Just eighty soldiers could not take on Cade's main force, though the narrow streets prevented them being easily crushed by huge numbers. Derry knew the Guildhall was poorly defended, with half the lords in London assuming Cade would go for the Tower. By the time they learned the truth, the Guildhall would have been gutted and the mob long gone.

As he rubbed his swollen face, Derry saw the flood of Cade's men break into a run as more of them vanished into the side streets. He craned his neck, wishing for more light, but there were cries of pain and rage not far off and the sounds seemed to be coming closer.

"What's going on back there?" Scales called to him.

Derry shook his head in confusion, then scowled. Coming around the corner and up the street was a marching rank of armored knights and men-at-arms, led by a man carrying the patterned shield of the Warwick family. The street continued to empty between the two groups, with the last of those between them casually spitted on swords as they tried and failed to climb out of trouble. In as many heartbeats, Derry saw a dozen men yanked down and butchered before the two groups faced each other, panting.

"Well met, Warwick," Scales said in delight to their young leader. "How many do you have?"

Richard Neville caught sight of Derry watching him and raised an eyebrow. He too had taken blows on his polished armor, but in the prime of his youth, he looked exhilarated rather than exhausted. He made a point of facing Scales to reply, ignoring Derry's sullen glower.

"I have my six hundred, Lord Scales. Enough to clear the streets of this rabble. Is it your intention to stand here until the sun rises, or may we pass?"

Even in moonlight and shadow, Derry could see Scales flush. The man had pride and his chin came up. There had been no offer to join their forces together, and Scales would not ask after such a comment from a younger man.

"The Guildhall is ahead," Scales said coldly. "Stand back, men. Back, there. Let Lord Warwick through."

Derry stood aside with the rest, watching as the earl's soldiers marched on with their heads high. Warwick led his six hundred armored men through them without a sideways glance, following the vanishing rear of Cade's Freemen.

"God save us from young fools," Derry heard Scales say to himself as they passed, making him smile.

"Where to now, my lord?" Derry said, pleased that at least his breathing was getting easier.

Scales looked at him. Both of them could hear the noise of moving men on all sides, creeping around their little force like rats in a barn. Scales frowned.

"If Cade himself is heading to the Guildhall, the choice is clear enough, though I'd rather not follow on the tail of such a Neville cockerel. Are you certain the Tower and the queen are safe?"

Derry considered.

"I cannot be sure, my lord, though there are king's men to hold it. I have runners—I don't doubt they are looking for me. Until I reach one of the spots they know, I'm as blind as that young Neville, with Cade's lot roaming all over London. I can't tell where they will strike next."

Scales showed his weariness as he rubbed a hand over his face.

"As tempting as it is to think of Lord Warwick running into Cade's bully boys, I should reinforce him. I cannot split such a small force further. Damn it, Brewer, there are just too many of them! Must we chase them all night?"

Derry looked round in time to see a rush of men come skidding round a corner ahead of them. With a great shout, they began to charge the group of men-at-arms, holding swords and billhooks.

"It seems they'll come to us, my lord," Derry shouted as he readied himself. "They're most obliging like that."

PADDY WIELDED a hammer as if his life depended on it, which he had to admit, it did. He'd been surprised when Jack took him aside in Southwark the night before, but it made sense. Jack would lead the king's men on a chase through the rest of the city, but to gain entrance to the Tower would take precious time. Running straight for it and then hammering at the gatehouse while every soldier in London converged on that spot would be a quick road to the Tyburn gibbets the following morning—and slit throats for most.

He paused for a moment to wipe the sweat that poured into his eyes and stung.

"Jesus, they built this door like a mountain," he said.

The men around him hacked heavy axes into the ancient wood, wrenching the blades back and forth to spit splinters as wide as a forearm out onto the stones. They'd been at the work for an hour of solid labor, with fresh men taking the weapons as each group tired. It was Paddy's third turn with a hammer and the men around him had learned to give him room after he'd knocked one down with broken ribs.

As he began to swing again, Paddy leaned back and tried to listen to the scurrying footsteps beyond the gatehouse. He knew they would be waiting, and he had no way of knowing if there were a few dozen or a thousand men making ready for him. The gatehouse had one weakness and he thanked God for it. Separated from the main walls, the stone mass of the gatehouse itself protected his men from arrows and bolts. He'd already heard the rattle of a portcullis coming down somewhere farther on, but a few of his lads had swum the moat and shoved iron bars through the drawbridge chains. It would stay down and, judging by the damage done to the outer door, Woodchurch had been right about one thing. Enough men with hammers and axes could smash their way through just about anything. Paddy felt the door give as he put all his strength and weight into another blow. The burly axemen had cut a long, thin hole in one of the iron-clasped beams. There were lights moving around across the moat in there and Paddy tried not to think of the damage archers could do shooting at him while he hammered away at an iron lattice. It would be brutal work and he'd called a few shield-bearers to dart in as best they could. It wasn't much, but it might save a few lives, his own among them.

With a great crack, one of the iron hinges failed. Somehow, the central lock stayed in place, so that the door yawned in at the top. With two others hammering between his blows, Paddy belted at the iron fastenings even faster, feeling great shudders go up his arms and his grip weaken.

"Come *on*, boy," he said, to the gate as well as himself. He saw the iron lock shear bright and clean and he almost fell through onto the jammed drawbridge with the power of his last swing.

"Mother of God," he said in awe then, looking across the walkway to an iron lattice twice his height. Arrows thumped into it from the courtyard beyond. Only a few came through, but Paddy's men were packed in around the broken door and two fell, swearing and shouting in pain.

"Shields here!" Paddy called. "Get a rhythm going—the boys will swing, then you step in with shields to guard us between each blow. We'll have that iron beauty down in an eyeblink."

They raced forward, roaring to frighten the defenders as they came up against the cold grid. It was made of straps of black iron, bolted together with polished spike heads showing at each junction. Paddy rested his hand on the metal. With enough force against the junctions, he thought the bolts could be broken.

Through the portcullis, Paddy could see the inner towers of the fortress. Above them all, the White Tower stood tall and pale in the moonlight, with dark shadows swarming around it. His eyes gleamed, both at the thought of the violence to come and the Royal Mint. He'd never stand as close to such wealth again, not if he lived for a hundred years.

MARGARET FELT goose pimples run up her arms as she shivered, looking down. The rain had stopped at last, leaving the ground a quagmire below her feet. Stamping and blowing in the cold, four hundred king's men were waiting for the besiegers to break their way in. From the height of the entrance to the White Tower, she could see them made black against the torches, line upon line of standing soldiers. She had watched them prepare, struck with awe at their calm. Perhaps this was why the English had crushed so many French armies, she thought. They didn't panic, even when the odds and the numbers were against them.

The officer in charge was a tall guard captain named Brown. Dressed in a white tabard over chain mail, with a sword dangling from his hip, he was a dashing figure, easily visible. He had introduced himself to her with an elaborate bow earlier that day, a man young for his authority who seemed to think the chances of Cade even reaching the Tower were slim. Margaret had been touched at the young man's attempts to reassure her. She noted Captain Brown had cultivated large black whiskers almost as fine as those of her brother-in-law, Frederick. The sight of them bristling as he moved his lips in thought made her want to smile every time she saw him. Even when news had come of the forces marching closer, Brown remained confident, at least when he reported to her. In just a short time, she'd come to value the brief moments when he returned to the bottom of the steps, his face flushed from checking on all the posts. With his head cocked, he'd look up to see if she was still there, then smile when she came out. If all those brief times were added together, they would have made less than an hour, but still, she felt she knew him.

Margaret had seen the captain's frustration when his archers on the walls found they had few targets. The mob outside had sent only a small group to hammer the gatehouse door and then break the portcullis, while the rest stayed back as a dark blot, waiting to come roaring in when they were given the chance. As the moon rose, Margaret could hear the occasional yelp as a crossbow bolt found its mark, but it was hard to aim well in the darkness and the hammering blows outside went on and on, first against wood and then the higher, ringing tones of strikes on iron.

Captain Brown had yelled for a group of crossbowmen to come down off the walls and do their work below. Margaret had found herself shuddering in the night air as he sent them right up to the portcullis, so that they put their weapons almost to the iron lattice before pulling the triggers. The hammering had fallen away to nothing for a time, as those outside arranged their shields against the iron. The speed of the blows had surely lessened, but they still came. One by one, the bolts and junctions sheared with a hard note, different from the striking blows. Margaret felt herself jump as each one failed, forcing herself to smile and stand still on the steps.

As the ranks of king's men took their positions to withstand the first rush, Margaret saw the white tabard of Captain Brown as he came striding back, looking up at his queen from across the open space. She waited for him, her hands gripping the wooden railing tightly.

"Your Royal Highness," he called up. "I'd hoped for reinforcements, but without a miracle, I think these men will be upon us at any moment."

"What would you have me do?" Margaret replied, pleased that she too could affect calm and that her voice didn't tremble.

"If you'll permit, my lady, I'll have a few of the men destroy these stairs. If you wouldn't mind standing back, we'll have them down in an instant. I have left six good men to hold the doorway of the White Tower. You have my word that you'll be safe, as long as you stay up there."

Margaret bit her lip, looking from the face of the earnest young officer to those waiting to withstand the flood.

"Can you not join your men here in the tower, Captain? I . . ." She blushed, unsure how to make the offer of sanctuary without offending him. To her surprise, he beamed up at her, delighted at something.

"You could order it, my lady, but, um . . . if you don't mind, I'd prefer it if you didn't. My place is down here and, who knows, we may send them running yet."

Before Margaret could speak again, a dozen men carrying axes and hammers had run up and Captain Brown was busy giving instructions.

"Stand clear now, if you please, Your Highness," he called from below.

Margaret took a step back, crossing from the wooden stairs to the open stone door of the tower, even as the steps began to shudder and shake. It was not long before the whole structure collapsed and Margaret watched from a height as the men set about reducing each piece to useless kindling. She found there were tears in her eyes as Captain Brown saluted her before returning to his men, all waiting for the portcullis to fail and the fighting to begin.

CHAPTER 28

Jack Cade came out of the Guildhall, winding a bit of rough hemp rope in his hands. He'd cheered with Ecclestone and the others when the king's own treasurer had been strung up to dance, the lord's face growing purple as they watched and laughed. Lord Say had been one of those responsible for the king's taxes and Jack felt no remorse at all. In fact, he'd cut the piece of rope as a keepsake and he was only sorry he couldn't find a few more of those who commanded the bailiffs and sheriffs around the country.

When he looked up from his thoughts, his eyes widened. There were still men coming into the open square around the Guildhall. Those who had been there for some time had found barrels of beer or spirits, that much was clear. Already drunk on violence and success, they'd used the time he'd been inside to loot every house around. Some of them were singing, others lying completely senseless, or dozing with their arms wrapped around cork-stoppered clay bottles. Still more were taking out their spite on the survivors of the last group to attack them. The few king's soldiers left alive had been disarmed and were being shoved back and forth in a ring of men, punched and kicked wherever they turned.

Jack glanced at Ecclestone in disbelief as he saw staggering men walk past with armfuls of stolen goods. Two of them were wrestling with a bolt of shimmering cloth, coming to blows and knocking each other down as he stared at them. Jack frowned as a woman began screaming nearby, the sound becoming a croak as someone choked her to silence.

Thomas Woodchurch came out behind Cade, his expression hardening as he viewed the chaos and blood-spattered stones.

"Sodom and Gomorrah, Jack," he muttered. "If it goes on, they'll all be asleep by dawn and they'll find their throats cut. Can you put them back in harness? We're vulnerable here—and drunken fools can't fight."

Cade was a little tired of Woodchurch believing he knew best all the time. He kept silent, thinking. His own throat ached for a drink, but it would wait, he told himself. The rainstorm had passed, but London was still reeling. He sensed his one chance was in danger of slipping away. He'd bowed his head to king's men all his life, been forced to look down from the hard eyes of judges as they put on the red or green robe and pronounced their judgments. For just a time, he could kick their teeth in, but he knew it wouldn't last.

"Come tomorrow, they'll appoint new men to chase us," he grumbled. "But what if they do? I have put the fear of God into them tonight. They'll remember that."

Woodchurch looked up at the Kentish captain, his irritation showing. He'd hoped for more than just a night of bloodshed and looting. With a fair number of the men, he'd hoped to change the city, perhaps even to wrench some sort of freedom from the hands of the king's men. They'd all learned King Henry was long gone by then, but it didn't have to end in drunken madness, not if Cade kept going. A few dead nobles, a few bits of cloth and pouches of gold. It was nowhere near enough to repay what had been taken.

"Dawn can't be far off now," Woodchurch said. "I'm for the Tower. If the king is gone as they say, at least I can leave London a rich man. Are you game, Jack?"

Cade smiled, looking up at the passage of the moon overhead.

"I sent Paddy there in the first rush. He's either dead or in by now. I'll walk with you, Tom Woodchurch, if you'll walk with me."

They laughed like boys then, while Ecclestone looked on sourly at this display of camaraderie. A moment later, Jack began ordering his men back to the streets. His voice was a bass roar that echoed back from the houses of aldermen all around.

Derry was exhausted. He knew he was a dozen years younger than Lord Scales and could only wonder at the source of the man's manic energy as they reached yet another alleyway and trotted down it in pitch darkness. At least the rain had eased off. They had four men out before and behind, calling warnings or opportunities as they found them. They'd been fighting in the streets for hours, and Derry had lost count of the men he'd killed in the black night, small moments of horror and fear while he cut strangers or felt the pain as their knives and clubs got through to him in turn.

He'd bound his leg where some nameless Kentish plowboy had stuck a spear into it. A spear! Derry could still hardly believe he'd been wounded by something that had decorative ribbons on the shaft. He carried the first few feet of it in his left hand by then, having ripped the last owner from life. A heavy seax was stuck through his belt and Derry wasn't alone in having picked up weapons from the dead. After so long struggling with strangers in the wind and dark, he was just desperate to see the sun again.

Scales's men were down to just three dozen from the original eighty. They'd lost only a few at a time before running straight into a couple of hundred looters. Those men had been stinking drunk, which was a blessing as it had slowed them down. Yet that little stand had left almost half Scales's men dying on their backs in filth and their own blood.

It was all falling apart, Derry could feel it. Cade's men had reached the heart of the city and whatever rage had brought them in had exploded into a desire to loot, rape, and murder while they could. It was something Derry knew well, from battles he'd seen, something about killing and surviving that put a shine in the blood and made a man wild. They might have been an army of Kentish Freemen coming in, but they'd become a savage and terrifying mob. Londoners crouched behind their own doors across the city, whispering prayers that no one would try to get in.

"East again," Scales ordered from up ahead. "My scouts say there are fifty or so ahead, by the Cockspur Inn. We can hit them while they're still bringing out the barrels."

Derry shook his head to clear it, wishing he had a drink himself. London had more than three hundred taverns and alehouses. He'd already passed a dozen he knew from his youth, buildings shuttered and dark with the owners barricaded inside. Licking dry lips, Derry would have given a gold coin for a pint at that point, especially as he'd thrown away his water flask after seeing it pierced. The thing had probably saved his life, but its loss left him dry as a panting dog.

"East again," he agreed.

Cade seemed to be heading back across the city and, in the condition they were in, all Scales and Derry could do was shadow him from a distance and pick off some of the smaller groups milling around in his wake—preferably the drunken ones, if they had a choice. Derry raised his head. He knew this part of the city. He took his bearings, rubbing his face with both hands to sharpen himself up. They were on

Three Needle Street, a haunt from before he'd begun shaving. The livery hall of the Merchant Taylors was close by.

"Hold there a moment, Lord Scales, if you would be so good," Derry called. "Let me see if there's anyone waiting for me."

Scales gestured irritably and Derry jogged off down the road, his feet squelching to the ankles. He'd been lost without his informants, but with the city heaving with knots of fighting, he'd been unable to find them. He reached the livery house and saw nothing. With a soft curse, he was turning to go back to the group when someone stepped out from a shadowed doorway. Derry jerked his spearhead up in shock at the sound, convinced he was about to be attacked.

"Master Brewer? Sorry, sir. I wasn't sure it was you."

Derry gathered himself, clearing his throat to cover his embarrassment.

"Who's that?" he said, his free hand resting on the hilt of the seax in his belt, just in case. Loyalty was in short supply that night.

"John Burroughs, sir," the shadow replied. Under the eaves of the houses above, there was almost no light.

"Well? You've found me, then," Derry snapped. "If you ask me for the password, I may just hand you your own entrails. Just tell me what you know."

"Right, sir, sorry. I came from the Tower, sir. When I left, they'd broken through the outer gatehouse."

Derry's eyes widened unseen in the darkness.

"Anything else? Have you heard from Jim or the Kellys?"

"Not since Cade's lot came in, sir, sorry."

"Run back, then. Tell them I'm coming with a thousand men."

Derry sensed his informant looking skeptically up the street to the ragged group with Lord Scales.

"I'll have more by then, don't doubt it. The queen is in the Tower, Burroughs. Bring anyone else you can find."

He watched as the man ran off at the best speed he could make through the reeking slop of the street.

"Christ, Cade, you cunning old sod," Derry breathed aloud. He began to run in the opposite direction, to where Lord Scales waited impatiently for news.

"They're attacking the Tower, my lord. My man said they were already inside the outer walls."

Scales looked up at the night sky. The first light of dawn was showing at last. His spirits lifted now that he could finally begin to see the streets around him.

"Dawn is almost here, thank the Lord. Thank you, too, Master Brewer. We'll leave that group at the Cockspur for someone else. Can you plot a course to the Tower from here?"

"Easy as winking, my lord. I know these streets."

"Then lead us in, Brewer. Stop for nothing. The queen's safety comes first."

PADDY LOOKED UP at the White Tower, oddly tempted to raise his hand in salute to those within, not that they would have been able to see it. His men had fought the king's soldiers to a bloody last stand, loping along the tops of the outer walls and taking them one by one or in small groups, offering no quarter. For all their fine swords and mail, he'd had the best part of two thousand charging around inside the fortress, breaking down doors and removing everything worth taking. He knew the best pieces would surely be within the massive walls of the White Tower, but there was just no way to reach them.

It stood unmarked, painted pale and gleaming in the moonlight. The only entrance was on the first floor, with the stairs reduced to kindling by the time he'd broken through the portcullis. It was such a simple thing to balk his assault. Given a day, Paddy thought he could have put something together, but the soldiers waiting inside the small entrance door could defend it easily and there wasn't enough time.

He looked around, chewing on his lip. He could see across the inner yard to the massive walls. Dawn was coming, and he had a strong sense that he should not be trapped within the complex of towers and walls when it came. As he stood and waited for the sun to rise, he saw two of his men staggering with the weight of an iron-bound chest.

"What do you have there, lads?" he called.

"Coins!" one of them shouted back. "More silver and gold than you would believe!"

Paddy shook his head.

"It's too heavy, you daft sod. Fill your pockets, man. Jesus, how far will you get with a chest?"

The man shouted back a curse and Paddy considered going after him to batter some sense into his head, before he mastered his temper. Jack and Woodchurch had been right about the Royal Mint, at least. Even without breaching the White Tower at the center, they'd found enough gold to live like kings, if they could just get it out of the city. Shining gold coins littered the stones and Paddy picked one up and stared at it as the light improved. He'd never held gold before that night and yet his pockets now bulged with the things. It was a heavy metal, he'd discovered, with a great weight of them resting on his shoulder, in a sack made from a cloak.

He wondered if they could find carts to carry their new wealth back across London Bridge. Yet the light was growing all the time and he feared the day. The king's men had been cut to pieces all night, but they'd surely come back with a vengeance when they could see the damage done to the city.

One of the men Paddy had placed high on the outer walls raised his arm and shouted. Paddy ran closer to hear, jingling with every step and dreading the news of an army come to relieve the Tower.

"It's Cade!" the man was yelling through cupped hands. *"Cade!"*

Paddy sagged in relief. Better than furious ranks of king's soldiers, at least. Within the Tower walls, he could not yet see the sun, but it was rising all the same, revealing swirling mists and corpses on all sides. Paddy began to trot to the broken gatehouse to greet his friend. Behind him, the soldiers in the White Tower called insults and threats from the windows. He ignored them all. They might have been untouchable behind walls fifteen feet thick, but that trick with the high door meant they couldn't come out and bother him, either. He waved cheerfully to them before going out through the gate to the street beyond.

JACK CADE was about dead on his feet after a night spent fighting and walking. His legs and hands were frozen, spattered with filth and blood. He'd crossed the city twice in the darkness and the rising sun revealed how battered and ragged his men had become, as if they'd been through a war instead of just one night in London. It didn't help that half of them were still drunk, looking blearily at those around them and just trying to stay upright and not vomit. He'd passed furious orders to leave the taverns alone, but most of the damage was already done.

By the time they reached the outer walls of the Tower, Jack was feeling a worm of worry in his gut, as well as his exhaustion. He cheered up when he saw broken chests of new gold and silver coins on the ground, but as his men rushed with raucous cries to grab their share, he could see some had lost or thrown down their weapons. Most of those still with him were too tired and red-eyed to push away a small child, never mind a king's man. A few hundred fresh soldiers would slaughter the lot of them. He looked up to see Woodchurch wearing the same worried expression.

"I think we should get back across the river, Jack," Thomas said. He was swaying as he stood there, though his son Rowan was as busy as the rest, collecting handfuls of gold and stuffing them about his person.

Jack looked up at the White Tower, hundreds of years old and still standing strong after the night they'd all been through. He sighed to himself, rubbing the bristles on his chin with one hand. London was waking up around them and half the men he'd brought in were either dead or lying in a drunken stupor.

"We made 'em dance a bit, didn't we? That was the best night of my life, Tom Woodchurch. I've a mind to come back tomorrow and have another one just the same."

Woodchurch laughed, a dry sound from a throat made sore by shouting. He would have replied, but the Irishman came jogging up at that moment, embracing Jack and almost lifting him off his feet. Woodchurch heard the jingle of coins and laughed, seeing how the Irishman bulged all over. He was big enough to carry the weight.

"It's good to see you among the living, Jack!" Paddy said. "There's more gold here than I can believe. I have gathered a share for you, but I'm thinking we should perhaps take ourselves away now, before the king's men come back with blood in their eyes."

Jack sighed, satisfaction and disappointment mingling in him in equal measures. It had been a grand night, with some moments of wonder, but he knew better than to push his luck.

"All right, lads. Pass the word. Head back to the bridge."

The sun was up by the time Jack's men were bullied and shoved away from their search for a few last coins at the Tower. Paddy had found a sewer-cleaner's cart a few streets away, with a stench so strong it made the eyes water. Even so, they'd draped it in an embroidered cloth and piled it high with sacks and chests and anything else that could be lifted. There was no ox to pull it, so a dozen men grasped the shafts with great good humor, heaving it along the roads toward the river.

Hundreds more emerged from every side road they passed, some exulting at the haul or with looted items they still carried, others looking guilty or shamefaced, or just blank with horror at the things they'd seen and done. Still more were carrying jugs of spirits and roaring or singing in twos and threes, still splashed with drying blood.

The people of London had slept little, if at all. As they removed furniture from behind doors and pulled out nails from shutters, they discovered a thousand scenes of destruction, from smashed houses to piles of dead men all over the city. There was no cheering then for Jack Cade's army of Freemen. With no single voice or signal, the men of the city came out with staffs and blades, gathering in dozens and then hundreds to block the streets leading back into the city. Those of Cade's men who had not already reached the river were woken by hard wooden clogs or enraged householders battering at them or cutting their throats. They had suffered through a night of terror and there was no mercy to be had.

A few of the drunken Kentish men scrambled up and ran like rabbits before hounds, dragged down by the furious Londoners as they saw more and more of what Cade's invasion had cost the city. As the sun rose, groups of Cade's men came together, holding people at bay with swords and axes while they backed away. Some of those groups were trapped with crowds before and behind and were quickly disarmed and bound for hanging, or beaten to death in the sort of wild frenzy they knew from just hours before.

The sense of an enraged city reached even those who'd made it to London Bridge. Jack found himself glancing back over his shoulder at lines of staring Londoners, calling insults and shouting after him. Some of them even beckoned for him to come back and he could only gape at the sheer numbers the city was capable of fielding against him. He did not look at Thomas, though he knew the man would be thinking back to his warning about rape and looting. London had been late to rouse, but the idea of just strolling back in the next night was looking less and less likely.

Jack kept his head high as he walked back across the bridge. Close to the midpoint, he saw the pole with the head and the white-horse shield still bound to it. It was mud-spattered, and the sight of it brought a shudder down Jack's spine as he recalled the mad dash under pouring rain and crossbow bolts the night before. Even so, he stopped and picked it up, handing his ax to Ecclestone at his side. Nearby lay the body of the boy, Jonas, who'd carried it for a time. Jack shook his head in sorrow, feeling exhaustion hit him like a hammer blow.

With a heave, he raised the banner pole. The men around him and on the bridge behind all cheered the sight of it as they marched away from the city and the dark memories they had made.

CHAPTER 29

Richard Neville felt blood squish in his armored boot with every step. He thought the gash under his thigh plate wasn't too bad, but being forced to keep walking on it meant the blood still dribbled, making his leggings sodden and staining the oily metal red and black. He'd taken the wound as his men stormed across the open square by the Guildhall, slaughtering the drunken revelers. Warwick had seen the lack of resistance and cursed himself for dropping his guard long enough for one of the prone figures to jam a knife between his plates as he stood over him. Cade had gone by then, of course. Warwick had seen the results of the man's "trial" in the purple features of Lord Say, left sprawled under the beam where they'd hanged him.

He felt as if he'd been fighting forever in the rain and dark, and as the sun rose, he was tempted to find a place to sleep. His men were staggering with exhaustion and he couldn't remember feeling so tired in all his young life. He just couldn't make a good pace, even to follow the host of Cade's men as they used the gray light before true dawn to push once more across the city.

Warwick cursed to himself as he came to the mouth of another silent road. After the rain, the damp coming off the river had filled some of the streets with thick mist. He relied only on his hearing to tell him the street was empty, but if there were men waiting in another silent ambush, he knew he'd walk right into it.

His soldiers were still among the largest forces of king's men in the city. Their armor and iron mail had saved many of them. Even so, Warwick shuddered at dark memories, of Kentish madmen rushing them from three or four directions at once. He'd lost a hundred and eighty killed outright and another dozen too badly wounded to go on with him. He'd allowed the most seriously injured men to enter houses, calling his rank and the king's name and then just kicking doors in when no one dared to answer.

London was terrified; he could feel it like the mist seeping beneath his armor and mingling with the blood and sweat of a night on his feet. He'd seen so many dead bodies, it was almost odd to pass a street without its complement of corpses. Far too many of them were liveried soldiers, wearing a lord's colors on their shields or on tunics plastered over bloody mail. The night dew had frozen on some of them, so that they sparkled and gleamed as if encased in ice.

As he trudged on, Warwick was coldly furious: with himself and with King Henry for not staying to organize the defense. God, it looked as if York was right, after all. The king's warrior father would have shown himself early and hit hard. Henry of Agincourt would have had Cade strung up by dawn, if the rebels had managed to get into the city at all. The old king would have made London a fortress.

The thought made Warwick stop in the middle of a street of butchers. The foulness underfoot was mostly red, thick with hog bristles as well as scraps of rotting flesh and bone. His nose had become used to treading in such things, but this particular lane had an acrid tang that almost helped to clear his head.

Cade's men were streaming east and south. It was true the bridge lay in that direction, but so did the Tower and the young queen sheltering within its walls. Warwick closed his eyes for a brief moment, aching to find a place to sit. He could imagine all too easily the relief that would flood his wrists and knees if he allowed himself to stop. The thought made his legs buckle, so that he had to lock his knees with an effort.

In the growing light, his closest men were looking back at him, eyes swollen, wounds bound in grubby cloths. More than a few had strapped their hands where they had broken small bones in wrists or fingers. They looked bedraggled and miserable, but they were still his, loyal to his house and his name. Warwick straightened, summoning his will with a massive effort.

"The queen is in the Tower, gentlemen. I'll want to see her safe before we can rest. The day is come. There'll be reinforcements this morning, bringing fire and the sword for all those who took part. There will be justice then."

The heads of his soldiers drooped as they understood that their young lord would not let them stop. None of them dared to raise a voice in complaint, and they pushed on through the mist, staring with bloodshot eyes as it swirled about them.

MARGARET SHUDDERED in the cold, staring out of the entrance door to the White Tower. Her field of vision was blocked by the outer walls, so that she couldn't see much more than the results of the night's battles around her stone fastness. Mist had begun to creep across the bodies lying on the ground below, moving on fitful breezes. It would burn off in the day, but for a time, the paleness crawled over the dead, touching them intimately and making them mere humps and hills in the white.

It had been a night of terrors, waiting for Cade's rough men to smash their way inside. She'd done her best to show courage and keep her dignity, but the soldiers in the tower had been just as nervous as they peered out and down into blackness, straining to understand every sound.

Margaret dipped her head, saying a prayer for Captain Brown, now lying sightless and still where he'd fallen in her defense. Her view of the fighting had been in spots and gleams of moonlight, a frozen witness to rushing, bawling shadows and a constant clash of metal that was like a whispering voice.

That voice had fallen silent as the hours passed, replaced by the loud talk and hard laughter of Cade's men. As the sun rose, she saw his followers running riot, breaking into the mint and staggering out under the weight of anything they could carry. She'd heard the mob hooting in delight and seen gold and silver coins spilled as carelessly as lives, to roll and spin untended on the stones.

There had been a moment when one of them stood and looked up at the tower, as if he could see her standing back in the shadows of the door. Whoever he was, the man stood head and shoulders above those around him. She'd wondered then if it was Cade himself, but the name she spat in her thoughts was called from the walls and the big man trotted away to meet his master. The sun was up and the tower had held. She gave thanks for that much.

Others came past the outer walls then, to stare up at the White Tower. Margaret could feel their gaze creeping over it and her, making her want to scratch. If she'd had crossbows, it would have been the time to order their use, but such weapons as they'd had lay in dead hands on the ground below. It was strange to look down on the enemies who'd assaulted the city and be unable to do anything, though they stood within reach and walked as if they owned the land around them.

By the time the sun cleared the outer walls, flooding gold light across the White Tower, they were marching away, carrying their spoils and leaving their dead behind for the Tower ravens to pluck and snag. The mist was thinning, and Margaret slumped against the frozen doorway, making one of the guards reach nervously out to her in case she fell. He caught himself before he laid hands on the queen and she never noticed the movement, her attention captured by the jingling sound of armored men coming through the broken gate.

It was with an odd sensation of relief that she recognized Derry Brewer walking at the head of a small group. As he spotted the bodies and broke into a lurching run, she saw how filthy he was, spattered to the thighs with all manner of foul muck. He came right to the foot of the tower, standing in the smashed wood of the stairs and looking up at the doorway.

Margaret came forward into the sunlight and she could have blessed him for the look of relief on his face as he caught sight of her.

"Thank God," he said softly. "Cade's men are on their way out of the city, my lady. I am pleased to see you well." Derry looked around. "It's difficult to think of a safer place in London at this moment, but I imagine you are sick of this tower, at least for today. If you'll allow me, I'll have men sent to find ladders, or to build them."

"Let down a rope to him," Margaret ordered the soldiers clustering behind her. "While they find me a way down, Derry, you can climb up."

He didn't question the command and only groaned quietly to himself, wondering if he had the strength. In the end, it took three men pulling on the rope above before he reached the lip and they were able to heave him over. Derry lay gasping on the stone floor, quite unable to rise until the guards helped him. He attempted a bow and almost fell.

"You are exhausted," Margaret said, reaching out to take his arm. "Come in farther. There is food enough, and wine."

"Ah, that would be very welcome, my lady. I am not quite at my best, I admit."

Half an hour later, he was seated in a room within the tower, wrapped in a blanket by the fire and chewing fat slices of cured ham as he fought against the desire to sleep. Outside, the noise of hammers told him Lord Scales was busying himself constructing rough steps. Some of the men inside had already climbed down to help with the work. Derry was left alone with the young queen, watching him with large brown eyes that missed nothing.

Margaret bit her lip with impatience, forcing herself to wait until he had satisfied his hunger and belched into his fist, the platter of ham polished clean. She needed to know what Derry had witnessed in the night. Perhaps first, she needed him to know what had been done for her.

"Captain Brown was a good, brave man," she said.

Derry looked up sharply, seeing the unnatural paleness of her face, the fear and exhaustion still showing in her.

"I knew him well, my lady. I was sorry to see he hadn't come through. It was a hard night for all of us."

"It was. Good men have died in my defense, Derry. And I live still. We have both survived—and the sun has risen."

Her voice firmed as she spoke, as she put her grief and weariness away for another time.

"How good is your information today, Master Brewer?" she asked.

He straightened in the chair, struck by the formality and understanding that it was a recall to duty. He was hard-pressed not to groan as every bone and muscle sent sharp warnings at the movement.

"Not as good as I would like, my lady. I know Cade has marched back to the bridge and over it. I have men watching him, ready to run back to me if something changes. For today, I would imagine he'll stay in Southwark to rest and count his spoils." His voice became bitter as he spoke. "But he'll be back tonight, I don't doubt. That is the burr, my lady. That is the thorn. I don't have the count of men lost, but from what I've seen and heard, there are precious few soldiers left in London. We have no more than a few hundred, perhaps a thousand men at most, from here to the west wall. With your permission, I will send riders out today to summon every knight and man-at-arms within range for tonight."

"Will it be enough?" she asked, looking into the flames of the fire.

He considered lying to raise her spirits, but there was no point. He shook his head.

"The lords of the north have armies to crush Cade and half a dozen like him, but we can't reach them in time. Those we can . . . well, there are not enough, not if he comes back tonight."

Margaret felt her fears surface at the despair she saw in him. Derry was never down for long, she knew that. He always bounced up when he was knocked onto his back. Seeing his hopelessness was almost more frightening than the dark murders of the night before.

"How is it possible?" she said in a whisper. It might have been a question she did not mean to ask aloud, but Derry shrugged.

"We were spread too thin, or the unrest was too wide to contain. My lady, it doesn't matter what has gone before. We are here today, and we will defend London tonight. I think you should get out of the city, either to Kenilworth or the palace in Greenwich. I can have boats brought before noon to take you. I will know then that you are safe, no matter what follows."

Margaret hesitated a beat before she shook her head.

"No. It has not yet come to that. If I flee the city, this man Cade will be calling himself king before tomorrow—or perhaps Lord York the day after, if he is behind this."

Derry looked sharply at the young queen, wondering how much she understood of the threats arrayed against her family.

"If York's hand is anywhere in this attack, he's been more subtle than before, my lady. I would not be surprised if there are agents working in his name, but I know for a fact that the man himself is still in Ireland."

Her voice was low and urgent as she replied, leaning closer in case they could be overheard.

"I am aware of the threat, Derry. York is the royal 'heir,' after all." Unconsciously, her hand dipped to run over her womb as she went on. "He *is* a subtle man, Derry. It would not surprise me if he were taking care to stay clear and untainted, while his loyal followers bring down my husband."

Derry blinked slowly at her, struggling against the weariness and warmth that threatened sleep, just when he needed to be sharp. He saw her thinking, sitting close enough to watch the pupils of her eyes contract and then widen.

"I saw them take the fresh-minted gold," she said, staring at nothing, "last night and this morning. Cade's men have found loot beyond their wildest dreams. They will be counting and gloating over it today, aware that they will never see such wealth again."

"My lady?" Derry said in confusion. He sat up and rubbed his face, feeling the calluses on his hands.

"They do not know how weak we are, how feeble the defense has become. They *must* not know." She took a sharp breath, making the decision. "I will send them a pardon for all their crimes, on condition they disperse."

"A *what*?" Derry said in shock.

He began to rise from his chair, but the queen pressed a hand on his shoulder. Derry looked at her in disbelief. He had fought Cade's men through a night that had lasted for an eternity and now she would pardon them all, let them all walk home with royal gold in their pockets? It was madness, and he searched for the least offensive way of telling her so.

"A pardon, Derry," she repeated, her voice firm. "In full, in writing, delivered to Jack Cade in his camp at Southwark. A chance for them to take what they have won and leave. Tell me of another choice that would achieve the same result. Can they be held back?"

Derry looked at her.

"We could destroy the bridge!" he said. "There is gunpowder in the armory here, not fifty feet from where we are now. With enough barrels, I could bring it down. How would they cross then?"

The young French queen blanched for a moment, considering her fortune that the rioters had not breached the powder stores and used them. She gave silent thanks, and then, after a time, shook her head.

"You would only provoke another attack. If we had a free day, perhaps you could bring it down, but Cade will cross again into the city the moment he sees barrels being rolled along the streets. *Listen* to me, Derry. Every man who entered London deserves to hang, but how many of them died last night? Thousands? The rest will imagine another night like it—and they will think of the wealth they have already gained. Some of them—God grant, *most* of them—will want so much just to go *home*. I will give them the chance to leave. If they refuse, we have lost nothing. If they take what I offer, we will have saved London."

She stopped, watching for his agreement and seeing only blankness. "Or will you let them come back in for another night of rape and slaughter? I heard their talk, Derry. I know what they have done.

Monsieur, I wish with every sinew of my heart to see them punished, but if there is another answer, I do not have it. So you *will* obey me in this, Master Brewer."

Derry was still staring in astonishment at the cold fury he was seeing when his attention was dragged away by shouting outside the tower. Margaret too looked up with an expression of sudden fear. His heart broke for her and he levered himself to his feet.

"Let me see what it is, my lady. Lord Scales is a good man, don't worry."

Derry cast the blanket aside rather than appear at the tower door like a frightened old woman in a shawl. He came out into the sunshine and looked down to see Scales arguing with Warwick, both men pointing up at the tower. Derry felt thoughts stir in the sluggish broth between his ears. He leaned against the door, looking down on them both as nonchalantly as he could manage.

"Morning, my lord Warwick. I see you survived, thank God. Better late than not at all, eh?"

Warwick looked up, his expression darkening at the sight of Derry grinning down at him from above.

"I will see the queen, Master Brewer. I will see for myself that she is unharmed."

"As you wish, my lord. Shall I let a rope down for you, or will you wait for stairs and ladders?"

"That's *exactly* what *I* was saying . . ." Lord Scales began indignantly.

Warwick glowered at both of them, but he was young and he shrugged at what might have been an indignity for an older man.

"Rope, Brewer. Right now, if you please."

Derry uncoiled the one he'd used himself. He saw Warwick come up it at surprising speed, feeling suddenly pleased the young earl had not been present when the soldiers had heaved him up like a sack of coal. As Warwick came to his feet on the lip of the doorway, Derry vanished back to the warmer rooms within. He reached the queen just a few feet ahead of the man behind.

"Your Royal Highness, it is my pleasure to announce Richard Neville, Earl of Warwick," Derry announced, stopping Warwick in his tracks while he was forced to bow. "On the matter we were discussing, I am of course your obedient servant." He stared off into the middle distance as he spoke. "I will attend to it immediately, my lady."

Margaret dismissed him with a gesture. The significance of the name Neville had not been wasted on her, but there were guards within call and she felt no fear facing such a battered and exhausted young man. Derry beat a retreat, followed down the corridor by Warwick's suspicious glare.

"As you see, I am safe, Lord Warwick. Are you able to stand, or would you like a chair and something to eat and drink? It seems I must be a nurse this morning, to you and perhaps to London."

Warwick accepted gratefully, pleased to find the young queen still in possession of her wits and dignity after such a night. He was not usually comfortable in the presence of women, preferring the bluff talk of men of his own station. Yet he was too weary even to feel embarrassed. With a stifled groan, he sat in turn, beginning his account of the night's events as servants prepared fresh cuts of ham and cool ale to slake his thirst. Margaret listened closely, questioning him only when he faltered or was unclear. He hardly noticed how much his manner warmed to her, as the sun continued to rise over the Tower.

CHAPTER 30

The afternoon sun beat down on the host gathered in Southwark, to the south of the city. For those who had come through the night unscathed, it was something to bless, a warmth that eased cramped muscles and made them sweat out the poisons of liquor and violence. For the wounded, the sun was a torment. Cade's army had no tents to keep the glare off their faces and sweat streamed from them as the pitifully small number of healers worked their way around the worst cases. Most had little to offer beyond a sip of water and bandages in great bundles of strips on their shoulders, giving them a hump as they appeared against the glare. One or two of the old women carried pots of unguent, oil of cloves, or a pouch of myrtle leaves they could grind into a green paste against pain. Those stocks were soon gone and the men could only turn on their sides in the open air and wait for the cool of evening.

Jack knew he was one of the lucky ones. He had examined himself in the upper room of his inn, removing his shirt and peering this way and that to see the extent of his bruising. His skin was a patchwork of puckered marks and stripes, but the few gashes were shallow and already clotted. Though it made him wince, he could still move his right arm.

Rather than let another man see him undressed, he pulled his stinking shirt back on when he heard footsteps on the stairs, slicking his hair down from a water bucket and standing to face whoever it was. The air was close and still in the small room and he could feel fresh sweat break out on top of the old. He thought wistfully of the horse trough in the inn yard, but the water there was being used to fill jugs for the wounded and it was likely already dry. He'd sent men back to the Thames to fill water skins, though there would never be enough for so many, not in that July heat.

As the door crashed open, Jack glanced guiltily at the jug of ale on the dresser, already half empty. There were perks in being the leader and he wasn't about to share his good fortune.

Woodchurch stood there, looking pale and dark around his eyes from lack of sleep. Most of the men who'd made it back from London had reached their camp and simply folded to the ground as soon as they found a good spot. Woodchurch and his son had kept going, organizing the village herbalists and doctors, sending men for water, and passing out coin to have food brought in. The men were starving after the night they'd had, but in that one thing they would be satisfied. With the king's gold, Woodchurch had purchased a dozen young bullocks from a local farmer. There were more than a few butchers among the Kentish and Essex men and they'd set to with a will and an appetite, dressing the carcasses and preparing enormous fire pits for the joints. Jack could smell woodsmoke on the archer as he stood there. He smiled at the thought. Gold in their pockets and the prospect of beef running with bloody juices. God knew, he'd had worse days.

"What is it, Tom?" he said. "I'm pissing blood and I ha'n't the strength for any more talk until I've eaten."

"You'll want to see this, Jack," Thomas said. He was still hoarse from shouting, his voice little more than a rasping growl. He held up a scroll in his hand and Jack's gaze fastened on it. Clean vellum and a blood-red seal. Jack's eyes narrowed, wondering if Woodchurch knew he couldn't read.

"What's that, then?" he said uneasily.

The written word had always been his enemy. Whenever he'd been flogged or fined or put in the village stocks, there had always been some white-faced scribe at the heart of it, scribbling away with his goose quill and ink. Jack could see Thomas was all in a flutter about something. The man was breathing hard and Jack knew by then that the archer wasn't one to get excited over nothing.

"They're offering us a pardon, Jack! A bleeding pardon! All crimes and misprisions forgotten, on condition we disperse." He saw Cade begin to frown and went on quickly before the obstinate man could start arguing. "It's victory, Jack! We knocked 'em bloody and they want no more of it! *God*, Jack. We've done it!"

"Does it say they'll dismiss the judges, then?" Jack asked softly. "Does it say they'll repeal the poacher's laws or lower the taxes on working men? Can you read those words in your little scroll, Tom?"

Thomas shook his head in disbelief.

"The messenger read it to me downstairs—and don't start that, Jack, not now. It's a *pardon*—for all crimes up to this day. The men can go home with gold and their freedom—and no one will come chasing us, after. You'll be the hero who took on London and won. Isn't that what you wanted? Come *on*, Jack. This is *good*. The ink still smudges, Jack, and it has the queen's signature on it. They've put this together in a morning."

Cade raised his hand to his neck and cracked it left and right, easing the stiffness there. Half of him wanted to whoop and holler, to respond with the same wild pleasure he saw in Woodchurch. With a grunt, he throttled that part to silence while he thought it over.

"We frightened them last night," he said, after a time. "That's the root of it."

"We did, Jack," Thomas replied immediately. "We showed them what happens if they ride too hard over men like us. We put the fear of God and Jack Cade into them, and this is the result."

Cade crossed to the door and yelled for Ecclestone and Paddy to come up. Both men were sound asleep on the ground floor of the inn. It took a while to rouse them, but they came at last up the steps, bleary-eyed and blinking. Paddy had found a stoppered jug of spirits and cradled it like a favorite child.

"Tell them, Tom," Jack said, turning back to sit on the low bed. "Tell the lads what you told me."

He waited as Thomas repeated himself, watching the faces of his friends closely as they began to understand. Not that Ecclestone gave anything away. The man's expression didn't change a whit, even when he sensed the silent scrutiny and glanced at Jack. Paddy was shaking his head in amazement.

"My whole life and I never thought I'd live to see something like this," Paddy said. "The bailiffs and sheriffs and landowning bastards, all quaking in fear of us. They've been on my back since I was a boy. I never saw them turn away, Jack, not once."

"They're still the same, though," Jack said. "We killed their soldiers and we strung up a few of the king's officers. We even took the head of the Kent sheriff. But they'll find new men. If we take this pardon, they'll go on just as they are and we'll have changed nothing."

Thomas understood the mingled fear and longing and delight in the big man, resting his powerful hands on his thighs as he sat there. Thomas felt the same caution, but he'd also seen the crowds of London line the streets as they left. No one in the inn would admit it, but there wasn't the heart in the Kentish Freemen for another attack, if they could even cross the bridge again in the face of strong resistance. The crowds of London had been moved to anger and there were more than enough of them. Yet as Paddy and Ecclestone looked at each other, Thomas knew both men would follow Jack again, even if he took them back into the city.

"We did our part, Jack," Thomas went on before they could speak. "No man could ask more. And they won't be the same, not after this. They'll tread careful, for a few years at least. They'll know they make their laws only as long as the people say they can. They still rule, all right, but with our damned *permission*. That's what they know now. That's what they know today that they didn't know yesterday. And if they ride us too hard, they know we'll gather once more. They know we'll be standing there in the evening shadows, ready to remind them."

Jack smiled at the words, enjoying Woodchurch's fervor and certainty. He too had seen the crowds gather as he'd crossed the bridge that morning. The thought of going back in was not a joyous one, though Jack would rather have died than admit it in that company. He wanted to be persuaded, and Thomas had given it to him. He looked up slowly.

"Is that all right with you, Paddy? Rob?"

Both men nodded and Ecclestone even smiled, his pale face creasing into unaccustomed seams.

Jack stood up and clapped both arms around the group of three men, squeezing them all together.

"Is the messenger still here, Tom?" he asked.

"Waiting outside," Thomas replied, feeling a growing sense of relief.

"Tell him we accept, then. Send him back and let the men know. We'll enjoy a bit of beef and ale tonight and then tomorrow I'm for home. I think I'll buy that magistrate's house and raise a glass to Alwyn bloody Judgment in his own kitchen."

"You burned it, Jack," Ecclestone muttered.

Cade blinked at him, remembering.

"I did, didn't I? Well, I can build a new one. I'll have my mates around and we'll sit in the sun and drink from a keg—and toast the dear old King of England, who paid for it all."

AT THE DAY'S END, Margaret stood on the wide wall surrounding the Tower of London, looking down on a city that had suffered. The setting sun turned the horizon the color of bruises and blood, promising a clear, warm day on the morrow. In truth, from that vantage point there was little sign of the destruction of the night before. The long summer day had seen the first stirrings of order in the capital, with men like Lord Warwick organizing teams of carts to collect the dead. She sighed, disappointed yet again that such an impressive young man should be a supporter of York. The Neville blood ran through too many of her husband's noble houses, she thought. The family would continue to be a danger to her, at least until her first child was born.

She tapped her hand lightly over her womb, feeling the ache of her fluxes and all the grief and frustration it brought. It would not be this month. She blushed as she recalled the small number of intimate meetings with her husband. Perhaps there would come a time when they were so many she would not be able to remember them all in great detail, but at that moment they were still events in her life, each one as important as her wedding day, or the assault on the Tower.

She prayed in a whisper, the soft words lost into the breeze and the city.

"Mary, mother of God, please let me grow with child. I am no longer a girl, given to foolish dreams and fancies. Let me be fertile, let me swell." She closed her eyes for a moment, sensing the vast weight of the city all around her. "Allow me a child and I will bless you all my days. Allow me a *son* and I will raise chapels to your glory."

When she opened her eyes once more, she saw a slow line of carts trundling along a road in the distance, filled with white-wrapped bodies. She knew great pits had been dug, each dead man or woman laid out carefully, with a priest to chant a benison over them before the laborers set to work covering them with earth and cold clay. Weeping relatives followed the carts, but it was vital to work fast in the heat of summer. Plagues and sickness would walk in the same footsteps. Margaret shuddered at the thought.

Across the river, Cade's host had begun a great feast, with bonfires visible as roaring points of light. They had sent their response, but she did not know yet if they would honor it, if they would leave. She did know Derry had made the bridge a fortress if they did not, setting teams of London men to building great barricades along its length.

She smiled to think of his mischievous expression that day, as he raided the Tower for weapons and barrels of powder. He would never have been allowed such a free hand before, but no one would stop him now, not after the previous night. She knew she should not depend on Cade going home, but it was hard to see Derry's bright malice and not feel confident in whatever he had planned if they rushed the bridge once more. The men of London had worked all day to be ready, sharpening iron and closing roads around the bridge. The news of Cade's pardon had not yet spread among them and she did not know how they would react when they heard. She did not regret the offer, not now it had been accepted. King Henry was not at her side and for a time the city was her responsibility, her jewel, the pounding heart of the country that had adopted her. Her father, René, could hardly have imagined such trials for his youngest daughter.

Margaret stayed on the wall until the sun went down and she could see the distant fires more clearly in the great camp across the Thames. Cade had thousands of his Kentish men there and she still did not know if he would come. The night air was cold and quiet as London held its breath and waited. The sky was clear and the moon showed low, creeping upward as the stars of the Plow rose.

Margaret said rosaries in her vigil, chanting the Ave Marias and Pater Nosters and lost in a trance so perfect that she did not even feel discomfort. She drifted, aware only of her pale hands on the rough-cut stone of the wall, anchoring her to the city. She wondered if this was the peace Henry found when he prayed from dawn till dusk, or even onward, through the night, until he could not rise without men to lift him up. It helped her to understand her husband, and she prayed for him as well.

The stars turned around the north and Cade did not come. As the moon crossed the city, she felt she could almost see the constellations move. Her heart slowed and in the silence that pressed against her she was filled with a sense of peace and presence. She bowed her head, giving thanks to God for delivering her city.

With care, she descended the steps down from the wall as the sun began to rise, feeling a dull ache in every joint. She crossed stones still marked with rusty spills of blood from the attack, though the bodies and the coins had been cleared away. She raised her head as guards fell into step at her back, following her from the shadows of the wall to the White Tower. They had waited with the queen through the dark hours, keeping vigil in their own way to ensure her safety.

In the White Tower, she walked down a corridor to where a smaller group had spent the night. Her arrival was heralded by the stamp and clatter of armored men standing to attention. If those men had slept, it didn't show as they stood and then knelt for the young queen. Margaret swept by them, taking her seat on a throne at the far end of the room and hiding the relief it brought to her knees and hips.

"Approach, Alexander Iden," she said.

The largest of the men rose from his kneeling position, walking to within a few paces of her before dipping down again. Like her guards, he had spent the night waiting for her, but he looked fresh enough, warmed by the fire burning in the grate. Margaret looked him over, seeing a hard man, with strong features and a trimmed beard.

"You were recommended to me, Master Iden," she began. "I have been told you are a man of honor and good character."

"With God's grace, Your Highness," he said, his voice deep and loud in the room, though he kept his head bowed.

"Derihew Brewer speaks well of your talents, Master Iden. I am of a mind to trust his opinions."

"I am grateful, Your Highness," he said, visibly pleased.

Margaret thought for a moment longer, then decided.

"You are hereby appointed as sheriff of Kent. My clerks have the papers for you to seal."

To her surprise, the big man kneeling at her feet blushed with pleasure, still apparently unable to look up.

"Thank you, Your Highness. Your . . . My . . . Your Highness does me great honor."

Margaret found herself wanting to smile and repressed the desire.

"Master Brewer has assembled sixty men who will accompany you to your new home in Maidstone. In the light of recent troubles, you must be kept safe. The authority of the Crown must not be flouted again in Kent. Do you understand?"

"Yes, Your Highness."

"By the Lord's grace, the rebellion of Kentish men is at an end. Pardons have been granted, and they are going back to their farms and villages with the wealth they have wrenched from London. What crimes they have committed are all forgiven and may not be brought before the courts." She paused, her eyes glittering over the man's bowed head. "But you have been appointed by *my* hand, mine alone, Master

Iden. What I have given, I can as easily take away. When I send you orders, you will carry them out swiftly, as the king's law, as the king's sword in Kent. Do you understand?"

"I do, Your Highness," Iden replied immediately. "I pledge my honor and my obedience to you." He blessed Derry Brewer for putting his name forward. It was a reward for a lifetime in service and war and Iden could still hardly comprehend what he had been given.

"Go with God then, Sheriff Iden. You will hear from me again."

Iden blushed with pleasure at hearing his new title. He rose and bowed deeply once more.

"I am your loyal servant, Your Highness."

Margaret smiled.

"That is all I ask."

THOMAS WOODCHURCH walked in silence through the echoing streets of London with his son, keeping a close eye out for anyone who might mark or recognize them. They'd stripped themselves of the green bows, keeping only a decent knife each to protect the pouches of gold they both carried. Jack Cade had been more than generous with the spoils, allowing triple shares for those who'd led the Kentish men. With the smaller pouch Rowan had hidden under his belt and tunic, they had enough to lease a decent-sized farm, if the right one could be found.

They'd crossed the Thames by ferryboat, rather than test the strength of the queen's pardon on those defending London Bridge. Thomas and Rowan had reached a landing place farther down the river, and then Thomas led his son through the dense and winding streets. Little by little, they grew more familiar in memory, until they reached the rookeries themselves, the slums Thomas had first known when his father had uprooted their little family from Kent and settled in the city to seek a living.

For Rowan, it was his first view of London in the daylight. He stayed close to his father as the crowds bustled around them, out to trade and talk as the sun rose. Already, the signs of fighting and destruction were fading, swallowed up by a city that always went on, regardless of the suffering of individuals. There were funeral processions blocking some of the streets, but the two archers worked their way around and through the maze, until Thomas came to a small black door, deep in the rookeries. That part of London was one of the poorest, but the two men did not look as if they had anything to steal and Thomas made sure his hand stayed close by his knife. He took a deep breath and hammered on the wood, stepping back into the muck underfoot as he waited.

Both of them smiled as Joan Woodchurch opened the door and stood there, looking up suspiciously at the hulking great figures of her husband and son.

"I thought you were both dead," she said flatly.

Thomas beamed at her. "It's good to see you too, my dearest angel."

She snorted at that, but when he embraced his wife, some of the hardness melted out of her.

"Come in, then," she said. "You'll be wanting breakfast."

Father and son went into the tiny house, followed shortly by the excited squeals of the daughters as they welcomed the Woodchurch men home.

CHAPTER 31

Jack stepped back, squinting at the line of mortar he'd pressed against the brick. With a steady hand, he ran his pointed trowel along the line, taking satisfaction from the way the walls were growing. As the long summer days began to shorten, he'd persuaded Paddy and Ecclestone to join him on the job. Neither of them had needed the work, but it had given him pleasure that they'd still come. Paddy was up on the roof, banging nails through the slates with more enthusiasm than skill. Jack knew his friend had sent some of his coins home to Ireland, to a family he hadn't seen for many years. Paddy had drunk away a heavy portion of the rest in every inn and tavern for miles around. It was a blessing that the Irishman was a reasonable drunk, given to singing and sometimes weeping, rather than breaking the tables. Jack knew his old friend was uncomfortable with having wealth of any kind. For reasons he could not completely explain, Paddy seemed determined to burn through his fortune and be penniless once again. It showed in the weight he'd put on and the sagging skin around his bloodshot eyes. Jack shook his head sadly at the thought. Some men could not be happy, that was all there was to it. There would come a day when Paddy had lost it all and was reduced to beggary, that much was certain. Jack hadn't said anything to him, but there would be a bed for Paddy then in the house they were building, or perhaps a warm barn on the land where the big man could sleep. It was better to plan for that, rather than see his friend freeze to death in a gutter.

Ecclestone was mixing more of the lime, horsehair, sand, and water, with a cloth wrapped around his face to counter the acrid fumes. He'd bought a tallow shop in town, learning the trade of candles and rough soap with a small staff of two local lasses and one old man. By all accounts Ecclestone was doing well with it. Jack knew he used his famous razor to cut the blocks of flecked white soap, while the girls looked on with horrified expressions. At times, a crowd would gather at the shop doorway, men and women who knew his exploits, come just to watch the terrible neatness of his cuts.

The work might have gone faster if they hadn't spent so much time laughing and talking together, but Jack didn't mind that. He'd employed three local men to raise the timber structure, cutting joints and pegs with the skill and speed of long experience. Another local man had supplied the bricks, each with the maker's thumbprint pressed into the clay as it dried. Jack thought he and his two friends would have the rest finished before winter, with the house as snug as a drum.

The new building was nowhere near as large as the one he'd burned down. The magistrate's land had been cheap enough with just blackened timbers standing in the gardens, but it hadn't felt right to build another mansion. Instead, Jack had laid out a place for a small family, with two big rooms on the ground floor and three bedrooms above it. He hadn't told the other two, for fear of their laughter, but news of his exploits in London had brought the interest of more than one unmarried woman. He had his eye on one baker's daughter in particular, from the local village. He thought a man could probably do worse than have fresh bread all his life. Jack could imagine a couple of boys racing around and swimming in the pond, with no one to run them off the land. It was a good thought. Kent was a beautiful county, right enough. He'd even considered renting a few local fields to grow hops. Some of the inns in town had begun selling various brews as Jack Cade's ale. It made sense to consider providing them with the real thing.

Jack chuckled to himself as he picked up another brick and slapped wet cement onto it. He'd be the proper man of business then, with fine clothes and a horse to ride into town. It wasn't a bad fate for a brawler and his mates.

He heard the tramp of marching men before he saw them coming up the long drive. Paddy whistled a warning overhead, already beginning to climb down. In response, Cade felt an old tremor in his stomach before he remembered he had nothing to fear, not any longer. He'd lived his entire life with the thought that the bailiffs might come for him one day. It was somehow hard to remember he'd been pardoned for all his crimes—and careful not to commit another. These days, Jack tipped his hat to king's men as he passed them in town, seeing their knowledge of who he was in their sour expressions. Yet they couldn't do a damn thing about it.

Jack laid his trowel down on the brick courses, tapping the seax in his belt from old habit, to reassure himself it was still there. He was on his own land, legally bought. Whoever they were, he was a free man, he told himself, with a written pardon to prove it. There was a wood ax not far off, with the blade buried in a stump to stop it rusting. Jack eyed it, knowing he would be happier even so with a decent weapon in his hand. It was a thought from the man he had been. It was not the thought of landowning, respectable Jack Cade, half engaged to be married, or at least thinking about it.

Paddy reached his side, blowing lightly after his scramble down from the roof. He held a hammer in his hand, a short length of club iron and oak. He pointed it at the soldiers.

"Looks like a couple of dozen, maybe more, Jack. Do you want to run?"

"No," Jack said shortly. He crossed to the ax and levered it out of the wood, resting his right hand on the top of the long ash handle. "You heard the new sheriff has come from London. I don't doubt he'd like to see us haring off through the fields, but we're free men now, Paddy. Free men don't run."

Ecclestone came to stand with them, wiping a streak of yellow-white lime from his cheek. Jack saw he had his razor concealed in a hand, an old habit he hadn't allowed to fall into disuse over the previous months.

"Don't do anything stupid, lads," Jack muttered as the line of marching soldiers came closer. He could see the sheriff's banner fluttering on a pole among them and he couldn't help but smile, thinking of the last one.

The three friends stood tall and surly as the soldiers fanned out, forming a half ring around them. The man who dismounted at the center wore a short black beard and stood almost as large as Jack and Paddy.

"Good afternoon," he said, smiling. "My name is Alexander Iden. I have the honor of being sheriff to this county."

"We know you," Jack said. "We remember the last one as well."

A shadow crossed Iden's face at that reply.

"Yes, poor fellow. Would you be Jack Cade, then?"

"I am, yes. You're on my land as well, so I'll be thanking you to state your business and be on your way. As you can see from the house, I have work to finish."

"I don't think so," Iden replied. As Jack watched, the man drew a long sword from the scabbard at his waist. "You're under arrest, Jack Cade, on orders of the Crown. The charges are unlawful assembly, treason, and murder of the king's officers. Now then, will you go quietly to London, or will you go hard? Tell me now; it'll be the same either way."

Jack felt a great calm come over him, a coldness that stole from his gut and made his arms and legs feel numb. He felt a surge of anger at the way he'd trusted the London lords and noblemen to keep their word. They'd written down the pardon and sealed it! *Written* words; words with authority. He'd had a local clerk read it to him half a dozen times, as solid and real as anything in the world. After his return to Kent, Jack had lodged it with a moneylender in town and he'd asked to see it twice since then, just to run his hand over the dark letters and know it was true. Even as his heart thumped in his chest and his face flushed, he held on to that slender reed.

"I've been pardoned, Iden. A paper with the queen's own seal and signature on it sits in a strongbox in town. My name is on it and that means you can't touch a hair of my *head*."

As he spoke, Jack raised the ax, gripping the shaft with both hands and pointing the big blade toward the sheriff.

"I have my orders," Iden said with a shrug. He looked almost amused at the outrage he saw in the rebel. "You won't come peaceably, then?"

Jack could feel the tension in his two friends. He glanced at Paddy and saw the big man was sweating profusely. Ecclestone stood as if he'd been carved, staring balefully at the sheriff's throat.

"You two should walk away," Jack murmured. "Whatever this oath-breaking fool is after, it ain't you. Go on."

Paddy looked at his friend as if he'd been struck, his eyes wide.

"I'm *tired* of running, Jack," he said softly.

All three had been given a glimpse of a different life those last few months, a life where they didn't have to go in fear of king's officials and county men. They'd fought in London and it had changed them. Ecclestone and Paddy looked at each other and both shook their heads.

"All right then, lads," Jack said. He smiled at his two friends, ignoring the soldiers staring them down.

The sheriff had been watching the exchange intently. As the three men showed no sign of surrendering, he made a chopping motion with his hand. His soldiers darted forward with shields and swords ready. There had been no warning but Jack had been expecting a rush and he swung wildly with his ax, smashing past a shield to crush the ribs of the first to lay a hand on him. The man screamed, a sudden and shocking sound in the garden.

Ecclestone moved fast, turning his shoulders and slipping between two mailed men as he tried to reach the sheriff. Jack shouted in grief as he saw his friend hacked down in one great blow, the sheriff's sword cutting him deep at the neck. Paddy was roaring, his big left hand tight in someone's jerkin as he used his hammer to smash a soldier's face and head. Jack continued to swing and strike, knowing already that it was hopeless, that it had always been hopeless. His breath came hard. He sensed the soldiers around him were trying not to land a fatal blow, but one of them caught him in the back with a blade, stabbing wildly. He heard Paddy grunt as the Irishman was knocked from his feet, his legs kicked away from him as he was struck from the side.

Another knife went between Jack's ribs, staying stuck there as he wrenched away from the pain. With a sense of wonder and shock, he felt his great strength vanish. He crashed down, quickly kicked and battered into a daze, with his fingers broken and his ax wrenched away from his grasp.

Jack was only half aware as they dragged him up for Sheriff Iden to stare at him. There was blood on Jack's face and in his mouth. He spat weakly as strangers held him in an unbreakable grip. His friends had been cut down, left in their own blood where they had fallen. Jack swore as he saw their bodies, cursing the king's men all around him.

"Which of you fools stabbed him?" Jack heard Iden snap. The sheriff was furious and the soldiers looked at their feet, panting and red-faced. "*Damn* it! He won't live till London with that wound."

Jack smiled to hear that, though it hurt him. He could feel his life pouring out onto the dusty ground and he was only sorry Ecclestone hadn't cut the new sheriff's throat.

"Tie this traitor onto a horse," Iden went on furiously. "God, didn't I *say* he should be taken alive?"

Jack shook his head, feeling oddly cold despite the warmth of the sun. For an instant, he thought he heard the high voices of children, but then it was gone and he sagged in the arms of the men who held him.

CHAPTER 32

Dawn rain drizzled across Windsor Hunting Park, cold and gusting April showers that did little to dampen the enthusiasm of the lords who had gathered at the king's command. Derry Brewer had been right about that much, Margaret had to admit, shivering slightly. Still yawning from what little sleep she had managed, she looked out across the vast fields, with the smudge of dark forests beyond. During the reign of her husband's father, royal hunts had been organized every year, with hundreds of nobles and their servants descending on the royal grounds to take deer or demonstrate their skill with falcons and dogs. The feasts that followed were still famous and when she had asked Derry what would bring even the Neville lords to Windsor, his response had been immediate and without thought. She suspected even a normal hunt would have brought them, after seeing so many flushed faces and the delighted pride in men like Earl Salisbury returning with his servants laden down by hares and pheasants, or the buck deer Lord Oxford had taken. Her husband had not ridden to the hunt in a decade and the royal grounds teemed with prey. The first two nights had been spent in lavish feasts, with musicians and dancing to keep their wives happy, while the men tore into the succulent meat they had taken, boasting and laughing at the events of the day. It had been a success in every way that mattered—and the main draw was still to come.

Margaret had been down to the stables of the castle to see the two captive boars they would release that morning. Duke Philip of Burgundy had sent the beasts as a gift, perhaps in part to mark his sorrow at the death of William de la Pole. For that alone, she blessed his name, though his offer of sanctuary to William meant she would always think of him as a friend. Male boars were the monarchs of the deep forest, the only animals in England capable of killing the men who hunted them. She shuddered at the recollection of the massive, reeking bodies and the fierce anger in their small eyes. In her childhood, she had once seen dancing bears in Saumur, when a traveling fair came to Anjou. The hogs in the stalls had twice the bulk of those animals, with bristles as thick as a bear's brown fur and backs as wide as a kitchen table. It made sense that as a gift between noble houses they would be fine examples of the breed, but she had still not been prepared for the sheer size of the grunting animals as they kicked and nudged the wooden stalls and made dust rain down from the roof. To Margaret's eye, they had as much resemblance to a succulent butcher's pig as a lion does to a household cat. The hunt master had spoken of them in awe, saying each one was said to weigh four hundred pounds and carried a pair of matched tusks as long as a man's forearm. Margaret had seen the near-mindless threat in the animals as they gouged the stalls with those tusks, gnawing and scraping, furious at being unable to reach their captors.

She knew Earl Warwick had taken to calling them Castor and Pollux, warriors and twins from ancient Greek tales. It was common knowledge that the young Richard Neville was intent on taking one of the heads home with him, though there were many others who eyed the great sweep of the tusks with delight and longing. True boars had been hunted almost to vanishing in England and there were few among the gathering in Windsor who had brought one down. Margaret had been hard-pressed not to laugh at the endless advice between the men on the subject, whether it was better to use the catch dogs to hold it steady, then seek its heart with an arrow, or whether a spear-thrust between the ribs was more effective.

She ran her hand over the swell of her womb, feeling again the intense satisfaction of being pregnant. She had endured the bitterness of having York named as royal heir, saying nothing for all the time it seemed Parliament had been right to prepare for the worst. Then she had felt the first signs and turned back and forth in front of mirrors, convinced she was imagining it. The bulge had grown with every week, a wonder to her and an answer to a thousand fervent prayers. Even the sickness was a delight to her as the child grew. All she had needed then was for the earls of England to see the signs, the curve of her womb that meant York's games had come to nothing.

"Be a son," she muttered to herself, as she did a dozen times each day. She longed for daughters, but a son would secure the throne for her husband and her line. A son would cast Richard and Cecily York out into the darkness, with all their plots in tatters. The thought gave her more pleasure than she could express and she found her hand was gripping her cup so tightly that the gemstones around the rim left a print on her palm.

Richard of York had not been invited to the Windsor hunt. Though he had inherited the title of Earl of March, he was the only one of the twelve English earls and "king's companions" not to be called to Windsor for the hunt. No doubt his supporters would consider it another insult to an ancient family, but she had made the decision even so. Let them think and say what they would. She did not want that man and his cold wife anywhere near her or her husband. Margaret still blamed

York for the death of Lord Suffolk and, though it had never been proved, she suspected him of involvement in Cade's rebellion and all the damage and pain it had caused. Cade's head sat high on a spike on the same bridge he had fought his way across. Margaret had gone to see it.

One of the hovering servants stepped forward to refill her cup, but she waved him away. For months, her stomach had clenched and protested at much of anything. Even watered wine had to be taken in small amounts, and most of her nourishment came in the form of thin broths that she would lose as often as she kept them down. It didn't matter. What mattered was that the Neville lords had seen her gravid state, her proof that King Henry's bloodline would run on and not be lost. The moment when Earl Warwick had frozen and stood staring on their first meeting in the castle had been one of the happiest of her life. York would be told now, she knew. Her husband may have lost France, but he had survived. King Henry had not been crushed by rebellions, riots, or plots—not even by the attack on London itself. Her husband lived, and all York's plans and maneuvers, all his bribery and flattery of supporters, had come to nothing as her womb swelled.

Margaret started as a great shout went up outside, realizing that the gathered lords had gone out to see the squealing hogs released into the royal forest. The king's huntsmen would chase the animals deep into the trees and then keep an eye on them while the hunters mounted and prepared their dogs and weapons. She could already hear the spurred boots of men clattering around downstairs. It was easy to picture the scene as excited nobles called and joked with each other, grabbing cold meats from the tables to break their fast.

Over the raucous tumult below, Margaret did not hear her husband enter the room. She jerked from her reverie when he was announced by his steward, rising to her feet with a slight gasp of effort. Henry was as pale as ever, though she thought he looked a little less thin. It pleased her to see there were no bandages on his left hand, where the wound had finally healed. A pink mark like a burn remained, ridged and hard compared to the smoothness of his skin elsewhere. There were still bandages on his right palm, a tight wrap of white cloth that was changed and cleaned every morning. Even so, she was pleased at any small improvement in him.

King Henry smiled to see his wife. He kissed her forehead and then her mouth, his lips dry and warm.

"Good morning, Margaret," he said. "Did you sleep? I had such dreams! Master Allworthy gave me a new draft that brought the strangest visions to me."

"And I would hear them all, my husband," Margaret replied, "but the great hunt is beginning. Your men have released the boars and your lords are gathering to go out."

"Already? I have only just risen, Margaret. I have eaten nothing. I will have my horse brought. Where is my stable master?"

Seeing Henry was growing agitated, Margaret smoothed her hands across his brow, a cool touch that always seemed to calm him. He subsided, his eyes growing vague.

"You are not well enough to ride out with them, Henry. You would risk a fall or an injury if your weakness came suddenly upon you. They understand, Henry. The boars are your gift to them and they are grateful for the sport."

"Good . . . good, Margaret. I was hoping to pray in the chapel today and I did not see how I could find the time."

He let himself be guided by her to a chair at a long table. A servant held it for him to sit and he settled himself as a steaming bowl of soup was placed before him. He picked up a spoon, eyeing the soup dubiously as Margaret's own servant helped her to take a seat at his side.

On the floors below, Margaret could still hear the loud voices of the lords, clattering about with their preparations. Outside in the drizzle, the baying of hounds was rising in intensity as the animals sensed they would soon be set free to race after the boars. During the night, half the earls she had invited had brought their best hounds down to the stables to take the scent of Castor and Pollux. From the resulting noise, the dogs had been driven almost to frenzy by the closeness of the monstrous beasts. Margaret had slept little with the din, but she had smiled as she dozed even so.

Margaret watched as her husband spooned the soup into his mouth, his eyes completely blank, as if he saw some other landscape among the cutlery and square wooden plates. The terrors that had almost destroyed him had lessened in the year after Cade's rebellion. She had made sure he saw and understood that the city of London was safe and peaceful once again, at least for a time.

Henry put down his spoon suddenly, rising from his place.

"I should go out to them, Margaret. As host, I should wish them luck and good sport. Have the boars been sent out?"

"They have, husband. Sit, it is all in hand."

He sat once more, though her sternness faded at the sight of him fiddling with his cutlery, for all the world like a boy denied the chance to run outside. Margaret raised her eyes, amused and indulgent.

"Go then, husband, if you think you must. Steward! The king will need a cloak. Be sure he puts it on before going into the rain."

Henry rose quickly, leaning forward to kiss her before leaving the room at something close to a run. She smiled then, settling down to her own soup before it grew too cold.

THE GATHERING of earls and their servants at the castle entrance might have resembled the preparations for a battle, if not for the laughter and general goodwill. Under a great stone arch out of the rain,

Richard Neville, Earl of Warwick, was discussing tactics with his huntsman and his father, while three more of his men readied four horses and a pack of savage, leashed dogs that snarled and barked at each other in their excitement. Warwick's falcons were not present. All his valuable birds were hooded and being looked after in his suite of rooms. He had no interest in fowl or fur that morning, just the two noble boars rooting around somewhere in the king's five thousand acres of meadows and deep forest. The squires for both father and son were ready with their weapons and the dogs would bring the boars to bay, gripping onto their flesh and holding them for the kill.

Earl Salisbury looked at his son, seeing the flush on his face despite the cold day.

"Is there any point in my telling you to be careful?" he said.

His son laughed, shaking his head as he checked the belly straps were tight enough on his mounts.

"You saw them, sir. The heads will suit my castle hearth, don't you think?"

The older man smiled ruefully, knowing that his son was set on reaching the boars first, no matter the risk. When the king's heralds blew their horns, they'd all be off, charging across the open fields and into the trees.

"Keep an eye on those Tudor lads," his father said suddenly. He waved off one of the huntsmen and clasped his hands together to help his son mount. "They're young and that Edmund is still so new an earl you can see the green on him. He'll do his utmost to please the king, I do not doubt it. And watch out for Somerset. That man is fearless to the point of stupidity." Against his better judgment, he could not help adding another word of warning. "Don't get between *any* of the king's favorites and a boar, lad, that's all. Not if they're holding a spear to throw or have an arrow on the string. You understand?"

"I do, sir, but I'll come back with one of those heads or both of them. There isn't a horse here to match my pair. I'll be on those boars before the rest. Let them worry then!"

Some of the older earls would count the kill even if their servants brought down the boar. Warwick intended to make the thrust himself if he could, with one of three boar spears he had brought for the occasion. They stood taller than he was, with blades sharp enough to shave. His father handed them up to him, shaking his head in amusement to hide his worries.

"I'll be along after you, with Westmorland. Who knows, I might get a shot with my bow when you young pups have exhausted yourselves." He smiled as he spoke and his son chuckled.

Both of the Neville lords turned their heads as conversations halted all around and the servants knelt on the cobbles. King Henry came out into the rainy courtyard, with his steward on his heels, still trying to drape the king in a thick cloak.

Henry stood and looked around at the gathering of earls and their hunt servants, forty or fifty men in all, with as many horses and dogs making a terrible noise between them. One by one, the noblemen caught sight of the king and bowed, dipping their heads. Henry smiled at them all, the rain falling harder, so that it plastered his hair to his head. He accepted the cloak at last, though it was already dark and heavy.

"Please rise. I wish you well, my lords. I am only sorry I cannot join you myself today."

He looked wistfully at the horses near to hand, but Margaret had been very clear.

"Good fortune to all, but I will hope to see at least one of those horns brought back by my brothers."

The assembled men laughed, looking over to where Edmund and Jasper Tudor stood, proud to have been mentioned. When they had arrived at court from Wales, Henry had wanted to make both men earls, honoring the children of his mother's brief second marriage. Yet half French and half Welsh as they were, there was not a drop of English blood in either of them. His reluctant Parliament had been forced to allow them the rights of an Englishman by statute before Henry could settle estates on his Tudor half brothers. The sight of them brought the memory of his mother's face to the fore. Tears came without warning to his eyes, washed away on the instant by the falling rain.

"I am only sorry our mother is not alive to see you, but she will be watching, I know."

Silence stretched then, growing uncomfortable as the noblemen could not leave for the hunt until they had been dismissed. Henry stared blankly at them, rubbing his forehead as a headache began. Some awareness seeped back into him slowly and he looked up.

"I will see you all at the feast tonight, to toast the victor of the hunt."

Earls and their men alike gave a great cheer at that, and Henry beamed delightedly before going back into the castle. He was shivering and his lips bore a tinge of blue from the cold. The steward who had brought the cloak was pale with frustration, knowing he would hear all about letting the king stand in the rain.

IN THE LAMPLIGHT, Henry shivered, feeling chilled. He had a blanket over his legs to keep him warm and he was trying to read, shifting uncomfortably in the armchair. Ever since his speech that morning, his head had throbbed with pain. He'd drunk a little wine at the feast, as well as picking at the great haunch of pork that steamed on his trencher. Richard of Warwick had been wildly drunk after his successful hunt. Through the pain in his head, Henry smiled at the memory.

Edmund Tudor had taken Castor, to Warwick's Pollux. Three dogs had been killed, opened from stem to stern by the boars' tusks. Two of Warwick's huntsmen had been gashed as well. They were being tended by Allworthy, stitched and dosed for the pain.

Henry had granted equal honors at the banquet, toasting the health of Warwick and Edmund Tudor from the head of the table. Margaret had squeezed his knee under the cloth and his happiness had been complete. He had worried for the longest time that his earls would bicker or even come to blows. They had seemed so very angry for a year or longer. Yet they had drunk and gorged themselves in good humor, singing along with the musicians and hooting at the actors and jongleurs he'd brought in to entertain them. The hunt had been a success, Henry knew. Margaret was pleased and even old Richard Neville had cracked his dour face in pride at seeing his son honored.

Henry looked away from the page, preferring to rest his gaze on the dark forests beyond the panes of glass. Midnight had passed long before, but he could not sleep with his head pounding and pressure all around the socket of his right eye. All he could do was endure until the sun rose and he could leave his rooms. He thought for a moment of calling Margaret, but remembered that she would be long asleep by then. Pregnant women needed to sleep, he had been told. Henry smiled to himself at the thought, peering again at the page that blurred as he stared at it.

In the silence, the king gave a small groan. He recognized the footsteps approaching, tapping closer on the polished wooden floors. Henry looked up in dismay as Master Allworthy entered, carrying his bulging leather bag. In his black coat and polished black shoes, the doctor looked more like a priest than a physician.

"I did not summon you, Doctor," Henry said, with less than perfect certainty. "I am resting, as you see. It cannot be time for another draft."

"Now, now, Your Grace. Your steward told me you might have

taken a fever, walking around in the rain. Your health is my care and it's no trouble for me to look in on you."

Allworthy reached out and pressed his palm against Henry's forehead, tutting to himself.

"Too much heat, as I suspected."

Shaking his head in disapproval, the doctor opened the bag and set out the tools and vials of his trade, checking each one carefully and adjusting their position until they were arrayed to his satisfaction.

"I think I would like to see my wife, Allworthy. I wish to see her."

"Of course, Your Grace," the doctor replied carelessly. "Just as soon as you've been bled. Which arm would you prefer?"

Despite his rising anger, Henry found himself holding out his right arm. It took an effort of will to resist Allworthy's chatter and he could not find the strength. He let the arm hang limp as Allworthy pushed the shirtsleeve up and tapped the veins. With care, the doctor laid the arm on the king's lap and turned back to his preparations. As Henry stared at nothing, Allworthy passed over a small silver tray, with a number of hand-pressed pills resting on the polished surface.

"So many," Henry murmured. "What are they today?"

The doctor hardly paused as he checked the edge of his curette, ready to be plunged into a vein.

"Why, they are for *pain*, Your Grace! You'd like the pain to go away, wouldn't you?"

An expression of intense irritation crossed Henry's face at hearing the reply. Some deep part of him hated being treated like a child. Even so, he opened his mouth and let the doctor place the bitter pills on his tongue to be swallowed. Allworthy passed the king a clay cup containing one of his usual vile liquids. Henry managed one small gulp before he grimaced and pushed it away.

"And again," Allworthy urged him, making the vessel clink as he pressed it against the king's teeth.

A little of the liquid dribbled down Henry's chin and he coughed, choking on it. His bare arm jerked up, knocking the cup away with a great crash as it shattered into pieces on the floor.

Allworthy frowned, standing completely still for a moment before he mastered his outrage.

"I will have another brought, Your Grace. You want to be well again, don't you? Of course you do."

He was rougher than he had to be as he used a cloth to wipe the king's mouth, making the skin pink around Henry's lips.

"Margaret," Henry said clearly.

Allworthy looked up in irritation as a servant against the far wall started into movement. He had not noticed the man standing there at silent attention.

"His Grace is not to be disturbed!" the doctor snapped across the room.

The servant paused in his rush, but only briefly. In a conflict of authority, his best course was to follow the king's orders over the doctor's. Allworthy tutted again to himself as the man vanished, clattering off down the corridors of the east wing.

"Now half the house will be woken, I do not doubt. I will stay and talk to the queen; don't worry. Give me your arm again."

Henry looked away as Allworthy cut a vein in the crook of his elbow, squeezing the flesh until a good flow of blood was established. The doctor peered closely at the color of it, holding a bowl under the king's elbow that slowly filled.

Margaret came before the bleeding had finished, dressed in a sleeping robe with a thick cloak over her shoulders.

Doctor Allworthy bowed as she entered, sensitive to her authority, but at the same time certain of his own.

"I am *so* sorry Your Royal Highness has been disturbed at this hour.

King Henry is still unwell. His Grace called your name, and I'm afraid the servant—"

Allworthy broke off as Margaret knelt at her husband's side, giving no sign that she heard a word the physician said. Instead, she eyed the slowly filling bowl with disgust.

"Are you unwell, Henry? I am here now."

Henry patted her hand, taking comfort from the touch as he struggled against a weariness that had stolen over him.

"I'm sorry to wake you, Margaret," he murmured. "I was sitting in the quiet and then Allworthy came and I wanted you to be with me. Perhaps I should sleep."

"Of course you should, Your Grace!" Allworthy said sternly. "How else will you ever be well again?" He turned to Margaret, addressing her. "The servant should not have run to you, my lady. I told him as much, but he didn't listen."

"You were mistaken," Margaret responded instantly. "If my husband tells you to fetch me, you drop your bag and *run*, Master Allworthy!"

She had never liked the pompous doctor. The man treated Henry like a village idiot, as far as Margaret could see.

"I cannot say," Henry replied, answering a question no one had asked him.

He opened his eyes, but the room seemed to be moving around him as his senses swam on acids in his blood. He choked suddenly, his mouth filling with green bile. Margaret gasped in horror as the bitter-smelling liquid spilled past his lips.

"You are tiring the king, my lady," Allworthy said, barely hiding his satisfaction. He used his cloth to collect the thin slurry coming from the king's mouth, wiping hard. "As the royal physician . . ."

Margaret looked up with such venom that Allworthy flushed and fell silent. Henry continued to choke, groaning as his stomach clenched and emptied. Foul liquids spattered from his mouth onto the blanket and his tunic. Blood continued to trickle from his arm, making bright beads around the bowl that sank instantly into the blanket. Allworthy fussed around the king, mopping and dabbing.

As Margaret clutched his hand, Henry lurched in his seat, showing tendons like wires in his throat. The bowl of blood went flying with a terrible crash, spilling its thick contents down the blanket and into a spreading red pool on the floor. As it came to rest upside down, Henry's muscles clamped tight all over his body and his eyes rolled up in his head.

"Your Grace?" Allworthy said, worried.

There was no response. The young king lolled to one side, senseless.

"Henry? Can you hear me? What have you *done* to him?" Margaret demanded.

Doctor Allworthy shook his head in nervous confusion.

"My lady, nothing I've given would cause fits," he said. "The same distemper has its hand on him, now as before. All I have done is to hold it back this long."

Hiding his panic, the doctor stepped into the spilled blood to loom over the king. He pinched Henry's cheeks, at first gently and then harder so that he left red marks.

"Your Grace?" he said.

There was no response. The king's chest rose and fell as before, but the man himself had fallen away and was lost.

Margaret looked from her husband's slack face to the doctor standing at his side, stains of blood and vomit on his black coat. She reached out and took a firm grip on the doctor's arm.

"No more of your foul drafts, your bleeding and your pills. No *more*, Doctor! One protest and I will have you arrested and put to the question. *I* will tend my husband."

She turned her back on the doctor, reaching for a strip of bandage to tie around the still-bleeding curette wound on Henry's arm. Margaret pulled it tight with her teeth, then gripped her husband by both arms. His head sagged forward, spit dribbling from his mouth.

Allworthy gaped as the young queen bit her lip in indecision, then raised her open hand and held it in the air, trembling visibly. She took a long, slow breath and slapped Henry across the cheek, rocking his head back. He made no sound at all, though a scarlet print spread slowly across his cheek to show where he had been struck. Margaret let him sag back into the chair, sobbing in frustration and sick fear. The doctor's mouth opened and closed, but he had nothing else to say.

EPILOGUE

L ondon could be beautiful in the spring. The sun made the sluggish river sparkle and there were fresh goods in all the markets. There were still some who came to see where Cade's ax had marked the London Stone, but even that scar was fading with time and the rub of hands.

At the Palace of Westminster, lords arrived from across the country, traveling by coach or horse, or ferried up the river in oared barges. They came alone or in crowds, bustling through the corridors and meeting rooms. Speaker Tresham had been sent by Parliament to greet the Duke of York as he returned from Ireland, but whatever the man had intended had been forgotten when the Speaker was killed in the road, apparently mistaken for a brigand. York's personal chamberlain, Sir William Oldhall, now held that vital post. It was he who had set the venue for his master's return and sent out the formal requests for attendance. Thirty-two out of fifty-five noble houses were represented in the London gathering, barely enough for the task ahead.

As the clock tower bell was rung for noon, Oldhall looked across at the gathered lords, separated from each other by a wide aisle. Sunlight shone through the high windows of the White Chamber, revealing velvets and silks, a mass of bright colors. York was not yet present and he could hardly begin without him. Oldhall wiped perspiration from his forehead, looking to the door.

RICHARD OF YORK walked calmly through the corridors leading to the White Chamber. He had a dozen men with him, all dressed in the livery of his house and marked with either the white rose of York or his personal symbol of a falcon with outstretched talons. He did not expect to be threatened in the royal palace, but neither would he come into the stronghold of his enemies without good swordsmen at his side. He heard the clock bell ring for noon and increased his pace, knowing his noble peers would be waiting for him. His servants matched him, checking every side corridor and chamber they passed for the first hint of trouble. The rooms were all deserted and York rounded the last corner at speed.

He drew to a sudden halt as he sighted a group standing close by the door he would take into the echoing chamber beyond. York could hear the mutter of conversation inside, but he had eyes only for the young woman who stood at the center of her pages and stewards, glaring at him as if she could set him on fire with just the force of her dislike. He hesitated only for a heartbeat before he put his right leg forward and bowed deeply, his men dipping with him for the Queen of England.

"Your Royal Highness," he said as he rose. On impulse, York stepped forward alone, raising an open palm to his men so that they would not be seen to threaten Margaret. "I did not expect to see you here today . . ."

His gaze dropped as he spoke, unable to avoid staring at the bulge of her dress. His mouth tightened as he saw her pregnancy for the first time. When he looked up, he saw she was watching his reaction.

"My lord York, did you think I would not come?" she said, her voice low and firm. "Today, of all days, when such great matters are to be decided?"

It was an effort for York not to show his triumph, but he knew it was unnecessary.

"Your Highness, has there been a change in the king's condition? Has he risen? I will give thanks in every church on my lands if it is so."

Margaret's lips thinned. For five months, her husband had been utterly senseless, almost drowned each day just to force enough broth into his stomach to keep him alive. He could not speak or react even to pain. Her child and his still grew within her until she felt she could not stand another day of the heaviness and discomfort. The triumph of the great hunt at Windsor seemed a lifetime away and now there was her enemy, the enemy of her house and line, home from Ireland once more. The whole country was talking of York's return and what it meant for England and the broken king.

Margaret's hands were swollen, made painful by the pregnancy. They still twitched as she wished that just once she might have the strength of a man, to reach out and crush another man's throat. The duke stood tall before her, his amusement showing clearly in his eyes. She had wanted him to see her gravid state, to know that at least there would be an heir. She had wanted to look into his eyes as he betrayed his king, but it was all ashes at that moment and she wished she had not come.

"King Henry improves by the day, Lord York. I do not doubt he will take up the reins of government once again."

"Of course, of course," York replied. "We all pray that it is so. Now, I am honored that you came to meet me, my lady. Yet I am called. If you will permit, I should go in to witness the vote."

He bowed again before Margaret could reply. She watched him sweep into the White Chamber, wilting as the will to face him faded.

Yet his men still observed her from under lowered brows and she raised her head, leading her entourage away. She knew what they intended, those lords who spoke so often of the need for strong rule, while her husband struggled and choked in his waking sleep.

As York entered, Oldhall puffed out his cheeks, desperately relieved to see his patron the duke both safe and present. As York took his seat on the ancient oak benches, Oldhall rose to speak, clearing his throat.

"My lords, if you would come to order," Oldhall called across their heads. He stood at a lectern in front of a gilded chair, raised above the benches so he could address them all. The noise fell away.

"My lords, it is my honor to give thanks for your presence today. I ask that you bow your heads in prayer."

Every man there either dipped his head or knelt on the floor at his seat.

"Lord, the God of righteousness and truth, grant to the king and to his lords the guidance of your spirit. May they never lead the nation on the wrong path, through love of power, or desire to please, but lay aside all private interests and keep in mind their responsibility to mankind and to the king, so may your kingdom come and your name be hallowed. The Grace of our Lord Jesus Christ, the love of God, and the Fellowship of the Holy Ghost be with us all. Amen."

The last word was echoed by those present. They sat back, knowing every detail of what was to come, but still attentive and alert. The gathering was simply the last part of months of negotiation and argument. The result was already set in stone, for all it had to be enacted.

"King Henry's state has remained unchanged for five months, my lords," Oldhall went on, his voice trembling with tension. "He cannot be roused and, in his illness, the king lacks the sense and capacity to rule. Therefore, for the good of the kingdom, I propose one among us be recognized as Protector and Defender of the Realm, to be arbiter and final authority until such time as King Henry recovers, or the succession is established elsewhere."

Oldhall swallowed nervously as he saw Lord York's mouth twitch. The queen's pregnancy was the only barb to prick his pleasure that day. The deals and alliances had all been made. It was done, the necessary result of her husband's blank stares and inability to speak. Oldhall cleared his throat to go on, his hands shaking so much that he gripped the lectern to hold them still.

"Before we proceed to a vote on this matter, who among you will offer himself as Protector and Defender to the kingdom for the period of the king's illness?"

All eyes turned to York, who rose slowly from his seat.

"With great reluctance, I offer my service to my lords and my king."

"Is there another?" Oldhall asked. He made a show of looking, though he knew no one else would stand. Those earls and dukes who were still staunch in their support for King Henry were not present on the benches. Somerset was missing, as were the king's half brothers, Edmund and Jasper Tudor. Oldhall nodded, satisfied.

"My lords, I call a vote. Please rise and pass to the division lobbies."

The two narrow rooms lay on either side of the White Chamber. To a man, the lords rose from their benches and walked into "Content," leaving the "Discontent" room empty. York was the only one of their number who remained in place, a small smile playing at the edges of his mouth. Clerks took the names, but it was a mere formality. When they returned, the mood was lighter and York was smiling and accepting congratulations from Warwick, Salisbury, and the rest of his supporters.

Oldhall waited for them to settle once again before he delivered the judgment.

"Richard Plantagenet, Duke of York, it is the will of the lords Temporal and Spiritual that you be appointed Protector and Defender of the Realm. Do you accept the appointment?"

"I do," York replied.

A cheer rose from the benches on either side of him and Oldhall sat back in relief, wiping his forehead. They'd done it. From that moment, York was king in all but name. Richard of York inclined his head to his peers. He stood tall among the assembly of noblemen, his pride showing clearly.

HISTORICAL NOTE

EDWARD III created only three dukes in his long reign. Earls were companions to the king, close supporters who provided armies of knights, archers, and men-at-arms in exchange for vast tracts of land and the "third penny" of the accompanying rents. The title of "Duke" was new to Edward III and untested as to the limits of its power. Two of Edward's sons died before him, so the only duke in his death chamber was in fact John of Gaunt, Duke of Lancaster. The other two sons would still have been known by earlier titles. Edmund of Langley, Earl of Cambridge, would be made Duke of York later on by his nephew, King Richard II. Thomas of Woodstock was Earl of Buckingham at the time of his father's death. He would also be made a duke by Richard II. Those five sons of Edward III would be the seeds for the conflict between houses that became known as the Wars of the Roses.

EDWARD III's oldest son may have died before the king, but the Black Prince was still the royal heir and his son became King Richard II in 1377, at just ten years of age. Richard's regent during his minority was his uncle John of Gaunt. When Gaunt died in 1399, King Richard was thirty-two and had been an unsuccessful and unpopular monarch. To ward off a threat to his throne from Gaunt's line, Richard exiled and then disinherited one Henry of Bolingbroke—John of Gaunt's son. Henry returned from exile with an army, invaded England, and deposed Richard, making himself King Henry IV. His son would be perhaps the most famous of the battle kings of England.

Henry V would triumph against appalling odds at Agincourt, in France. Successful both at home and abroad, the Lancaster line from John of Gaunt would have been set in stone and history if he had lived just a little longer. Instead, Henry V died in 1422 from sickness, at the age of just thirty-five. He left a nine-month-old son to be King Henry VI, with regents to rule until the infant reached adulthood. Unfortunately for the Lancaster line, Henry VI was nothing like his martial father. He was the last English monarch who could properly be described as King of France, though the title was still used by English and then British kings and queens until 1801. As I have described here, Henry VI's reign saw the loss of all French territory except for the fortress of Calais.

IT WAS WHEN I was looking through the details of the plan to give up Maine and Anjou in exchange for a twenty-year truce and a wife for Henry VI that I realized there had to be a guiding mind behind such an outrageous scheme. Though the name of the individual has not survived, *someone* had to have known the French aristocracy and the house of Anjou in tiny detail—as well as being close enough to King Henry VI to influence major events. Thus, Derry Brewer was born. A man something like him must have existed.

The French king, Charles VII, would not give up a daughter to an English king. He had seen two sisters sent over the Channel, and the result was a strengthened English claim on his own realm. Yet the only other princesses on French soil were in Anjou—a family with no love of the English. René of Anjou was brought to the negotiating table by the only thing that mattered to him: the return of his ancestral lands.

As a point of interest, the French chronicler Bourdigné gives a harrowing account of the indictment and conviction for blasphemy of an elderly Jew in the area controlled by René of Anjou. Though the Jewish community appealed to Duke René personally, the execution went ahead and the man was flayed alive.

A NOTE on Margaret's French "marriage": It is true that Henry VI was not present for the first ceremony, which must presumably be called a "betrothal," as he wasn't in the building. William de la Pole, Lord Suffolk, said the vows on Henry's behalf and placed the ring on the fourteen-year-old Margaret's finger. William de la Pole was already married to Alice Chaucer—granddaughter of the writer Geoffrey Chaucer. The ceremony actually took place at the church of St. Martin in Tours and not the cathedral. We do not know why Henry VI wasn't present, though it seems reasonable to suspect his lords didn't want him anywhere near the French king, French territory, or French soldiers.

IT HAS always been a problem for historical fiction that true events often took place over a much longer timescale than I would like. So, for example, the retaking of Anjou by the French took the best part of a year and the crisis in Maine didn't occur until a fifteen-year-old Margaret was properly married to Henry in Westminster Abbey. After a delay in Calais for some five months, that second wedding took place in April 1445. I have compressed the timeline because months of "not very much happening" do not make for interesting chapters. In the same way, I felt it necessary to reduce the time between Cade's rebellion and York becoming Defender of the Realm. The reality was that something like three dull years passed, with King Henry's health worsening and York's supporters growing stronger and more bold.

I COULD FIND no record of the actual vows used between Henry VI and Margaret of Anjou, so I used well-attested details of noble weddings from the fifteenth century. We do know Henry wore cloth-of-gold and that the ruby ring he put on her finger was the one he'd worn at his coronation. The vows are reproduced from a form used at the time, with slight modernization of spelling. Draping the bride and groom with a shawl tied with a cord is an accurate detail. It is also true that there would have been no chairs in the main church and that the altar would have been hidden from the congregation by a screen. How close one came to the altar depended on status. Henry and Margaret were indeed married in the abbey of Titchfield, which was destroyed in the sixteenth century and rebuilt as a Tudor mansion. Part of the old abbey survives as a gatehouse. Margaret went from there to Blackheath in London, entering the city in a procession that passed over London Bridge and halted there to witness pageants in her honor. She was finally crowned in Westminster Abbey. There is no record of Henry being at her side for that ceremony.

I COULD NOT resist using the name of Baron Strange, just as I couldn't resist mentioning René of Anjou's "Order of the Croissant" though I put it some five years before its historical creation. The rest of that French story line is fictional—though based around true events. English settlers in Maine resisted the French occupation and began a disastrous conflict that ended with the loss of all Normandy up to Calais. The title of Baron Strange did exist at this time, though was later in abeyance for three centuries. There is, in fact, a current Baron Strange, and it has been one of the odd things about setting a novel in England that all the main characters have descendants who are still alive today. Nonetheless, the name was just too good to omit. Lord Scales was also involved in the defense of London.

NOTE that sugar was available in England from the twelfth-century crusades. By the fourteenth century, it was imported into Europe and England from the Middle East—specifically, Lebanon. It would have been an expensive treat compared to honey. The reference to blood and sugar being given to children is an old continental treat, unfashionable today but still popular just a few generations ago.

A NOTE on codpieces: Although usually associated with the later Elizabethan era, the first codpieces came into fashion in the fourteenth and fifteenth centuries. There is one tale of Edward III that he had an enormous one made during the Hundred Years' War and then commanded his knights to do the same. The legend goes that the French were terrified by such "well-equipped" knights.

It's ALSO worth noting that the modern-day Palace of Westminster would have looked very different in the fifteenth century. At the time of Henry VI, it was still an important residence of monarchs. The Commons and Lords both existed as political entities, though in the main to control the collection of taxes and advise the king. The Commons consisted of 280 members in 1450, made up of Knights of the Shires (two from each of thirty-seven counties) and 206 "burgess" members (two from each city or borough and four from London). With no permanent place to call their own, they met most often in the octagonal Chapter House attached to Westminster Abbey, across the road from the Palace of Westminster. The Painted Chamber in the palace was also used, and I have represented it here as the hub of administrative activity it was slowly becoming. I have taken some liberty with the Christian prayers described at the beginning of a parliamentary meeting. The formal prayer was introduced later, and I have mingled the modern wording from both Commons and Lords. It is certainly true that a prayer would have been said in the fifteenth century, but I believe the exact wording is unknown.

The House of Lords was a much smaller gathering, consisting of fifty-five Lords Temporal: dukes, viscounts, earls, and barons, and the Lords Spiritual: the bishops. They met in the White Chamber in the Palace of Westminster in meetings overseen by the lord chancellor. Westminster was also the site of law courts, such as the King's Bench and the Court of Common Pleas in the fifteenth century, and would have been a bustling place of judges, lawyers, and a multitude of shops.

Cardinal Henry Beaufort was de facto prime minister during the last part of his life, though no such formal post existed at the time. By that I mean that he was the most senior man in the Commons, with a link to the church in Rome as well as high secular status. Beaufort was not only the second son of John of Gaunt, but he had been lord chancellor to Henry IV and Henry V, presiding over both the courts and the assembly of lords. It is true that Beaufort ruled on the fate of Joan of Arc and it's an odd coincidence that he was actually born in Anjou, France. I could not omit a character with such a fascinating history from the story, though I took a liberty with the history by keeping him alive past 1447. The real man could not have been involved with the accusation of treason against William, Lord Suffolk, in 1450.

SIR WILLIAM TRESHAM was the Speaker of the House of Commons and, by 1450, had served in twelve parliaments. The Jewel Tower where I wrote his meeting with Derry Brewer still stands today. It was built originally to house the valuables of King Edward III, complete with moat, high walls, and guards. It is true that William, Lord Suffolk, was held there during his trial for treason. The text of a letter he wrote to his son John survives and is fascinating as an example of advice from a man who thought he was going to be executed.

HISTORICAL FICTION sometimes involves filling in the gaps and unexplained parts of history. How is it that England could field fifty thousand men for the Battle of Towton in 1461 but was able to send only four thousand to prevent the loss of Normandy a dozen years earlier? My assumption is that the unrest and riots in England put such a fear into the authorities that the main armies were kept at home. Jack Cade's rebellion was only one of the most serious uprisings, after all. Rage at the loss of France, coupled with high taxes and a sense that the king was weak, brought England close to complete disaster at this time. Given that Cade breached the Tower of London, perhaps the court and Parliament were right to keep soldiers at home who could have been used to good effect in France.

KING HENRY VI's illness is difficult to pin down at the distance of five and a half centuries. Given his eventual collapse, it is reasonable to assume there were some warnings and symptoms before that disastrous event. Descriptions of him from the period suggest that he was weak-willed, "simple," and biddable. Any man can be weak-willed, of course, but his long near-catatonic state suggests some sort of physical damage. No matter the cause, he was not the son his father, Henry V, should have had. While the Wars of the Roses had many fathers, one of them was Henry's utter weakness as a king.

It is true that Henry was present in Westminster when William de la Pole was accused of treason for his part in the loss of France. As was typical of the time, a long list of crimes was prepared and read. Lord Suffolk denied them all. It is interesting to note that King Henry did not speak his judgment. It was not a formal trial, though forty-five lords (that is to say, practically all the noblemen in England) were present in his personal chambers at Westminster. The judgment was read by the king's chancellor, and Suffolk was banished for five years. One reading of the events is that William de la Pole was a perfect scapegoat to conceal the involvement of the king in the failed truce. The fact that he received such a light sentence suggests Henry was on his side to the end.

It was not enough for William de la Pole's accusers. Parliament wanted Lord Suffolk to be the one held responsible. In the next formal session, a bill to formally declare him a traitor was suggested but defeated in a close vote. Lord Suffolk was allowed to flee by night, barely avoiding an angry mob.

I have no doubt at all that the "pirate" ship that overtook him as Suffolk left England was in the pay of another faction, if not the most likely culprit, York himself. Suffolk was beheaded on deck, where true pirates could have held him for ransom, as was common practice. It was a tragic end for a decent man who had given his all for king and country.

THE REBELLION led by Jack Cade was one of many that began around 1450. In part it was an outpouring of anger and sorrow over the loss of

French territories, resulting in brutal French raids along the Kent coast. Cade's list of grievances also included being blamed for the murder at sea of William de la Pole, as well as injustices and corruption. It is astonishing that Cade managed to gather so many thousands of angry men to march on London, forcing the king to flee the capital to Kenilworth. Some sources put his followers as high as twenty thousand.

Very little is known for certain about Cade. He may have been Irish or English, and John or Jack Cade was almost certainly not his real name. At that time, "Jack" was commonly used when a son's name was the same as his father. When Cade struck a sword on the London Stone in Cannon Street, he gave his name as Mortimer and used either that or John Amendall. His men did indeed storm the Tower of London, getting through the outer defenses and failing only to breach the central White Tower. In a semiformal trial at the Guildhall, Cade and his men executed the king's treasurer, Lord Say, as well as his son-in-law, William Crowmer. It is true that Cade put the head of the sheriff of Kent on a pole. Yet it was more than just another peasant rebellion. Cade's most famous demand was that the king dismiss his favorites because "his lords are lost, his merchandise is lost, his commons destroyed, the sea is lost, and France is lost."

Henry's weakness was not a steady state. At times, he played a more active part than I have given him, before, during, and after Cade's rebellion. It is true, however, that Queen Margaret was the one who remained in London, and it was she who negotiated the truce and pardon. In the interests of historical accuracy, I should say that she wasn't in the Tower of London when it was breached. She stayed at Greenwich, then known as the Palace of Pleasance. It is also true that pardoning Cade's men was her idea and her command. Cade agreed to the pardons. He slipped away as royalist forces regrouped and it was some months later when the newly appointed sheriff of Kent finally caught up with him. Cade was mortally wounded in his last fight and died on the journey back to London. His corpse was hanged, drawn, and quartered before his own head was put on a pole on London Bridge. Many of the other rebels were tracked down and killed over the following year.

A NOTE on roses: One of the symbols of the house of York is a white rose. Richard of York also used a falcon and a boar. Both Henry VI and Margaret used a swan as a symbol.

The red rose was one of many heraldic symbols for the house of Lancaster (from John of Gaunt, Duke of Lancaster). The concept of a war between the roses is a Tudor invention and there was no sense of white versus red at the time. The actual struggle was between different male lines from Edward III: men of great power, who were all in reach of the throne. Yet it was King Henry VI's weakness that made his enemies bold and plunged the country into civil war.

CONN IGGULDEN
London, 2013

LIST OF CHARACTERS

ALBERT Servant of de Roche family, in France

MASTER ALLWORTHY Royal physician to Henry VI

BARON DAVID ALTON Officer in France, with William, Duke of Suffolk

MARGARET OF ANJOU/QUEEN MARGARET Daughter of René of Anjou, wife of Henry VI

YOLANDE OF ANJOU Margaret of Anjou's sister

JOHN, LOUIS, AND NICHOLAS OF ANJOU Margaret of Anjou's brothers

MARIE OF ANJOU Queen of France, aunt of Margaret of Anjou

RENÉ, DUKE OF ANJOU Father of Margaret of Anjou

HENRY BEAUFORT Cardinal, son of John of Gaunt, great-uncle of Henry VI

EDWIN BENNETT Man-at-arms to Baron Strange, France

BERNARD Old friend of Thomas Woodchurch

SAUL BERTLEMAN (BERTLE) Mentor of Derihew Brewer

DERIHEW (DERRY) BREWER Spymaster of Henry VI

CAPTAIN BROWN Officer defending the Tower of London against Jack Cade

PHILIP, DUKE OF BURGUNDY Offered sanctuary to William, Duke of Suffolk

JOHN BURROUGHS Informant to Derry Brewer

JACK CADE Kentish rebel

CHARLES VII King of France, uncle of Henry VI

LIONEL, DUKE OF CLARENCE Son of Edward III

BEN CORNISH Present at hanging of Jack Cade's son

JOHN SUTTON, BARON DUDLEY Present at "trial" of William, Duke of Suffolk

DUNBAR Kentish smith

ROBERT ECCLESTONE Friend of Jack Cade

EDWARD III King of England, great-great-grandfather of Henry VI

FLORA Kentish innkeeper

COUNT FREDERICK Betrothed/husband of Yolande of Anjou

THOMAS, DUKE OF GLOUCESTER Son of Edward III

HALLERTON Servant to Derry Brewer

HENRY VI King of England, son of Henry V

SIR HEW Knight at Agincourt

BARON HIGHBURY Vengeful lord, in Maine, France

HOBBS Sergeant-at-arms, Windsor

ALEXANDER IDEN Appointed sheriff of Kent

JAMES Younger torturer in the Jewel House

JONAS Banner boy at Cade's London Bridge crossing

ALWYN JUDGMENT Magistrate, Kent

EDMUND GRAY, EARL OF KENT Present at "trial" of William, Duke of Suffolk

JOHN OF GAUNT, DUKE OF LANCASTER Son of Edward III

BARON LE FARGES Part of French army, Maine, France

SIEUR ANDRÉ DE MAINTAGNES Knight in French army, Maine, France

JEAN MARISSE Officer of the court, Nantes

PADDY/PATRICK MORAN Friend of Jack Cade

REUBEN MOSELLE Financier in Anjou

SIR WILLIAM OLDHALL Speaker of the House of Commons

JOHN DE VERE, EARL OF OXFORD Present at "trial" of William, Duke of Suffolk

JASPER TUDOR, EARL OF PEMBROKE Half brother of Henry VI

ALICE PERRERS Mistress of Edward III

RONALD PINCHER Kentish innkeeper

CAPTAIN RECINE Soldier from Saumur Castle who arrested Reuben Moselle

EDMUND TUDOR, EARL OF RICHMOND Half brother of Henry VI

RICHARD WOODVILLE, BARON RIVERS Present in London during Cade assault

BARON JEAN DE ROCHE Part of French army, Maine, France

RICHARD NEVILLE, EARL OF SALISBURY Head of Neville family, grandson of John of Gaunt

JAMES FIENNES, BARON SAY Present in London for Cade's assault

THOMAS DE SCALES, BARON SCALES Present in London for Cade's assault

SIMONE French maid at Saumur Castle

EDMUND BEAUFORT, DUKE OF SOMERSET Friend of William, Duke of Suffolk, supporter of Henry VI

BARON STRANGE Neighbor of Thomas Woodchurch in Maine, France

WILLIAM DE LA POLE, DUKE OF SUFFOLK Soldier and courtier who arranged the marriage of Henry VI and Margaret

ALICE DE LA POLE, DUCHESS OF SUFFOLK Wife of William, Duke of Suffolk, granddaughter of Geoffrey Chaucer

JAMES TANTER Scottish supporter of Jack Cade

TED Older torturer in the Jewel House

SIR WILLIAM TRESHAM Speaker of the House of Commons

RICHARD NEVILLE, EARL OF WARWICK Son of Earl of Salisbury, later known as the Kingmaker

RALPH NEVILLE, EARL OF WESTMORLAND Present at Windsor hunt

JOAN WOODCHURCH Wife of Thomas, mother of Rowan and two daughters

ROWAN WOODCHURCH Son of Thomas and Joan

THOMAS WOODCHURCH Farmer, archer, leader of Maine rebellion

EDMUND OF LANGLEY, DUKE OF YORK Son of Edward III

RICHARD PLANTAGENET, DUKE OF YORK Head of House of York, great-grandson of Edward III

CECILY NEVILLE, DUCHESS OF YORK Wife of Richard, Duke of York, granddaughter of John of Gaunt

SELECT BIBLIOGRAPHY

Henry VI by Bertram Wolffe, Eyre Methuen, 1981

The Wars of the Roses by Desmond Seward, Constable, 1995

The Wars of the Roses: A Concise History by Charles Ross, Thames and Hudson, 1976

Blood Sisters by Sarah Gristwood, HarperPress, 2012

She-Wolves by Helen Castor, Faber and Faber, 2010

The Medieval Household by Geoff Egan, Boydell Press, 2010

Elizabeth Woodville by David Baldwin, Sutton, 2002

Duke Richard of York 1411–1460 by P. A. Johnson, OUP, 1988

Richard III by Charles Ross, Eyre Methuen, 1981

Edward IV by Charles Ross, Eyre Methuen, 1974

Richard III by Paul Murray Kendall, Allen and Unwin, 1955

Henry the Fifth by A. J. Church, Macmillan, 1889

The Fifteenth Century 1399–1485 by E. F. Jacob, OUP, 1961

Cassell's History of England, vols. I and II, Waverley, n.d.

English Men of Action: Henry V/Warwick, Macmillan, 1899

TURN THE PAGE FOR AN EXCERPT

AS TRAITORS ADVANCE, A QUEEN DEFENDS.

For more than a year, King Henry VI has remained all but exiled in Windsor Castle. His fiercely loyal wife and queen, Margaret of Anjou, safeguards her husband's interests. While Henry is all but absent as king, the Duke of York extends his influence throughout the kingdom. But when the king unexpectedly recovers his senses and returns to London to reclaim his throne, the balance of power is once again thrown into turmoil. The clash of the Houses of Lancaster and York may be the beginning of a war that could tear England apart . . .

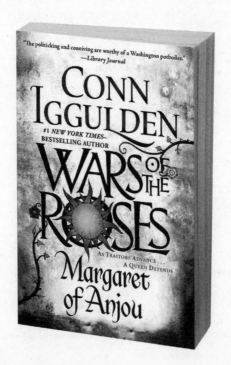

Penguin
Random
House

PROLOGUE

Vicomte Michel Gascault was certainly not a spy. He would have scorned the name if he had heard it used of him. Of course it went without saying that the French ambassador to the English court would report anything of interest to his monarch on his return. It was also true that Vicomte Gascault had considerable experience in the royal palaces of Europe as well as the field of war. He knew what King Charles of France might want to know and, with that in mind, Vicomte Gascault took careful note of all that went on around him, little though it was. Spies were grubby, low-born men, given to hiding in doorways and hissing secret passwords at each other. Vicomte Gascault, *d'un autre côté*—"on the other hand," as the English said—was a gentleman of France, as far above such things as the sun above the earth.

Those and similar thoughts were all he had to amuse him in his idle hours. He was certain to mention to King Charles how he had been ignored for three full days, left to kick his heels in a sumptuous chamber in the Palace of Westminster. The servants sent to attend his person were not even well washed, he had noticed, though they came promptly enough. One of them positively reeked of horse and urine, as if he found his usual employment in the royal stables.

Still, it was true Gascault's bodily needs were met, even if his ambassadorial ones were not. Each day began with his own retainers dressing him in the most gorgeous raiments and cloaks he possessed, choosing them from among the garments pressed into the enormous trunks he had brought from France. He had not yet been forced to repeat a combination of colors and if he had overheard one of the English scullions refer to him as the "French Peacock," it bothered him not at all. Bright colors raised his mood and he had precious little else to while away the time. He did not like to think of the food they set out for him. It was clear enough that they had engaged a French cook; equally as clear that the man had no love of his countrymen. Gascault shuddered at the thought of some of the flaccid things that had appeared at his table.

The hours crept by like a funeral and he had long ago read every scrap of his official papers. By the light of a candle-lamp, he turned at last to a dun-colored book in his possession, marked throughout with his notes and comments. *De Sacra Coena* by Berengarius had become a favorite of Gascault's. The treatise on the Last Supper had been banned by the Church, of course. Any argument that strayed into the mysteries of body and blood brought the attention of Papal hounds.

Gascault had long been in the habit of seeking out books destined for the fire, to set his thoughts aflame in turn. He rubbed his hands over the wrappings. The original cover had been stripped and burned to ashes, of course, with those ashes carefully crumbled so that no questing hand could ever guess what they had once been. The rough, stained leather was a sad necessity in an age where men took such delight in denouncing each other to their masters.

The summons, when it came at last, interrupted his reading. Gascault was used to the booming bell that rang each hour and half hour, startling him from sleep and spoiling his digestion at least as much as the poor pigeons that lay so limply on his dinner platter. He had kept no count but still knew it was late when the horse-servant, as he thought of him, came rushing into the rooms.

"Viscount Gas-cart, you are summoned," the boy said.

Gascault gave no sign of irritation at the way he mangled a proud name. The boy was surely a simpleton and the Good Lord expected mercy for those poor fellows, set among their betters to teach compassion, or so Gascault's mother had always said. With care, he laid his book on the arm of the chair and rose. His steward, Alphonse, was only a step behind the lad. Gascault let his eyes drift back to the book, knowing it would be enough of a signal for his servant to keep it from other hands in his absence. Alphonse nodded sharply, bowing low while the horse-boy stared in confusion at the dumb show between the two men.

Vicomte Gascault strapped on his sword and allowed Alphonse to drape his yellow cloak around his shoulders. When his gaze dropped once more to the chair, the book had somehow vanished. Truly, his servant was the soul of discretion and not simply because he lacked a tongue. Gascault inclined his head in thanks and swept out behind the boy, passing through the outer rooms and into the chilly corridor beyond.

A party of five men awaited him there. Four of them were evidently soldiers, wearing a royal tabard over mail. The last wore a cloak and tunic over hose, all as thick and well made as his own.

"Vicomte Michel Gascault?" the man said.

Gascault noted the perfect pronunciation and smiled.

"I have that honor. I am at your service . . . ?"

"Richard Neville, Earl of Salisbury and lord chancellor. I must apologize for the late hour, but you are expected, my lord, in the royal chambers."

Gascault fell easily into step at the man's side, ignoring the soldiers clattering along in their wake. He had known stranger things than a midnight meeting in his career.

"To see the king?" he asked mischievously, watching the earl closely. Salisbury was not a young man, though he seemed wiry and in good health to the Frenchman's eyes. It would not do to reveal how much the court of France knew of King Henry's poor health.

"I am sorry to report that His Royal Highness, King Henry, is suffering with an ague, a temporary illness. I hope you will take no offense, but I am to bring you to the Duke of York this evening."

"My lord Salisbury, I am so *very* sorry to hear such a thing," Gascault replied, letting the words spill out. He saw Salisbury's eyes tighten just a fraction and had to repress a smile. They both knew there were families in the English court with strong ties to France, whether by blood or titles. The idea that the French king would not know every detail of King Henry's collapse was a game to be played between them and nothing more. The English king had been near senseless for months, fallen so deeply into a stupor that he could not be raised to life. It was not for nothing that his lords had appointed one of their number as "Protector and Defender of the Realm." Richard, Duke of York, was king in all but name and, in truth, Vicomte Gascault had no interest in meeting a royal lost in his dreaming. He had been sent to judge the strength of the English court and their willingness to defend their interests. Gascault allowed his pleasure to sparkle in his eyes for just an instant before snuffing the emotion. If he reported that they were weak and lost without King Henry, Gascault's word alone would bring a hundred ships from France, to raid and burn every English port. The English had done the same to France for long enough, he reminded himself. Perhaps it was time at last that the devil had his due of them as well.

Salisbury led the small group along an endless stretch of corridors, then climbed two flights of stairs to the royal apartments on the floors above. Even at such a late hour, the Palace of Westminster was ablaze with lamps set just a few paces apart. Yet Gascault could smell damp in the air, a reek of ancient mold from having the river so close. As they reached the final, guarded door, he had to control the desire to straighten his cloak and collar one last time. Alphonse would not have let him leave with anything awry.

The soldiers were dismissed and the door opened by guards within. Salisbury extended his hand to allow the ambassador to enter before him.

"After you, Vicomte," he said. His eyes were sharp, Gascault realized, as he bowed and went in. The man missed nothing and he reminded himself to be wary of him. The English were many things: venal, short-tempered, greedy, a whole host of sins. No one had ever called them stupid, however, not in all the history of the world. If God would only make it so! King Charles would have their towns and castles in his grip in just a single generation.

Salisbury closed the door softly at his back and Vicomte Gascault found himself in a smaller room than he had expected. Perhaps it was only right that a "Protector and Defender" would not allow himself the trappings of a royal court, yet the stillness of that room made a shudder pass down Gascault's back. The windows were black with the night outside and the man who rose to greet him was dressed in the same color, almost lost in the shadows of low-burning lamps as he came forward.

Richard, Duke of York, extended his hand, beckoning Gascault further into the room. The Frenchman felt his hackles stand up in superstitious fear, though he showed no sign of his discomfort. As he stepped forward, he glanced behind, seeing nothing stranger than Salisbury watching him steadily.

"Vicomte Gascault, I am York. It is my pleasure to welcome you and a source of great distress that I must send you home so soon."

"Milord?" Gascault asked in confusion. He sat where York gestured and gathered his wits as the man took a seat across the wide table. The English duke was clean-shaven, square-jawed, and yet slim enough in his black. As Gascault stared, York pushed loose hair off his forehead with one hand. He tilted his head as he did so, yet his eyes never left Gascault's own.

"I'm afraid I do not understand, my lord York. Forgive me, I have not yet learned the correct term of address for a Protector and Defender." Gascault looked around for some sign of wine, or food, but there was nothing in sight, just the deep golden oak of the table, stretching bare before him.

York regarded him without blinking, his brows lowering.

"I was the king's lieutenant in France, Vicomte Gascault. I am certain you were told as much. I have fought on French soil and I have lost estates and titles to your king. All this you know. I mention it only to remind you that, in turn, I know France. I know your king—and, Gascault, I know you."

"My lord, I can only assume—"

York continued over him as if he had not spoken.

"The King of England sleeps, Vicomte Gascault. Will he wake, at all? Or will he die abed? It is the talk of all the markets here. I do not doubt it is the talk of Paris as well. Is this the chance for which your king has planned and waited for so very long? You, who are not strong enough to take Calais from us, you would dream of England?"

Gascault shook his head, his mouth open to begin a denial. York held up his hand.

"I invite you, Gascault. Throw your dice. Take your chance while King Henry drowses. I would walk again on lands that once were mine. I would march an army on French earth once more, if I had the chance. *Please*, consider my invitation. The Channel is just a thread.

The king is just a man. A soldier, well, if he is an English soldier, he is still a man, is he not? He can fail. He can fall. Come against us while our king sleeps, Vicomte Gascault. Climb our walls. Set foot in our ports. I welcome it, as our people will welcome you all. It may be a rough welcome, I grant you. We are rough folk. But we have debts to repay and we are generous with our enemies. For each blow landed on us, we give them three and we do not count the cost. Do you understand me, Vicomte Gascault? Son of Julien and Clémence? Brother to André, Arnaud, and François? Husband to Elodie? Father to two sons and a daughter. Shall I name them, Gascault? Shall I describe your family home, with the red plum trees that bracket the gate?"

"Enough, *monsieur*," Gascault said quietly. "Your meaning is clear enough."

"I wonder," York said. "Or should I send an order to wing faster than you can ride, faster than you can sail, so that you understand my meaning, as well and as fully as I intend it, when you return to your home? I am willing, Gascault."

"Please don't, my lord," Gascault replied.

"Please?" York said. His face was hard, darkened by the dimming lamps as if shadows crept over his jaw. "I will decide, after you are gone. There is a ship waiting for you, Gascault—and men who will take you to the coast. Whatever news you report to your king, I wish you all the fortune you deserve. Good night, Vicomte Gascault. God speed."

Gascault rose on trembling legs and went to the door. Salisbury kept his head down as he opened it for him and the Frenchman took a deep breath in fear as he saw the soldiers gathered beyond. In the gloom, they had a menacing aspect and he almost shrieked as they allowed him out and turned in place to march him away.

Salisbury closed the door softly.

"I do not think they will come—at least, not this year," he said.

York snorted.

"I swear, I am in two minds. We have the ships and the men, if they would follow me. Yet they wait like hounds, to see if Henry will wake."

Salisbury did not reply at first. York saw his hesitation and smiled wearily.

"It is not yet too late, I think. Send for the Spaniard as well. I will speak my lines to him."